Praise for *God's War*

'Kameron Hurley's a brave, unflinching, truly original
writer with a unique vision – her fiction burns right
through your brain and your heart'
Jeff VanderMeer

'Hurley's world-building is phenomenal... [she]
smoothly handles tricky themes such as race, class,
religion, and gender without sacrificing action'
Publishers Weekly

'An aggressively dark, highly original SF-fantasy novel
with tight, cutting prose and some of the most
inventive world-building I've seen in a while'
FantasyLiterature.com

'Kameron Hurley is ferociously imaginative – with the
emphasis on the ferocious. She writes novels that are smart,
dark, visceral and wonderfully, hectically entertaining'
Lauren Beukes

'…where some writers might focus on high-tech weapons or
explosive battles in space, Hurley brings things down to a
personal level, recalling more the toughminded realism of
Chris Moriarty's *Spin State*…'
New York Review of Science Fiction

ALEXANDRA PARK

D0264135

KAMERON HURLEY

GOD'S WAR

DEL REY

3 5 7 9 10 8 6 4 2

First published in the US in 2011 by Night Shade Books
First published in the UK in 2013 by Del Rey, an imprint of Ebury Publishing
A Random House Group Company

This edition published in 2014

Copyright © 2011 by Kameron Hurley

Kameron Hurley has asserted her right to be identified as the author of this
Work in accordance with the Copyright, Designs and Patents Act 1988

This novel is a work of fiction. Names and characters are the product of the
author's imagination and any resemblance to actual persons,
living or dead, is entirely coincidental

All rights reserved. No part of this publication may be reproduced,
stored in a retrieval system, or transmitted in any form or by any means,
electronic, mechanical, photocopying, recording or otherwise, without the
prior permission of the copyright owner

The Random House Group Limited Reg. No. 954009

Addresses for companies within the Random House Group can be found at:
www.randomhouse.co.uk

A CIP catalogue record for this book is available from the British Library

The Random House Group Limited supports the Forest Stewardship
Council® (FSC®), the leading international forest-certification organisation.
Our books carrying the FSC label are printed on FSC®-certified paper.
FSC is the only forest-certification scheme supported by the leading
environmental organisations, including Greenpeace.
Our paper procurement policy can be found at:
www.randomhouse.co.uk/environment

Printed and bound in Great Britain by Clays Ltd, St Ives PLC

ISBN 9780091952785

To buy books by your favourite authors and register for offers visit:
www.randomhouse.co.uk

For Jenn and Patrick

Haringey Libraries	
AA	
Askews & Holts	22-Oct-2014
AF	
	science fiction

Listen to me, you islands;
hear this, you distant nations:
Before I was born God called me;
from my birth he has made mention of my name.

He made my mouth like a sharpened sword,
in the shadow of his hand he hid me;
he made me into a polished arrow
and concealed me in his quiver.

He said to me, "You are my servant,
Israel, in whom I will display my splendor."

But I said, "I have labored to no purpose;
I have spent my strength in vain and for nothing.
Yet what is due me is in the Lord's hand,
and my reward is with my God."

(Bible, Isaiah 49:1-4)

"Say: My prayer and my sacrifice and my life and my
death are surely for Allah, the Lord of the worlds…"

(Quran, 6.162)

PART ONE

BIG GAME

Nyx sold her womb somewhere between Punjai and Faleen, on the edge of the desert.

Drunk, but no longer bleeding, she pushed into a smoky cantina just after dark and ordered a pinch of morphine and a whiskey chaser. She bet all of her money on a boxer named Jaks, and lost it two rounds later when Jaks hit the floor like an antique harem girl.

Nyx lost every coin, a wad of opium, and the wine she'd gotten from the butchers as a bonus for her womb. But she did get Jaks into bed, and—loser or not—in the desert after dark, that was something.

"What are you after?" Jaks murmured in her good ear.

They lay tangled in the sheets like old lovers: a losing boxer with a poor right hook and a tendency to drop her left, and a wombless hunter bereft of money, weapons, food, and most of her clothing.

"I'm looking for my sister," Nyx said. It was partly the truth. She was looking for something else too, something worth a lot more, and Jaks was going to help her get it.

The midnight call to prayer rolled out over the desert. It started somewhere out in Faleen and moved in a slow wave from mosque muezzin to village mullah to town crier, certain as a swarm of locusts, ubiquitous as the name of God.

"Don't tell anyone," Nyx said, "what I'm about to tell you…"

*

Nyx woke sometime after dawn prayer with a hangover and what felt like a wad of cotton in her belly. Dropping the womb had bought her some time—a day, maybe more if the butchers were smart enough to sell it before her bloody sisters sniffed her out. She'd shaken them in Punjai when she dumped the womb, along with the rest of her coin.

Jaks was long gone, off to catch a ride to Faleen with the agricultural traffic. Nyx was headed that way too, but she hadn't said a word of that to Jaks. She wanted her next meeting with Jaks to be a pleasant surprise. Mysterious women were attractive—stalkers and groupies were not. Nyx had tracked this woman too long to lose it all by being overly familiar.

Some days, Nyx was a bel dame—an honored, respected, and deadly government-funded assassin. Other days, she was just a butcher, a hunter—a woman with nothing to lose. And the butcher had a bounty to bring in.

The sun bled across the big angry sky. The call box at the cantina was busted, so Nyx walked. The way was unpaved, mostly sand and gravel. Her feet were bruised, bleeding, and bare, but she hadn't felt much of anything down there in a good long while. Back at the butchers', she had traded her good sandals for directions out of the fleshpots, too dopey to figure the way out on her own. Under the burnous, she wore little more than a dhoti and breast binding. She had an old baldric, too—her dead partner's. All the sheaths were empty, and had been for some time. She remembered some proverb about meeting God empty-handed, but her knees weren't calloused anymore—not from praying, anyway. She had already been to hell. One prayer more or less wouldn't make any difference.

She hitched a ride on the back of a cat-pulled cart that afternoon. The cats were as tall as her shoulder. Their long, coarse fur was matted and tangled, and they stank. The cats turned leaking, bloodshot eyes to her. One of them was blind.

The woman driving the cart was a cancerous old crone with a bubbling gash that clove the left half of her face in two. She offered Nyx a ride in exchange for a finger's length of blood to feed the enormous silk beetle she kept in a covered cage next to her left hip, pressed against her battered pistol.

Nyx had the hood of her burnous up to keep off the sun; traveling this time of day was dangerous. The crone's skin was rough and pitted with old scars from cancer digs. Fresh, virulent melanomas spotted her forearms and the back of her neck. Most of her nose was gone.

"You coming from the front, my woman?" the crone asked. Nyx shook her head, but the old woman was nearly blind and did not see.

"I fought at the front," the crone said. "It brought me much honor. You, too, could find honor."

Nyx had left her partner, and a lot more at the front—a long time ago.

"I'd rather find a call box," Nyx said.

"God does not answer the phone."

Nyx couldn't argue with that.

She jumped off the cart an hour later as they approached a bodega with a call box and a sign telling her she was fifty kilometers from Faleen. The old woman nattered on about the wisdom of making phone calls to God.

Nyx made a call.

Two hours later, at fourteen in the afternoon on a day that clocked in at twenty-seven hours, her sister Kine pulled up in a bakkie belching red roaches from its back end.

Kine leaned over and pushed out the door. "You're lucky the office picked up," she said. "I had to get some samples at the war front for the breeding compounds. You headed to the coast? I need to get these back there."

"You've got a leak in your exhaust," Nyx said. "Unlock the hood."

"It's been leaking since the front," Kine said. She popped the hood.

The bakkie's front end hissed open. Waves of yeasty steam rolled off the innards. Nyx wiped the moisture from her face and peered into the guts of the bakkie. The bug cistern was covered in a thin film of organic tissue, healthy and functioning, best Nyx could tell by the color. The hoses were in worse shape—semi-organic, just like the cistern, but patched and replaced in at least a half-dozen places she could see without bringing in a speculum. In places, the healthy amber tissue had blistered and turned black.

She was no bug-blessed magician—not even a standard tissue mechanic—but she knew how to find a leak and patch it up with organic salve. Every woman worth her weight in blood knew how to do that.

"Where's your tissue kit?" Nyx said.

Kine got out of the bakkie and walked over. She was shorter than Nyx by a head—average height, for a Nasheenian woman—but they shared the same wide hips. She wore an embroidered housecoat and a hijab over her dark hair. Nyx remembered seeing her with her hair unbound and her skirt hiked up, knee deep in mud back in Mushirah. In her memory, Kine was twelve and laughing at some joke about conservative women who worked for the government. Rigid crones, she'd call them, half dead or dying in a world God made for pleasure. A farmer's daughter, just like Nyx. A blood sister in a country where blood and bugs and currency were synonymous.

"I don't have a tissue kit," Kine said. "I gave it to one of the boys at the front. They're low on supplies."

Nyx snorted. They were low on a lot more than tissue kits at the front these days.

"You're the only organic technician I know who'd ever be short a tissue kit," Nyx said.

Kine looked her over. "Are you as desperately poor as you look? I know a good magician who can scrape you for cancers."

"I've been worse," Nyx said, and shut the hood. "Your bug cistern is in good shape. It'll breed you enough bugs to power this thing back to the coast, even with the leak."

But the leak meant she'd get to Faleen just a little bit slower. If there was one thing Nyx felt short on these days, it was time.

Nyx slid into the bakkie. Kine got behind the steering wheel. For a moment they sat in stuffy, uncomfortable silence. Then Kine turned down the window and stepped on the juice.

"What's her name?" Kine asked, shifting pedals as they rolled back onto the road.

"Who?"

"I can smell her," Kine said, tightening her hands on the steering wheel. Her hands had the brown, worn, sinewy look of old leather. Her lip curled in disdain.

"I'm working a note," Nyx said. "What I do to bring it in isn't your business."

"A note for a deserter, or one of those dirty bounties you deal in? If you're bringing in a deserter, where's Tej?"

Tej, Nyx thought, and the shock of it, of hearing his name out loud, of thinking *Tej, my dead partner*, was a punch in the gut.

"I couldn't get him back over the Chenjan border," Nyx said. Another boy buried in the desert.

A clerk the color of honey had given Nyx a bel dame's note for a boy named Arran nearly three months before, after he'd deserted his place at the front and sought refuge in Chenja. His officer had called in the bel dames because she believed he'd been exposed to a new Chenjan burst, a delayed viral vapor that hid out in the host for up to four months before triggering an airborne contagion. The contagion was capable of taking out half a city before the magicians could contain it. Nyx had gone into the bel dame office and been inoculated against the latest burst, so all she had to do was bleed on the boy to neutralize the contagion, then cut off his head and take him home. Even clean, the penalty for desertion was death. Boys either came home at forty or came home in a bag. No exceptions.

This was Nyx's job.

Some days, it paid well.

So Nyx and Tej had tracked Arran. Arran had gone over the border into Chenja. That part was easy to figure out. Where in Chenja, though, that was harder. It took tracking down Jaksdijah so Hajjij first. Arran had been a house boy of Jaks's mother, a coastal boy raised in the interior. Jaks was the last of his known, living kin. Nyx and Tej found Jaks boxing for bread at an underground fighting club thirty kilometers inside the Chenjan border. The mullahs didn't like Chenjans fighting foreigners—which made Jaks's fights illegal—but it paid well.

Tej and Nyx bided their time for a month, waiting for Arran to show up while their money ran out. Arran didn't disappoint. Tej was on watch the night a hooded figure knocked on Jaks's door. Just before dawn, Jaks and Arran were headed back to Nasheen.

Tej and Nyx followed.

But Tej hadn't made it back.

"He was the only one of your partners I liked," Kine said, and pursed her lips, probably to hold back words God wouldn't permit her to say. Then, "You should partner with men more often."

Nyx snorted.

They blew back out onto the road. The shocks in the bakkie were going out too, Nyx realized, leaking vital fluid all over the desert. She hoped Kine knew a good tissue mechanic at the coast.

"Where am I taking you?" Kine asked. Sand rolled across the pavement.

"Faleen."

"A bit out of my way."

Nyx let that one go and looked out the window, watching flat white desert turn to dunes. Kine didn't like silence. Give her a long stretch of stillness and eventually she'd change the subject.

Kine was government now, one of the breeding techs who worked at the compounds on the coast. She had some kind of slick security clearance that went well with her hijab and lonely bed. Nyx saw her only when she was ferrying samples to and from the front—just another blood dealer, another organ stealer.

"A ship came into Faleen this week," Kine said as she rolled up the window. Nyx saw the wide sleeve of her burnous come down, flashing a length of paler skin from wrist to elbow—dusty sand instead of sun dark. "If you're looking for magicians to help you bring in this deserter, there are a whole mess of them gathering in Faleen. I hear even the lower sort are there, the sort who might—"

"Where from?"

"The magicians?"

"The ship."

"Oh, yes. The ship is from New Kinaan."

Colonists had been barred from Umayma for a thousand years. Nyx hadn't even seen a ship in a decade. Umayma sat at the edge of everything; most of the sky was dark at night. All she ever saw moving up there were dead satellites and broken star carriers from the beginning of the world.

"I've corresponded with them for some time," Kine said, "for my genetics work. They fight another of God's wars out there in the dark, can you believe it?"

"Does the radio work?" Nyx asked. Knowing aliens were out there killing each other for God, too, just depressed her. She leaned forward to fiddle with the tube jutting out of the dashboard.

"No," Kine said. She pinched her mouth. "How did you lose Tej?"

Nyx wasn't sure she could answer that question herself, let alone give Kine a good answer.

"You have any weapons?" Nyx asked.

Kine's face scrunched up like a date. "If you can't tell me that, then tell me who's tracking you."

"You giving me the fourth inquisition?"

"Nyxnissa," she said, in the same hard tone she used for quoting the Kitab.

Nyx dipped her head out the open window. The air was clearing up.

"Raine," she said.

Kine's hands tightened on the wheel. She shifted pedals. The bakkie rattled and belched and picked up speed. Dust and dead beetles roiled behind them.

"You're doing black work, aren't you?" Kine said. "One of your dirty bounties. I don't like dealing with bounty hunters. Raine is the worst of them, and you're no better, these days. I'll drop you at the gates of Faleen, but no farther."

Nyx nodded. The gate would be good. More might get Kine killed.

Raine would bring Nyx in if he had to cut up half of Nasheen to do it. Nyx had been a part of his team, once, and it had been a great way of picking up skills and paying off some magician-debts for having her body reconstituted. After a while, though, he'd started to treat her like just another dumb hunter, another body to be bloodied and buried. When she started selling out her womb on the black market, well, that had made the animosity mutual. He had good reason to track her down now. Reasons a lot less personal than cutting off his cock.

"Tej was a good boy," Kine said, "You kill good men for a lost cause just like Raine."

"Raine always got us back over the border."

"Raine isn't a bel dame. He's a bounty hunter."

"There's not much difference."

"God knows the difference."

"Yeah, well, we all do it our own way."

"Yes," Kine said, and her hands tightened on the wheel. "We're all trying to cure the war."

Spoken like a true organic technician, Nyx thought.

"But there is a difference," Kine said, turning to look at her again, hard and sober now. "Bel dames enforce God's laws. They keep our boys at the front and our women honest. Bounty hunters just bring in petty thieves and women doing black work."

Women like me, Nyx thought.

Her black market broker, Bashir so Saud, owned a cantina in Faleen. The cantina was first. Even on a botched delivery, Bashir owed her at least half what it was worth. If Nyx had taken the job in Faleen instead of through Bashir's agents in Punjai, she'd have half her money now and wouldn't be so hard up. As it was, her pockets were empty. The last of her currency had been eaten with Tej.

They turned off the paved track and onto the Queen Zubair Highway that bisected Nasheen from the Chenjan border to the sea. The road signs were popular shooting targets for Chenjan operatives and Nasheenian youth. Most of the metal markers were pocked with bullet holes and smeared in burst residue. A careful eye could spot the shimmering casings of unexploded bursts lining the highway.

If dropping the womb kept Raine and Nyx's sisters busy long enough trying to track it down so they could tag and bag it, she could collect her note, call in some favors from the magicians, and maybe find a way to clear up this whole fucking mess.

Maybe.

A three-hundred-year-old water purifying plant marked the edge of the old Faleenian city limits. The city itself had lapped at the organic filter surrounding the plant for half a century before a group of Chenjan terrorists set off a sticky burst that ate up flesh and metal, scouring the eastern quarter of the city and leaving the plant on the edge of a wasteland. The government had rebuilt the road and the plant, but the detritus of the eastern quarter remained a twisted ruin. Chenjan asylum seekers, draft dodgers, and foreign women had turned the devastated quarter into a refugee camp. A colorful stir of humanity wove through the ruins now, hawking avocados and mayflies and baskets of yellow roaches. Nyx caught the spicy stink of spent fire beetles and burning glow worms.

As the dusty ridges of the refugee camps turned into the walled yards and high-rises of what passed for the Faleenian suburbs, the massive ship from New Kinaan came into view, rearing above the old gated city center of Faleen like some obscene winged minaret.

Faleen was a port city, the kind that took in the ragged handfuls of off-world ships that sputtered into its archaic docking bay every year looking for repairs, supplies, and usually—directions. Faleen wasn't the sort of place anybody off-world came to on purpose. Most of the ships that rocketed past Umayma were so alien in their level of technology that they couldn't have put into the old port if they wanted to. The port design hadn't changed much since the beginning of the world, and most everybody on Umayma wanted to keep it that way.

They drove past women and girls walking along the highway carrying baskets on their heads and huge nets over their shoulders. Bugs were popular trade with the magicians in Faleen. Professional creepers caught up to three kilos a day—striped chafers, locusts, tumblebugs, spider wasps, dragonflies, pselaphid beetles, fungus weevils—and headed to the magicians' gym to trade them in for opium, new kidneys, good lungs, maybe a scraping or two to take off the cancers.

Kine pulled up outside the towering main gate of the dusty

city, scattering young girls, sand, and scaly chickens from her path with a blast of her horn. Another cloud of beetles escaped from the leak in the back and bloomed around the bakkie. Nyx batted away the bugs and jumped out.

She took one long look at the main gate, then swung back to look at Kine. She half opened her mouth to ask.

"I'm not giving you any money," Kine said.

Nyx grimaced.

"Go with God!" Kine yelled after her.

Nyx raised a hand. She'd left God in Chenja.

Kine shifted pedals and turned back onto the highway, heading for the interior.

Nyx turned toward the two giant slabs of organic matting that were the main gates into Faleen. Rumor had it they'd seen better days as compression doors on some star carrier the First Families rode down on from the moons.

Nyx pulled up the hood of her burnous and bled into the traffic heading through the gate. She passed the broken tower of a minaret and walked through narrow alleys between mud-brick buildings whose precipitous lean threatened a swift death. She didn't much like the stink and crowd of cities, but you could lose yourself in a city a lot more easily than you could out in farming communities like Mushirah. She had run to the desert and the cities for the anonymity. And to die for God.

None of that had worked out very well.

Bashir's cantina was at the edge of the Chenjan quarter, and the ass end of it served as the public entrance to the magicians' gym and fighting ring. Bashir made a pretty penny on fight nights when all of Faleen's starving tailors, tax clerks, bug merchants, and renegade printers crowded in through the bar to watch the fight. The ones who couldn't get into the main fighting area contented themselves with drinking cheap rice wine and whiskey, listening to the steady *slap-slap* of gloved fists meeting flesh and the damp thumping of sweaty bodies hitting the mat.

Bashir also made a little money on the side as a black work broker.

Two tall women with shoulders as wide as the doorway stopped Nyx at the cantina stoop.

"You have an appointment?" one of them asked. "It's private business only until we open for tonight's fight."

"Do I look like I have an appointment?"

"Who the fuck are you?"

"Tell her I'm the bel dame."

The women shifted on their feet. "I'll get her," the biggest one said.

There was a time when Nyx had enjoyed throwing that title around on a job. "Yeah, I'm a bel dame," and "bel dames—like *me*." These days the whole dance just made her tired. She'd cut off a lot of boys' heads over the last three years. Draft dodgers, mostly, and deserters like this Arran kid who came back into Nasheen still contaminated with shit from the front.

Nyx pushed at her sore belly and rocked back on her heels. She wondered if Bashir sold morphine before noon.

The bouncer came back and said, "She'll see you."

Nyx ducked after her into the dark, smoky interior of the cantina. Dust clotted the air, and bug-laced sand covered most of the floor. It was good for soaking up blood and piss.

Bashir sat at a corner table smoking sweet opium. Nyx could taste it. The smell made her nauseous. Bashir had two bottles of sand-colored whiskey at the table, and someone had left behind a still-smoking cigar that smelled more like marijuana than sen. Bashir had two teenage boys beside her, both just shy of draft age, maybe fifteen. They were sallow and soft-looking and kept their hair long, braided, and belled. Somebody had kept them out of training. Letting adolescent boys go that soft was illegal in most districts, even if they were prostitutes. They wouldn't last a day at the front—the Chenjans would mash through them like overripe squash.

"Nyxnissa," Bashir said. She exhaled a plume of rich smoke. "Thought I'd seen the last of you."

"Most people think that," Nyx said, sliding next to one of the boys. He flinched. She outweighed him by at least twenty-five kilos. "Until I show up again."

"How was your trip?" Bashir asked. She wore red trousers and a stained short coat but kept her head uncovered. Her skin was a shade paler than those who worked in the desert, but the tough, leathery look of her face said her wealth was recently acquired. Like the boys, she was getting fat and soft at the edges, but unlike the boys, she'd fought it out on the sand with the best of them in her youth. There was muscle under the affluence.

"Not as smooth as I hoped," Nyx said. She pulled off her hood.

Bashir looked her over with a lazy sort of interest. "A bug told me you don't have what we bargained for."

"I need a drink," Nyx said, "and half of what you owe me." She hailed the woman at the bar, but Bashir waved her woman back.

"The bug says you dropped the purse at the butcher's."

"I did," Nyx said. "It was a high-risk job. You knew that when your agent gave it to me." She'd been carrying genetic material worth a nice chunk of money in that womb. Bashir wasn't going to let it go easy, no, but bel dames made good black market runners which made them valuable to people like Bashir—until they got caught. Word got around when you did business with gene pirates.

Being unarmed made it easier to resist the urge to shoot Bashir in the head and demand the contents of the cantina's till from the barmaid. She was too close to the magicians' gym to get away with that.

"It was a substantial purse," Bashir said.

Nyx leaned back against the seat. The boy next to her had a

hold of his glass, but wasn't drinking. Like many Nasheenian women, Bashir was known to like boys, but these ones were a little young and soft for a desert matron.

"Where'd you pick up these two?" Nyx asked.

"Lovely, eh?" Bashir said. Her dark eyes glinted in the low light. The place was too cheap for bulbs. They were still using worms in glass. "They were a gift. From a friend."

Bashir didn't have friends. Nyx cut a look at the door. The bouncers had closed it. The woman at the bar was still wiping the same length of counter she'd been mopping when Nyx dropped in. I shouldn't have come, Nyx thought. She should have gone straight to the magicians and asked for sanctuary. It had been only a matter of time before turning Nyx in was worth more than a black market purse. But, fuck, she'd needed the money from this job.

Nyx knew the answer but asked anyway.

"Who gave them to you?"

Bashir showed her teeth.

"You'll get shit from the magicians for crossing a bel dame," Nyx said. They could take her money, her shoes, her sword, her *bloody fucking partner*, but they couldn't take her title. "How much did you get for selling me out? I'm worth a lot more than a couple of fuckable boys."

"Your reputation's been tumbling for a good long while, Nyxnissa. The bounty hunters have your name in a hat now, and if you're lucky, it'll be Raine who brings you in and not some young honey pot trying to prove something by cutting off your head. What would your sisters say?"

"Leave the bel dame family out of it."

"There's been some stirring in the bel dame council. Rumor has it they want to clean up this little mess with you internally, the way Alharazad cleaned up the council. They'll cut you up and put you in a bag."

"Then you and your pirates are losing a good ferrier."

"You don't deliver enough to make yourself worth the risk. And now you dropped your womb, so I don't have anything invested. Putting out a note on you got me a good purse for reporting a pirate. Delivering you to the bounty office and claiming my own bounty makes us even."

So Bashir had turned her in for bread.

"How much am I going for?" Nyx asked. Her hands itched for a blade that she no longer carried. She was good with a sword. The guns? Not so much.

"About fifty," Bashir said.

Well, that was something.

The boy beside Nyx took his hand away from his drink.

The woman behind the bar moved toward the kitchen.

All right, then.

Nyx kicked up onto the tabletop before the boy could steady the pistol in his other hand. The gun went off with a pop and burst of yellow smoke.

She threw a low roundhouse kick to the other boy's face and leapt off the table before Bashir could get her scattergun free.

Reflex sent her running for the back door, kicking up sand behind her. She shouldered into the kitchen, knocked past a startled Mhorian cook, and ran headlong out the open back door and into the alley.

A strong arm shot out and slammed into her throat. The blow took her off her feet.

Nyx hit the sand and rolled.

Still choking, Nyx tried to get up, but Raine already had hold of her.

He twisted her arm behind her and forced her face back into the sand. She spit and turned her head, gulping air. She saw two pairs of dirty sandaled feet in front of her. She tried to look up at who owned them.

Little ropy-muscled Anneke hadn't broken a sweat. She stood chewing a wad of sen, one arm supporting the weight of the rifle she kept lodged just under her shoulder. She was as dark as a Chenjan, and about the size of a twelve-year-old. The other feet belonged to the skinny half-breed Taite, who wasn't a whole hell of a lot older than thirteen or fourteen.

"You must be desperate," Nyx said, spitting more sand, "to use Taite and Anneke as muscle."

"That's all the greeting I get?" Raine asked. He pulled her up, kept a grip on her arm, and tugged off her burnous.

"Where did you lose your gear, girl? I taught you better than that." He shook the burnous out, probably thinking she'd hidden something in it.

Raine was a large man, a head taller than Nyx, just as dark and twice as massive. His face was broad and flat and stamped with two black, expressionless eyes, like deep water from a community well. The hilt of a good blade cut through a slit in the back of his brown burnous. He was pushing Bashir's age—one of the few who'd survived the front.

She grunted.

He took off her baldric and passed it to Anneke for inspection.

"Nothing here," Anneke said, and tossed the baldric at Nyx's feet.

"You're clean," Raine said, half a question. "You know how much you're going for?"

"More than fifty," Nyx said.

He took Nyx by her braids and brought her close to his bearded face. The beard was new, a Chenjan affectation that would get him noticed on the street and pegged as a political radical. "Do you know what the queen does to bel dames who turn black?" he asked. "When they start selling zygotes to gene pirates? Those pirates will breed monsters in jars and sell them to Chenjans. But you don't care about that, do you? You need pocket money."

Raine had recruited her from the magicians' gym after she was reconstituted. They'd spent long nights and longer days talking about the war and his hatred for those whose work he saw as perpetuating it. Gene pirates—selling genetic material to both sides—were no better to him than Tirhani arms dealers.

Raine released her.

"I didn't train you to be a bel dame," he said. "I taught you to be a bounty hunter, to fight real threats to Nasheen like young bel dames who sell out their organs to gene pirates."

"I got issued a bel dame note for a contaminated boy. I know he's in Faleen. I needed the cash from the womb to bring him in."

"You should have given the note to a real bel dame."

Nyx looked him in the eye. "I don't give up notes."

"Taite," Raine said, holding Nyx with one strong arm while reaching toward the boy. Taite had the half-starved look of a kid who had grown up outside the breeding compounds. He reached into his gear bag.

They were going to truss her up and sell her.

Nyx stood in the back alley of Bashir's cantina. At the end of the alley she could clearly see the back entrance to the magicians' gym. Anneke was leaning against the wall now, rifle still in hand. Getting shot would hurt.

Getting trussed up and hauled into the Chenjan district, though… that would be the end of the job. And probably a lot more.

Nyx tensed. Taite pulled out the sticky bands from his gear bag and threw them to Raine.

Nyx twisted and swiveled in Raine's grip while he tried to catch the bands. She palmed him in the solar plexus. He grunted. His grip loosened. She pulled free and bolted.

Anneke jumped to attention. Nyx pushed past her.

The rifle popped.

Nyx felt a sharp, stabbing thump on her right hip, as if someone had set a sledge hammer on fire and hit her with it.

She staggered down the alley and clutched her hip. A burst of mud-brick exploded behind her. She heard two more rounds go off.

The red door of the magicians' gym appeared at her right. She stumbled and pounded on the door.

"Sanctuary!" she yelled. "Bel dame! My life for a thousand! Sanctuary!"

She heard Anneke yell, "Fuck!"

The pack of them ran toward her. Raine's face was dark. Nyx screamed, "My life for a thousand!" and pounded on the door again. There was nothing easier to shoot than a stationary target.

Anneke was a hand breadth away. She reached for Nyx's hair.

The magicians' door opened. A waft of cold air billowed into the alley, bringing with it the stink of sweat and leather. Nyx fell inside, into darkness. She tucked her feet underneath her, pulling them across the threshold.

"Fuck!" Anneke said again.

Nyx lay at a pair of bare feet cloaked by yellow trousers. She heard a low buzzing sound, and a soapy organic filter popped up over the doorway. Through the filmy gauze of the filter, Nyx saw Raine standing behind his crew, her burnous still in his hand.

She looked up the length of billowing yellow trousers and into the sapphire-eyed face of Yah Reza.

"You're bleeding all over my floor, baby doll," Yah Reza said, and shut the door.

2

Rhys had never fought at the front. He'd been through it, yes. But he had never picked up a blade or a burst or dismembered a body. He had gone to great lengths to avoid doing so.

He had once walked across a rubbish-strewn street with his father, anxious to keep up with the long-legged man, and some piece of glass or serrated tin had lodged in his shoe. He had kicked free of it and limped on despite the pain. When he arrived home after morning prayer, he had pulled off his shoe and found it full of blood. It had taken his mother and sisters nearly a quarter of an hour to stir him from a dead faint, and by then they had cleaned and bandaged the wound. He did not look at it again until the skin had healed clean. He threw out the shoes.

When Rhys crossed the great churning waste of the desert, he'd been running not toward his father but away, across the disputed border between Chenja and Nasheen. The sky had lit up every night with deadly green and violet bursts. The world had smelled of yeast and mustard and geranium. He had stayed as far from the contagion clouds as possible, but when he stumbled through Chenja and into the nearest Nasheenian border town, he was hacking up his lungs in bloody clumps, and his skin burned and bubbled like tar.

What woman took him in then, he did not know, but he knew it was a woman. Everyone alive in Nasheen was a woman. They sent all their men out to die at the front. They had no family heads, no clans. They were godless women who murdered men and bred like flies. The Nasheenians took him for a deserter, but because they called in their magicians before they called in their order keepers, they had saved him from a cold, bloody death in an interrogation room somewhere in the Nasheenian interior.

The magicians had arrived with sleeves full of spotted fungus beetles and cicadas in their hair, and when Rhys next opened his eyes, he was in a bed at the center of a circular room deep in the magicians' quarters. A lightning bug lamp beside him brightened and dimmed, brightened and dimmed, until he thought his vision must have been lost somewhere in the desert along with his name. He moved his hands over the lamp, and the bugs ceased their intermittent dance and glowed steadily.

"Is it better or worse, in the light?" one of the magicians had asked, emerging from the darkness of the doorway. From the raised bed, he could see that the doorway opened into more blackness.

The woman magician spoke to Rhys in accented Chenjan, and she had brought him a strange still-wriggling stew of grubs and gravy. She was a tall, bony woman with eyes the color of sapphire flies; not their real color, she assured him.

"We know a thing or two about illusion in Nasheen," she had told him. He remembered how strange it was to see her eyes at all. He had heard that Nasheenian women did not wear veils, but he still found her vanity surprising, decadent. Chenjan women could submit to God and wield a rifle with equal ease, but Nasheenian women had allowed their propensity for violence to pollute their beliefs. Wielding a rifle, they believed, made them men in the eyes of God, and men did not have to practice modesty or submission to anyone but God. Nasheenian women had forgotten their place in the order of things.

The woman's mouth had worked constantly at the wad of sen she kept in it. Her teeth were stained a bloody crimson. She turned to the lightning bug lamp and laughed.

"You've figured it all out, haven't you, baby doll?" she had said, gesturing at the bugs. "We may find some use for you yet."

It was then that he realized he had asked the bugs to light the room, something only a magician could do. They knew what he was, then.

Her name, she said, was Yah Reza. She said she would help him work on his Nasheenian and that hiding his ability with bugs from another magician would have been like trying to pretend he wasn't Chenjan. She could see the difference. Now, she had said, he was hers, unless he wanted some other life—wanted to get sold off to gene pirates or the breeding compounds, or become a venom dealer or some mercenary's translator.

"There are worse fates," she had said, and something on the stuccoed wall behind her had shifted, and Rhys realized it was an enormous butterfly, big as his hand. "But I can make you a magician."

A magician.

A *Nasheenian* magician.

"One that can practice in Nasheen?" he had asked, because he could not go back to Chenja. Something in his chest ached at the thought of it.

He remembered rubbing at the backs of his hands where his father had beaten him with a metal rod when he had refused him. But the magicians had healed those wounds as well, and the skin and bones were mended now, erasing the physical history of that night, those words. But not the memory. His or God's.

"I can even get you a proper sponsor, once you're trained. Better, I won't ask what brought you across the border in the dead of night or how you did it. You get on with the magicians, you get immunity from the draft and the inquisition. What do you think of that?"

Rhys did not fear the Nasheenian draft—Nasheenians didn't draft foreign men—or the inquisition; he was too smart for them. But Yah Reza offered him magic. In Chenja, to reveal his skill would have meant immediate training for the front, no matter that he was his father's only son. As a standard, his father's lack of sons had given Rhys a place at home. Men still headed families in Chenja. They still owned companies, acted as mullahs, ran the government. But as a magician, he would have been forced to the front.

"I'll stay," he had told her.

He spent some months among the magicians, learning the intricacies of bug manipulation and organic tech. His Nasheenian improved. He learned to look away from the women in the hall as he passed. They stared at him openly, like harlots. It was up to him to allow them to maintain some shred of honor. When he asked to leave the cavernous labyrinth of the magicians' quarters and boxing gym to go sightseeing in Faleen, Yah Reza told him he was not yet ready. She encouraged patience. But her words did nothing to distill the growing sense that he was a prisoner there, kept at the discretion of Nasheen's magicians until he proved worthless or useful. He did not know what they would do with him when they decided which he best embodied.

Yah Reza caught him by the elbow one afternoon as he hurried back to his rooms after another embarrassing encounter with a magician teaching him transmission science. He was not used to a world where women put their hands on him without reservation and regarded him as if he were a young but dangerous insect. Chenja was full of women, of course, but no Chenjan woman had ever grabbed him in the street, not even the lowliest of prostitutes. And no Chenjan woman had ever done the things to him that the women in the border towns had done before their magicians showed up. They would not have dreamed of it. They would have been killed for it.

He was still trembling when Yah Reza grabbed him.

"Come with me, baby doll," she said. She wore a billowing

saffron robe and smelled of death and saffron. A furry spider the size of Rhys's thumb crawled along her sleeve, and a whirl of tiny blue moths circled her head.

He tried to quiet his trembling.

Yah Reza beckoned him. Rhys followed her through the long, twisting halls of the magicians' quarters—cool, windowless corridors that suddenly opened into niches and vaulted chambers filled with locusts and cocooned creatures, lit sporadically by glow worms and fire beetles and the ever-present lightning bugs flaring and dying in the dark.

The preponderance of bugs in the magicians' quarters made his blood sing, as if he was attuned to a bit of everything, able to touch and manipulate pieces of the world. He felt more alive here than he had anywhere else in his life, among those who spent their days coming up with new and interesting ways to kill his people.

I'll take what I need from them and return, he thought. I'll make it right.

The boxers' locker rooms were three steps to the right of the transmission rooms, a corridor away from the internal betting booth, and three long bends of the hall from Yah Tayyib's operating theater, where magicians and bel dames came to receive treatment for cancer and contagion. The corridors within a magicians' gym were never the same length, never quite in the same location. Beneath each gym, the world was bent and twisted. The distance-bending corridors were relics from the times before Umayma was habitable, back when magicians lived belowground while they remade the world. This made it possible to step into a gym at the coast and emerge a few minutes later at a gym in Mushtallah or Faleen and Aludra. Practical for long distances, but dizzying over short ones.

As they approached the locker room for outriders, Husayn—the magicians' favorite boxing nag—passed them in the hall, heading one twist of the hallway down to her own locker room. Husayn was a stocky woman with a face like a shovel. A novice magician scurried after her, carrying her gear.

"Hey, chimba!" Husayn called at Rhys. Too loud. The women in this country were all too loud.

Rhys did not look at her.

"Those magicians haven't been able to wash that gravy stink off you, you know it?" Husayn persisted.

"I am still perplexed as to why it is that Chenja retained the veil and Nasheen discarded it," Rhys said. "Perhaps Nasheen's women sought to frighten away God with their ugliness."

"Well now, if all your boys are as pretty as you, your *boys* best start covering up too," Husayn said. "Ah, the shit I'd like to do to you." She laughed.

What a fool, Rhys thought. Chenjan mullahs taught that men's bodies were clean, asexual. Closer to God. Women, real women, were not stirred to sin at the sight of men. If these godless Nasheenian women were stirred at the sight of anything, it was blood.

Yah Reza shooed her away. "Come, now, this isn't a whorehouse."

Husayn cackled and moved on.

Rhys ducked into the other locker room. Inside, the light was dim, and a lean woman sat hunched on one of the benches, staring into her hands.

When he stepped in, she looked up. She was long in the face, like a dog, and she had narrow, little eyes and a set to her mouth that reminded Rhys of one of his sisters, the look she got when she wanted something so badly she made herself sick. He hoped this woman didn't vomit. He knew who would have to clean it up.

Yah Reza moved past him and greeted the outrider.

The outrider stood. She looked uneasy, like a cornered animal—a dog-shifter in form, or maybe some scraggly adolescent sand cat. He might have guessed her for a shifter if he had seen only an image or picture of her, but in person he was able to see clearly that she was not. The air did not prickle and bend around her as it did a shifter. She was just some kid, some standard—just another part of the world.

Yah Reza talked low to the girl and rubbed her shoulders. She spit sen on the floor. Rhys knew who would have to clean that up too.

"This is Rhys. Come here, boy," Yah Reza said, and Rhys walked close enough to see that he was a head and shoulders taller than the outrider.

"You bring your wraps?" Yah Reza asked the girl.

The outrider stabbed her fingers toward two long, dirty pieces of tattered muslin on the bench next to her.

Yah Reza spit more sen. "Rhys," she said.

Rhys went to the locker at the back of the room, where they kept the extra gear. He unraveled a couple of hand wraps. He grabbed some tape and took a seat on the bench and finished unraveling the wraps.

"He know how to box?" the outrider asked, and even Rhys, with his non-native Nasheenian, noticed her mushy inland accent. Where had they picked her up? Working some border town? The magicians were notorious for pushing girls into the ring before they were ready. It made the fights bloodier.

"I don't believe in violence," Rhys said.

"A shame too," Yah Reza said. "He's a damn fine shot with a pistol. But don't worry none about his technique. He's a magician, girl. He knows hands. You get on, and I'll meet you in a quarter-hour. We got some fancy visitors want to meet you and Husayn before the fight."

Yah Reza petted the outrider's cheek.

The outrider sat back on the bench and eyed Rhys like he was a beetle turned over on its back, not sure if it was harmless or just playing at docility until she got close.

Rhys asked for her right hand.

She hesitated, and he thought that was odd from a woman who was about to go toe to toe with a seasoned fighter in a magicians' gym. He realized then how young she was, maybe seventeen. It was hard to tell with Nasheenian women. They grew up fast, bore the marks of their short, brutal childhoods on their bodies and faces. Most of them were broken old crones at thirty.

He taped the wrap in place and began to loop it around her wrist and between her fingers. She had her palm flat and her fingers wide.

When he had first come to Nasheen, he'd thought he would hate all of its women for their ugliness, their vanity, but as he put the wraps on this little dog-faced girl, he found himself admiring her hands. She had strong, beautiful fingers, calloused knuckles and palms, and he saw her scars, and the dirt under her bitten nails. There was something splendid and tragic about her all at once.

He tied off her right hand and moved to the left. When he took her left hand in his, something about the way she held it, the way it felt beneath his fingers, made him hesitate. He pulled at her fingers.

She winced.

"You've done an injury to this hand?" he asked.

"Nothing," she said.

"An old injury," he amended as he pressed his thumb against the back of her hand, rubbed her knuckles, pushed in slow circles up to her wrist. She had hairline fractures in the small bones of her left hand. Some had healed, but badly. It was a brittle hand.

"You shouldn't be fighting with this," he said.

She pulled her hand from him, and her mouth got harder. Her shoulders stiffened. "I can wrap myself. They told me magicians used tricks."

"I didn't say I wouldn't finish." He took her hand in his again. His ability to diagnose illness and injury had been the first sign that he'd inherited his father's skill as a magician. A more talented magician might have been able to heal her hands, if the injuries weren't so old, but Rhys's skill was limited, his knowledge incomplete. The longer he stayed among the Nasheenian magicians, the more he worried things would stay that way.

"Does your family approve of you boxing?" he asked to fill the cool silence. Three locusts climbed up his pant leg. He moved his hand over them, and they dropped to the floor.

"Don't have much family," she said. "Where you learn to wrap hands? They teach you that in magic school?"

"My uncle took me to fights in Chenja," he said, "when I was too young to know better. I wrapped his hands."

"You got soft hands. You aren't a fighter. You never fought?"

"I don't believe in violence."

"You ain't answered the question."

He finished taping her bad hand. He squeezed her fist in his palm. "There, that good?"

She made fists with both hands. "I been taped worse."

"I'm sure," Rhys said. He hesitated. If she had had a proper husband, or a brother, or a son, that man would have told her not to fight. He would have taken care of her. "You shouldn't fight with that hand," he repeated.

"I been doing it a long time. It's fight or die where I'm from. Sometimes you have to run away just to live. I suppose you know something about that."

Rhys did not answer.

"I don't mind you're black," she said, magnanimously.

"It doesn't matter what we mind," Rhys said. "God sorts all that out."

"Our God says your god is false."

"They're the same God." He had not always believed that, even when he pressed his head to the ground six times a day in prayer and intoned the same litany in a dead language, the language of Umayma, brought down from the moons with the Firsts at the beginning of the world: *In the name of God, the infinitely Compassionate and Merciful...*

For years he had believed what the Imams told them, that Nasheenians were godless infidels who worshipped women and idols brought in from dead worlds, worlds blighted by God for their own idolatry. But when the muezzin called the prayers here, those who were faithful went to the same mosque he did with the other magicians, prayed in nearly the same way, and spoke in the same language—God's language—though his birth tongue was Chenjan, and theirs, Nasheenian.

They were all Umaymans, the people from the moons who had waited up there a thousand years while magicians made Umayma half-habitable—all but the Mhorians, Ras Tiegans, the Heidians, and the two-hundred-odd Drucians, who had come later. Survivors of other dead worlds, worlds out of the darkest parts of the sky.

In the mosque, forehead pressed against the floor, Rhys never understood the war. It was only when he raised his head and saw the women praying among him, bareheaded, often bare-legged, shamelessly displaying full heads of hair and ample flesh, that he questioned what these women truly believed they were submitting to. Certainly not the will of God. On the streets he saw widowed women reduced to begging, girls like this one earning money with blood, and bloated women coming in from the coast after giving birth to their unnatural broods of children. This was the life that Chenja fought against. This godlessness.

Whenever the bakkie got sick or the milk soured, his mothers would blame "those godless Nasheenians, daughters of demons."

"Rhys?"

He looked up from the outrider's hands to see Yah Reza in

the doorway. A dozen fungus beetles skittered past her into the room. The outrider flinched.

"Yah Tayyib needs you in surgery," Yah Reza said.

Rhys squeezed the girl's fist a final time. "Luck to you," he said.

"We have some visitors come to see you boxers," Yah Reza said. "You up for it?" She was slipping further into whatever vernacular the girl spoke.

"What sort of visitors?" the girl asked.

Rhys stood, and put away the tape. He walked toward the door.

"The foreign kind. They don't bite, though, so far as I can tell."

"Yeah, that's fine, then."

Yah Reza clapped her hands. "Come."

Rhys turned past the magician and walked into the dim outer corridor. He saw a cluster of figures outside Husayn's locker room and paused to get a look at them.

Two black women wearing oddly cut hijabs spoke in low tones. Though the hijabs were black, their long robes were white, and dusty along the hem. They wore no jewelry, and instead of sandals they wore black boots without a heel.

Despite their complexions, he knew they were not Chenjan, or even Tirhani. They were too small, too thin, fine-boned, and the way they held themselves—the way they spoke with heads bent—was not Chenjan or Tirhani but something else.

One of them looked out at him and ceased speaking. From across the long hall, he saw a broad face with high cheekbones, large eyes, and dark brows. It was a startlingly open face, as if she was not used to keeping secrets. Her skin was bright and clear and smoother than any he'd seen save for the face of a child. She was old, he knew, by her posture and her height, but the clarity of her skin made him want to call her a girl. It was not the face of a woman who had grown up in the desert or even a world with two suns. Unless she was the daughter of a rich merchant who had kept her locked in a tower in some salty country, hidden from the suns by dark curtains and filters for a quarter century, she was not from anywhere on Umayma.

"You're very young to be a man," she said, and laughed at him. Her accent was strange—a deep, throaty whir swallowed all of her vowels, and when she laughed, she laughed from deep in her chest. It was a boisterous sound, too loud to come from a woman with such a narrow chest.

"You're not from Nasheen," he said.

"Nor are you."

She was not from anywhere in the world. But that was impossible. The Mhorians had been the last allowed refuge on Umayma, nearly a thousand years before. They had brought with them dangerous idols and belief in a foreign prophet, but they claimed to be people of the Book, and custom required that they be given sanctuary. It was a custom soon discarded, though, and the ships that followed the Mhorians were shot out of the sky. Their remains had rained down over the world like stars.

Were these women people of the Book?

"You're an alien," he said, tentative, a question.

She laughed again, and the laughter filled the corridor. "Your first?"

He nodded.

"Not the last, I hope," she said.

And then Yah Reza and the outrider entered the hall and blocked his view, and Rhys turned away and walked quickly past a bend in the corridor, where he could no longer hear the alien woman's voice.

The memory of her laugh tugged at something inside him, something he thought he'd left back in Chenja. He wanted to pull back her hijab and run his fingers through the black waves of her unbound hair. He squeezed his eyes shut, shook his head. He had been too long in Nasheen.

When he arrived at Yah Tayyib's operating theater, he saw blood spattering the stones, hungry bugs lapping up their fill. Another hard-up bel dame had come to collect *zakat*. Another godless woman was destined to die.

3

Nyx struggled out of a groggy half dream of drowning and fell off the giant stone slab in Yah Tayyib's operating theater. The floor was cold.

Yah Tayyib helped her up. One curved wall of the theater was lined with squat glass jars of organs. Glow worms ringed the shelves and hugged the glass. Nyx noted the long table at Yah Tayyib's left and the length of silk that covered his instruments, but her gaze did not settle there long. She was interested in the medicine wardrobe at the back. The one with the morphine.

She was naked. Blood trickled down one leg.

"How do you feel?" Yah Tayyib asked. He wore a billowing blue robe. Carrion beetles clung to the hem. He was a tall thin man, well over sixty and gray in the beard. His face was a sunken ruin, the nose a mashed pulp of flesh. But his hands, his all-important magician's hands, were smooth and straight-fingered.

Nyx wondered how she was supposed to respond to that. Her head felt stuffed with honey.

"You were missing a kidney," Yah Tayyib said. "I replaced that as well."

"I traded it for a ticket out of Chenja. The other one wasn't mine either."

"I didn't think it was," he said.

"Why not?"

"I put it in there six months ago."

"Ah," Nyx said.

"I'm quite sorry about the womb," Yah Tayyib said. "It was your original, you know, and uniquely shaped. Bicornuate. I would have bought it myself, though for much less than you likely sold it." He always talked about body parts like bug specimens—dry and purely academic.

"I don't care much how it's shaped or whose it is," she said. "I care about what it can do for me. What time is it? I've got Raine on my tail."

She looked around for her clothes. They were stacked neatly next to the operating slab. She started to get dressed, slowly. It was like trying to work somebody else's body. She was still a big woman, but she was down to her dhoti and binding, and both were tattered and loose, hanging off her like a shroud.

"You have a price on your head," Yah Tayyib said, and turned to wash his hands at the sink. Flesh beetles clung to the end of the tap, bundling up drops of water in their sticky legs.

"Yeah," she said. "More than fifty, apparently."

"You should turn yourself in to your bel dame sisters. The bounty hunters won't be so generous. They say it's black money this time. Gene pirates." He wiped his hands dry on his robes and regarded her. "What were you carrying?"

"Zygotes," Nyx said. "Ferrier work. I was supposed to hand it off on this end, but I had to drop it and sell it to some butchers to keep my sisters busy. I figure they lost at least half a day trying to figure out where I dropped it. No womb, no proof, no way to fully collect their note on me."

The fist in her belly tightened, contracted. She felt dizzy, and leaned back against the stone altar.

"You've indebted yourself to us again," Yah Tayyib said. "This is not the place to settle a blood note. Yours or theirs. Keep your bloody boys and your bloody sisters out of my ring."

"Still got something against bel dames?"

"You've never been a boy at the front."

"I can't imagine you being frightened of anything, Yah Tayyib."

"We all manage our grief differently," Yah Tayyib said. "Three dead wives and a dozen dead children make me more human, not less. You have chosen your path. I have chosen mine. This is the last time I do this for you, Nyxnissa."

"You say that every time. Is it too late to bet on the boxers?"

"What in this world do you own to bet?"

Nyx prodded at the red scarring tissue on her right hip. "I've got good credit," she said. She always paid her debts to the magicians… eventually.

"I doubt that," he said. "You've nothing more than rags and flesh."

She shook her head. Her vision swam. "I'll get paid when I've cleared the blood debt. I can buy whatever I need after that."

Yah Tayyib sighed. He walked over to the big wardrobe next to the medicine cabinet.

"Am I done bleeding?" Nyx said.

Yah Tayyib pulled out a deep mahogany burnous. "You'll expel the usual bugs in a few hours. They're aiding in the last of the repairs. Here, this is the most inconspicuous I have."

Nyx donned the burnous. It was surprisingly soft.

"Organic?" she asked.

"Yes. It will breathe for you, if you need it to."

"Great," she said, as if that would make any difference tonight. "Walk me out?"

Yah Tayyib escorted her back through the labyrinthine halls of the magicians' quarters, all windowless. He took her to the internal magician's betting booth, where a young woman Nyx knew from her days at the gym stood at the window collecting baskets of bugs.

"I still have credit here, Maj?" Nyx asked.

"You always have credit," Maj said.

Yah Tayyib huffed his displeasure as Nyx set down a bet on Jaks so Hajjij for fifty.

"You're a madwoman," he said as Nyx picked up her receipt and then pushed back through the crowd of magicians.

"Maybe so," she said. But this would get her Jaks, and Jaks would get her the boy, and the boy would put money in her pockets—and save some Nasheenian village from contamination.

That was the idea, anyway.

Yah Tayyib brought her back to the gym, which had been transformed into a fighting arena. The lights outside the ring were dim. The last of the speed bags had been put away. A man who looked remarkably like a Chenjan dancer moved under the ring-lights and it took Nyx half a minute to realize the dancer really *was* Chenjan—and male. Some instinctual part of her thought he'd look a lot better blown up, but there was something she liked about him, something about the way he moved, the delicacy of his hands.

She and Yah Tayyib negotiated the crowd to a bench at the back, along the edges of the darkness. Nyx kept her eye on the dancer.

"Who's he?" Nyx asked.

"The boy?"

He was probably eighteen or nineteen, old enough for the front. Not so much a boy, in Nasheen.

"Yeah," she said.

"A pet project of Yah Reza's," Yah Tayyib said. "A political refugee from Chenja. He calls himself Rhys."

"What kind of a name is that?"

"A *nom de guerre*," he said, using the Ras Tiegan expression. "Yah Reza tells me he used to dance for the Chenjan mullahs as a child. When his father asked him to carry out the punishment of his own sister because he himself was unable, Rhys refused, and was exiled. That's the story he tells, in any case."

"Does he do anything besides dance?"

"He's not a prostitute, if that's what you're asking," Yah Tayyib said.

"Then what's he do?" she asked.

Yah Tayyib folded his hands in his lap. "He's good with bugs."

"A bel dame could use someone good with bugs."

"He's worth three of you."

"You saying I'm a bad girl?"

Yah Tayyib's expression was stony. "I'm saying you're less than virtuous."

Well. She'd been called worse.

The dancer slowed and stilled. The match was about to start, and his time was up.

Nyx scanned the crowd for Raine and his crew, in case they'd gotten in through the cantina entrance. Her gaze found a handful of very different figures instead. Three tall women with the black hoods of their burnouses pulled up, the hilt of their blades visible at their hips, moved through the throng of spectators, sniffing at glasses of liquor and brushing bugs from their sleeves.

Her sisters.

Not the kind she was related to by blood.

Nyx hunkered on the bench. Her insides shifted. She winced. "How much longer until it starts?" Nyx asked.

"A moment. The visitors wished to speak with the boxers."

"The visitors?"

"There's a ship in from New Kinaan. Had you not heard?"

"What do they care about boxing?"

"Not only the boxing," Yah Tayyib said. "The magicians. Ah, there she is."

At the far end of the room Yah Reza stood in a door that opened into blackness. Husayn strode in from the darkness, followed by a wave of purple dragonflies that coasted out over the heads of the spectators and swarmed the ring lights. Nyx had known Yah Tayyib's blind-eyed boxer for years. They'd trained together back when Nyx came in from the front. Husayn was a decade older than Nyx, big in the hips and thighs, with the beefy legs of a woman who spent most of her days running—from what or to where, only Husayn knew. She had a mashed-in pulp of a nose and a misty right eye that wasn't commonly talked about. Husayn kept a long list of dead men and women in her locker—the ones she'd served with at the front.

The spectators were finding their seats. Nyx watched her sisters take up a position along the far wall. They did not sit. They would look for a lone woman congratulating the winner at the end of the bout—Nyx knew enough about the game not to bet on losers.

Unless she wanted to.

Jaks appeared from the more traditional entrance, the one from Bashir's cantina. She was a tough, skinny little fighter with a face like death—long and hard and forgettable. She was so sun sore she looked Chenjan. She had her chin tucked and her shoulders rolled, and she walked with her hands up. She had no patron, no cut woman, no manager. She walked alone and looked just the way she should: like a scared kid pulling her first fight in a magicians' gym.

Another of the magicians, Yah Batool, stepped up into the ring and announced the fighters.

Jaks and Husayn touched fists. The stir of dragonflies circled the lights, casting wide, weird shadows over the faces of the crowd.

When the buzzer sounded among the caged insects kept just below the gym's water clock, Jaks leapt forward and opened with a neat right double-jab-cross-hook combination. She was young, and overeager. She could probably outlast Husayn if she wanted to, but when the bugs signaled the end of the round, Jaks was already breathing hard, and her face was bloody. Husayn had clipped her open. Yah Batool sealed the cut and sent her back out.

Rounds were three minutes long, and in a magicians' ring, the boxers fought it out until somebody was knocked down for the duration of a nine-second count or tapped out in their corner. Nyx had seen outriders go down three seconds into the first round. She'd also stayed up all night watching two magicians pummel each other until one of them had an eye dangling from its socket and the other was spraying blood every time she exhaled.

Jaks's bleeding made Husayn arrogant. Jaks knocked Husayn down in the third round. The knockdown sent Yah Tayyib and the rest of the crowd to their feet. The air filled with a collective roar of dismay.

Nyx took the opportunity to slip past Yah Tayyib's elbow and make her way toward the back of the room.

Yah Batool started the count.

Nyx circled around to the front of the cantina, keeping to the darkness at the rear of the ring and avoiding her sisters. Behind her, Nyx heard the crowd give a yell at the count of seven, and she turned to see Husayn back on her feet.

Husayn wouldn't lose this fight. It was why Nyx *hadn't* bet on her. Jaks would visit the betting booth to collect her money for the night, and like every new boxer at a magicians' gym fight, Jaks would want to know who had bet on her. Jaks would check the books and see Nyx's name. There was no faster way to get a losing boxer to take you home than to bet on her when nobody else did. And if Nyx had done her job the night before, Jaks would be giddily looking for Nyx in the bar later.

The bodies inside the cantina were packed so tight that Nyx had to shoulder her way through to a free patch of counter space. She edged a smaller woman out of a seat and ordered a whiskey from a slim half-breed barmaid.

Nyx perused the bar. She saw Anneke standing outside the

door to the street. Raine and his team were likely worried the magicians had filtered the place against them. Bashir should have been looking for Nyx too, but Bashir spent fight nights watching the fight, and business dictated that she attend the postfight parties with the local tax and gaming merchants. She wouldn't be running the bar.

Nyx looked for a good way to blend in with the chattering locals and decided to flirt with the sour-faced woman at her left, who turned out to be a gunrunner from Qahhar.

Nyx heard the fight end in round five. A wave of celebratory dragonflies cascaded from the arena and into the cantina through the open door. They brought with them a wave of scent—lime and cinnamon—that drowned out the musky stink of sweat-slathered women and warm beer. Dragonflies meant the magician-sponsored fighter had won.

The bar got louder. The winning betters bought rounds of drinks, and the gunrunner started weeping into her beer, grieving for her wayward girlfriend. She bid Nyx good night.

Nyx watched Anneke leave the doorway. Anneke would take up a position on higher ground, where she could get a better view as the cantina began to clear out en masse.

Jaks came through the door half an hour later, both eyes going purple, lip swollen. Blood oozed through a heavy wad of salve smeared above her brow. She walked like she had the last time she lost a fight—like a woman who believed she'd never see another break.

When Jaks got close, Nyx tugged her hood back so Jaks could see her face.

"Buy you a drink?" Nyx asked.

Jaks grinned. It wasn't an improvement on her face. "I suppose I owe you money," she said. "I saw that you bet on me."

Nyx shrugged. "Seemed like a fine idea at the time. What kept you so long?"

"Those off-world women chewed my ear clean off with all their talk," Jaks said.

"What, the ones from New Kinaan?" Yah Tayyib hadn't been shitting, then. What kind of alien came all the way out to this blasted rock to talk to boxers?

Jaks sat next to her. "Yeah. What about you, what the hell you doing in Faleen?" Jaks asked.

"Looking for you," Nyx said. She had never been a good liar, so whenever the truth worked, she used it. "What are you drinking?"

"Whatever you are," Jaks said. She was still beaming, and Nyx had a twinge of something like guilt. She let the feeling slide away, like oil on the surface of a cistern.

The barmaid brought their drinks. Nyx moved closer to Jaks, so their knees touched. "You have family in Faleen?" Nyx asked.

Jaks chattered about her kin. They lived just outside Faleen, she said. She'd been trying to build up to a magician's fight since she was fourteen. She had two sisters and a handful of house brothers. Her mother was on the dole, the *waqf*, and not well off.

"Boxing keeps me in bread," Jaks said, polishing off her third whiskey. Like Nyx, she drank it straight. "And it's good for picking up girls," Jaks added.

"I don't have a place," Nyx said. "You empty tonight?"

"Mostly," Jaks said. She was grinning like a fool now, like a kid. She was probably sixteen. She'd never been to the front, never been a bel dame. You could see the difference in the grin, in the eyes.

Jaks leapt from her seat and bounced around. She paid the tab and said, "Let's get out of here."

Nyx hunched and shifted her weight to alter her usual walk as they crossed the bar. Jaks moved out the door, and Nyx looped an arm around her narrow waist and turned to press her lips to Jaks's neck, letting her hood shield her profile. She saw a stir of figures hanging around outside but couldn't catch their faces in the dim night. Her sisters would be figuring out soon that she had bet house credit on the wrong boxer and wouldn't be showing her face at the betting booth to collect.

Jaks was only a little drunk; the liquor made her happy.

"Listen," Jaks said as they stumbled down the alley, groping at each other. "We need to be quiet. I've got company."

"I'm a spider," Nyx said.

Jaks took her down a dead-end alley near the Chenjan district. Something hissed at them from a refuse heap. Nyx reflexively pushed Jaks behind her. Three enormous ravager bugs, tall as Nyx's knee, scurried out from the refuse pile. One of them stopped to hiss at them again. It opened its jaws wide. Nyx kicked it neatly in the side of the head, crushing an eye stalk. The bug screeched and skittered off.

Jaks laughed. "I should have warned you. They don't spray around here. Lots of mutants."

They climbed a rickety ladder to the second floor. Nyx felt like she'd been running forever, since the dawn of the world. Time stretched.

A boy's sandal hung from the top rung of the ladder. In that moment, Nyx saw the pile of Tej's things again, the detritus the Chenjan border filter had left of him. A sword, a baldric, his sandals.

Nyx caught her breath as she peered into the little mud-brick room. A couple of worms in glass lit the place. There were two raised sleeping platforms on either side of the room. A boy looked down at her from the one at her right. He looked nothing like Jaks. He was large and soft where she was small and hard. His hair was curly black and too long for a boy his age.

"My house brother," Jaks said. "Arran. Sorry, he doesn't do tea."

He didn't look like he'd spent a day at the front, but he was the right age. Nyx had expected to feel something when she saw this one. Rage, maybe; bloodlust. But he was just another boy. Another body. Another bel dame's bounty.

Along the far wall was the kitchen space: a mud-brick oven, all-purpose pot, two knives, and a sack of what must have been rice or maybe millet, knowing a boxer's take.

Arran rolled back into the loft.

"Come up," Jaks said.

Nyx came.

She kissed and licked Jaks in a detached sort of way. It was like watching two people she didn't know having sex.

Nyx lay awake after, until Jaks slept. She was aware, vaguely, of being hungry. She moved like a dream, smelling of Jaks, and slunk down the ladder and into the darkness near the oven. She reached for the biggest of the kitchen knives and put it between her teeth.

She climbed up the ladder to Arran's loft.

He came awake before she reached him. She heard the straw stir. She took the knife from her mouth, cut her palm, and as she met the top of the ladder, said, "Arran."

Following Jaks to find this boy had cost Nyx a kidney, her womb, and a year's worth of *zakat* from Yah Tayyib.

It had cost Tej his life.

Nyx shoved her bloody hand against the boy's mouth and brought up the other hand with the knife.

When infected boys came home, they jeopardized the lives of women like Jaks and Kine and little Maj. It's what she told herself every time. It's what she told herself now as she shoved her knife fast and deep into Arran's naked armpit three times.

Arran flailed in the straw. Nyx listened for Jaks. Sex and liquor and a hard fight would send even the worst of sleepers into a dead quiet, but anybody who lived like Jaks might be able to shake off worse.

Arran tried to catch her wrist with his other hand. Nyx

rolled the rest of the way up onto the platform and pinned him still. She waited until the strength bled out of him, then began to saw at the neck with her stolen knife. For a stretch of time while she cut off Arran's head, she wasn't a bel dame at all—just another body hacker, another organ stealer, another black trader of red goods. The only difference was, when she brought this boy in, her sisters would forgive her. Her sisters would redeem her.

She had collected the blood debt this boy owed Nasheen.

Nyx tugged off her burnous with sticky fingers and bundled up the head. She was an hour's walk from the local collector's. Her feet were numb, and her legs ached.

This was all she knew how to do.

She got lost somewhere outside Jaks's place and turned around in circles, listening to the scuffle of feet and bugs. She remembered what Jaks had said about the mutants. Dark shapes hissed and skittered through the alley, some of them big as dogs—only without the cozy fur. She stumbled over a head-size ravager gnawing on a human hand. It caught hold of the end of her bloodied bag and tried to jerk it out of her hands. She bludgeoned the enormous bug to death with Arran's head.

Light and noise from the apartments hanging above her seeped into the street. Her bundle grew heavier as she walked. She kept losing her grip, and the head thudded onto the dusty street, picking up more sand. The organic burnous would eat most of the blood, but not for much longer. Even bugs got full.

She'd just turned off onto a lane she recognized when she caught the sound of footsteps behind her. She didn't turn, only picked up her pace. Her insides were hurting again. She needed a second wind, but she'd already spent her fourth getting into Faleen.

The footsteps behind her broke into a run.

Nyx ran too.

The way was mostly dark, cut through with rectangles and lattices of light. She ducked in and out of darkness. Bugs hissed and scattered around her.

She was twenty-four years old, a bottom-feeder among the bel dames, and she was about to be far less than that.

"Nyx! Nyx!"

She kept running. *Just keep going.*

Two shadows leaked out of the alley ahead of her. She knew their shapes before they leapt—a fox and a raven. Shifters tracked better in animal form. The third would come from behind. She put one arm over her head to deflect some of the blow.

Her sisters cloaked her from all sides.

I'm a fool, Nyx thought as she hit the dirt, suffocated by the weight of her sisters' bodies. It took three of them to pry the burnous from her clenched fingers.

Nyx howled. She twisted, found an opening through fur and feathers and long, black burnouses.

They shot her. Twice.

Nyx heard her sisters' voices in hazy snatches, little clips of song and breathy whispers. Rasheeda, the raven, had once been an opera singer. A soprano. Nyx had never much cared for opera. It was all about virgin suicides and widowed martyrs. She got enough of that in real life.

The air was sultry and smelled of death and lemon. Nyx saw tall women wearing the white caps of Plague Sisters moving through the hall. She could hear the click and scuttle of insectile legs. The Plague Sisters were a guild of magicians specializing in the decontamination of bel dames and the refurbishment of discharged soldiers. Nyx had been among them before, back when her carcass was hauled in from the front, charred and twisted. But she'd been too ruined even for the Plague

Sisters, and they'd sent her to Yah Reza and Yah Tayyib, two of the country's most skilled magicians. Nyx's first memories of reconstituted life were of Faleen. The sound of cicadas. Yah Reza's eyes, the color of sapphire flies.

Fatima minced into the room with a white raven on her shoulder… Rasheeda the raven. Fatima spent a moment fussing with the gas lamp near the bed. Fatima was picky about things, and had gone so far as to pose her bodies for pick up. She also dabbled her fingers in bel dame politics. She had the patience for it, and the bloodline. Bel dames ran through every generation of her family.

Gas lamps meant they were in Mushtallah or Amtullah, one of the major cities in the heart of Nasheen. If that was true, it meant Nyx had been out a long time—and she was in a lot of trouble. Behind Fatima was a long, thin window that looked down onto a street the color of foam. Extravagant figures cloaked in peach and crimson milled past the smoky glass like burned jewel bugs. Nyx no longer wondered if she was still half asleep. Her dreams were never so colorful.

"She's coming around again," Fatima said to the raven.

The raven shivered once, hopped from Fatima's shoulder, and began to morph into her sister Rasheeda. A few minutes later, Rasheeda was mostly human again, naked, covered in mucus, tossing her head of dark hair and snickering. Feathers rolled out across the floor.

Rasheeda came alongside the bed and wiped the worst of the mucus from her face and neck with one of Nyx's bedsheets. She had a peculiar way of cocking her head that put Nyx in mind of the raven.

"You look terrible," Rasheeda said.

"You helped," Nyx said.

Nyx tried to sit up. Rasheeda snickered again. Unlike Fatima's illustrious line, Rasheeda's was nothing special—she'd been just another grubby kid from the coast whose mother was into career breeding. Nyx heard that Rasheeda had gone mad at the front, ripping out entrails and eating Chenjan hearts. There was only one suitable occupation for a madwoman from the front after she was discharged.

Nyx gazed down the length of her own body. She swam in the black nightdress of the Plague Sisters. She pushed up the sleeves and saw her own tawny wrists and arms, like sticks. She dared not look at her belly or legs. The bullets her sisters shot her with had been tipped with bugs. They'd whittled her down to almost nothing.

"Get me something to eat," Nyx croaked, and Rasheeda laughed.

One of the Plague Sisters strode into the room, white skirt trailing behind her. A cloud of spiders clung to her hem, darkening the fabric.

The Plague Sister fussed with Nyx's bedding and probed at her arm with the puckered snout of a semi-organic needle, which blinked at Nyx with half-dumb eyes. Nyx flinched. The sister gave her a disapproving frown and pulled away from her arm, taking the blood sample with her.

"I'll mark her for final analysis," the sister said, "but the venom should be out of her system." She walked back out, her entourage of insects pooling behind her.

"Are you all they sent?" Nyx asked.

Rasheeda snickered again, still sticky and naked.

"They couldn't spare any more of us to go running after a rogue sister," Fatima said. She was tall, skinnier and darker than Rasheeda, almost Chenjan in color, and stronger in the face and shoulders. She bore a perpetual frown on her long countenance.

"Dahab's here," Rasheeda said absently. "Luce went for sodas."

Dahab and Luce. If they'd sent Dahab, it was a wonder Nyx

was still alive. Four mad, skilled bel dames had tracked her across the desert. Why the fuck was she still breathing?

"What am I doing in the interior?"

"A suit's been filed," Fatima said.

"Catshit. You don't have anything on me."

"I know a number of butchers outside Punjai," Fatima said. "One of them even bought a womb that matches your tissue samples. She sold it back to us."

"That doesn't prove—"

"We have Yah Tayyib," Rasheeda said.

"Yah Tayyib's taken an oath. He wouldn't testify. About black work or anything else."

"Wouldn't he?" Fatima said. "He knows the place of a bel dame. He knows we're just as happy to haul in rogue magicians as black sisters. We used to hunt magicians when they went rogue too. Black bel dames ruin our reputation."

Nyx lay back on the bed. Yah Tayyib, who had mended her when she was barely human, who recalled her body and mind from the front when she thought she had lost both there. The man who taught her to box.

"He wouldn't make a charge," she said.

"There was another complaint," Fatima said. "Not as potent as Yah Tayyib's, but a formal complaint nonetheless."

"Raine," Nyx said.

Fatima raised her brows. "You expected it?"

"I've been expecting him to file a formal complaint ever since I cut off his cock."

"It was deserved," Rasheeda said.

"Deserved or not, he's filed a formal complaint about a bel dame doing black work," Fatima said.

"Lucky you left him his balls," Rasheeda said, "or you'd get a fine for reproductive terrorism." She waggled her index finger and snickered.

"So what happens now?" Nyx asked. "You give me some kind of probation?"

"No," Fatima said. "We terminate your contract and send you to prison."

"What?" Nyx said. Prison was for draft dodgers and terrorists. Prison was for *men*.

"The sentence came from the queen."

"I'm bored," Rasheeda said. "Where's my soda?" She went naked into the hall, calling for Luce.

Nyx stared into her skinny, veined hands again. It was like she'd woken up with someone else's body.

"How long do I serve?" she asked.

"A year, maybe less. We could have had you sent to the front."

"How did you find me?"

"We had Rasheeda posted at Jaks's residence."

Of course. She'd seen only three of them at the fight. "So you knew about Jaks?"

"We looked up your note," Fatima said, then wrinkled her nose. "You look and smell like death. I'll get you something to eat." She walked into the busy hall.

Prison, Nyx thought, with all the criminals Raine and people like her had put there.

Nyx tried to pull her legs off the bed. They were numb. How long had she been here? The window overlooking the street was barred, and the walls were solid stone. How the hell could she get bars out of stone?

But Fatima was coming back into the room with a Plague Sister bearing a tray of something that smelled a lot like food, and Rasheeda had her arms full of bottles of soda. If there was a way out of this one, Nyx couldn't think of it. Didn't even know if she wanted it. Her body was done.

"Here," Rasheeda said, throwing her a bottle. Nyx's reflexes were off. She ducked instead of catching it. "You won't get any of those in the box."

"When she's done eating," Fatima told the Plague Sister, "I have a team coming to get her."

Nyx didn't finish eating, but they still came for her.

And prison was pretty shitty.

4

"It's time," Yah Reza said.

Rhys entered the plague hall. Yah Tayyib and two other magicians sat at a large circular stone table at the center of the room. Three Plague Sisters, the hems of their white robes dripping with spiders, sat across from them. Like Yah Tayyib's operating theater, the plague hall was a cavernous room lined with jars of mostly human organs. And like the magicians' quarters, the whole room hummed with the sound and feel of bugs. Rhys's skin prickled. He had waited some time for this.

Yah Reza followed Rhys inside and bid him stand next to her within a pace of the table.

Three months after Rhys saw his first alien, Yah Reza had deemed him ready for a magician's trial. He had come to the interior and been independently tested by the Plague Sisters. He had read his performance in their faces, in the hard line the bugs themselves drew against him. The Plague Sisters kept a diverse colony of insects within their care, but he should have been able to manipulate them far more effectively than he had. If the organs and entrails he'd mended on the slabs had been those belonging to real human beings, he doubted his patients would have entirely recovered. Some may not have lived. He knew the outcome of his evaluation even before Yah Tayyib spoke.

"We have spent some time discussing your evaluation," Yah Tayyib said. "My fellow magicians and Plague Sisters agree that you have some skill in the arts. No doubt Yah Reza would not have undertaken your tutelage if she did not believe you were gifted." He carefully pressed the tips of his fingers together. "Unfortunately, we have not deemed your talent sufficient to grant you a practicing government license."

Rhys exhaled. What had he expected, that a Chenjan man in his prime would be given leave to walk through a palace filter and perform surgery on the Queen's ministers? There would be no easy road, no well-paying government job. But hearing it out loud felt better than he thought it would. Something, some expectation, had been cut away. Hope, maybe.

"However," Yah Tayyib said, "we find it acceptable to grant you a provisional license that allows you to practice so long as you are employed. Yah Reza has expressed interest in keeping you on at the magicians' quarters as a teacher, if you wish it. Otherwise, you're free to take up gainful employment with whatever employer you see fit. Do you have any questions?"

Rhys looked over at Yah Reza. She smiled her sen-stained smile. She intended on keeping him prisoner for the rest of his days, then.

"Yes," Rhys said, turning back to Yah Tayyib. "Is the denial of my government license based on my talent or my race?"

The old magician shook his head. "Rhys, if you were as talented as Yah Reza hoped, we would have no choice but to grant you a government license. Nasheen could not turn away one with such skill. But your talents are middling. We have no place among the palace magicians or within the First Families for a mediocre Chenjan magician. You are better suited for the private sector."

Rhys swallowed his words. What was there left to say? His father had cursed him the night he refused him. Cursed and abandoned him. *This is my penance,* Rhys thought, *this time among godless Nasheenians.*

"Thank you," Rhys said finally.

Yah Reza led him out.

When the door closed behind them, she said, "It is not such a terrible thing, to teach Nasheenian magicians. You are capable with children and the teaching of standard arts."

"I will not be staying long," Rhys said. "I'll find employment elsewhere."

"Of course," Yah Reza said, and he should have realized then that she knew something he did not.

The magicians did no end of business with bel dames and bounty hunters. Both groups often came to the gym looking for new recruits—petty magicians and women just back from the front. Government officials frequented the fights as well, recruiting veterans and magicians as order keepers. Rhys spent week after week at the gym acting the part of a cheap harlot, trying to sell his services. But no bel dame would have him, and the order keepers, of course, would not even speak to him. The magicians could afford to pretend not to notice his accent and his coloring, but the rest of Nasheen... the rest of Nasheen saw him for what he was—a Chenjan man, an infidel, an enemy.

Yah Reza caught up with him one afternoon in his chambers as he penned a response to an ad for a tissue mechanic he had found in the morning's newsroll. If they wouldn't hire him on as a magician, he would spend his days digging into the guts of bakkies in Mushtallah. It was better than a lifetime of servitude to Nasheenian magicians. Most tissue mechanics were just like him—failed magicians working for bread and bugs.

"Why not give this up, baby doll? Are things in my gym so bad?"

"A well-appointed prison is still a prison," Rhys said.

Yah Reza clucked her tongue. She waved a hand toward his lamp and increased the light. Rhys felt the message she sent the bugs, the chemical tingling in the air. Why did it take so much more effort for him to produce the same reaction? Why gift this stubborn old woman with enough skill to raise the dead but relegate him to the role of messenger, with the occasional talent for staunching blood and fighting infection? God did not grant talent indiscriminately.

Gift or curse, it was not enough.

"I keep you on for your protection," Yah Reza said. "Nasheen will eat you alive, boy. Even if you had the talent for the real stuff, how long do you think you'd last in Mushtallah among the First Families? How long before a gang of women cuts you up and feeds you to the bugs? This isn't Chenja, doll, where all you men get a free pass. Boys play by rules here. Chenjan boys don't play at all."

"I'm going mad," Rhys said.

"Weren't you already? No sane man would be sitting there in that chair—not unless I was interrogating him."

Rhys met her look. Yah Reza was an old woman, but how old? Always hard to tell in Nasheen. Sixty or more, surely.

"How long were you at the front?" he asked. She had never spoken of it.

"Thirty years," she said. "Give or take. Intelligence, you know. Taught Yah Tayyib back when he was just Tayyib al Amirah, eh? One of my best students."

"You mean torture and interrogation."

"Oh, there was some of that," Yah Reza said absently. She sat across from him. Three cicadas leapt out of the wide sleeves of her robe and crawled across Rhys's letter. "Yah Tayyib lost three wives to the war, you know it? And all of his children. You think he would give *you* a license? If you were his charge, he'd have turned you over to interrogation from the start. You'd be bleeding out in the interior right now."

"Why didn't you do the same?"

"Me? Ah, doll." Yah Reza spit on the floor, and a dozen blue beetles scurried out from under the end table and lapped at the crimson wad of spittle. "More death doesn't cure the war, eh? Just makes it drag on a while longer. Yah Tayyib, yes, he would do whatever it took to end the war. He would end it one Chenjan at a time. But then, so would most men. Women too. That's why this war never ends. Nobody lets go."

"You're letting go?"

"Completely? Ah, no. Maybe one Chenjan at a time."

He leaned toward her. "Then let me go."

She gave him a sloppy smile. "You aren't a prisoner." She stood, and the cicadas flew back up into her sleeves. "Go see Nasheen. But don't expect it to love you."

Yah Reza set him up with his passbook and paid his train fare to Amtullah. The interior. He did not use the space-twisting magicians' gyms to travel. He had wanted to see the country, to be on his own. If he'd made himself an exile, he needed to live as one.

When he arrived in the city, he set up several interviews with merchants looking for magicians to accompany their caravans north, through the wastelands.

During the day, Amtullah was a raucous mass of humanity, full of half-breeds and chained cats and corrupt order keepers and organ hawkers and gene pirates. He had trouble following the accented Nasheenian of the interior, and the fees for everything—from food and lodging to transit—were far higher than he'd anticipated. At night, the sky above Amtullah lit up with the occasional violet or green burst, remnants of a border barrage that managed to get through the anti-burst guns. The sound of sirens sent him to bed most nights, as regular as evening prayer.

But when he went to his interviews, he was cast off the porch or stoop or simply turned away at the gate more often than not.

His color was enough. They did not wait to hear his accent. A little more talent, perhaps, and he could have perfected a version of Yah Reza's illusory eyes to mask the obvious physical evidence of his heritage. As it was, he kept his burnous up and his hands covered when he traveled, and spoke only when he had to. It saved him harassment on the street, but not from his potential employers.

He spent many months in Amtullah getting thrown off doorsteps and turned away from tissue mechanic shops. Hunger made him take up employment as a dishwasher at a Heidian restaurant in one of the seedier parts of Amtullah, the sort of place he did not like walking around in at night and liked living in even less. He worked fourteen-hour days, six days a week, and came back to the buggy room he rented smelling of sour cabbage and vinegar. The other three days of the week he spent at the local boxing gym looking for real work—magician's work—something that made his blood sing.

And every day, six times a day, he prayed. He submitted all that he was, this life, everything, to God.

He was pinched and spit on at work and on the street. His overseers were Heidian women, mostly indifferent, but the patrons were a mixed group, largely Nasheenian, and when he walked among them uncovered he was jostled and cursed and jeered. Retaliation would have meant the loss of his job. A few women, it was true, were disinterested—some were even kind—but the daily indignities of being a Chenjan man in Nasheen began to wear him down. He spent less time at the boxing gyms looking for work. He spent most nights with his forehead and palms pressed to the floor, wondering if his father had cursed him not to death but to hell.

One late night, he decided to walk home from work down a street that would take him to the local mosque in time for midnight prayer. The streets were quiet that night, and the air tasted metallic, like rain. Or blood.

A group of four or five women walked toward him on the other side of the street. He paid them no attention until they crossed over to his side of the empty road and called out to him.

"You have the time?" one of them asked, and as they neared he could smell the liquor on them. They were young women.

"I'm sorry, I do not," he said. "It is near evening prayer."

"The fuck's that accent?" one of them said.

Rhys picked up his pace.

"Hey, man, I said, what's that accent?"

The tallest girl pulled at his burnous. She was stronger than she looked. The tattered clasp of his burnous snapped, and it pulled his hood free. He staggered.

"Fuck, you're kidding me!" the tall one said.

They started to crowd him. Like all Nasheenian women, they seemed suddenly larger there together, in the dark along the empty street. And they spoke in loud voices. Always too loud. Overwhelming.

"That's a fucking Chenjan!"

"Smells like a pisser, though. You a cabbage-eater, Chenjan man?"

"Look at that face! Not a day at the fucking front."

He made to push through them, but their hands were on him now, and their liquored breaths were in his face. He raised one arm to call a swarm of wasps. One of the girls grabbed his arm, twisted it behind him. The pain blinded him.

"Where you going, black man?"

"You know what Chenjans do in the street after dark?"

"Fucking terrorist."

He didn't know which of them threw the first punch. Despite their belligerence, he hadn't expected it. He never expected violence from women, even after all this time in Nasheen.

She caught him on the side of the head, and a burst of black-ness jarred his vision. He stumbled. Someone else hit him and he was on the ground, curled up like a child while they kicked him.

"Turn him over!"

"Get that off!"

One of them had a knife, and they cut his clothes from him. They cut a good deal more of him.

The midnight call to prayer sounded across Amtullah.

Rhys recited the ninety-nine names of God.

Rhys took what was left of his money and his ravaged body and shared a bakkie with eight other hard-luck passengers to Rioja, a northern city, closer to the sea. Towering above Rioja was the Alhambra, a fortress of steel, stone, and ancient organic matting built at the top of a jagged thrust of rock of the same name. Rhys painted portraits in the cobbled square that lay in the shadow of the Alhambra. He sold them for ten cents apiece. At night, he slept in the steep, narrow streets among creepers, black market grocers, and junk dealers. When he was cold, he called swarms of roaches and scarab beetles to cover him. When he ran out of money for canvas and paint, he sold bugs to creepers and the local magicians' gym. And when he was too poor to eat—or the creepers were no longer buying—he ate the bugs that made his blood sing, the bugs that tied him to the world.

He dreamed of his father. Of his house in Chenja. The smell of oranges.

A woman threw a coin at him one morning while he sat huddled in a doorway in his stained, tattered burnous.

"Find yourself a woman," she said. She wore sandals and loose trousers, and her face had the smooth, well-fed look of the rich.

"I used to dance for Chenjan mullahs," Rhys said.

The woman paused. The morning was cool and misty; winter

in Rioja. Damp wet her face, beaded her dark hair. He suddenly wanted this strong, capable woman to hold him, Nasheenian or not. He wanted her strength, her certainty.

"But you don't dance for them anymore," the woman said. "Let me tell you, boy: Whatever you were in your past life, you aren't that any longer."

She continued up the narrow street.

In the end, it was not so hard to return to Yah Reza.

Rhys walked to the magicians' gym in Rioja and asked for her at the door. He waited on the street in front of the dark doorway for some time while they found her there, somewhere within the bowels of the twisted magicians' quarters, the world with so many doors.

When she entered the doorway, she was wearing her yellow trousers and chewing sen, unchanged though it had been well over a year since he last saw her.

"Hello, baby doll," Yah Reza said.

"Sanctuary," Rhys said.

Yah Reza smiled and spit. "I put on some tea for you."

She gave him some tea and sent him to Yah Tayyib.

Yah Tayyib dewormed him and cut out the old scars from his assault in Amtullah. He did not ask about what had happened.

"I have seen far worse," Yah Tayyib told him. "You were lucky they just cut flesh and not entire body parts—though I have plenty of those to spare as well."

Rhys ate his grubs and gravy. After a time, he no longer urinated blood, and his persistent cough eased. One morning he found himself in the locker room the outriders used, and he stood there in the doorway thinking about the little dog-faced girl and her beautiful, imperfect hands. The old stale smell of sweat and leather filled the room.

Soon he would go back to teaching magic to Nasheenian children. He would lose himself again to the dark bowels of this prison. Hell on Umayma. But was it any worse than the hell outside these walls?

"Rhys?" Yah Tayyib asked.

Rhys turned and saw the old man approaching from the direction of the gym.

"I need you to wrap a woman for me."

"You don't wish to do it?"

Yah Tayyib pinched his mouth in distaste. "I have no time for her."

Rhys walked out into the boxing gym. He saw Husayn in the ring, surely on her last legs as a magician-sponsored fighter. The last year had not been kind to her either. She was well past thirty, too old to make much more money for the magicians. She was gloved and warming up.

It was the other woman who caught his attention. She stood in the near corner of the ring, and she turned as he entered. She was as tall as he was, broad in the shoulders, and heavy in the chest and hips. She wore a breast binding, loose trousers, and sandals. Her hair was jet black, braided, and belled. It hung down her back in one long, knotted tail. She put both hands on the ropes and leaned forward, looking him straight in the face. The boldness of the look stopped him in his tracks. He didn't know if she wanted to cut him or kiss him.

"I know you," she said.

"You're a bel dame," he said. He knew it the same way he'd known the dog-faced girl had a bad hand, the way he knew a magician or a shifter by sight on the street.

"Was," she said. "Not anymore. I'm Nyx."

Husayn bounced over to the former bel dame's side and punched her on one of her substantial shoulders. "Let's go, huh?" Husayn said.

"You're a dancer," Nyx said.

"Was," he said.

Nyx let go of the ropes. She looked out behind him, toward the entrance to the magicians' quarters. Rhys followed her gaze and saw Yah Tayyib in the doorway, watching her with black eyes.

A broad smile lit up Nyx's face. It made her almost handsome. "You need a job?" she asked Rhys.

"Doing what?" he asked.

"Bugs," Nyx said. "It's what you can do, isn't it?"

"Yes," he said. He'd discovered that he could do little else. "I'm not the most skilled, but… I've been told it's enough for petty employment."

"I'm a hunter. I need a team. Magicians get ten percent."

"On a two-person team? No less than twenty-five."

"There's three of us for now, but it'll be five, eventually. Fifteen."

"Five ways is twenty."

"That assumes we're all equal. Nasheen's not a democracy, and neither's my team."

"Fifteen. I won't kill anyone for you."

"Fifteen, you don't kill anybody, and you sign a contract today."

Rhys turned again to look at Yah Tayyib. The old magician moved out of the doorway, back into the darkness.

"Yes," Rhys said.

She squatted and reached through the ropes for him. He started, expecting violence. Instead, she clasped his elbow. He recovered quickly and clasped hers in turn. And in that one moment, that brief embrace, he felt safe for the first time in more than a year.

"You'll do all right with me," Nyx said, straightening.

"You think so?"

She grinned again. Her whole face lit up. It was dynamic. "If you don't, I'll cut your fucking head off. It's what I'm good at."

"Not so good as all that, if you aren't a bel dame anymore."

She caught hold of the ropes and leaned back, still grinning.

PART TWO

IN THE DESERT

Nyx came out of her year in prison with all of her limbs and organs intact, though she had a new appreciation for open sky and food that hadn't been grown in a jar. After that, time licked by in a blur of boys and blood. Seven years of putting together a crackerjack bounty hunting team, starting with Taite, her com tech, then her Chenjan magician. Seven years of boys and blood—girls too. Bounty hunters took up notes on girls and women, and that's all she had a license to be anymore, just another body hacker. Another organ stealer. In Nasheen you hacked out a living or spent your last days hacking out your lungs.

She knew which she preferred.

The war still raged along the ever-changing border with Chenja. Nyx started up her storefront with the dancer and com tech in Punjai, a border city at the heart of the bounty-hunting business. While she was in prison, Punjai had been swallowed by Chenja for six months, then "liberated" by a couple of brilliant Nasheenian magicians and an elite terrorist-removal unit. Chenjan corpses burned for days. All of the city's prayer wheels were burned and the old street signs were put back up. There had been air raids and rationing and a couple more poisoned waterworks, but, as ever, the war was just life, just how things clicked along—one exhausting burst and bloated body at a time.

It was a fitting way to look at time, Nyx figured, as she opened up her trunk one hazy morning while the yeasty stink of bursts blew in on the wind. She and her team were still three bounties short of rent.

She found a headless body inside the trunk.

"You should have put some towels down," Rhys said. It had been worth the look on Yah Tayyib's face the day she signed Rhys, though his cut was still substantially more than anybody else's on the team.

And she liked his hands.

There had been dog carcasses in the alley behind her storefront this morning, fat rats squealing over tidbits, old women netting roaches for stews. The accumulated filth of rotting tissue, blood, sand, and the stench of human excrement had sent Rhys out onto the veldt for dawn prayer, and Nyx had grudgingly agreed to take the bakkie out to pick him up. She made sure to arrive well after the end of prayer, because watching Rhys praying was about as uncomfortable as the idea of catching him masturbating—if he even did that sort of thing.

In any case, she hadn't thought to check the trunk.

"Whose is it?" Nyx asked. She was due to pick up a bounty in a quarter of an hour. She needed the trunk space.

The body was draped in the white burnous of a clerk, gold tassels and all. The feet were bare. Though he had no head, a red newsboy cap was cradled under the left arm.

Nice touch, that.

"Khos's," Rhys said.

She should have recognized his work.

Nyx glanced over at Rhys, trying to read him. His dark face was pinched and drawn.

She watched him gather his gear. "I'll put this in the cab. I forgot about the body," he said.

"Khos won't get anything without the head."

"He says the body's got a birthmark."

"Khos is an idiot." Khos, her big Mhorian shifter. Substantial in *so* many ways. She teased that thought back out of her mind. Shit, it had been a while.

Rhys pinched his mouth. Nyx waited for a word of affirmation, but he said only, "Khos said this one was on the boards for black work. He had me open a file."

Nyx shut the trunk.

"Somebody's going to revoke my hunter's license 'cause Khos can't burn his bodies," she said. It wouldn't be the first time. She'd had her bounty hunter's license revoked twice in her seven years as a hunter—once for accidentally shooting a diplomat's assistant, who'd been within range of her actual target, and again for employing Khos without a shifter's license. Shifters were expensive.

Nyx moved around to the cab of the little bakkie, kicked the latch loose, and propped open the door. She took the driver's seat, adjusted the sword strapped to her back to make it easier to sit, and pumped the ignition pedal. A growl came from under the hood. She'd gotten the bakkie off a hedge witch working in the fleshpots on the Tirhani border. Nyx knew all about what it was like to be hard up for bugs and bread.

"Hit the grille," Nyx said. Sometimes you had to get the beetles riled up before they'd feed.

Rhys banged the flat of his hand on the grille. Not much weight behind it. Fucking *dancers*.

While she waited, Nyx watched a burst from the front ignite across the sky over Punjai. One of the anti-burst guns stowed in the minarets along the perimeter fired. The heavy *whump-whump* of the guns made her ears pop. The burst burned up over the city. Bursts were a lot prettier from a distance.

"Would you put some shit behind it?" Nyx yelled. "You want to go back to whoring-out portraits?"

Rhys kicked the grille. Better.

The bugs hissed, and something inside the semi-organic cistern belched.

"In, in, let's go!" Nyx called.

Rhys leapt in as the bakkie began rolling down the dusty hill toward Punjai.

There was a hot desert wind blowing in from the western waste, pushing out the city's black shroud of smog and settling a misty cloud of red silt over the cityscape. The double dawn had risen; the orange sun overpowered the wan light of the blue sun, and the silt-filtered light caught the world on fire.

Nyx shifted pedals as the road straightened out. They hit gravel, and a couple of roach nymphs wiggled free from the leak in the hose by her feet and flitted through the open windows.

They came over the top of a low rise, and Punjai spread before them like a jagged wound, a seething black groove torn out of the red wash of the veldt. Three years before, the front had been closer, and all of the minarets outside the Chenjan quarter of the city had been bombed. Truckloads of dead and dying men were still carted into the city during the worst of the skirmishes, but for the most part, magicians liked to patch up their charges at the front. The more men that got away from the front, the more likely it was that somebody would figure a way to smuggle them out—and the greater the danger they posed to the city if they were contaminated. Bel dame business was brisk in Punjai. Not that Nyx was licensed to do that type of thing.

But it didn't keep her from thinking about it.

At the edges of the city, the desert stirred, set free by centuries of bug storms and heavy warfare. Bursts had seared the veldt and carved deep pockets into mud-brick ruins and heaps of rock the color of old blood. At the center of the city rose the old onion-shaped spirals of the remaining minarets, long since converted to more practical watchtowers equipped with long-range anti-burst weapons and scatterguns. The only minaret that still called the faithful to prayer in Punjai was a crumbling black spiral in the Chenjan quarter.

"Taite briefed you on the file?" Rhys asked as he buckled on his dueling pistols and shrugged into his black burnous.

Nyx watched him fiddle with the frogged tie at his collar.

"Yeah," she said, "I looked over the file. Some Chenjan terrorists. Expected to be armed. Good boxers. I sparred with one of them in Aludra a couple of years ago."

"I expected they'd be friends of yours," Rhys said.

"I run with a lot of questionable characters," Nyx said, giving him a sidelong look. "We're stopping at the storefront. I need to off-load your body."

"It's Khos's body. Is Anneke in?"

"She's already posted. Less picky about where she spends morning prayer." Anneke had been one of the easier additions to her crew, once Nyx made up her mind to cannibalize Raine's team. All Anneke had wanted was a bigger gun.

"I hate this city," Rhys said.

Nyx nodded at the radio tube jutting out of the dash. "Find something useful on. You have some sen?"

He obediently switched on the tube. It vomited a misty blue-green wash. A cacophony of low voices muttered at them. Local politics. Queen Ayyad had abdicated to her daughter Zaynab four months before, and the talking heads were still preoccupied with what that meant for relations between Nasheen and Ras Tieg. Nyx was more interested in what Zaynab's policies would be regarding the capture of terrorists. Queens and bel dames did not, traditionally, get along, and the livelihood of mercenaries and bounty hunters didn't even show up as a line item during the low council meetings. The queen got on best with her decadent group of high-council nobles—representatives from the richest houses in Nasheen, descendants of the First Families. It was a hazy kind of history, and Nyx didn't remember half of it. Most of her schooling consisted of adding and subtracting bullets and calculating the trajectory of burst guns, interspersed with some theology from the Kitab and exaltations about the power of submission to God—dead words from some other dead world. Actual Umayman history was usually just a nod to how everything that ever went wrong on Umayma was the fault of the Chenjans.

Nyx changed the station. The air tingled, and the voices were briefly garbled, but then cleared up. More news: local gossip. Talk about the upcoming vote on whether or not half-breeds should be drafted. A couple of serious-sounding women discussed the arrival of a ship that had put down in Faleen. Where were all these antiquated wrecks coming from? Nyx thought. When was the last time I saw one?

When you went to prison, she remembered. She grimaced and turned the radio off. It was a night she didn't like to dwell on. The mist receded. Sound faded to silence.

"You know I don't poison myself with narcotics and pollutants," Rhys said, and she realized he was talking about the sen.

Nyx hoped he'd start ranting about submission and God and pollutants. She could use the diversion.

He rarely disappointed her these days.

"I only drink the blood of my enemies," Nyx said, "and maybe some whiskey and water. Beer with a little lime."

Rhys snorted.

She considered selling him to a mardana, a brothel populated entirely by men. It was one of her more frequent fantasies.

The hunched black smudge of the city grew closer. Umber-clad women moved along the side of the road, balancing baskets on their heads. Girls herded giant spiders and a couple of dogs along the drainage ditches flanking the road. Some creepers in blue and gold carried baskets of beetles and grasshoppers in tiny wooden cages. Giant drooping nets hung over their lean shoulders.

They passed under the burst-scarred main gate and into Punjai.

Nyx parked outside their storefront, badly, and pushed into the reception area they called the keg. Before Nyx sold bounty services out of the storefront, she had sold kegs of beer to wedding parties and war veterans. Taite started calling it the keg the fourth time a drunken government clerk came looking for cheap booze in the middle of the night.

Taite, another crew member scalped from Raine, was working her com now. Upon her arrival, the skinny pock-faced kid ducked his head out of the gear room in the back and widened his eyes. He was a crackerjack with the com, but he still cringed in the face of her moods, and there were days she wished he had a straighter spine. He must have been in his early twenties now, but in her head he was still just the fourteen-year-old refugee of Raine's with the Ras Tiegan accent.

"Khos?" he said hopefully.

"Khos," she said.

"He's already posted at the location."

"Fucker," Nyx said. "Let Rhys know if that fucker calls off. If he gets tangled up with his whores before this job, I'm going to tear up his contract."

She went back out to get Rhys to help her with the body. The two of them hauled it down into the freezer under the gear room.

When they came back up, Taite was looking jittery. He usually only looked that way after he'd talked to his sister, another refugee half-breed. Nyx had seen her once, looking down at the bakkie from a dirty window when Nyx dropped Taite off. She was prettier than Taite, though just as fine-boned and frail. Neither of them had been inoculated, and they were allergic to everything.

"There's a problem, Nyx," Taite said.

"I hate problems."

"Anneke says Raine's there trying to pick up our bounty. Khos moved without your leave. She thinks Khos lost the bounty."

"Shit," Nyx growled. "Get in the fucking bakkie, Rhys."

She and Raine had been netting each other's prime catches for years, ever since she stole Taite and, later, Anneke from him. Taite was the only com tech she knew who could keep a line secure without resorting to venom addiction, but whoever Raine was using now consistently hacked Taite's com. She had lost her last two bounties to Raine, and now the cockless fuck was pushing for another one.

"Keep your ear to the com. I'm headed there now," Nyx said.

Nyx hit the juice on the bakkie and plowed through the narrow streets of Punjai. Rhys had the sense to strap himself in and hang on tight. She figured he knew better than to push her when she was pissed off, because he was quiet the whole time.

She drove out to the bounty's residence, a brick one-level squeezed between three-storied apartment buildings with more modern tiled façades.

The door was already bashed open. Nyx saw scattered parrot feathers all over the street.

She jumped out of the bakkie and ran across the busy street, dodging cat-pulled carts and sinewy rickshaw drivers. She half-reached for her sword but pulled her pistol instead. In close quarters, sword fighting got tricky. She pushed inside.

Lithe little Anneke crouched next to the crumpled body of a blue-eyed boy still covered in feathers and mucus. Anneke jerked her head and rifle up when Nyx came in but relaxed when she saw who it was.

Nyx saw a dead dog with two naked human legs sprawled near the broken lattice of the window.

"Where's Khos?" she asked.

She heard a stir outside the window, and a big blond dog leapt inside. In dog form, Khos was only about as tall as her hip. The dog shook off the dust and started to shed dog hair all over the floor. Watching shifters change generally put Nyx off lunch, so she looked away as Khos shifted. When she looked again, he was wiping mucus off his immense naked body. Khos was a head and shoulders taller than she was, broad in the face and chest, and when he shook his head, the last of the dog hair purled out around him in a cloud, leaving him with a head of thick blond dreadlocks.

"What the fuck happened?" Nyx asked.

"Raine's team moved for the—" Anneke began.

"I don't give a fuck what Raine did. Which of you moved off point first?"

Anneke spit on the floor and looked over at Khos.

Nyx regarded him. A fine webbing of spidery blue tattoos—the same color as his eyes—wound around Khos's pale limbs and torso. Some kind of Mhorian thing. He was still wiping mucus from his face. In a quarter hour, he was going to be starving for protein. Shifters were fucking *expensive*.

"They were going to sweep that bounty right out from under us," he said. "I moved because—"

"And did you get a transmission from Rhys or Taite telling you I wanted you off point?" she said.

She heard somebody come in behind her and turned, pistol in hand. But it was only Rhys, the hood of his burnous drawn up, a cloud of red beetles circling his head.

"Taite says Raine and his crew are already headed toward the Cage. With the bounty," Rhys said.

Nyx grimaced and looked at the body on the floor. "Can we get anything for this one?"

"Yeah, boss," Anneke said, "but he isn't worth so much as the others."

"He'll have to do. Somebody's gotta feed Taite's sister this month. Bundle him up."

ALEXANDRA PARK

"Boss?" Anneke said.

"We're taking him to the Cage," Nyx said. "Any more questions or suggestions? I don't run a democracy here. This isn't some Mhorian brothel, you get that, Khos?"

He made a face and looked down at the body. She had another body to talk to him about, later.

Nyx holstered the pistol.

Khos sighed over the body and muttered, "God be merciful."

"You'll find I'm bloodier than He is," Nyx said.

"I don't doubt that," Khos said.

"Prove it," she said, and walked outside to get the trunk ready for the next body.

Nyx dropped Rhys off at the keg and then followed the old elevated train tracks uptown to the Cage. Khos rode shotgun, but it was Anneke who rode armed. She sat up in the bowl of the roof, her feet dangling over the trunk, a shotgun over one of her lean shoulders.

Punjai's border security office and bounty reclamation center—aptly known as "the Cage" by those in the business—was in the heart of upper Punjai, on the other side of the city from the Chenjan district.

They pulled up outside the Cage. Raine's bakkie was already there, along with half a dozen others belonging to rival hunters.

As she waited for Khos and Anneke to unload the body, Nyx looked across the parking lot to the *other* reclamation office. The bel dame collection center was a tall four-storied building with a façade of painted mud-brick and amber. The motto above the lintel of the main entrance was in the raised script of the old prayer language: *My life for a thousand.*

She remembered swearing an oath with that at its core: My life for yours, for ours, for Nasheen. *My life for a thousand.*

"Boss?" Anneke said.

Nyx looked back at them. Khos had the bundled body in his arms—the body of some dumb half-breed kid who'd run with the wrong crowd—but he'd keep them in bread for another day.

My life for a thousand.

She didn't risk her life for all that much, these days.

Nyx reached into the bakkie and palmed some sen from her stash, then squared herself in front of the low building. Hunters were slipping in and out, gutter feed in tow. Little operations like those had to take in half a dozen terrorists a week to make a profit. She'd gotten out of the small time years ago. She wanted to stay out of it.

Nyx spit red, and led her team in.

Shajin was working behind the lattice of the front desk. She was a squat, serious woman with flinty eyes and a bad complexion. She sat gazing stonily at a new hunter who sounded like she was having trouble understanding the monetary restrictions on her catch.

Shajin, unimpressed, replied in her booming monotone, "Read the fine print. Says here you only get sixty if this particular catch is live. They preferred him dead and would have paid you a hundred for it. I'm not killing him for you, so you take him out back and shoot him or take your sixty. If there's something you don't understand about that, you need to go back to state school. Get your skinny ass away from my desk. Move."

The hunter pulled out her pistol and then dragged her catch out the door.

Nyx stepped up. Shajin relaxed in her seat.

"And what do you want, my wandering woman?" Shajin asked.

"How's business?" Nyx said.

"Poor. Full of men and self-righteous mercenary runts. They upset my digestion." She patted the great swell of her stomach.

"I've got a poor piece for today, then."

"File number?"

Nyx told her.

Shajin grimaced. "You're in the dregs again, my woman."

Shajin passed the file number on to one of the little desk

clerks—a betel-nut-colored, boyish girl named Juon who had a sassy walk.

Nyx leaned over the desk so her nose nearly touched the latticework. "When are you coming home with me, Juon?"

Juon marched into the back.

Shajin grinned. "She'll have none of you, my woman. She just got a letter from that boy of hers at the front."

Nyx snorted. "Probably six months dead. The flies have him."

Amid the low murmur of exchange and the occasional outburst from an irate hunter or wheedling bounty came a deep, familiar voice.

"So the huntress returns," Raine said.

Nyx took half a moment to loosen up her suddenly rigid body. She turned and showed her crimson teeth.

Raine stood near the main door with three of his crew. On a good day, he had a dozen veterans and half as many irregulars.

She saw Raine around the Cage a lot and more around the local pubs, but—not being half a fool—he avoided her personally. He usually sent out his veterans to harass her. She had sent the last one back without an ear.

"I see you've gotten better at eavesdropping on our com," Nyx said.

"Taite's security is terrible," Raine said. "I taught him everything I know."

"Which must not have been much," Nyx said.

"There is much more I could teach you, Nyxnissa, if you could set aside your arrogance."

"You're the one who thinks he's some fucking prophet 'cause he had a shitty time at the front. I heard you got arrested during a protest in Sahlah. I'm surprised nobody's put you in prison yet for blasphemy. Why hasn't your mother gutted you, the way she did the council?"

"I know faith and belief are concepts you have a difficult time understanding, Nyxnissa, but some of us have an interest in righting wrongs, not perpetuating them."

"I believe in myself. That's enough."

"For you? And your crew?"

"Why don't you go off and get married and settle down like a good little war vet, huh? I'm sure you could find some dumb bitch to put you up."

"We're a sorry pair of veterans, aren't we? I think you have as much interest in becoming a kept thing as I do."

"Hey, hunters!" Shajin said. "You take your personal business outside."

"I've got a file," Nyx said.

"I have mine," Raine said. He clapped his hands. His three regulars headed for the door.

"Watch yourself," Raine said. He put his back to her and walked out.

"Watch your regulars," Nyx said. "I may find a use for them."

She wasn't the only one Raine was stirring the pot with these days. It wasn't just the protests in small cities like Sahlah. Rhys had word of Raine at rallies in Mushtallah and boys' rights gatherings in Amtullah. Those were bad places to be seen protesting anything that had to do with God or the queen or the bel dames. It was like he was presenting himself to a butcher and asking them to chop something else off. But he had taught her how to drive, how to use a sword, and how to patch a bakkie—this old man with the dead eyes and bizarre family history who couldn't leave the war alone.

She supposed there must be something redeemable about him.

Khos spit on the floor next to Nyx.

"Those three were ours," Anneke said. "Honest, boss, I had them."

"Well, you don't have them now, do you?" Nyx said, too sharply. She turned back to the desk.

Juon handed Shajin the file.

"Says here you get thirty for a live catch," Shajin said, "and twenty for a dead. Too bad." She filled out the pay receipt. "You know the routine."

Nyx handed the receipt to Anneke, who followed Khos through the throng to the body drop-off and cashier.

Juon leaned over and whispered into Shajin's ear.

"What's that? Ah, yes. You have a note," Shajin said.

Juon went to the sorting cabinet behind Shajin and plucked out a red letter.

Nyx's heart skipped. The old bullet wound in her hip throbbed.

Red letters were straight from the desk of the queen. The queen only sent red letters to nobles, ambassadors... and bel dames.

Juon handed the letter to Shajin. Shajin handed it to Nyx.

Nyx's fingers trembled. She took the letter and tucked it carefully into the top of her dhoti. A pardon from the Queen? Back to bel dame work? Back to prison? Had she fucked anything up recently?

"Thanks," she said.

"They've been giving them out to the top hunters," Shajin said. "Must be somebody pretty important."

"Oh," Nyx said. Not a pardon, then. "If it's that important, they'd give it to the bel dames, not the hunters."

Shajin shrugged. "I don't make policy. Come now, you're holding up the line, my woman."

Nyx pushed away from the counter.

She waited for Anneke and Khos, and when they returned with the bounty money, she tucked that, too, into her dhoti and told Khos to drive.

Nyx rode shotgun. She pulled out the red letter. Khos looked at her as he started the bakkie.

It took a long time to read the letter. If she went too fast she got the characters backward. By the time they reached the keg, she'd read it twice.

The letter read:

> We, God's Imam, Queen Zaynab sa Boliard so Amtullah, on the forty-eighth day of the Sahfar in the year nine hundred eighty-nine, hereby summon God's servant Nyxnissa so Dasheem to the Al-Ahnsalus Palace at Mushtallah on behalf of Almighty God and the people of the Holy Empire of Nasheen.

> In view of the authority conferred to us by God, and to further the glory of God and His servant Nasheen, we seek the covert recovery of a fugitive, to be apprehended by God's servant Nyxnissa so Dasheem and whose recovery will be rewarded most graciously.

> God's servant may exchange this imperial summons at the nearest train repository for complimentary roundtrip tickets to God's seat, Mushtallah.

Someone had written in, at the bottom, using the same pen stroke as the queen's signature:

> Recompense for the apprehension of the agent is negotiable. Details forthcoming when you arrive. Discretion advised.

The second part was a lot easier to read, and much more Nyx's style. It made her wonder how much of her file they'd read before sending the summons.

Back at the keg, Nyx handed Rhys the red letter.

"This for real?" she asked.

He ran his hands over it. "It appears genuine," he said.

"Best you can tell, right?" she said.

He grimaced. "You pay me for an acceptable level of talent. You get what you pay for."

"I want you to go with me," she said.

His dark eyes widened—pretty eyes with long lashes. There were days when she couldn't get enough of them, and days she wanted to cut them out for the same reason.

"The Nasheenian court? Palace Hill? You must be joking," he said.

"Listen. I take Anneke or Khos with me, they don't speak very good, all right? I take Taite, and you know he gets sick when he's nervous. I want you there."

"Nyx, I—"

"Thanks," she said. "Just don't worry about it." She turned away from him before he said any more. She needed Rhys, her mediocre magician. There were other things he was good at: well-read, well-spoken, well-mannered. He was Chenjan, sure, but she didn't know anybody else around with his manners. He never missed a prayer; he talked about God all the time and drank tea instead of whiskey. He made her look good. He made the whole team look good.

Nyx walked into her office and dumped her gear onto her desk. As she saw Khos walk in to the keg she hollered that she wanted to talk to him. Rhys was still standing near the door, at the ablution bowl she had set out for those who wanted to wash themselves before and after they spoke to her. Her business had that effect on people. Rhys had his hands in the water, sleeves up.

She turned back in to her spare office, kicking her chair away. It wasn't even noon, so the light coming through the latticed windows was low. She climbed up on to her battered desk and propped open the old entrance in the ceiling.

Better.

Khos knocked on the open door.

"Get in here," Nyx said.

She climbed down from the desk as Khos came through the doorway. He needed a wash.

"Funniest thing," Nyx said. "I had a body in my trunk this morning."

"Yeah."

"Sit."

Khos lumbered over to one of the backless chairs in front of her desk. They were mismatched chairs, trash she and Taite had picked up years before when they moved out of their firebombed storefront in the Chenjan district and onto the east side. He'd been allergic to the original upholstery, and she'd had to redo most of it herself.

Nyx took off her burnous and draped it over her chair. She removed the most extraneous of her weapons and piled them up next to her for cleaning.

"You want to step away from the crew?" Nyx asked.

If Taite was a good but fragile kid, Khos was like the kid's lumbering, towheaded older brother. Nyx had picked up Khos Khadija at a brothel outside Aludra three years before. They were both there to see the same girl and had bumped into each other on the stairs. When she found out he was Raine's new shifter, she hired him at twice the cut Raine was giving him. She'd been very drunk. She'd also been very drunk later, when she slept with him. She didn't like big men all that much, but it had been a hot fuck for all that. She knew it had been a while since she'd been to bed with anybody at all, because right about now he was starting to look half good again.

Khos shrugged. If the seat had a back, he would have slumped. "It was side work. I forgot about it."

She climbed into her chair and perched up on the back, her feet on the seat. She leaned forward.

"You were supposed to wait on me and Rhys. Instead, you panicked and moved too soon, and we lost our take."

"I told you, Raine showed up and they were heading out. We would have lost all of them if I hadn't gone in when I did."

"So instead, all three of them lit out the back window, right into Raine's ambush, and we ended up with some dumb kid who was worth more alive than dead."

"I wasn't—"

"Is this your crew? Did I sign a contract of yours, or did you sign one of mine?"

He grimaced.

"Answer me."

"No, it's not my crew."

"You know how many hunts me and Anneke have been on? A hell of a lot. There's nothing we haven't seen."

"Nyx—"

"I don't want to hear about Mhorian chivalry. You don't like working with women, you shouldn't be in Nasheen. As I heard it, it's your love of women that got you here in the first place. Women can fight as well as fuck, you know it?"

He shifted in his seat, looking toward the window. She knew he hated it when she swore. Mhorians were a strange bunch of refugees, a late addition to Umayma. They'd been given some of the shittiest, least developed land in the world, and the vast majority of them had died within the first year of landing. A thousand years worth of hard living had made them a prickly, stubborn sort of people. Most of them were religious zealots, worse than any Chenjan, obsessed with laws and prescriptions about marital relations and the segregation of men and women. A full three-quarters of their Book dealt with rules about marriage, sex, and birth. Nyx had been with Khos the first time he saw a topless woman on the streets of Nasheen, burning an effigy of the Queen in protest of some new regulation about births completed off-compound. The look on his face had been worth a thousand notes.

Mhorian women also cost money, like bugs. Nyx supposed that in a society where most of you were dying and you didn't have much initial bug tech, women's wombs would go for more. Khos had lit out of Mhoria looking for a good wife he didn't have to pay for, and he hadn't had much luck in Nasheen. Who wanted to shack up with some Mhorian shifter and push out useless half-breed babies? Half-breeds didn't get free government inoculations. The vast majority died within the first three years as a result. Nyx figured it was why Khos spent most of his time in brothels. Maybe he thought those women were hard up? What he didn't seem to get was that women in Nasheen who made a living as prostitutes were usually doing so for political reasons, not because they were desperate for money or anxious about having husbands. Women in Nasheen didn't grow up looking for husbands. They grew up looking for honor and glory.

"I need to know you'll follow the plan," Nyx said. "If I can't count on that, I cancel your contract. I can get another shifter, you hear me?"

"I hear you."

"Yeah?"

"Yeah."

"Good. Go sit with the others in the keg. We've got to prep for another pickup."

He heaved himself out of his seat, and shut the door softly behind him. For a man his size, he moved with surprising quiet.

She took a deep breath, exhaled, and pulled the letter out of her dhoti.

Recompense for the apprehension of the terrorist is negotiable.

She closed her eyes. She was thirty-two years old, and every bone in her body hurt, every joint, every muscle. Some mornings, she woke up so stiff she had to roll herself out of bed and stretch for a quarter-hour just so she could stand without pain.

Nyx sat on the edge of the desk. She didn't have the money to replace any more body parts, and she wasn't so sure that any magician could tell her what needed replacing even if she could afford it. Yah Tayyib once told her she needed a new heart.

She'd thought he was serious.

This bounty wouldn't buy her a new heart. It wouldn't fix anything she'd broken. But it might get her out of this hole and working closer to the wealthy Orrizo district in Mushtallah, dressing real fine, getting patched up by the best, and getting all the good notes. *My life for a thousand.*

She wanted a new life: a life she could trade for something more worthwhile than twenty bloody notes and the contempt of a bunch of refugees.

7.

At dawn, Nyx made Khos drive her and Rhys out to the central train station in Basmah, following the long scar of the elevated tracks the whole way. The local, intercity trains didn't run anymore, and hadn't in about three years. The Chenjans had taken out the main line between Punjai and Basmah so many times that the Transit Authority had stopped sending out tissue mechanics to fix it. They used to come back at least one woman short after every run. Most of the busted tracks were planted with mines and bursts now.

The threat of Chenjan terrorism kept train tickets on the working long-distance lines exorbitant. Nyx had ridden the train only twice in her life—to and from the front.

Khos got them within a hundred yards of the station before the crowd of bakkies, rickshaws, and pedestrians brought them to a standstill. Half a dozen security techs dressed in red burnouses prowled the station with enormous sand cats on heavy chains.

Nyx shouldered her pack and slammed the door. She said to Khos through the open window, "Don't give Anneke any shit. Taite's in charge. If he says fuck off, you do it."

"He knows where to find me," Khos said, and grinned. He and Taite were fast friends, disparate brothers from foreign countries who went to mixed brothels together, back before Taite had a boyfriend. Nyx wasn't sure why the friendship annoyed her. Maybe because she didn't understand it. When had she ever had a friend close enough to go to brothels with? Not since grade school.

"Just don't blow all your money on girls and wine. I need you to keep your head clear for whatever I bring back. Don't throw it all away on some green girl."

"I like them green."

"Virgins are boring," Nyx said. "What is it with Mhorians and virgins?"

She caught Khos blushing before he turned away. It was remarkable how red he could get. Nyx waved him off. He gave a blast of the horn and backed away from the station. She watched him go. She was worried about what all that time at the brothels meant. She was worried, too, about the team, about how long she could keep them working for so little. It had been a long time.

Nyx turned and saw Rhys standing at the edge of the crowd. They didn't give him much space. He kept a firm footing, though creepers bumped into him with their nets and at least one child spit at him. He was the only black man in view for as far as Nyx could see—a black roach skittering along a sea of sand.

The station reared up behind him, gold-colored stone perched on a series of pointed arches that the bustling mob slowly pushed through on their way to the platforms and ticket desk.

Nyx elbowed her way into the swarm and looked back once to make sure Rhys was following unmolested. The arches leading into the station were plastered with martyrs' letters from women who'd volunteered for the front. A couple of pushy women dressed in the prophet's green were handing out copies of the latest propaganda sheets and shiny carcasses of pretty holiday beetles, insects known for their cowardly aversion to loud noises.

Nyx shouldered past, and the look she gave the green-clad women was enough to make both of them jerk their hands away from her, withdrawing their insulting little beetles.

Once inside the station, Nyx found some room by the empty fountain and shuffled around the tickets.

Rhys looked at her dubiously. "You do know how to use those, right?" he asked.

Nyx turned the tickets over a couple more times until she matched the gate numbers at the station to the ones on her card.

"Fuck off," she said.

They got lost on one of the platforms and had to double back. Once they were on the right platform, Rhys bought himself a purified water. Nyx bought a whiskey, straight.

Rhys watched her take a swig with his usual distasteful eye.

"I can get you a soda," he said.

"I've had enough of soda," Nyx said. She wanted to be drunk by the time the train arrived in Mushtallah. She knew Mushtallah. She had done all of her bel dame training there. Most magicians and bel dames worked out of the capital, and she expected she was going to run into a lot of women she knew. In the border towns she was somebody to fear, to loathe—a former bel dame who brought in every bounty with the same determination and brutality she'd taken in her bel dame notes. But in Mushtallah, she was just another criminal. Nobody. Nothing. Just like she'd been when they threw her in prison.

Rhys pulled out a slim volume of what looked like poetry from his robe.

A voice came on over the platform radio, and a misty woman's head came into view just over the train tracks.

"There will be a slight delay due to unrest along the Bushair line running north-northwest. This will affect lines Zubair, Mushmura, and Kondija. Thank you for your patience."

Somebody had blown up another track along the Bushair line, then. Nyx allowed herself a minute to wonder how many people had died. She wondered if it mattered.

She sipped her drink and watched Rhys while he read.

"Would you mind reading out loud?" she asked, hoping she sounded nonchalant. It felt too much like she needed something.

He raised his gaze above the ends of the pages and looked at her.

Nyx kept staring at the tracks. She wanted to do something with her hands.

"You nervous?" he asked.

"I'm never nervous."

"Of course not," he said. "This is *Petal Dancing*."

"Oh, God, this isn't something soft, is it?"

"Not everything that's beautiful is weak."

"No, it just makes you that way."

He smiled. "We disagree, then."

"We do," she said.

Nyx cupped her glass in both hands. Rhys began to read, in that voice that could calm her during the worst days—days when bugs got into the money bin and bodies piled up in the freezer like cheap popsicles. Time stretched. His accent had gotten better since she'd started asking him to read out loud. It had been a couple years now, she supposed. She insisted he read in Nasheenian, not so much to improve the accent but because hearing him speak Chenjan—hearing him speak the same language as the people she'd spent two years throwing bursts at on the front felt obscene, and there wasn't much anymore that made her feel so fucked up down to her bones.

After a time, Nyx stopped her fidgeting. She let herself forget some of the worst of the fear. Another announcement came on over the station radio. The delay had been extended.

She finished her drink.

They boarded the train two hours later and found their way to a private first-class cabin whose bench seats were nonetheless so close that if they sat directly across from each other, their knees touched. They didn't sit that way.

Rhys opened his copy of the Kitab, and Nyx fixed herself at the window and watched the Nasheenian desert roll past them in a blur of umber brown and violet blue. The sky was a pale amethyst today, bruised purple along the western horizon, the direction of the front.

"How fast do you think these go?" she asked.

"A hundred, hundred and twenty kilometers an hour," Rhys said.

"Huh," Nyx said. She wasn't going to argue. "You know anything about courts and royalty?" she said.

He did not raise his eyes from the Kitab. "I thought bel dames held intimate soirees with queens and politicians all the time. You should be an old hand at this."

"We don't flirt and whore ourselves out like dancers," she said. He flinched. Why did she always want to twist the knife with him?

"Just make it look good, all right? It's bad enough you're Chenjan."

"I didn't ask to go along. If you take offense at the—"

"It's your fucking accent I can't stand." Something roiled up in her, something old and twisted. She hated it even as the words slipped out. She pressed her fist to her belly.

He shut his book and stood. "Excuse me."

"Sit down."

"I signed an employment contract with you," he snapped. "You did not obtain a writ of sale. I'll be in the dining car." He rolled open the door. It banged behind him.

Nyx rubbed at her face. The worst of her troubles always started with what came out of her mouth.

She heard a knock at the cabin door. She stood and slid it open, trying to come up with something that sounded nice but not like an apology.

But it was not Rhys at the door. A young woman wearing a

blue Transit Authority uniform offered her a complimentary newsroll.

The scrolling text that slid across the translucent projection of the newsrolls was even tougher to read than static text, but Nyx figured Rhys would want to read it when he got back. An offering. She could look at the pictures. Her teachers at the state schools had called her dead dumb because she got all her letters backward. Some of the better newsreel companies had an audio option, but this wasn't one of them.

"Thanks," she said, taking the roll.

She sat back down, but before she twisted the news back into its thumbnail-size roll, she looked over the projection. Bundled between two articles about border skirmishes near Aludra was a picture of the gates of Faleen. The nose of a star carrier reared up behind them.

Nyx stared at the carrier a long time. She'd seen that carrier before. She tried to find an article with it, but all she noted was a short blurb before the picture scrolled over to the next image of three beaming young boys heading for the front.

Star carriers didn't get lost in Faleen twice, and even if it was a different carrier than the one she'd seen the last time she was there, it was the same make as the last one. Aliens interested in boxers were back in Nasheen. What the hell was up with that?

Nyx spent a long while staring at the scrolling pictures, but the image of Faleen didn't pop up again.

What did an off-world carrier want in Faleen? What did the queen want with her in Mushtallah? Being a bel dame had taught her that there were no coincidences, only cause and effect.

She was going to need another drink.

8

Rhys could recite the Kitab by heart, but he never quoted it at Nyx.

He sat in the dining car reading for hours, yet no one came to wait on him. He even stayed long enough for the waitstaff changeover. Three women gave him openly hostile stares as they passed his table. A Transit Authority agent asked to see his papers. The few times he'd dared to go off on his own outside the Chenjan district since joining Nyx's team, he'd been beaten up, cut, and much worse. He didn't travel alone anymore. Much as he hated it, knowing Nyx was just two cars away was somewhat comforting, though her sharp tongue was not.

What finally drove him back to the cabin was the conductor's announcement that they were nearing Mushtallah and were about to go through customs. Customs agents were as violent with Chenjan men as security agents and order keepers.

Rhys put his things away and passed between cars. The stricken Nasheenian landscape rolled by. The world outside did not look so different from Chenja here: There were fewer minarets, and some of the older, mostly untouched villages were tiled in ceramic and still bore huge gold-gilt inscriptions from the Kitab above the lintels to all of their village gates, groceries, and the wealthier houses. He saw old contagion sensors sticking up from the desert, half buried, some of them with the red lights at their bulbous tips still blinking. There were fewer old cities in the Chenjan interior. The oldest relics, Rhys supposed, would be farther north, in the Khairian wasteland, where the first world had been created and abandoned. Out here, though, was the most he had seen of old-world Nasheen. He had never been to Mushtallah.

Rhys knocked at the compartment door. As Nyx pulled it open, a passing member of the Transit Authority paused in the hall at the sight of him and asked Nyx if Rhys was bothering her.

"It's all right," Nyx said. "He's mine." The Transit Authority agent gave them both a good long look before moving on again.

Rhys shut the door.

"Here, I kept the news for you," Nyx said. She tossed him a newsroll. He pocketed it. She had the red letter in her hands again. He pretended not to notice. He had spent six years with her—five and a half longer than he'd expected. She was supposed to be his way out of the boxing gym and on to more lucrative contracts with universities and First Families. But even with an employer on his résumé, his middling talent was not great enough to make up for his ethnicity.

Rhys glanced out the window and decided it was almost thirteen in the afternoon, about time for noon prayer. He rolled out his prayer rug. Nyx went off to find the bathroom.

Despite—or because of—her prison record, Nyx had a good reputation with just about every border agent inside Nasheen. Rhys had crossed into enough cities with her to know. During his more cynical moments, Rhys wondered if she got through customs so easily because she'd slept with all of the agents. It had taken him some time to realize just how terrible Nasheen's problem with same-sex relations had become. Though sex between two men was not only discouraged, but illegal, what passed for sex between women was actively celebrated, and Nyx used sex as freely and easily as any other tool on her baldric. What women found appealing about her, he could not say. She was coarse and foul-mouthed and godless. She was also the only woman who would employ him.

The customs agents slid the door open. They both stared hard at him and told him to raise his arms.

Rhys felt a gut-churning moment of terror.

Nyx appeared just behind them and leaned against the doorway. She smirked. The fear bled out of him.

"Go easy on him," she said. "He's mine."

She said it like he was her bakkie or a prized sand cat.

The bigger woman asked for Nyx's passbook.

"I'm already coded for Mushtallah," Nyx said. "I'm Nyxnissa so Dasheem."

The woman clucked at her. "Who'd you kill to get you back in Mushtallah, Nyxnissa?"

"All the same sorts of people," Nyx said.

"I haven't seen you here since you went to prison."

"For good reason, then," Nyx said.

The matron laughed. "It's not the prettiest city, but it's still our best. Good women in prison, too." She pulled up a sleeve and revealed a badly drawn tattoo of a sword and scattergun on a round shield.

Nyx snorted. "Gunrunning?"

"Good money," the woman said. "Tirhanis don't mind selling so long as we do all the work lugging it through the pass—and the time if we get caught."

"So I hear," Nyx said.

She would know, Rhys thought. How many gunrunners had Nyx slept with?

Both agents went through Rhys's pockets. They didn't find the pockets that kept his bugs, which improved his confidence in his ability to conceal items by altering the composition of the air around them. The skill had not been one of his best back in Faleen. Not that he was going to be able to keep the bugs on his person much longer. Mushtallah would take care of that.

One of the women, an ugly matron with a face the color and texture of boot leather, paged through his passbook. "You a resident alien?" she asked.

"I'm employed," he said. "Everything is in order."

She looked him up and down and made a moue of her mouth, as if contemplating whether or not to spit on him. Nyx pushed farther into the crowded room, arms crossed, and grinned at her.

The customs agent closed her mouth. "No doubt you are," she said to Rhys, and dropped her eyes back to his passbook.

The one patting him down found his Kitab and laughed as she looked through it. "It's the same damn book as ours. Same language and everything. You a convert?"

"No," he said. "Chenjans have always had the same book. Unlike Nasheenians, however, we follow its teachings."

"You speak the dead language?" the ugly one asked, ignoring the jibe.

"Only as much as you do."

"Huh," she said.

The language of the Kitab had been the same since the First Families brought it down from the moons. Even godless Nasheenians should have known that. Who taught the schools here? Atheists like Nyx? They killed atheists in Chenja.

The other one gave back his Kitab. They didn't always. He'd lost a number of Kitabs going through customs.

The ugly one turned to Nyx. "You vouch for him, my woman?"

"You think I'd bring a terrorist into Mushtallah?"

"Only if you're cutting off his head," the ugly one said, and laughed again.

The matron finally pressed a thumb to the organic paper at the back of Rhys's passbook.

"You keep hold of that," she told him, "or the filter will eat you. No permanent residency, no permanent bio-pass into

Mushtallah." She flashed her teeth and gave Nyx a nod. "Good luck, my woman."

The customs agents went back out into the hall. The door rolled shut behind them.

Rhys tugged at his coat, and returned his Kitab and passbook to his breast pocket.

Nyx sat at the window and put her feet up. "They were just flirting," she said. "You don't see a lot of men this far inland. And sure not Chenjan ones."

"That's not flirting."

"You've seen worse."

He turned away from her. "It doesn't excuse them."

"Stop mewling." She paused, then relented. "You know I'll do what I can to make it easy."

"I know," he said.

Rhys liked to think she defended him out of some kind of loyalty or affection, but most days he felt she guarded him the same way she did everything in her possession: *He's mine.* He was just another thing to be owned and retained. Just another thing she could lose.

Once the customs agents were off-loaded, the train chugged into the station just outside Mushtallah. Rhys and Nyx gathered their things and then stepped onto the sandy platform overlooking the city.

"The most boring city in Nasheen," Nyx declared, and trudged down the steps and onto the paved road.

Rhys had read that before Nasheen's revolution two hundred fifty years ago, the gutters were full of dead babies and the mullahs wore vials of virgins' blood to ward off the draft. They'd bred sand cats for fights in the train workers' ward, and the stink and smog of the city sent the First Families who lived up in the hills to the countryside every year during high summer.

The wealthy still fled the city in the summer—it looked deserted from the platform—but there weren't any dead babies that he could see, and the last of the male mullahs had been drafted two centuries ago, right after the queen decreed that God had no place for men in mosques unless they had served at the front.

Mushtallah had been built on seven hills, but that was for beauty and breezes, not for defense. When Mushtallah was founded, there hadn't been much to defend the city from but wild sand cats and some of the more virulent strains of bugs that had gotten away from their magicians or bled down from the twisted mess of the Khairian wasteland in the north. That had all changed, of course, when the war started.

The first wall that rose around the city was an organic filter that kept foreign bug tech out. Every ten yards, a hundred foot faux stone pillar jutted up from the packed, sandy soil. The bug filters that stretched from pillar to pillar made the air shimmer like a soap bubble. Organic filters were a necessity in a country bombarded by all manner of biological, half-living, semi-organic weaponry. Destruction entered cities as often through contaminated individuals as it did through munitions. Filters were magician-made and could be tailored to keep out anyone and anything organic. It was a matter of introducing the bugs powering the filter to the unwanted contagion or—in the case of Mushtallah—only coding the filter to allow in particular individuals. The fact that Rhys had gotten through customs unmolested was a testament to how highly regarded Nyx was by the customs agents.

As they approached the filter, Rhys called up a handful of flying red beetles. He held out his hand, and a dozen swarmed about his fingers.

"We'll be out of contact, Taite," he said. "We're going into Mushtallah."

"Sure thing." Taite's voice carried just over the singing of the beetles, a second song. "Tell me when you come back to civilization."

Rhys flicked his wrist, and the beetles dispersed. He dug through his pockets and released three locusts and a couple of screaming cockroaches he kept in magicians' cages for emergencies. All the bugs had sense enough to head away from the filter. He would need to call or buy more when they got back to Punjai.

Nyx turned in time to see the swarm recede. "You clean?" she asked.

He showed her his empty pockets.

Nyx bled through the gate.

Rhys took a deep breath. Nyx stood on the other side, whole, and stopped to look back at him. He still wasn't entirely convinced about the safety of entering Mushtallah. How far would those agents take their "flirting"? Far enough to tell him that the filter had been coded to let him through, then stand at the train windows and laugh as he stepped through the filter and disintegrated into gray ash?

There are worse ways to die, Rhys thought distantly, and stepped forward.

The filter clung to him, slightly sticky, until he pushed through. He came out the other side with a delicate *pop*. He reflexively patted at his arms and his hips—and smoothed the robe over his groin—to make sure everything was still blessedly intact.

The first twenty yards inside the filter was a stretch of bare soil that lapped against Mushtallah's second wall. The second wall encircling the city, made of stone, had little practical value. It had no working gates anymore, just great gaps in the masonry where travelers passed through and locals kept tchotchke booths. The poor and underemployed spread out their wares on mass-produced blankets given out by the same wholesaler who doled out their identical figurines of Queen Zaynab, and their cheap model palaces and star carriers. The petty merchants and beggars were all women, which was not so different from Chenja, he supposed, but in Chenja all of these women would have had husbands and brothers or sons who were responsible for them, even if those husbands looked after forty or fifty wives. Instead, Nasheenian women all came to adulthood with the terrible knowledge that they had to fend for themselves in this terrible desert.

Ahead of him, Nyx pushed past the throng of traders clinging to the old stone wall, and he slipped through in her wake. The heart of the city spread before them in what had once been a neat grid. As the city grew, new buildings had moved out onto the streets, and finding a straight path to any address was like trekking through an unmapped jungle.

Nyx paid a rickshaw waiting outside a bookshop to take them to Palace Hill.

As they rode through the city, burnouses pulled up to ward against the suns, Rhys tried to call up a swarm. The magicians in Faleen had told him he'd be lucky to find anything living in a clean city. There should have been no bugs in Mushtallah except for the local colonies of flies sealed in when the filter first went up. But as Rhys tried to summon the bugs, he found various colonies at hand, isolated so long from those outside the filter that they must have been different species. He found no bugs suitable for transmissions. The filter would have kept them from broadcasting, anyway. Media had to come into the city via newsrolls or archaic forms of audio-only radio.

The rickshaw pulled them through the crowded street and under a renovated arch that nonetheless looked like it had seen better days. It was checkered with bullet holes. Two centuries before, the Chenjans had poured into the interior and nearly burned Mushtallah to the ground. In retaliation, the Nasheenians had razed a swath of Chenja's agricultural cities, and a hundred and fifty thousand Chenjans died.

After about an hour, the rickshaw pulled them onto the busy main street that ran outside the palace.

Nyx alighted from the rickshaw and held out her hand to help him down. It was an odd gesture, and he gave her a look. She seemed startled, as if the move had been unconscious, and pulled her hand away, turning to face the palace compound on the other side of the street, her body suddenly rigid. He had seen Nasheenian women offer such courtesies to Nasheenian boys, but never to foreign ones. He wondered what her memories were of Mushtallah. Had she courted boys here? He couldn't picture Nyx as a young, bright-eyed girl opening doors for boys.

Rhys got down from the rickshaw and stood next to her. The palace walls were twelve feet high, spiked and filtered. Two women in red trousers stood outside a filtered gate that shimmered in the heat. He pulled again at the hood of his burnous to make sure it was all the way up. His dress was just as much an adherence to Chenjan modesty as it was a practical barrier against the violent suns. He had never been scraped for cancers. Chenjans still boasted the lowest rate of cancers of any people on Umayma.

Nyx crossed the street, striding ahead into the press of people and vehicles with the dumb confidence Rhys suspected would someday get her killed. He followed, stepping over a heap of refuse and ducking away from a sand cat pulling a rickshaw. The women around him turned to stare as he passed. There was not much of him visible outside the burnous, nothing but his hands. Perhaps they could peer into his cowl for a look at his face, but he suspected there was something else giving him away. Some kind of stance or Chenjan affectation that he had never been able to mask or alter. Or maybe he was just intensely paranoid. He had a right to be.

Nyx presented the women at the gate with her red letter. They pointed Nyx and Rhys in the direction of another, smaller, gate. The women posted there let them into an inner yard and through an organic filter. Inside the filter, the world suddenly smelled strongly of lavender and roses. Rhys had a startling memory of the front—of bright bursts in the sky, the smell of oranges and geranium, and this, somewhere, this smell of lavender. He trembled and stilled.

Nyx looked back at him. "Come, now," she said softly. "It's real lavender. It smells different. Come on, I bet they have a garden in here." She, too, had been to the front.

He wanted to take her hand. He shook his head, sighed deeply through his nose, and followed after her.

They were given over to a woman in yellow, who took them through yet another gate and into a massive courtyard. The smells dissipated.

Spotted sand cats prowled the yard, not one of them tended by a chain or a trainer. Women ran through military drills along the far side of the square, dressed in the long, green, organic trousers and gauzy sandals of the Queen's guard.

They wound up a broad staircase flanked by statues of some sort of muscular maned sand cat and into an airy compound with a fountain at the center. Water ran out in four directions along grooved channels carved into the brightly tiled floor. A couple of tall trees with serrated leaves and giant orange blossoms filled the yard. The trees had recently dropped some sort of fruit into the water channels. Rhys realized he had no idea what kind of fruit it was.

"I'll announce you," the woman said. "It may be some time. Tea?"

"Do you have whiskey?" Nyx asked.

"Tea will be fine," Rhys said.

The woman called a servant, and left them.

Nyx stood in front of a carved stone bench. Rhys looked at the wall behind her. Tiled mosaics covered it: images of the first of the Nasheenian monarchs speaking to a white-veiled figure that was likely supposed to be the Prophet. Rhys found depictions of the Prophet distasteful at best, even those that veiled his face. Finding the image of *any* living thing in Chenja was difficult. Most of the books produced before the war had had the pictures cut out and the faces blackened. Chenjans and Nasheenians should have followed the same rulings of the same Prophet, but words, even the words of the prayer language, were open to interpretation, and when Nasheen had disbanded the Caliphate and instituted a monarchy, existing divisions in those interpretations had reached a violent head.

We were always two people, Rhys thought, gazing at the veiled face. It's what his father had told him when Rhys first questioned the war. Rhys had heard it said that Nasheenians and Chenjans came from different moons, believers from different worlds, united in their belief of God and the Prophet and the promise of Umayma. For a thousand years they had carved out some kind of tentative peace, maneuvered their way around a hundred holy wars. They had agreed to shoot colonial ships out of the sky, back when that was still possible, but this? It was too much. Chenjans would submit only to God, not His Prophet, let alone any monarch who wanted to sever God and government. That final insult had resulted in an explosion of all the rest, and the world had split in two.

The other walls presented the more traditional forms of decoration—elaborate raised script, passages from the Kitab carved into the walls and painted in bright colors. Through the airy wooden grating of the windows lining the courtyard, Rhys saw other waiting areas and long hallways. He heard the sounds of more water beyond them, hidden gardens, perhaps. The smell of roses and lilac. Pervasive. It made his eyes water.

"Not so bad a place, huh?" Nyx said.

Rhys sat on the bench. The air was cool. The open center of the courtyard must have been filtered. He pulled back the hood of his burnous.

"Nasheenians spend too much time worshipping images," he said.

"Yeah, well, I never read anything in the Kitab about prayer wheels being the quickest way to get a response from God either. I thought you're supposed to submit, not ask Him for things."

"We don't all use prayer wheels," Rhys said, and grimaced. There was nothing worse than a Nasheenian mistaking him for a Chenjan purist instead of an orthodox. At least no one asked if he was a follower of Bahay anymore. The mullahs had wiped out that sect three years before. "When did you ever read the Kitab?"

Nyx looked away from him, back toward where they'd come in. "Doesn't everybody read it? Man, I could use a whiskey."

"How can you read such a beautiful book and turn your back on it?"

"Never said it wasn't a beautiful book. I just don't believe there's some man up there in the black who gets off on watching us pound our head on the pavement six times a day."

Rhys watched her. "And yet you must have believed there was a God, at some time. You did go to the front."

"I went to the front for my brothers," she snapped, and the force of the response surprised him.

The servant returned with tea and a decanter of whiskey for Nyx. Nyx walked over to the lip of the fountain and sat, square in the sun, her burnous pushed back over her shoulders. Though Rhys was reasonably certain of the filter, he guessed that Nyx would have sat there uncovered regardless. He had never met anyone so casual with their life. Most people that careless or arrogant were dead before thirty. How she continued to elude a violent death while actively courting it still mystified him.

"You must have had a powerful belief once, to take you out there," he persisted. "If I'd ever been called, it would have been difficult to answer." Saying it that way, saying "if," had become such a natural thing, such a natural story, that it fell off his tongue without a hitch. It was easier to say in Nasheenian.

Nyx barked out a little laugh. "Oh, yeah? You saying that if your mullahs told you God wanted you to go, you wouldn't have? Don't be an ass, Rhys. You would have gone. You would have dressed up for it."

He looked down into his lap so she could not see his face. Sometimes he wondered how two people could work together for so long and still know nothing about one another.

They sat waiting an hour more before another yellow-clad woman summoned them. The woman was tall and lean, with a blunt, bold face and keen stare. When she walked in, Rhys knew she was a magician, though she dressed in the same uniform as the queen's other attendants. The look she gave him confirmed that she knew he was a magician also, and they held each other's attention for a brief moment. She turned to Nyx.

Nyx had finished most of the whiskey.

"She will see you now," the woman said as four more women turned out from the arched doorways to join her. They were a formidable bunch, dark-haired and dark-eyed, with the backs and shoulders of women who could pull rickshaws and swing swords with equal ease. They were very Nasheenian.

"I am Kasbah," the woman said. "We will, of course, need to search your persons for weapons and contaminants. Weapons will be returned when you exit her presence."

Rhys unbuckled his pistols. He turned over the loop of ammunition he kept at his belt and the dagger at his hip.

Watching Nyx disarm was a more drawn-out affair. There was the sword she kept strapped to her back, her pistol, her whip, the garroting wire she kept strung in her dhoti, the bullets sewn into her burnous, the bullets strung around her neck. The dagger strapped to her thigh, the pistol strapped to the opposite calf, the three poisoned needles she kept in her hair. He noted she kept the garroting wire she used to tie her sandals, but she pulled out the razor blades tucked into the soles.

The women must have been used to bel dames and bounty hunters, because they did not blink at the pile of weaponry she handed over. Though the filters had cleared them both of bugs, the women searched their pockets. Kasbah neatly found and turned out Rhys's hidden bug pockets. She was, most certainly, a magician.

"We'll also need to perform an organics search," Kasbah said. She did not look at him, but she had just pulled her hands from his hidden pockets.

Rhys flinched. Nyx looked over at him. "Can't we skip that?" she asked.

"I'm sorry," Kasbah said, "but particularly when"—she gave Rhys another open look—"we have those trained in the art of assassination within her presence, we must perform a search. If you'll come with me, Nyxnissa, I will have your companion searched separately."

Rhys said, "No. I'll stay here." He had been through many a Nasheenian organics search. The kind by women like the ones on the train. He felt a sharp tightening in his chest. Sweat broke out across his brow. I've been here too long, he thought.

Nyx was fiddling with her red letter. "I'll be in the next room," she said, but from the tone of her voice, even she knew that would not be enough.

"No." He pulled his burnous more tightly around him. The fear was in him now, the memories of half a hundred organics searches during the years he'd lived in exile. They did not just use their fingers to search every cavity, orifice, and wound on his body for hidden organics, but far more invasive tools. They were never gentle. These cold women on the interior knew little of the war and had seen few Chenjans. They would enjoy venting their rage and frustration onto his black body.

"Can I go with him?" Nyx asked. "What if I go with him?"

"These aren't customs agents," Rhys snapped at her. She couldn't flirt or fuck her way out of everything. He felt the blood rush into his face. He began to recite the ninety-nine names of God, silently. Stillness, he thought, silence. This is all temporary.

Nyx shot him a dark look.

Kasbah clapped her hands. "Come, now. You wish to be searched together? This is acceptable. Many women worry over their men. I understand."

"That's fine," Nyx said.

"Nyx, I'm not—" Rhys began. He tripped over the names of God, lost count. Started over.

Nyx stepped up and took his elbow. The names of God fell away. She was about his height, but heavier, solid, and when she took his arm, the fear, too, bled away. Her touch filled him with an emotion so complex that he could not name it. The same woman who could cut the head off a man with a dagger in sixty seconds could ease his mind in the face of a thousand angry Nasheenian women. She could banish all thoughts of God, of submission. Some days she made him feel like an insect, a roach, the worst thing to crawl across the world. And then there were the times, like now, when she brought him a stillness he had known only with his forehead pressed to a prayer rug.

She said to him, "We'll be all right." To Kasbah and her women, "We'll be all right."

Kasbah led them to the examination room. Rhys's pulse quickened. He would have bolted if not for Nyx's hand on his arm.

"You'll be all right," she said. She would know the sorts of things Nasheenian women had done to him before. She had likely done work like that herself.

What had this exile made him? What was he becoming? He prayed; God, how he prayed. But he dreamed, often, in Nasheenian now, and the memories of his father's face had slipped away long ago. How could one forget his father's face? It was like forgetting the face of God.

The women stripped Nyx first, searched her, and when she was putting her clothes back on, told him to strip. And he obeyed them, as he had before, as he would again.

When he had been in Rioja, he found out what Nasheenians did to unescorted Chenjan men. He dreamed now, some nights, of Nasheenian women and boys, bloody mouths, screaming. *His* blood. *His* screaming.

He turned his back to Nyx and stared at the wall. When they bent him over the table, he felt Nyx's hand on his back.

"You'll be all right," she said. "I'm here."

The ninety-nine names of God…

He gripped the table so hard his hands hurt.

When he was clothed again, Kasbah led them back to the courtyard. Nyx and Rhys stayed several feet behind her, walking gingerly. As they walked, their hands touched. Rhys knew he should be the one to step away an appropriate distance, to maintain a modicum of modesty even after all that, but he didn't have the energy to break away from her. It was the history of their… partnership? Alliance? Contract? His inability to pull away was all that kept him next to her. But what kept her here? Her arrogance, her selfishness, her desperate need for a magician, even a poor one? She hated him as much as any other Nasheenian did, but she had hired him and kept him, long after his usefulness as a sly slap in the face to Yah Tayyib had expired.

She strode next to him with her usual confidence, a hard but neutral look on her face. She was impossible to read.

"This way," Kasbah said. She took them back to the courtyard and through one of the archways. The air beneath it shimmered as they passed, although, unlike the other two filters they'd walked through, it was transparent when undisturbed. They moved into another courtyard teeming with succulents, shielded from the suns by an opaque filter. Rhys took a deep breath. The air was warm and humid. At the other end of the yard—along a path that curved through the broad-leafed plants and heavy flower heads lining the stone path—were two latticed doors.

Kasbah opened the doors onto a broad terrace, also shielded by an opaque filter. Inside, a short, squat woman sat at a table on the terrace.

Kasbah announced them.

"Nyxnissa so Dasheem, and her companion, Rhys Dashasa."

The woman on the terrace did not stand. She turned a soft, slightly sagging face to them, her mouth a thin line. She had the flat, broad nose of a Ras Tiegan and the strong jaw and deep brown complexion of a Nasheenian. As she watched them, she turned up the corners of her mouth. "Rhys Dashasa isn't a Chenjan name," she said. The voice made her sound older than the look of her face.

"It's not supposed to be," Rhys said.

Everyone on Nyx's team had their secrets. Nyx said nothing of her time at the front, though Rhys had seen a public copy of her military records, which indicated she had been reconstituted and honorably discharged. Her honor was not one she spoke of. Taite had never told any of them why he'd run from Ras Tieg, and when his sister mysteriously arrived in Nasheen eight months ago, pregnant, he simply said that he was her only means of survival and refused to elaborate. Khos's time at the brothels was too extensive for traditional reasons, even if Mhorians were as sex-crazed as they were purported to be. Anneke had blown up more things than even she would admit to, and Rhys suspected she'd spent a lot of time in prison. She had no public record at all. He knew. He had checked.

On Nyx's team, the matter of Rhys's real name was a small thing, hardly worth comment.

It was another reason he stayed.

9.

Nyx had seen images of the queen before, of course—misty blue images from high council meetings and patriot-act ads on the radio—but most of those were doctored. As Nyx walked closer, the queen stood. She barely reached Nyx's shoulder. She was a plump, matronly figure with a wispy cloud of graying hair. Her face was too young for the hair—she might have been forty. The desert and the suns sucked the youth from most women, but the queen had grown up rich, and the rich—the sort of people on the high council and of the First Families—didn't get exposed to much sun. They didn't age as quickly as everybody else, so it was worth her while to keep her hair white. Older women were well respected in Nasheen. If it didn't show in her face, she'd need to show it somewhere. She was the fucking Queen, after all.

Nyx caught Rhys looking at her. She had the peculiar feeling he was reading her mind. One never knew with magicians, even bad ones. He still sometimes surprised her.

"May God bless you. Please, be comfortable," the queen said, gesturing to the two seats on the other side of the polished white table. Nyx didn't see the advantage of having a white table. She supposed it made sense if you had somebody around to clean up after you all the time. Back when she was growing up in Mushirah, her mother and aunts had employed a Ras Tiegan servant to help out with taking care of Nyx and her siblings and doing little stuff around the house. The woman had lived out back in the bug storage shed and taught Nyx how to swear in Ras Tiegan and beat her brothers at strategy games. Nyx wondered if the Queen remembered any of her servants' names.

As she sat down across from the Queen, Nyx realized *she* had forgotten the Ras Tiegan servant's name.

"I guess I should say I'm sorry about your mother," Nyx said. "About her abdicating."

Nyx hadn't cared much for the old half-breed hag and the bureaucratic tape she wound around the apprehension of terrorists. It had cut into Nyx's business in a bad way. The current queen being a half-breed hadn't been terribly popular either.

"My mother realizes what is best for her health," the queen said, "and the health of Nasheen."

"That's good to hear," Nyx said, and wondered what she was trying to say with that. Rumor had it Zaynab was an enterprising sort of queen. She'd been running the country on her own for years while her mother dabbled in astrology and sand science.

"Nyxnissa so Dasheem," the queen said.

"Nyx, yeah."

"Nyx, a pleasure."

"Uh, thanks."

"Thank you for answering my summons," the queen said. There was something on the table at her elbow, a transparent globe. An information globe. Nyx hadn't seen one of those in more than a decade. "I was told that you served at the front."

"A long time ago." Nyx glanced over at Rhys and clenched her left hand, the one he'd brushed during their long walk from quarantine to the queen's chambers. What little she knew about Rhys she hadn't learned from him but rather from the magicians and boxers in Faleen. He was from some rich family, and he'd spent time at the Chenjan Imam's court. He was used to dealing with mullahs and politicians and First Families. It explained his uptight dressing practices and strict manners. She hoped he was a lot more comfortable right now than she was, even if he was the Chenjan.

"Volunteered?" the queen said.

"Yeah."

"Two years of service, honorably discharged at nineteen, so I've read."

Nyx stiffened. It was a bit early in the interview to be bringing up her file. She had managed to keep a lot of things out of that file, and even more out of the public one—things she didn't talk about with anybody, especially not her team. She didn't look at Rhys.

"You came back with burns over eighty percent of your body," the queen said.

Nyx opened her mouth to cut her off. The queen kept talking, minor details, and Nyx saw her looking at the globe, checking her notes.

"Your military file says you were put into the care of the magicians for reconstitution." The queen paused to eye Nyx over, as if looking for evidence that Nyx had once been a charred, blackened husk of a woman. "Is that right?"

"Yeah, I guess."

She remembered the mud between her toes, the taste of the rain in the yeasty air and the way the wet made the long grass shine. They had been in Chenia, in Bahreha, sweeping for mines. She went barefoot when she was doing sapper work; she liked to feel the ground under her, the way it responded to her weight. She believed it gave her a better idea of where the Chenjans had set the mines. Her whole squad had been there, sweeping up from behind her. She led, pushing farther into the muddy grass, until she reached the end of the cleared field. That's where she had gone down on her belly, a knife in one hand and her other palm flat on the ground, a mantis at work. She remembered finding the mine, a flat green disk the size of a bottle cap, the same as half a hundred others she'd cleared from the same field. Nothing special. Nothing different.

She had been good at what she did.

Until that day.

"I had a good magician work on me. The best in the business," Nyx said. *And then he fucked me over and sent me to prison,* Nyx thought. But that was in the file too. No need to repeat it.

"I went against the advice of my best counselors in asking you here," the queen said, and now she wasn't looking at the globe anymore. She smiled, but it was a too-sweet grandmotherly smile, like she was doing Nyx a favor. A favor she'd want repaid real soon.

It all started to click together in Nyx's head now. The aliens from Faleen, the queen's recent abdication, the fact that the queen was calling in Nyx—a hunter, not a bel dame.

This might get tricky.

"Sorry I'm not more popular," Nyx said. She was better at killing her own people than getting rid of foreigners. Nobody liked to hear that, but it was true.

"They told me that you served some time in prison for black work. You were delivering zygotes to gene pirates."

Yeah, that one had definitely gone into the file.

"I did," Nyx said. She was being tested. But for what? Her loyalty to Nasheen? To the queen? The queen's laws? To what end?

"You have some sympathy for illegal breeding? We have no need for rogue mixers or illegal half-breeds, like Ras Tieg or Druce. Our compounds perform those functions. It's disappointing to see a woman waste her womb on a single birth."

"Your mother was a half-breed, wasn't she?" Nyx asked.

Rhys made a strange little choking sound that might have been a laugh.

"Excuse me," he said, "may I have some water, Honorable?"

The queen cocked her head at him. She raised a fleshy hand,

and Kasbah called in a retainer. They gave him a plain glass of water. Nyx and the queen were silent through the whole performance.

Nyx's mother and all the rest who were authorized for child rearing had to go through the filtration and inoculation process on the coast. Just as Umayma had been tailored to suit the people on it, the people on Umayma had been tailored to suit the world. Half-breed illegals like Taite had a tougher time getting around. They burned more easily, died sooner, and suffered from more cancers and diseases. Most of Taite's childhood stories were about things experienced while bedridden. The former queen and her children wouldn't have had that problem, of course. The high council would have approved their pairing and gotten them the inoculations they needed. It strengthened Nasheenian ties with Ras Tieg.

"I was into black work because it paid all right," Nyx said, getting back into safer territory.

"More than being a bel dame? Collecting blood debt is rewarding."

"Only if you're good at it," Nyx said. "I wasn't."

Rhys shifted in his seat and gave her a pointed look. "Nyxnissa is being modest," Rhys said. "She brought in every note she was assigned. Her final note as a bel dame prevented an outbreak of what we now know was blister fever. I believe a similar contaminated soldier was responsible for the deaths of more than four hundred people in Sahlah last year."

"Indeed," the queen said. "And who is this Chenjan man in your company, Nyxnissa?"

Nyx said, "He's my magician."

"I read that your other partners did not last long while you were a bel dame."

"It's a good thing I changed professions, then," Nyx said.

"Nyxnissa is many things," Rhys cut in, "including stubborn.

Determined. If you're looking for a woman to stick to a note until the bitter end, you've summoned the proper woman. She has a black mark—the black work—yes, but she was also young and foolish then. She's tempered a good deal since."

Rhys was a much better liar than she was.

"Stubborn, yeah," Nyx agreed. "But maybe just stupid."

"Neither of us has gotten where we are by being stupid," the queen said.

"Oh, I've done some pretty stupid things," Nyx said. Going to the front had been one of them. This conversation with the queen might be another. "I heard you've called in a lot of hunters for this note. Not just me."

"Hunters, yes. A few mercenaries. Most have already given up the hunt, however."

"You haven't called in any bel dames to pursue the note?" Might as well ask, Nyx thought.

"I have my reasons for keeping bel dames out of this particular affair. I need someone…."

"Desperate?" Nyx suggested.

Rhys pressed his lips together and looked at the table. He discreetly covered his mouth with his hand. Being blunt shocked him.

Maybe selling herself as desperate wasn't a great idea either. Nyx closed her eyes, and behind her eyelids she saw the mine explode again, felt something wet against her skin, a hard slap. Then the whole world was full of filth, offal; she watched half a dozen boys blow apart.

She had been good, once.

Nyx opened her eyes.

Recompense for the apprehension of the terrorist is negotiable.

How negotiable? Getting back her bel dame title negotiable?

Duty. Honor. Sacrifice. *My life for a thousand.*

"These days, I only risk my life for cash," Nyx said, opening her eyes.

Duty. Honor. Cash.

"Tell me, why did you volunteer for the front?" the queen asked.

"My older brothers died at the front. When they called up my youngest brother, I joined so I could watch his back."

"A family woman, then," the queen said.

"Not really," Nyx said. "He died of dysentery during basic training."

When she'd gotten back from the front after being reconstituted, the government had plowed over her mother's homestead in Mushirah and put up a munitions factory. The locals later burned the factory down and reclaimed the farmland, but her mother had died of Azam fever when she relocated to a breeding farm on the coast. She was dead and buried long before Nyx was reconstituted.

"Let's go ahead and talk money," Nyx said.

"Money isn't an issue," the queen said. "Bring me the woman I want—alive—and we can negotiate the rest. I have half a dozen estates and twice as many servants, if you wish it. Women, of course." She looked at Rhys. "Unless you'd prefer half-breeds. We have no end of male half-breeds."

"Until we start sending half-breeds to the front," Nyx said. "You want to know why women risk illegal pregnancy and keep pirates elbow deep in organs? Half-breeds who aren't inoculated—who aren't rich Firsts—don't get drafted. They'd fall like rotten wasp nests at the front."

"Perhaps we can eliminate the need for the draft altogether."

"What do you mean?" This was the dangerous part. No legitimate note was ever pointedly removed from the bel dame queue.

"The woman I'd like you to retrieve can help us end the war."

Nyx gave a soft grunt. And who would be more interested in ending the war than a former bel dame and war veteran who'd lost everything to it? Somebody just as good as a bel dame but with publicly severed ties to the council? Somebody the queen could put in her pocket?

Pocket, my ass, Nyx thought.

"We could put something together," Nyx said. "Who is she?"

"A foreigner. An off-worlder called Nikodem Jordan."

Fuck, Nyx thought. The carrier in Faleen. The boxers. Jaks. Prison. Her sisters. Aliens. A boy's head in a bag. No coincidences.

Cause and effect.

The queen pulled the globe off the table and called up a still. She handed the globe to Nyx. "This gives her likeness and background. You'll need to change the password."

Nyx took the globe. It fit neatly in the palm of her hand. Nikodem's images had date and time stamps. Nyx saw that several of the stills were dated eight years before. Just as she'd suspected. The same carrier. The same aliens.

Nikodem was a small woman, Chenjan in coloring, with a broad nose, wide cheekbones, and gray eyes. It was an arresting face, not so much alien as exotic. She had the smooth, unblemished skin of someone who'd never stood under the suns of Umayma. She was too little and big-eyed for real beauty, but there was some strength in that face—and cunning. It was the sort of face that kept others out, kept secrets.

"I'll need to know everything about her," Nyx said. She looked up from the projections, reluctantly. "How long has she been gone? Does she have friends? Other travelers with her? Who did she meet with when she was last here? Looks like that was eight years ago."

Rhys tilted his head slightly and peered at the images projected from the globe. She saw his eyes widen, and he sat back. The woman wasn't *that* pretty. Nyx frowned and peered at the stills again. Then Nyx remembered where Rhys had been eight years ago. She looked at him again. Their gazes met. One long, tense moment.

Then the queen was talking, and Rhys looked away, and Nyx tried to listen. Nikodem had been missing for a month, the queen said. She came to Nasheen with three others. The off-worlders had come to Faleen for the first time sixteen years before, and they had come speaking the language Chenjans and Nasheenians used for prayer. Only mullahs spoke that language with any competence anymore, and most people would debate just how competent it was.

"What did they come here looking for?" Nyx asked.

"Some of that is confidential," the Queen said. "What I can say is that they were very interested in finding other followers of the Kitab and its sister books. They have offered an exchange of technologies in the spirit of our shared faith. We've been in negotiations for nearly two decades."

"They from New Kinaan?" Nyx asked.

"Yes. You know it?"

"Heard it secondhand. My sister works with foreigners on the coast," Nyx said. Kine might be able to fill her in on what they were up to, though she hadn't spoken to Kine since she got out of prison. Kine had wanted even less to do with her after the black mark. "I know that when we get in off-worlders, we're always real interested in hauling them down to the breeding compounds and getting new tech from them."

"You say they are followers of the Kitab. A sister book. But have you read it?" Rhys asked.

Nyx looked at him sharply. She didn't know what that had to do with anything.

"As with any people, they believe they are the only true believers of the one God, the only people who know and understand Him through the words of His many prophets," the queen said.

"God is unknowable," Rhys said. "That is His nature. For them to claim to know God is arrogance at best. For them to claim more than one prophet isn't heresy, but to claim there was another after ours... I couldn't imagine doing business with such a people."

That dagger was a little too sharp for Nyx's taste. She opened her mouth to tell him to shut up.

"At one time, Nasheen and Chenja did business," the queen said, "and it wasn't called heresy then. It is no business of mine to tell my women how to worship. I do not require a call to prayer in any city. That is up to the mullahs and the people who elect them. Your Chenjan mullahs may be elected, but I am not. When our mullahs overstep, I intervene." She smiled thinly. "Our balance of power has kept the soldiers at the front, the bel dames at work, and the mullahs sticking to matters of God. We have done this successfully for nearly three hundred years, while doing business with people of the Book."

"You say you give your people freedom to submit to God," Rhys said, and Nyx wondered if he'd hoped to have this conversation with the Queen of Nasheen his whole life, "yet you have barred men from serving as mullahs unless they return alive from the front. I see some contradiction in that. How can you deny a man the right to submit to God as he believes God has directed him?"

Nyx sucked her teeth.

"We have different views of God, you and I," the queen said.

Which explains that whole war business, Nyx thought.

"So, when can I see these Kinaanites?" Nyx asked.

The queen turned from Rhys and regarded her a long moment, as if she'd forgotten Nyx was even there. "Kasbah will take you to them," she said.

10

The off-worlders were having supper, which Nyx found somehow reassuring. As she and Rhys stepped into the room behind Kasbah, the call to prayer rolled out over Mushtallah. The keening cry sounded close, and Nyx figured it was pumped into the palace grounds through some kind of local radio.

Rhys found an ablution bowl near the door and began to wash in preparation for prayer. Nyx continued on into the airy little room. There were plush divans and tall succulents in striped pots. Some kind of gauzy curtain draped down from the ceiling in soft folds, which cut some of the filtered light from the open shaft above them.

The off-worlders were gathered around a faux wood table set near four glass doors that led out onto a balcony overlooking the spread of Mushtallah. Nyx could see the blue light of the second sun begin to push dusky evening across the city. Glow worm lamps had been unshuttered, and the minarets were lit up with red beacons, an old but useless tradition. The beacons just made the minarets better targets.

The aliens at the table were small, bony women. Two were black as pitch, and one was whiter than a Mhorian, which Nyx figured wasn't healthy. The white one wore a visible silver X-shaped pendant, like a Ras Tiegan, and they all wore dark hijabs that covered their hair and wrapped around their necks like overgenerous turbans. They were covered from wrist to ankle in a variety of housecoats and loose trousers.

Though she ate with her fingers, the white woman wore gloves. Nyx wondered if the white pigment was some sort of skin condition.

Rhys had pulled the prayer rug from his back and took up his kneeling position, facing north. As he professed his intention to offer salaat and began to go through the gestures of the niyat, she could still follow along with him, the words and movement so familiar to her body. She wished he would carry a sword instead of a rug. When bullets ran out, rugs weren't much good for beating people off.

Kasbah introduced Nyx to the off-worlders.

"You don't pray?" Nyx asked the women.

"We pray," the more delicate of the black women said in heavily accented Nasheenian. "Just not so publicly, not in ordinary spaces, and not so frequently. We are people of the Good Book, but our book is… different from yours. I must admit, even among followers of your book… what is it you call it here, the Kitab? Even among followers of your Kitab on other worlds, your interpretation is… exceedingly unique. Yours is the first post-Haj world to—"

"I sometimes wonder what he has left to say to God," Nyx interrupted, nodding toward Rhys.

"There is always something left to say to God," the woman said. She gestured to the table. "Join us. I am Danika Chaba."

The other two introduced themselves. The other black woman was Solome Hadar, and the white one was Keran Yarkona. The white one's Nasheenian was so bad that Nyx could barely understand her.

"You're the tenth mercenary to talk to us," Danika said.

"I'm a bounty hunter," Nyx said.

"Oh? Is there a difference?"

"Yeah," Nyx said. She could hear Rhys reciting, not in Chenjan or Nasheenian but the ancient language of prayer:

"In the name of God, the infinitely Compassionate and Merciful. Praise be to God, Lord of all the worlds."

"Were you all with Nikodem the last time she was in Nasheen?" Nyx asked. She was hungry, and they had a lot to go over.

Keran and Solome exchanged looks, but Danika did not blink as she replied, "I was. Solome stayed aship, as she had not yet been inoculated against your contagions. Keran had not yet graduated."

"Graduated?"

"Off-world studies, diplomacy. She has done some work for us in-system."

"In-system?"

Danika clucked her tongue. In Nasheen, that was a reproach, but Nyx suspected she meant it differently.

"We have two viable worlds in our star's system, and a colonized moon. We have some experience in negotiating with others who are not as we are."

"It was smart to send women to Nasheen, then."

Danika gave a tight smile. "It was not all politics. We have sent skilled technicians before us, but most were unable to adapt to the peculiar contagions of your world, and perished. Nikodem and I are now the top technicians in our field."

"And what field is that?" Nyx asked.

"Organic sciences."

Rhys finished the prayer with his feet tucked under his thighs, his palms splayed on either knee.

"Peace and blessings of God be upon you," he murmured, turning to look over his right shoulder, where one of God's angels was supposed to be recording all your good deeds. He then looked over his left shoulder, to the angel making note of all his wrongs.

What wrongs had Rhys ever committed, Nyx wondered? Again, he murmured, "Peace and blessings of God be upon you." He began to roll up his prayer rug.

She noted that he had added no personal prayers to the beginning or end of his salaat.

Angels and demons and a great man in the sky who took the time to listen to a whole world abase itself. There had been no angels at the front. Chenjans were the only demons, and sacrificing herself to God had proved nothing, saved no one.

What bugged her was that Rhys hadn't figured that out yet.

She heard him get up and turned to watch him walk over. Kasbah brought another chair from the back of the room, and Rhys joined them at the now crowded table. The white woman, Keran, flinched away from him as he sat next to her. What did she have to be afraid of from another believer? Maybe they all had something against aliens. Nyx wondered how often these people had dealt with other worlds. If they had whole schools for "off-world diplomacy," they must do it a lot. Nyx had a long moment of vertigo. How many worlds were out there?

Lord of all the worlds…

"Competitive field on your world?" Nyx asked. "Organic sciences?"

"In our country, yes. But you did not come here to talk of science," Danika said.

Nyx leaned back in the chair and thought: *You did though, didn't you?* But that wasn't the note Nyx had accepted.

"Can you think of anyone Nikodem met last time who would give her harbor?" Nyx asked. "Any place she'd want to go?"

A black woman in Nasheen might stick out even if she holed herself up in the Chenjan quarters with the refugees. Though her color would match, her foreign look and accent would give her away as something other than Chenjan, especially if she went out unveiled or looked too many men in the face. These women had no problem looking Rhys in the face—only Keran seemed to actively dislike him—but that may have been them bowing to Nasheenian custom. In any case, the other hunters this group had spoken to would have started in the Chenjan district. If so many had already given up the hunt, it was likely Nikodem wasn't there.

"We have a more detailed itinerary on the globe the queen issued you," Danika said. "We spent a good deal of time here in the palace meeting with bel dames and dignitaries."

"Which bel dames did you meet?"

"Do you remember their names?" Danika asked Solome.

Solome's voice was deep, sultry. Nyx was impressed to hear that voice come out of such a small woman.

"I believe we spent time with Dahab so Batir and Fatima Kosan. Who were the others? Inan so Khada, and someone called Blake, a half-breed from Ras Tieg."

"Blake's not a bel dame, she's a bounty hunter like me," Nyx said. "Half-breeds can't be bel dames." Ah, Blake. So the young upstart was still around. Nyx knew Inan too. They had gone through bel dame training together.

"There were magicians, also," Danika said. "We met with a great deal of magicians over the course of our stay. The nature of our work demanded it. That list is in your file also."

"I heard you saw a boxing match in Faleen," Nyx said, casually. She suspected that little detail wasn't on the queen's globe.

Danika grimaced. "Boxing, yes. A bit of parting vulgarity for Nikodem during her last visit. She has a peculiar obsession with violence."

"Does she?" Nyx said, interested.

"Why is it you are not taking notes?" Solome asked.

"I was trained as a bel dame," Nyx said. "We don't take notes." What she didn't say was that she learned everything by rote because she was dead dumb with books. It was why she could still recite the Kitab by heart nearly two decades after she'd last picked one up.

"Then this man is not your assistant? Is he a magician?"

Solome asked, and Nyx watched her eyes. It was a hungry look, but not one of physical desire. She hadn't looked at him much until now.

"I have some training with bugs," Rhys said, "My practicing license is provisional."

"On what?" Solome asked.

"On my being employed with a local hunter or bel dame," Rhys said.

"I find this ability to manipulate organisms through will alone fascinating," Solome said. "We have tried to replicate it in our system, but... The ability to alter pheromones, to... effectively reprogram insects at the cellular level, seems to be something innate, peculiar to this world."

"It's inherited," Nyx said, "like shape shifting."

"It was not something we carried with us from the moons," Rhys said.

Nyx, startled, looked at him. "Where'd you hear that?"

He shrugged. "My father was a hobby historian."

Solome said something in a bizarre syrupy language to Danika. Danika nodded and replied in the same language.

Solome said, "Perhaps you could tell us of your father. We're much interested in those with knowledge of this world. Most Nasheenian libraries and records were burned or culled during one of your many wars."

"My father is dead," Rhys said.

"Ah," Solome said, "a small tragedy, but not unexpected. How is it you tolerate living in the country of your enemies?"

Nyx watched him.

Rhys did not look at her but met Solome's steady gaze. "I am a political refugee. Nasheen tolerates my presence because I am a magician."

"Tirhan cherishes magicians and shifters alike, does it not?" Solome asked. "Surely that country, being one only recently estranged from Chenja, would have been a better fit for one such as you."

"Nasheen was… closer," Rhys said carefully. Nyx saw him start to play with his hands. Such a good liar, until he had to lie about himself.

"Anyhow, Tirhan split from Chenja two hundred years ago," Nyx said. "The split isn't exactly new. Don't they speak some southern dialect?"

"They know Chenjan," Solome said. "Chenja allows them passes to visit their martyr's grave each year."

Nyx had heard something about that at some bug party back in bel dame training. Rhys was still playing with his hands.

"Tell me," Solome said, leaning in slightly now, suddenly a bit more animated. "This sixth prayer of yours, what is its purpose? No other followers of your book have a midnight prayer."

"The midnight prayer—" Rhys began, but Nyx had had enough talk of religion.

"Tell me more about Nikodem and her love of violence," Nyx said.

Solome settled back into her chair again.

"I wouldn't call it a love," Danika said, picking up for Solome. "Perhaps a peculiar obsession. In our country, on New Kinaan, we are born into our classes. Nikodem was born to a scholarly class, organic sciences. She wished she had been born one of God's soldiers."

"It's overrated," Nyx said.

Danika knit her brows.

"Never mind," Nyx said. "You say she wanted to see the boxers?"

"Nikodem asked the court's lead magician, Yah Hadeel, to arrange for her to see a fight before we departed. The only one that fit into our schedule was the fight in Faleen. It was a dull thing."

"I was at that fight," Nyx said. "I heard she talked to the boxers."

Solome made a noise of distress.

Danika shushed her. "I let her speak to them."

Solome snapped something in their language, and Nyx rearranged the women's hierarchy in her mind.

"She spoke to both boxers before the fight," Danika said. "She was very interested in why they would choose to get hit in the face."

"There's good money in boxing," Nyx said.

"In our country," Keran piped up, tugging at the fingers of her gloves, cutting off all the ends of her words with rolling "shhhh" sounds, "the State ensures that all are employed and cared for. One need not resort to violence."

"Uh-huh," Nyx said. The sand was always cleaner just over the next dune. These women were reminding her more and more of First Family matrons. "So if your world's so sweet, what are the lot of you doing out here collecting bug tech?"

All three women stilled. There was an uncomfortable moment of silence. Then Danika looked at Solome, and Keran reached for her cold tea with her gloved hands.

"We have an interest in all of God's worlds," Solome said. "Nikodem more than most. Surely you trust the judgment of your queen—God's appointed leader of your world?"

"I wouldn't take her purported divine right to the title that far," Rhys said.

"What about the magicians you met up with here at the palace?" Nyx said, before Rhys started derailing them again. "You sure Nikodem ran and wasn't kidnapped? Not every magician on the Queen's payroll is clean."

Altruism. Shared resources. Catshit. It wasn't only their intentions they were lying about. Some of the fact-by-fact reporting may have been because Danika had told the story so often, but Nyx wasn't betting on it, not with some of the other answers they'd given her. Nikodem just "disappeared"? Went rogue? What kind of society trained and employed people based on genetics, had their own interstellar diplomacy school, and then "accidentally" lost one of their diplomats? Umayma was a long way to come for a couple of bugs and a boxing match.

But that's none of your concern, she thought, and grimaced. She only needed the note. She needed Nikodem. It wasn't her job to figure the intentions. That was for the queen and her security techs.

I hate this note already, Nyx thought.

"It's true that the magicians understand the importance of our work," Danika said. "It's possible that one of them could have approached her once she left Mushtallah, but I don't believe a magician would take such a risk. Those who were aware of her talents would understand her importance to your country and the disastrous consequences if she was acquired by your rivals."

"So she disappeared from here, not from Faleen?"

"Oh yes," Danika said. "Queen Zaynab's security bugs recorded her departure."

"Footage can be doctored," Nyx said, turning to Rhys. "Right?"

"It can," Rhys said. He looked back at Kasbah. "Can we view it?"

"I've had that footage uploaded to your globe," Kasbah said from her place near the door, but she looked at Rhys as she said it, which was odd for a Nasheenian security tech. When you wanted to put black boys in their place, you talked to their owners—or employers—not to them.

"I would need to see the originals," Rhys said.

"Can we do that?" Nyx asked.

"I can authorize that," Kasbah said.

"Great," Nyx said. She stood and nodded to the aliens. "Thanks. I can contact you here if I have any other questions?"

"Certainly," Danika said. "A contact pattern has been designated for us and uploaded to your globe. Kasbah says the call is routed through palace security."

All three women stood, and pressed their hands together and bowed.

Nyx made a quick, sloppy mirror of the gesture and watched Rhys make a far more elegant bow alongside her. Nyx had never bowed to anybody in her life. It was the sort of thing people only did in cheap historical dramas. Who ran all these other worlds? Where did all the people come from? Motes of stardust, just like Nasheenians and Chenjans? Refugees from dying worlds like the Ras Tiegans or asylum seekers from planets that hated the people of the Book, like the Mhorians? But then, where did the people who hated the people of the Book come from?

Theology looked a lot better the more questions you started to pile up. Saying it was all just God's plan gave you neat answers for everything.

Give it a fucking rest, she thought, and turned to Kasbah. "Let's go," she said.

Kasbah took Nyx and Rhys into the belly of the palace. The way grew darker as they descended. The floors were still brightly colored tile, but the doors were no longer made of intricately carved wood. These were solid, made of twisted metal and bug secretions. Nyx wondered what kind of fallout shelter they had down here. She knew the main bug bank for Mushtallah's filter was on Palace Hill, which required a lot of security.

"Who else was on this job?" Nyx asked Kasbah. "I'll need to know how they fucked up, when they gave up, what they found out. If you don't have that information, I need to go to them directly. I don't want to reinvent their work."

"We've hired only one bounty hunter who's still on the note, but the list of mercenaries is somewhat classified," Kasbah said. "We already find it politically distasteful to work with bounty hunters. Admitting publicly that we've hired foreign mercenaries as well may be disastrous."

"Then at least give me the list of bel dames you've hired," Nyx said. She was still having trouble with the idea that they'd cut out the bel dames.

"We cannot involve the bel dame council in a note such as this. You, of all people, should know this."

"I know what the line is, Kasbah. I also know this is Palace Hill."

"You do perhaps overestimate the power of the queen or, perhaps, overestimate her interest in agitating the bel dame council over a matter even such as this."

"Seems a little funny. This note is so important, but she won't piss off a couple old ladies on the council to get them to put some women on it?"

"Perhaps it is best the old ladies *don't* understand the importance of this note."

Nyx gave Kasbah a good sidelong look. "Don't tell me the queen's after somebody the bel dames want dead."

"Let us say it is best for Nasheen if we acquire this woman without exciting the bel dame council."

Nyx let that settle in her head. This could be bad.

Kasbah led them through several sets of security doors, past two guards, and through another filter. Then they stepped into a small viewing room. The room itself was no different than any other security viewing room Nyx had seen, only colder. She wondered how far underground they were.

Kasbah stepped into the next room to find the security techs.

Rhys's expression was grim. "I don't like the sound of this note, Nyx."

"That's why it pays so well, Rhys," she said, but her chest was tight.

The last time she pissed off the bel dames, they'd sent her to prison. What the fuck was the queen doing running a high-risk note under the noses of the bel dames? Why not hire them to do it? If she was going to bleed, Nyx wanted to know who and what she was bleeding for.

Kasbah returned with a couple of security techs. One of them held a transparent thumb-size case filled with amber fluid. She shook it and put it into the viewing tube.

The tube vomited a misty rain of particles that coalesced into four round moving images.

"I thought your filter kept out transmission bugs," Rhys said.

One of the techs, an older woman with a wash of white-peppered hair, said, "It does. These are native to Mushtallah, something we put together with the palace magicians."

Like com techs and hedge witches, most security techs had some paltry talent that made them more adept at working with bugs. Nyx figured about the only advantage of having an affinity for bugs was that it increased your job prospects.

Nyx focused on the round views, broadcasts from the lenses of tailored bugs plotted around the city.

The first showed an image of the main courtyard they'd entered earlier where all the women had been training.

"She starts here," the tech said, pointing to the staircase. It was a bad wide shot. Everything that came in via bugs was in shades of gray, so the woman moving down the stairs could have been any dark woman. She walked with two other figures.

"Who are they?" Nyx asked.

"Magicians," Kasbah said. "Yah Inan and Yah Tayyib."

"Yah Tayyib of Faleen?" Nyx asked.

"Yes. You know him?"

"Here," the tech said, as the figures disappeared from the eye's view. She pointed to the next eye, a view of the deserted main street outside the palace. Nyx saw that the time stamp had them moving during the darkest part of the night, the thirteenth hour. With the moons in recession, it was even darker than usual, and hazy by the look of the gas lamps left running on the windowsill inside the main window of each of the apartments above the storefronts.

"Did she have a lot of midnight sorties with magicians?" Nyx asked.

"It wasn't unusual," Kasbah said. "Nikodem got on well with them."

The younger tech nodded. "We saw nothing odd about this night, not until here, when we picked her up going through the filter, alone. But of course we didn't see that until later. The bug jumps here, changes position."

She pointed to the eye that showed the dark figure moving through the filter. The bug indeed shifted position, a back-and-forth motion that made the picture wobble. The woman stepped into a bakkie waiting on the other side of the filter. The picture was bad, and Nyx couldn't make out any distinguishing features—no tags, no strange markings. She couldn't even gauge the bakkie's state of health. It was a newer model, not yet sand-gutted or sun-sick. It might have had tinted windows.

"So she had help," Nyx said.

"Or she called a bakkie before she left," Kasbah said. "The Kinaanites aren't wholly ignorant of how to get around in Nasheen."

"We're talking about a woman who had confidential information of great interest to magicians," Nyx said. "I don't think she headed out alone to watch a little boxing in the border towns."

"The magicians have been extensively interrogated," Kasbah said, but it wasn't the voice of a woman of absolute faith. Nyx had heard those voices enough to know what they sounded like. "They understand the nature of this project. They know what would happen to Nasheen if we lost this woman to the Chenjans."

"Tell me what would happen to Nasheen," Nyx said.

Kasbah looked at her. Her mouth was a thin line. "If she could end the war in our favor, she could also end it… not so much in our favor, couldn't she?" Kasbah said.

The images began looping on all four lenses: the courtyard, the street, a bookshop where Nikodem seemed to have gone off on her own, the filter, the bakkie.

Nyx glanced over at Rhys. He was examining the image of the bakkie. When he caught her looking at him, he nodded. One of the images was doctored, then. Mercenaries generally didn't work with magicians, so any of the ones who'd viewed this before Nyx may not have caught that, but if Kasbah had a lot of her own security techs and magicians working on this, *she* should have known it.

Nyx looked over at Kasbah. Kasbah had her arms crossed as she stared at the security screens. She did not meet Nyx's look.

Nyx asked Rhys, "You need to see anything else?"

He shook his head.

"I think that's it, then," Nyx said. "Unless I can speak to Yah Inan."

"She is away at the magicians' quarters," Kasbah said. "She was scheduled for a sabbatical many months ago."

"You've already talked to Yah Tayyib?"

"He says he left Nikodem at the bookshop. He and Yah Inan went out for a late supper with her and paused to look at some organics books. She said she was going to visit an acquaintance living above the bookshop. She asked them to escort her home at mid-morning prayer. When they returned the next day, they found that no one lived above the shop. That's when I had my technicians go through the security lenses."

"She's been gone a month now?" Nyx asked.

"Yes."

"She could be dead."

"That may be. If she is, we'll need her body. As a former bel dame, you know how important it is for us to retain at least her head, for our own purposes. However, I doubt she is dead. If kidnapped or coerced, as you believe, her keepers would understand her importance to the war."

"She's not contaminated, is she?"

"Not so far as I know."

"So you've had a bunch of hunters and mercenaries looking for her in Nasheen for a month, the sorts of people who'd have access to every low-end cantina and fighting ring in the country, and they haven't found her. We're going to have to widen the net, then."

"That is what the other bounty hunter said," Kasbah said.

"The other bounty hunter?" Rhys asked.

But Nyx didn't have to ask. She knew which one.

"Raine al Alharazad. You know him?" Kasbah asked.

"Intimately," Nyx said.

Rhys got to his feet, keeping his hands on the back of the chair. "When you say widen the net—"

"I hope Anneke's getting some sun," Nyx said. "We're going to Chenja."

11

The burst sirens went off as Nyx and Rhys stepped out onto the busy main street. The palace filter over the sally port door popped behind them, and for a minute Nyx thought the keening cry of the sirens had something to do with the ringing in her ears from the quick succession of filters.

Rhys looked skyward, and Nyx touched his arm, nodding back down the street. "Let's get inside and get some food," she said. "You hungry?" The queen had given them a generous starting allowance, and she wanted to make the most of it. "I haven't had good food in ages."

"Starving," he said, tucking his hands beneath his burnous, hunching his head and shoulders as if his guarded posture would ward off the blow from some burst.

Nyx heard the heavy *whump-whump* of the anti-burst guns, somewhere just to the north of them, and though she knew better, she picked up her pace. Inside or outside, a direct hit killed you, but it might be more comfortable getting hit inside. She'd be drunk.

As they walked, Rhys said, "I think Danika's lying."

"So do I," she said. "I'm just not sure about what."

She ducked into a café on the south side of the palace called the Grim Matron. She knew it from her year of training in Mushtallah as a bel dame. Rasheeda had loved their little green drinks.

Nyx and Rhys both pulled off their hoods as they entered, and the bar matrons all lifted their heads from their beer glasses and opium pipes and plates of fried grasshoppers. The hush of low conversation in the dim room ceased, and the smoky air suddenly felt a lot heavier.

Nyx pushed her burnous back over her shoulders, so her weapons were visible, and stepped up ahead of Rhys. She pushed through the scattering of tables to a tall, latticed booth at the back, seeming to ignore the gazes that followed after Rhys, but tracking every one of them with her peripheral vision, waiting for somebody to move.

Rhys followed her, careful not to touch anything, maneuvering his slim body around the tables and matrons.

Just as Nyx reached the table, a grizzled woman, one arm larger and darker than the other, her face a drooling mass of scarred flesh, hacked a gob of spit at Rhys's face. Rhys caught the spit in his hand. Nyx appreciated that. The woman began to get up, opened her mouth to say something.

Nyx pivoted and tugged her whip from her hip. She caught the woman around the throat with it and stood behind the woman's chair, holding her taut against the seat back. Rhys said he was going to find an ablution bowl to clean up.

Nyx leaned over and said, loud enough for the women at the nearest three tables to hear, "This man belongs to me. What you do to him, you do to me. Understand, my woman?"

The woman gurgled something, and Nyx watched the faces of her table companions. They were grizzled old war veterans as well, hard-faced and battle-scarred, and the looks they gave her were equal parts hatred and respect.

Nyx released her hold and knocked the woman back into her seat.

The woman grabbed at her throat and muttered something.

Nyx wound her whip back up.

"You don't see many women carrying a whip," one of the other women at the table said.

"It's good for stealing weapons and drinks and tying boys up," Nyx said.

"You use it a lot, then?"

Nyx saw Rhys returning to their table.

"You wouldn't believe," Nyx said.

She turned away from them and slid into her seat across from Rhys. There were partitions between the tables, which helped muffle the sound. The three veterans at the nearest table got up and went to the bar; the spitter still rubbed at her throat, muttering.

"Was that really necessary?" Rhys said, shrugging out of his burnous. Nyx caught herself admiring the breadth of his shoulders. If he wasn't dancing anymore, how was he keeping in shape?

"This is Mushtallah," Nyx said. "They push, you push back, or they'll mow you over." She pressed a hand to the table. The tiny bugs inside the tabletop displayed the menu in response to the warmth of her touch. "You think that last lens was doctored?"

Inside, the sound of the sirens was muffled, a dull whine. The stink of the opium was making Nyx nauseous.

"Yes," Rhys said, "and worse. Any magician, including Kasbah, could tell that was a doctored bug. Some other magician with access to the same bug transmissions the palace uses doctored that last image of Nikodem and the bakkie, probably so they could edit themselves out. My concern is that Kasbah knew that and didn't tell us."

"Maybe Kasbah doctored the footage herself?"

"She's not a complete imbecile," Rhys said. "If she doctored the footage, we wouldn't have been authorized to see the originals. She wanted us to know it was doctored but feared saying it out loud. She feared even putting that information on the globe."

"Which means Nikodem probably went out with one of the

palace magicians and didn't come back," Nyx said, "and the palace magicians doctored the footage."

"So the palace has black agents, maybe black magicians," Rhys said, shaking his head, "and she doesn't want your bel dames on this note. I don't like this, Nyx, and I don't like where this note might take us."

Nyx thought of Yah Tayyib. If Nikodem had been friendly with Yah Inan and Yah Tayyib, either of them could have set her up with someone to get her out of the country.

"I don't see a motive for the magicians she was friendly with," Nyx said.

Rhys made a noise that sounded like a laugh. "Magicians remember a time when they ruled the world. It's the same with mullahs and magicians in Chenja. However, the queen isn't paying you to take care of her internal security issue. She's paying for a head, preferably attached to a living body."

"More body swapping. I'm not keen on getting cut up over this note, but you know how that is. Wish I had my original womb. Bet I could get Yah Tayyib out of retirement to come and deal for it."

"Why?"

"He liked it. Said it was shaped funny."

Rhys quirked an eyebrow. "Shaped funny?"

"Yeah, some big word. Biocurate. Biocarbonate. Bicoital. Something."

"Bicornuate," Rhys said. "A heart-shaped uterus."

"What?"

"Most wombs are balloon-shaped. Bicornuate wombs are heart-shaped." He used his fingers to draw a picture in the air of a stylized heart. "Makes delivery more difficult. It's best you had it replaced."

"No shit? I should have sold it for a lot more. I knew a kid who made good money selling mutant organs to magicians." She moved her hand back over the menu. "What are you eating?"

Rhys looked down at the table and dithered over his choices. "Why doesn't anyone in this country serve fish?"

"Unclean animals. All that water."

"That's the silliest thing I've ever heard. Fish farming is a highly lucrative business in Chenja."

The bar matron finally came over, looking like she was trying real hard not to stare at Rhys. Nyx stared at her instead. The bar matron brought them beer—local stuff—without them asking, the way Nyx would have been served water at the coast. Nyx remembered some things from the coast, little snatches. She'd spent the first three years of her life there, but most of her memories were of inoculation regimens: blinking syringes, yellow fluid, the stink of sulphur.

"None for him," Nyx said. "Can you bring him tea?"

The matron moved to take away his beer.

"No, I'll drink that too," Nyx said. "Can I get something with a lot of meat? Like a slab of dog and some curried sweet potatoes?"

Rhys grimaced. "Soup, please," he said. "The curried noodle. Do you have protein cakes?"

"Do I have what?" the matron asked.

He asked for that Chenjan shit at every inn, café, restaurant, and cantina Nyx had taken him to for the last six years. In Chenja, they served that wood-chip-tasting crap with rice and some kind of brown sauce. When she was passing time across the border or as part of Raine's crew, Nyx had fed that stuff to the dogs.

"Never mind," Rhys said. "Just the soup and some bread. Plain bread."

The matron nodded and left them.

Nyx took a slug of her beer and kept her eye on the front door. This was bel dame country, and the war vets at the bar had moved off. Word of a Chenjan man in a café would get around.

"I need to have Taite hack Raine's com," Nyx said. "I want to see how far the old man's gotten on this one."

"Do you want me to find out who the other mercenaries are on this note? I'm sure there's a record at the Cage."

"Call up Taite once we're outside the filter and have him send Anneke and Khos to do that. I want that information in a file when we get back to Punjai."

"You think Khos will stay on?"

"I can't afford to spend time looking for another shifter."

Nyx heard the burst siren dying off. She felt her body start to unwind. Fucking siren.

Then she heard someone snicker.

It was a very familiar snicker.

Nyx had kept an eye on the front door, but the two women had come in the back.

Rasheeda was older—not as beautiful as Nyx remembered, though that wasn't because of her age. Warm, crinkle-eyed, matronly women were some of the most sought-after bed partners in Nasheen. But Rasheeda lacked the warmth.

Rasheeda was still shrugging her shoulders, shivering, as if she had just finished shifting. Luce stood next to her, head just reaching Rasheeda's shoulder. She had a grim little face.

Nyx leaned back in her chair. She saw Rhys's hands twitch toward his pistols. It was illegal to kill a bel dame, but using whatever force necessary short of killing to subdue them in self-defense was all right. Bel dames were tough to kill.

Nyx knew.

Rasheeda kicked one of the chairs around and sat backward on it, folding her arms over the headrest. Luce slouched in the chair next to her and let her burnous fall back to reveal the ivory hilts of her pistols. Rasheeda didn't usually wear weapons—it made shifting easier, and she didn't have to worry about losing anything when she made a quick escape. Not that Rasheeda being unarmed was any comfort. Nyx had watched her claw out women's eyes and eat them.

Rasheeda snickered again.

"Small town," Nyx said. "You two had your fill of the local boys?"

Luce hadn't bedded a boy in her life. They made her nauseous, as Nyx recalled. Rasheeda usually just ate them.

"You had business with the queen," Luce said.

"I did. And that business is none of yours."

"Funny woman," Rasheeda said. "You know we know all business."

"The council asked us to tell you that working on this bounty isn't in your best interest," Luce said.

"Well, then, let me hang up my guns," Nyx said. "You know what high regard I have for the council." And some fucked-stupid queen who couldn't keep bel dame bugs out of her palace. If the council had bugs in the palace, it meant the animosity between the queen and the council was a lot deeper than Nyx realized.

Not your problem, Nyx reminded herself. But staring into her sisters' faces, she had a hard time figuring out why it wasn't her problem if what she didn't know ended up getting her killed.

"Drop the commission and Dahab won't drop you," Rasheeda said.

"Sister, where's your sense of subtlety?" Nyx asked. "How about *you* fuck off? I'm working a queen's bounty. You try to pin some silly shit on me and I'll have your heads."

The matron brought Rhys's tea.

"Can I get a little green drink?" Rasheeda asked.

"What kind?" the matron asked.

"A Green Beetle," Rasheeda said.

"That's not their best drink," Nyx said. "I recommend the Holiday Beetle. I'm sure you know it."

Rhys sipped his tea. His other hand stayed near one of his pistols.

"Just drop the fucking bounty, Nyx," Luce said. "The last time you pissed the council off, you lost everything, and you have a lot more to lose this time."

Nyx took a pull of her beer. "I don't drop notes."

"It's not a note," Luce said. "You aren't a bel dame. It's a bounty. There's no honor in bounties."

"I know what I am. Does the council have you working actual notes, or are you just here to bully like a couple of border toughs?"

"We're always working on notes," Rasheeda said. She snapped her teeth at Rhys. "I ate a Chenjan just yesterday."

"I hope you choked," Rhys said.

"Keep your mouth locked, black man," Rasheeda said. "My business isn't with dumb bags or baby stealers."

"Try to close it," Rhys said.

Nyx grinned at that. She wanted to see Rhys shoot an organic target. He was a good shot.

"I heard you were fucking Chenjans," Luce said, "but I didn't believe it."

"You women paying for lunch?" Nyx asked. "Or is that all?" Rhys might have an aversion for hurting living people, but she didn't.

Luce said, "You think the council's joking?"

"No," Nyx said. "I think everything you honey pots could think of to do to me has been done. You stripped me of my bel dame license and sent me to prison. What, you want to set me on fire? Cut off bits and pieces and sell them to collectors? Send me to the front? It's all been done. Fuck off."

"We have other ways to hurt you, Nyx," Luce said quietly.

"No, you don't. My mother and brothers are dead. The only blood sister I have thinks I'm headed straight for hell. God left me in a trench outside Bahreha. You're all the sisters I have, and you're the ones who sent me to prison. Have a nice night."

Luce kicked Rasheeda. "Up," she said.

Rasheeda said, "I haven't gotten my little green drink."

"Get it at the bar," Luce said.

The bel dames stood.

Nyx watched them walk to the bar.

The bar matron arrived with their food. There was soup for Rhys, and a steaming heap of meat for Nyx that made her even more nauseous than the opium smoke. She drew her dagger and stabbed at the hunk.

"Why haven't they killed you yet?" Rhys asked.

"Nobody likes to kill bel dames," Nyx said. And she was a lot more valuable to them alive. "I've been inoculated against every known contagion, and I can pass through any filter in the country. I can power down a city with one good burst slapped together with bug juice and scattergun acid." Nobody killed a bel dame. At worst, you were thrown out. Or permanently imprisoned and cocooned.

"So there's someone on that council who wants you alive to use for later."

"Yeah. It's why I went to prison and not back to the front."

"Who is she?"

"I don't know. Some old lady, probably."

"But they don't like the queen. Do you think some of them would kill you anyway?"

"And piss off the old ladies? Luce won't. Fatima would arrange an accident. Dahab and Rasheeda might. Others, no. They'd stick to clean notes."

Nyx stared at the hunk of meat on her plate. It had taken four bel dames to bring her down last time. She had been on her own then, without a com tech, a shape shifter, a magician, or any kind of hired gun.

"So what do you think this alien knows that makes the queen *and* the bel dames want her so badly?" Rhys asked.

"What it is isn't as important as what it can *do*," Nyx said. "If it could end the war, it could end it in favor of either side. Think of her like a weapon we need to get back." She considered. "I need to go to the coast and talk to my sister. She was passing information with New Kinaan at about the time Nikodem was last here. She might know something that'll help." Kine could also tell her a lot more about the aliens—and maybe their real motives—than they'd tell her themselves.

"I can go to the archives," Rhys said.

"Too conspicuous."

"I mean, the archives in the Chenjan district. I won't be conspicuous there."

"Hold off until I get back." Nyx poked at her food.

"What's wrong?" Rhys asked.

Nyx sighed. "I really wanted to get into a fight."

Outside, the heady whine of the burst sirens started up again. The building shook.

"Bloody fucking Chenjans," Nyx muttered, but she didn't look at Rhys when she said it.

12

"You're telling me that one of the mercenaries on this list is the Chenjan under ice in our fridge?" Nyx asked.

"I think so," Khos said. He shuffled his feet.

Nyx had sent him and Anneke out to the Cage to butter up Shajin. Shajin had all the records of which mercenaries were given the queen's note. There was more than one way to dig a hole.

When Nyx got back from Mushtallah, Khos had handed her a list and told her what they'd found out about all twelve people on it. None of the information was worth much, but from the look of the packages Anneke had hauled in from the bakkie, the bad news hadn't stopped them from picking up enough weapons from a local dealer to fight a small war. Anneke had a habit of overspending on gear.

"You think so, or you know so?" Nyx stood in her office packing fist-sized bursts into airtight containers. She had just enough time to repack her gear and head out to Kine's.

"I think I know," Khos said. "The one I wanted was a Chenjan doing black work. I thought this was him. It's not. This is a mercenary. He's got a similar birthmark. I had Juon look up his vitals in the directory of resident Chenjans. The one I wanted was worth about seventy. The one in the fridge is just some petty mercenary."

"The price for black work has gone up," Nyx said, and snorted. "Where did you find him?"

"At a bar in the Chenjan district. Working on some kind of deal. I took him when he came out the back."

"He have anything on him?"

"I didn't have time to check. I was being followed. That's why I dumped the head and stowed him in the trunk."

She hadn't checked the body either, when they dumped it at the keg before driving out to the botched bounty job. "Let's look, then."

There was a trapdoor in the hub—the gear and com room—in the back that led down to the freezer in the basement. They passed Taite, who was still working at hacking into Raine's com. Sweat beaded his brow. He was looking a bit shaky, and Nyx figured she'd tell Khos to get the kid some food. When he didn't eat on time, he passed out, and the last thing she needed right now was a comatose com tech.

She and Khos went down into the basement, and Nyx unlocked the fridge. The body was pushed up against the wall, alongside the head of a local magistrate whose sister had never paid them for the bounty she'd put on her. That particular bounty hadn't exactly been legal. Nyx wasn't so surprised the sister hadn't come to collect.

Nyx crouched by the body and pulled open the burnous. She checked the obvious pockets and seams first, finding three in notes and another buck in change. She opened up a bug box and found a lethargic locust. She handed that to Khos.

"Make sure Rhys gets that," she said.

Then she checked the waistband, found some garroting wire and some black papers. Looked like at least one of the contracts the mercenary was pursuing was a contract that ran boys out of Nasheen, probably to Tirhan or Heidia. Ras Tieg was under contract to send back draft dodgers. Nasheen's other neighbors weren't.

Hell of a thing to die for.

She handed the papers to Khos.

"You think he was part of the underground?" Khos asked, and Nyx heard something odd in his voice, something nervous. She wondered how many of his whores knew something about the underground. Most of the women who permitted themselves illegal pregnancies were whores. Pay a hard-up hedge witch and you could get your viability hex turned back on—everybody had it shut off at the breeding compounds when they were kids. It came with the inoculations.

"Looks like it," she said.

Nyx tugged out a purse from the front of the man's dhoti and opened it. Another ten in notes and loose change. They might be able to afford to feed Taite's sister this month after all.

Inside was another bug box. Nyx shook this one before she opened it, and heard a satisfying sloshing sound. He had a recording.

"Tell Rhys to warm that up and translate it."

She wiped over the obvious places on the body where he might have kept organics, hidden documents, or internal transmission bulbs, but came up with nothing.

"Burn his clothes, cut him up, and feed him to the bugs," Nyx said. They had a composting bin on the other side of the basement. "The last thing we need is a dead mercenary in our fridge."

Khos went out to get the butchering equipment.

Nyx climbed upstairs.

Taite was still in the hub working at the com. His dark hair was held clipped back with converted bug clips—the jawed ends from a couple of mud beetles. A stack of books sat at his elbow, half of them written in Ras Tiegan, and he kept an idol of one of the Ras Tiegan demigods—he called them saints—named Balarus or Baldomus or something unpronounceably Ras Tiegan like that. Old Baldo was the demigod of locksmiths, apparently.

"You hack Raine's system yet?" she asked.

"I need another half day," Taite said. He looked up from his work. "Are you voting this week?"

"What?" she said, letting the door drop. She wiped her hands on her trousers.

"The vote. Queen Zaynab's asking for a public vote about whether or not to draft half-breeds. She's bypassing the low council and going directly to the people. You remember?"

"Queen does what she wants no matter what we vote. This isn't a democracy."

Nyx walked toward her office. Taite followed her.

"It matters," he said. "If she thinks there's overwhelming disagreement with the policy, she'll back down. Things are hot right now between her, the bel dames, and the high council. The vote might actually sway her this time. Only you and Anneke are eligible, so I thought—"

"Why not have your boyfriend get his sister to do it?" Technically, Taite's boy-boy love affairs were illegal, but Nyx had seen enough boyish affection at the front that she didn't have much of a problem with it.

Taite flushed. "She already is. But I need—"

"Taite," Nyx said, getting back to her desk. She tried to find something to do with her hands. "You get drafted and die and your sister gets a pension. What's the difference if you die on the road with me or at the front?"

"My sister can barely make it on the eight I give her every month. And the baby's not here yet. You know how much a pension is?"

Him and his fucking pregnant sister. What was that fool woman doing, getting pregnant outside a breeding compound? And what fool man had she been cavorting with? Ras Tiegans had absolutely no control over the fecundity of their citizens. Nobody—male or female—ever got bugged or permanently severed, and just like the Mhorians, none of them was legally compelled to give birth at a compound that would properly inoculate their children. It was like some kind of human dice game.

They're fucking refugees, she reminded herself, but some of that old anger stirred, her school-taught aversion for wasted reproduction. There were a lot better things Taite's sister could be doing with her womb. Single births thrown away on a kid who likely wouldn't live past five were a waste. Hell, Nyx could justify selling her own womb to gene pirates who'd take the zygotes out and build better zygotes for some compound somewhere, but spread her legs with the intent of getting pregnant? What the hell for?

"Didn't it go up to seven?" Nyx said. She honestly had no idea what pensions were running these days.

"Four. Four a month for a half-breed woman and her illegal kid. Come on, Nyx. It's two minutes of your day."

"Anneke will vote. Tell her you'll buy her a big gun."

"Think about how much of your team you'd lose. You work with more men than any other hunter."

She packed the last of the bursts, and tied her bag closed. "I've gotta go," she said.

"If they draft half-breed men today, they'll take resident foreigners next," Taite said, and his tone got wheedling. She hated it when he did that. "They'll take Rhys."

"I'll be in Jameela for a few days," she said. "Transit's about a week turnaround. Rhys is in charge of the keg, but you'll need to back him up if there's security trouble. Khos has a transmission for Rhys to sort out. You'll need to help him. And finish hacking into Raine's com."

"You driving all the way to the coast?"

"Yeah. You'll need to take a local caravan if you have to get out." She dug into her pocket and pulled out three of the notes she'd pawned off the body. "You get that to your sister. Tell her if we make a bag on this note I'll get her kid inoculated." Nasheen didn't inoculate foreign kids for free.

"You'll vote?"

"Don't push me."

Nyx went out into the keg. Rhys was sitting at the front desk doing paperwork, bleeding bugs onto greasy pages.

"You have the keg," she said. "I'll be back in about a week."

He glanced up. Looked at her with his dark eyes. She remembered listening to him pray, back at the palace. Had she ever heard him give a salaat that included personal prayers? They'd worked together for six years, and for six years she'd managed to be in some other room or smoking out on the street or patching together a bakkie every time he prayed. What did he pray for, all those times she wasn't listening?

"Nyx?" he said.

God, she wouldn't mind standing there a while longer while he looked.

She hated that.

Nyx dropped her bag, and splashed her face with water from the ablution bowl near the door.

"Are you all right?" he asked.

"Never better."

Her whole body ached. She hadn't slept well on the train, and she'd had dreams about that old boxing match in Faleen—Jaks the outrider and stocky-legged Husayn bashing each other's heads in, blood soaking into the organic matting of the ring, the whole first row of spectators covered in blood and saliva, their faces animated, jubilant. She had dreamed of her womb, a perfect heart, cut up on a butcher's block somewhere between Punjai and Faleen.

"Make a couple of calls to some people you know in the Chenjan districts. Just make sure Nikodem's not there."

"I will."

"And keep everybody on high security. The bel dames might move on you here. Not likely, but it's possible. Council can't find its own ass some days, and it'll take them a long time to agree on whether or not we're worth killing. Hopefully we'll be in Chenja by then and they won't touch us. Not even bel dames like running the border. Where's Anneke?"

"Getting lunch."

"Keep her on point this afternoon. And you double-lock the doors and set up an organics net. Taite and I were burned out of our first office before you came on board. I don't want to take any chances."

Nyx picked up her bag and pushed out the door and onto the hot, reeking street. She rolled under the bakkie and checked it for bugs, bursts, and regular explosives. The organic guts surrounding the hoses and wires were clear, and the pulse was good. She opened up the trunk to make sure Khos hadn't left any more bodies in there. She saw nothing but some bloody blankets and toolkits, but she knew Anneke better than that. She reached into the trunk and pushed back the blankets. Anneke had two long rectangular boxes shoved in the back, tied with brown paper. Regular, not organic. Nyx shook her head and threw the blanket back over them. She might end up needing the guns anyway, and if Anneke had forgotten about them, it might make her sweat a little knowing they weren't in her hot little hands.

She tried to open the passenger side door. Jammed. She tossed her bag in through the window. She needed to get Anneke to fix that.

Nyx hopped in, kicked up the engine, and headed east, to Jameela. To the sea.

To the bloody fucking sea.

13

Nyx blew out of Punjai and hit the radio a couple times with her palm, but all she got was misty blue static.

It was going to be a long ride.

She spent the night in the bakkie after making good time; she got about halfway to Mushtallah. She passed the sand-swallowed ruins of old cities, now no more than irregular bulges in the desert, marked only by the tall rusted poles of the cities' contagion sensors. Rogue swarms and viral bugs leaking in from the north had blighted whole cities back in the old days. There were still wild places in the Khairian wasteland, and the border cities still had working contagion sensors that warned the unfiltered inside when the mutant monsters of the red desert wandered too far south or some sand-crazed magician who had gone out there searching for her soul came back with half her head missing, muttering in tongues. Most magicians stayed concentrated in the big cities to keep them clean of virulent swarms. The borderlands just limped along, mostly on their own. There was homesteading to be done for the poor and desperate, still, in the north and south and throughout Ras Tieg and Heidia and Druce. Three thousand years old, and Umayma was still an untamed place.

Nyx had kept as far off the road as she could without getting stuck in the sand and sat out a benign locust swarm just before dawn. Once it passed she was back on the road, out past Mushtallah and the central cities, where the gas lamps lit up every window. She landed another night on the road, then climbed over the low mountains that divided the coast from the interior.

As she came up over the other side, the terrain began to change. Sand gave way to choked crabgrass. The desert bled to scrubland, then long-needled pine trees, then tall oak hybrids with leaves the size of Nyx's head, low ferns with thorns, tangles of wild roses, snake maples, amber ticklers, patches of low-spring wildflowers. The kinds of bugs changed, too. Fewer beetles and roaches; more ladybugs and spider mites and mayflies. There were less hospitable bugs too, the farther she got from the interior: giant plate-size cicadas and acid-spraying chiggers as long as her arm.

Nyx found it all pretty claustrophobic. The trees were so enormous they blocked the sky, the suns. She couldn't see beyond the turns of the road. She checked her mirrors more often.

She came out of the mountains and into rolling fields of red-tipped wheat, saw the broad dirt runs for the kept dogs. Farmsteads dotted the landscape. Swarms of locusts, red flies, and ladybugs mobbed the fields, tailored to devour the less friendly bugs and fungi that ruined the staples.

Nyx found a motel that night at the Amber Stalk crossroads, named after some dead magician who'd saved the valley from mutant cicadas. There was a living plaque up under the road marker. Nyx figured she'd saved a lot more lives than he had, but nobody had ever named anything after her. She wondered how spectacular your death had to be to come out the other side with a plaque.

She parked her bakkie out front alongside flatbeds and rickshaws and a cart hitched to the front end of a converted bakkie. The bakkie had smoky black patches on its semi-organic exterior; the first signs of sun-sickness. Along the edges of the parking lot, she saw a head-size mutant flower chafer scuttling back into the brush. If she had to deal with giant bugs out here, she preferred benign ones like the chafers.

Inside the motel, she splurged on good food and a bath. The only upside to coming out to the coast was all the cheap food and water.

Nyx didn't linger long in the bath. She just scrubbed herself off and rubbed at old wounds that had started biting and aching as the weather cooled. It was colder on the coast.

She missed the desert.

When she crawled into bed, her sheets weren't full of sand.

She couldn't sleep.

Nyx grabbed her pillow and moved to the floor. She lay there for a couple of hours staring at the shiny green roaches scuttling along the ceiling, half the size of the ones in the desert and the wrong color. A couple took flight, landing on her arms and her face. She flicked them away.

There was a call box downstairs, but she had no one to call. If she called Kine, it was likely her sister would tell her not to come. If she called the keg, she could make small talk with Taite or Anneke about how they were handling security, but she'd be repeating herself, and they'd see through it. They'd see some kind of weakness. Maybe fear.

Nyx got up and went to the bar.

The motel had an "honor" bar, the kind with liquor bottles affixed to the wall upside down and a little book to record how many shots you'd pulled so they could bill you for them later. Nyx didn't intend on taking shots.

Nyx pulled out her dagger, pried a bottle of whiskey from the wall, and went out and sat on the front porch. The sky was big, and the stars were the clearest she'd seen since she was a kid in Mushirah. She drank, leaned back in the chair, and tried reading the constellations. Tej had been good at that.

Tej. A lifetime ago. Been a long time since she'd thought of him too. She touched her baldric absently. Blood and death and aliens—it all went back to that night in Faleen.

A noise from the parking lot drew her attention. She went still. The night was clear, but the big bloody moons were at the far end of their orbit, meaning they looked about the size of her thumbnail in the night sky. Ten years from now, they would look about three times the size of the sun.

But that didn't help her out much tonight.

The figure was dawdling next to Nyx's bakkie. Nyx had parked close to the motel so she could keep an eye on it. The figure crouched for a long while, then rose and moved off. She thought it might be some kind of giant leaf insect, but as Nyx watched, the figure shrank, dwindled. She heard a sneeze, and then a white bird was flapping off toward the road.

Nyx swore.

She clutched the bottle and went back to her room and bolted herself in. She sat on the edge of the bed. Her hands shook.

Bloody sisters. Bloody *Rasheeda*.

Nyx took a deep breath, drank more. Find your nerves, woman, she thought. Find your damn nerves. It took four of them to take you out last time.

But they might not be so nice this time.

She closed her eyes and tried to calm down. It was possible they'd only sent Rasheeda. She could deal with Rasheeda. But not Dahab. Not Fatima. Not all of them together. Not again.

Nyx opaqued the windows.

The room was dark.

She could not sleep.

She pulled her dagger from the sheath on her thigh, picked up the bottle with her other hand, and crept downstairs. She went back to the call box and dialed the pattern for the keg. She wedged herself into a corner underneath it.

The line buzzed and buzzed and buzzed.

Pick up, she thought. Pick up. Nyx closed her eyes. She was on her own out here. It would take four of them to get her. Fuck, she didn't need a fucking team, what kind of catshit was this?

"Peace be unto you."

Nyx opened her eyes.

Rhys's voice.

Nyx wet her mouth again with the whiskey, found some words. "You read to me?" she asked.

A long pause. She thought maybe she'd lost the connection.

"Are you drunk?" he asked.

"Rasheeda's here," Nyx said.

Another pause. She heard him moving around. He must have come from bed and into her office, where the call box was.

"Should I send someone?"

"Can you just read?"

"All I've got is the poetry."

"Fine."

He sighed. He was always sighing at her, making faces at her, disapproving, her pious Chenjan. "Do you know what time it is?"

She didn't answer.

"How drunk are you?"

"Drunk enough to ask," she said.

Rhys read to her for a long time.

The fear started to bleed away. It was like loosening up a garroting wire pulled taut. She clutched the transceiver to her ear as if it, too, were a weapon, as effective as the dagger. But, after a while, her death grip eased up. She realized her hand hurt.

Sometime later, Rhys's voice began to soften, grow quiet. Finally he said, "I'm going to bed, Nyx."

"All right."

"Nyx?"

"Yeah?"

"You can take Rasheeda."

"I know." She wanted to ask him what he prayed for.

She hung up.

Nyx took a last pull from the bottle, returned it to the bar, and held out the rest of the night in her room with the door bolted. She slept in front of it.

The next morning, honey-headed hungover, Nyx made an inspection of the bakkie and turned up an ignition burst and a cut brake line. It looked like Rasheeda had tried to disable the main hose connecting the pedal mechanisms to the cistern as well but had only nicked it, cutting a secondary hose instead. Some dead beetles and bug juice pooled beneath the bakkie, but the severed organic artery cushioning the line had already scabbed over. She knew how to properly fuck up a bakkie without leaving behind any obvious traces. Rasheeda hadn't wanted to stop Nyx, just announce herself and slow Nyx down.

Nyx disarmed the ignition burst. She opened the trunk and took out one of the toolkits. She patched the leak, cut out and sewed in a new brake hose, and got back onto the road.

This time, she kept an eye on the road behind her the whole way.

She stopped at a dusty station just past a couple of farmsteads at the foot of the coastal hills and filled up on bug juice. Dead and dying bugs—some of them the size of small dogs—littered the periphery, wallowing in a citron-and-cinnamon smelling mixture of pesticide and repellent the owner had put down to protect the station.

The woman who popped open her tank was a soft, fleshy coastal type with a plump mouth.

"You come in from the desert?" she asked.

Nyx wondered where else there was to come in from. As the woman pumped the feed into the tank, Nyx gazed out at the road. She saw a black bakkie crawling around a bend in the road, coming in from the direction of the motel. Following her.

It didn't parse. Rasheeda was a shifter—she didn't need to

send a bakkie after Nyx. She would have followed in bird form. So who the fuck were *these* people?

Nyx turned her face away, but noted the movement of the bakkie in the station windows. The bakkie slowed as it passed the station, then sped up again. Nyx saw three figures. She slumped in her seat, wondered if they'd open fire.

But the bakkie sped on. She looked after it.

"Friends of yours?" the attendant asked. She capped the tank.

"I hope not," Nyx said. She leaned over, opened her pack, and rolled a few bursts onto the passenger seat. Just in case.

She paid the woman and then got back onto the road.

Three kilometers on, she saw the bakkie parked at the side of the road.

Waiting.

Nyx switched pedals, kicked the bakkie a little faster. The other bakkie turned out onto the road after her.

Nyx didn't know the coast well, and unlike the cities, the place was wide open, no cover. About all the cover she had were the hills, and some woods, if she could find them. She switched pedals again, reached for the clutch. She hadn't had to use the clutch in a long time. She wondered if it still worked.

The dark bakkie kept just within her rearview mirror range. They knew they'd been seen. Either they didn't know where she was going and wanted to pin her there, or they were waiting for a good turn in the road to take her out.

She sped up. They sped up.

She watched the image of the black bakkie grow larger in the mirror.

She fucked with the clutch. It made a nasty grinding sound. The bakkie wheezed.

"Come on, you fucker," she said.

It clicked.

She switched pedals. The bakkie shuddered. The speedometer

climbed. She saw a turnoff on her left that went up into the hills. Nyx did a neat brake, twisted the wheel, and hit the speed as she came out of the turn.

The bakkie screamed under her. She caught the smell of burning bugs, death on the road. She glanced back and saw smoke and dead beetles roiling out from the exhaust. The way was narrow and twisted, and as she climbed, the grasslands turned to a forest of oak hybrids. She took the turns too fast.

Nyx kept checking the mirror. She spent a moment too long looking and nearly lost herself on a narrow turn. She'd seen the other bakkie.

They were still behind her.

She kept a sharp eye out for turns off this road. She didn't want gravel tracks or logging roads. The bakkie would get stuck, and she'd be for shit.

The black bakkie was right behind her. She could just see their faces now. The big woman in the driver's seat was definitely Dahab. Not a doubt in her mind. Dahab had a new team with her—and not bel dames from the look of them.

And she had a real good feeling they weren't with Rasheeda. That threw a whole other contagion into the mess.

Nyx twisted around another curve. Raine had taught her to drive when she was nineteen. It was the first thing he taught every member of his crew. She knew how to pedal her way out of a tight spot.

Nyx heard a shot, and ducked. Checked the mirror again. The woman riding shotgun with Dahab was doing what people riding shotgun did.

Nyx dared not take her hands off the wheel. Even if she could clip off a couple shots with her pistol, the odds of her hitting anything in or around that bakkie were slim.

She reached a crossroads. Right would take her further up into the hills. Left was down into the coastal valley. Down meant she would have to put a lot of faith in her repair of the brake line.

Fuck it.

She veered left and barreled down the hill. She disengaged the clutch.

Heard another shot.

Something exploded against her back window.

That wasn't good. Organics. A fever burst? Something worse?

She grabbed at one of the bursts on the seat next to her and lobbed it out the window. Heard a satisfying pop as it exploded on the road.

The bakkie squeezed around another narrow turn. The cover of the woods was thinning out. She saw a house set back away from the road. If she couldn't lose them, she had to fight them.

Fight Dahab.

Nyx ignored the house and kept on the road.

She came down a long stretch and turned. The road abruptly changed from pavement to gravel. Logging road.

The bakkie skidded on the sudden raw stretch. Nyx hit the far left and far right pedals, and all four wheels twisted sharply, giving her some traction.

She looked back. Missed a turn. She spun the wheel and tried to recover, but she was trying to recover on gravel.

The bakkie slid clean off the road.

For a long, hopeful moment, she thought she'd be all right. But as she braked and twisted the wheel, she saw she wasn't going to avoid the big tree in front of her.

The bakkie smashed into the oak hybrid with a loud, wet crunch: a giant crushed melon. Bugs exploded from the hood. A rain of leaves dropped onto the windshield. Nyx's torso thumped into the steering wheel, knocking the breath from her.

The sound of hissing beetles and spitting fluid filled her ears.

Adrenaline flooded her body. Nyx pushed at the door but

couldn't find the handle for some reason. She leaned over and reached for one of the bursts on the floor.

The barrel of a very large gun pointed in at her through the passenger side window.

"Don't fucking move," Dahab said.

14.

Nyx didn't move. She was still trying to get her breath. Her fingers clutched empty air.

Dahab's two squirts were opening up the driver's side door.

"Let her out," Dahab said. "Watch her hands."

Dahab was an imposing woman—not just tall, but broad and fat. She could bench about a hundred twenty kilos, if Nyx remembered right. She'd lost an arm at the front, so her right arm was a lighter color than the left, courtesy of some dead foreigner. She had a wide flat-cheeked face and piercing eyes. Her teeth were stained red.

Dahab gestured with the gun. "Out, Nyx."

The squirts each took one of Nyx's arms and hauled her out of the cab. The council had moved a lot faster than Nyx anticipated, but she didn't know yet what the decision was. Dahab hadn't blasted her face off in the cab, so they probably wanted her alive. But there was a lot you could do to a woman and keep her breathing.

And she still wasn't sure where Rasheeda fit.

Nyx's chest hurt—a dull, throbbing ache. She hadn't heard anything break, but what would she have heard above the crunch of the bakkie?

She loved that fucking bakkie.

Beetles crawled over her feet.

While the women held Nyx, Dahab reached into the cab and pulled out Nyx's pack. Nyx hadn't brought anything with her relating to the off-worlder, but then, Dahab likely knew more than she did about Nikodem Jordan.

"Rasheeda and Luce told you to fuck off, Nyx," Dahab said.

Nyx sized up the women next to her. One was a stocky battle-scarred runt who looked like she'd just come off the front. The other one was a pretty half-breed woman who could have sold blood to bel dames. What was she doing collecting notes? She could have been a radio star.

Something buzzed at Dahab's hip. She grabbed at it, shook it, and put the transceiver to her ear. "Yeah," she said. "Uh-huh. We'll be there." She put it away, said, "Put her in the trunk of the bakkie. We're late for a meeting."

"Leave her here?" the pretty one said.

"You're staying with her. Suha and I will meet up with you in an hour. I can't have her going where we're going. They'll check our rig. Get her weapons off first."

The women took off Nyx's pistols, took her extra ammunition, took her whip, found the dagger and pistol strapped to either thigh.

Then they dragged her to the trunk and popped it open.

Nyx thought about trying an escape. Instead, she looked down the barrel of Dahab's rifle and got in.

It was a tight fit. Nyx lay curled up on one side. They shut the trunk. It all went dark except for a rusted-out patch in the floor near her head. She pulled at the blanket covering the rest of the hole and peered through. She couldn't see anything but the churned soil around her bakkie's tires.

A sharp edge dug into her shoulder from behind. She twisted around so that she faced the rear of the trunk. She pulled back the blankets and kicked the toolkits down around her feet. Sometimes Anneke's manic obsession for collecting guns did more than empty Nyx's bank account.

Nyx felt a jabbing pain in her sternum and stopped and took a deep breath.

Dahab had known Nyx when she was a skinny little bel dame without any idea of how to arm herself. Dahab had cleared her of the obvious weapons, the sort of stuff some young kid would carry, but Nyx had learned a thing or two since then.

Nyx brought her heels up behind her and reached her hands back. She worked one of the razor blades out of the sole of her sandal and used it to cut open the package.

She heard the other bakkie start up, heard muffled voices.

She pulled open the package and reached inside. Her fingers met cold metal. She unwrapped the gun and ran her hands over it to get a feel for what it was.

X80 scattergun, dual organic acid barrels.

Tirhani made, if she guessed right. Those fucking sheet-wearing martyrs had claimed neutrality for more than a century and still sold the best firearms on the planet.

Nyx checked to see if it was loaded. No, but when she shook it, she could hear liquid in the barrels. The acid part worked, anyway.

She held the gun to her chest and waited until she heard the bakkie pull away. When it was well gone, she got to work shifting both her body and the gun toward the other side of the trunk.

The squirt pounded on the trunk. She froze.

"You're kinda quiet!" the girl yelled.

Nyx didn't answer.

Nyx waited and listened. When nothing else came, she went back to moving.

Organic acid wasn't a fun thing to use in a tight space. She pulled her burnous over her face and torso. She took a deep breath and wedged her feet up against the trunk.

She pressed the barrel of the gun against the trunk lock. The other end got stuck on the trunk hinge in the back.

Nyx flipped the trigger mechanism to what she hoped was acid-only and squeezed.

The gun went off.

Fluid from both barrels hit the trunk and hissed as the compounds came together.

The blast sent a splatter of fluid back at her. She kicked at the trunk. Kicked again. Acid was eating through her burnous.

"Goddammit!" Nyx yelled, and kicked again.

The trunk popped open, and she came out gun first, tossing away her burnous as she did.

The girl had her gun out.

Nyx shot first.

The girl squealed and clawed at her face.

Nyx grabbed the girl's discarded gun and shot her in the face again, this time with bullets. It was red and messy.

Nyx pulled out her toolkits and wiped them down. She wiped the trunk clean too. She took out the other mystery package and found a second weapon, a 42.40 sniper rifle. No ammunition, though.

She searched the dead squirt and came up with some change and some extra rounds for the gun. No paperwork, no transmissions. Dahab wouldn't have left that sort of thing on a squirt. Nyx wiped the blood off her sandals.

She put the bakkie in neutral and pushed it away from the tree and surveyed the damage. There were a couple of broken hoses and a giant red gash in the cistern that bled bug juice and lube. She could work a temporary patch, but from the look of all the dead and dying beetles floating in the pooling organic feed at her feet, she wasn't going to have much of a colony to work with, and she needed more coagulant. The gash in the cistern wasn't healing over right.

She needed to work fast. Dahab would be back.

It took just under an hour to get the bakkie sewn up enough to start and another half hour to let the bugs rejuice. Even then, Nyx had to push the bakkie onto the road. Her chest hurt, and she had to stop and rest twice to catch her breath and ease the ache.

Dahab had taken the duffel bag out of the cab, but Nyx still had a buck in notes sewn into her dhoti and some cash stowed under the dash. The bag had contained the last of her sen, though. She was going to have to finish this trip sober.

She walked around the front of the bakkie to get in and came face to face with a giant, flat-backed millipede busily devouring the spilled contents of her cistern. The insect was a good meter long. It reared up at her and hissed.

Nyx reflexively jerked the acid spray on her rifle. The insect made a high-pitched whirring sound and started to smoke. She finished it off by bashing in its fist-size head with the butt of her rifle.

Fuck, she'd be glad to get back to the interior.

Nyx got the bakkie moving. It broke down twice. She stopped at a farmhouse and asked for directions to Jameela. She hadn't had a chance to see her face, but it probably didn't look great. The bakkie was worse. It was no wonder the coastal folk looked at her funny.

She finally turned in to Jameela, a bustling seaside town that supported the towering breeding centers looming behind it—row upon row of barracks, courtyards, labs, health centers, mess halls, and a single mosque. The first time the Chenjans blew up a breeding center, Nasheen had nearly given up the war.

Nyx dropped her bakkie at a local tissue mechanic's and walked the rest of the way to Kine's complex.

Kine lived in a tenement three blocks from the breath of the ocean. Nyx didn't know how she could stand the salty death stink of the sea. After Nyx followed her brothers to the front and their mother died at the compounds, Kine had retired to the coast and gone into organic tech. She studied reproductive theology, working on a cure for the war.

We all fight the war our own way, Nyx thought idly as she

climbed the stairs. She knocked at the heavy door. When no one answered, she pressed her palm to the faceplate on the door. Bugs stirred beneath her fingers, lapped up the secretions on her skin. Working at the breeding compounds got Kine extra security. All that time at the coast—at the compounds, nose in a book, moving magician-trained bugs across a dish, locked safe behind secure doors at the edge of a soupy sea, her only company the words of the Kitab and the violently conservative women she shared her days with—it was no wonder Kine had come back wearing a hijab to mark her as one of the fundamentalist followers of the Kitab, the Kitabullah.

Kine had, however, tailored the house to admit blood kin. Nyx was the only blood kin Kine had left. Their mother had borne the five of them—three boys, two girls—in one pregnancy at the breeding compounds. She hadn't been interested in having any more. That was before women had quotas.

The door slid open. Automatic doors creeped Nyx out.

The first thing Nyx saw was one of Kine's long coats and a crumpled hijab on the floor. Kine didn't leave her clothes on the floor. Her place was always immaculate.

Nyx didn't call out for Kine. She unshouldered the scattergun. She tended to be a better shot with fluid at short range. She stalked into the flat.

I'm a bloody fucking fool, she thought. Of course the council wouldn't have authorized killing Nyx in so short a period of time. But they would have happily authorized the slaughter of everyone around her. Her chest hurt. She needed to find Kine and call the keg.

There was a broken lamp in the main room. Dead glow worms littered the floor. Nyx nudged one of them with the toe of her sandal. They were still soft. It had been an hour, maybe two. She had missed them by an hour.

Nyx poked around the kitchen, found a couple of drawers

open. Had Kine been looking for a weapon? Had she known there was someone in the flat?

Nyx checked behind all the doors as she moved, cleared each room. Kine had put up blank-faced portraits of the prophet in the living area, and hung some gaudy inscriptions from the Kitab alongside them. In her bedroom, though, Kine kept pictures of the five of them, her kin, embedded in the walls—glowing, partially animated portraits of better days. If you got too close, you could see that what made the images move were multi-colored layers of rug lice. The faces of their brothers laughed back at Nyx: Amir, the oldest by an hour; brilliant Fouad; and skinny little Ghazi, the runt.

By seventeen, all the boys were dead.

Nyx pushed open the bathroom door.

Kine lay in the tub, mouth open, one arm flung over the edge. The water was rusty and full of shit. The room stank. Congealed blood blackened the floor.

Nyx got close enough to see that most of the blood had come from a long tear in Kine's gut. Her bowels had let loose—before or after she expired, Nyx didn't care to know. Kine's eyes were black holes of blood and eye pulp. They'd finished her off with two shots to the head.

There was blood in the bowl of the sink. They'd washed their hands, after.

Under the sink was a single white feather.

Nyx looked at her sister's body for a long minute. Nyx's palms were wet. The flat was cool.

She dared not make any calls from inside the flat. They'd likely bugged it.

Nyx did a pass through the last room, Kine's study. They'd gone through the desk, opened up jars and boxes of bugs. The dead and dying insects littered the floor or clung to the ceiling. Smears of velvet black—blue, violet—ran across the floor. Torn organic papers, bleeding those same colors, were crumpled and scattered around the window.

What did Kine have that they'd wanted? If the only reason they killed her was to get to Nyx, why go through the—

We're all trying to cure the war.

Nyx turned abruptly and ran back to the bedroom. She felt along the edges of one of the animated photos of her, Kine, and their brothers until she found the catch. The depiction was not soldered to the wall. It popped free and swung out.

For a conservative like Kine, images of living things of any kind were vulgar, obscene. An affront to God. If she had them around, it was to tell somebody something. Or remind herself of something.

Inside the hidden cabinet were Kine's real records: papers and bug recordings of her work in the compounds. Nyx found a satchel and stuffed the lot of them into it without looking. Rhys would help her sort them out. She put the picture back in place. Her siblings grinned at her. Kine winked. Nyx wiped down the frame.

On her way out, she cleaned the faceplate as well. She walked quickly but didn't dare run.

Back at the mechanic's, she found a call box. She flipped the switch that agitated the bugs and plugged in the pattern for the keg.

The bugs chattered for a long time. She heard someone on the other side of the building and ducked behind the box.

"Pick up, you fuckers," she muttered. She saw a sudden clear image of Anneke with her head blasted in, Taite with a sword through his gut, Rhys's hands—

"Peace be unto you," Rhys's voice carried to her from the desert.

"You listen to me," she said. Her voice shook. She stilled it. "You tell Taite to get his sister to a safe place and cut free his boy. Tell Khos to get his whores to another house, and if Anneke gives a shit about anybody, you tell her to get them a train ticket. Anybody we care about, get them out of the city or out of their places. And start packing up our stuff. You know the regrouping point. You put a filter up and get out of there. You hear me?"

"Are you all right?"

"Kine's dead."

He inhaled sharply. "Nyx—"

"You go get anybody you care about, Rhys. Tell them to clear out."

"Everyone I care about is on this team," Rhys said.

"Then they need to move," Nyx said, and hung up.

15

Burst sirens wailed out over Punjai; brilliant green burst tails lit up the black sky. Taite and Khos walked quickly, side by side, through the Mhorian district, one of the few parts of Punjai where neither of them stood out much. The faces were paler, the noses flatter, the shoulders broader, and most of the women on the street covered their hair with white scarves. A pity, really. The Mhorian district was the one place Taite ever saw hair that wasn't black.

"How are we for time?" Khos asked.

Taite shook his head. He knew they were running a little late, and he knew he should have gone to his sister's first, but he had set up this night with Mahdesh three days before. Mahdesh had been unreachable since then, out poking around some fallen space debris in the desert. Taite needed to speak to him in person. Inaya would have to wait.

Taite stepped over the threshold and into the Lunes Dansantes, a Ras Tiegan café that served Mhorian honeyed tea and kosher food for Khos in addition to saucy, spicy Ras Tiegan cuisine.

They both took off their sandals and piled them at the door with the others. Inside, the light was low, fresh glow worms in glass, and a woman sat with a small string band on a raised platform at the back of the café, singing a Ras Tiegan love song in a high, clear voice.

Taite looked out over the heads of the cigar-smoking crowd, a mixed group of men and women, mostly expatriates like him and Khos. He saw Mahdesh's familiar shaggy head and slim profile and felt a surge of relief. Of course he would be here. Of course everything was all right.

"I'll get us some drinks," Khos said.

Taite nodded, and picked his way among the tables to Mahdesh's side.

Mahdesh caught sight of him and grinned. He had the sort of grin that could fill a room. A smile that made Taite feel as if he were the only man in Nasheen.

They touched lips to cheeks, twice. Mahdesh kept hold of his elbow, still grinning. He was a little taller than Taite, broader in the shoulders, and had the clear, pale skin and even teeth of a half-breed inoculated Mhorian. Mhorians had no qualms about inoculating their half-breeds.

"Dangerous night?" Mahdesh asked, nodding toward Khos as they sat.

Taite sat close enough so their knees touched. It was as much prolonged public contact as they dared, even in the Mhorian district. Some Nasheenian women took violent offense to overly friendly men, no matter where they sat.

"Yes, I have to be quick tonight," Taite said.

Mahdesh leaned back in his chair, winked. "I'm getting used to that."

"We're having some trouble with a note."

"You mean Nyx is having some trouble with a note."

Taite swallowed. "Yes."

Khos arrived with drinks. Clear liquor for Taite and Mahdesh, amber honeyed tea for himself.

"How are you, stargazer?" Khos asked. He held out a hand to Mahdesh. They clasped elbows, and Khos leaned in and kissed his cheeks.

"I've been better. The city's too hot for me."

"It's a good time to get out, then," Khos said, and sat. "You told him yet?" he asked Taite.

"Nyx's note is in trouble," Taite said. "You and Inaya should leave the city tonight. Nyx's sister was killed. She thinks whoever did it may be coming after our kin next."

"Are you going to hold my hand, Taitie?" Mahdesh asked.

Taite felt himself redden. "I—"

Mahdesh reached under the table, squeezed his knee, and sobered. "I know. I'll be all right. What does your sister think about it?"

"We're going there after," Taite said.

Mahdesh raised a brow. "Hope Khos is staying in the bakkie."

Khos snorted. "I'm doing it for Taite."

"She doesn't hate you, Khos. You just make her nervous," Taite said.

"She hates me. She hates herself."

"Don't say that," Taite said. God, his sister. "She needs to be looked after, all right? Khos, don't fuck with me on this. Anything happens to me, look after her, will you?"

Mahdesh shook his shaggy head. "When will you let her grow up, Taitie? She's nearly a decade your senior."

"Take care of her," Taite repeated, still looking at Khos.

Khos shook his head. "Come on, you'll be fine. It's why I'm out tonight." He pulled down his tea in one swallow. "You two catch up. I'll meet you outside. That singer's voice grates."

He stood, and moved back through the crowd.

Taite looked back at Mahdesh. Their eyes met. Mahdesh's were steely gray, large and liquid. Taite wanted to stay there forever.

"This note… Inaya…"

"I understand," Mahdesh said. "I have some work to do in Faleen at the docks, muddling over some repairs and doing some translation. I can bide my time until things here cool down. The border's been a little warm anyway."

Taite nodded. He reached for his drink and realized his hand was shaking. Why was he always such a coward when it came to these things? Why not say it all out loud?

Because they could kill us for it, Taite thought.

Mahdesh put his hand over Taite's. "Go on. She needs you more than I do. I'll be all right."

Taite nodded. He stood. "We'll be at a safe house. I'm not sure for how long."

"Contact me when you can."

"I will."

Taite wanted to kiss him. The singer's voice trailed off. The café patrons began to clap. Taite turned away and pulled up his burnous, even though it was dark and too warm. He didn't want Mahdesh to see his face.

Taite left Khos with the bakkie and walked the two blocks over from the Mhorian district into the Ras Tiegan district. The change was subtle: a narrowing of the lanes, brighter colors out on the balconies, and the smell of curry that slowly came to dominate the stench of the streets as he walked.

A gang of women sat outside a bar and jeered at him as he passed. Most women didn't bother him, even in the Ras Tiegan quarter, but he'd had some bad nights since he arrived in Nasheen a decade before: fourteen years old and starving, his only talent a predisposition for mucking around effectively inside the mechanical and organic bits of a com unit.

There were more men in this part of the city, but the crime rate was about the same as anywhere else in Nasheen. In Nasheen, Chenja, and most parts of Tirhan, stealing got you a limb chopped off, and a second offence barred you from replacing it. Blinding was popular for black market offenses, and he had gone just once to a public execution where a woman had her head cut off for killing a local magistrate who'd come to register her son for the draft. There had been a crowd at the execution, but they had not jeered or clapped or reveled in their bloodlust the way he thought they would. No, it was a sober occasion, somber, like a funeral. After, they had wrapped the woman in white and set her on fire.

Fewer people stayed for that part.

He found his sister's tenement building—a squat brick-and-tile construction that must have dated back a century. Most of the tile had been stolen, leaving wounds of brick and mortar behind. The only renovations going on in Punjai were on the gun towers in the mosques and the military headquarters to the south.

Taite walked past the building on his first pass. He hung around the corner and waited to see if anyone had followed him. His parents had taught him a good deal before they'd managed to smuggle him out of Ras Tieg just ahead of the military police. He remembered how black the night was; remembered the protestors on the streets, the pictures of mutilated babies, the men on their podiums shouting, telling the crowd that the women of Ras Tieg were murderers and adulterers. He remembered the children—boys and girls—handing out pamphlets of crushed fetuses and mangled children, remembered their innocent smiles, as if they were handing out hard candy.

When he decided there was no one following, Taite buzzed his sister's place and waited some more.

Inaya was slow coming down the stairs. He had managed to get her passage into Nasheen eight months before by calling in a lot of favors and relying on some of Nyx's friends in customs. Inaya had been roughed up at the border crossing but said she would never be able to recognize her attackers. There'd been too many. Whether her pregnancy was her former husband's or some border tough's, she never said. He had not asked. She was a woman of a hundred secrets—a Ras Tiegan woman—and he let her keep them. The last time they'd seen each other, they were ten years younger, and she, eight years his senior, was rushing through a hasty marriage of necessity while their friends' houses burned.

They both knew she could have made an easier crossing into Nasheen, but she would have rather killed herself than given in to shifting. For any reason. No matter their parents' politics, Inaya thought shifters were dirty and diseased. She thought their miscarriages of nonshifting children were murder. She thought her mother was a murderer for not getting Taite and her inoculated, for not somehow saving the five bloody fetuses that their mother had lost and mourned for five bloody years.

Taite hadn't blamed their mother for shifting at night, going out to copulate with dogs, living some other life in some other form. He understood something of it, that need to escape one's body.

He had never been able to shift, and a lack of shifting ability for many Ras Tiegans resulted in poor health. Nyx liked to tell him he was allergic to air, and she was only half joking. Much of his memory of Ras Tieg was of a dark room, breathlessness, and the smell of stale urine in a pot.

When Inaya had started to get sick, she told them all it was just allergies, like Taite's. The headaches, the skin rashes, the nausea. She had nearly killed herself the day she realized her asthma was not from a lack of inoculants but one of the initial symptoms of a maturing shifter about to come into her ability. Taite had never seen her shift. The day she first shifted, he had been young and remembered only screaming, the smell of saffron. He learned later that magicians used saffron to discourage shifters from changing. It mangled their senses, the way the smell of oranges confused transmissions between bugs and magicians.

Inaya opened the door. The swell of her belly made it difficult to maneuver the narrow stairwell. In the dim light from the street, he saw how pale she was.

She'd gotten factory work in neighboring Basmah, but couldn't afford to live there. She rode a bus an hour there and an hour back. She worked two split eight-hour shifts—eight hours, three hours off, then another eight hours—which meant she didn't get much time to sleep during a twenty-seven-hour day.

"What's happening?" she asked.

He hadn't been to see her in a week. "We'll talk upstairs," he said.

She nodded, a woman used to secrecy and discretion. Her black curls were tied up with a vermilion scarf, keeping her hair out of her face. Her enormous belly looked far too large for her little frame. He and Inaya were both built like their Ras Tiegan father—narrow in the hips and shoulders, fine-featured. Inaya, by all counts, was prettier and had been darker before she started the factory work that kept her out of the suns.

Inaya started back up the sandy stairs. She wore a long skirt and loose blouse and went barefoot. The building manager was usually gone for months at a time. Taite preferred it that way. She meddled less often.

"Things with Nyx are all right?" Inaya asked as they climbed. Three flights.

"I still have a job, but some things have come up." Inaya always asked about Nyx first, the job second. Over the months Inaya had picked up Taite's employer's first rule: If Nyx was happy, everyone was happy.

Inaya pulled open the door of the little three-room flat. Kitchen, greeting area, bedroom. The toilet was down the hall. A palace, for most refugees. Nyx had found the place through a network of old bel dame contacts and offered it to Taite at a rate he could not refuse. The walls were hung in tapestries and bright bits of fabric Inaya had secreted home from the textile factory. She loved color. Her loom took up one corner of the greeting room. She made some extra money selling her brilliant woven tapestries of Ras Tiegan jungles to rich merchants in Basmah.

There were cushions on the floor and a pressboard box covered over in a sheet, which served as a table.

Inaya moved over to the radio and turned it off. She was breathing hard, and sweat beaded her upper lip. The windows were open, but the room was still too warm. Summer had breached the city a month before. Taite heard the steady whir of the bugs in the icebox.

"When will the results of the vote be in?" Taite asked.

"Soon," Inaya said.

Taite sat on one of the cushions. Inaya waddled into the kitchen to make tea. She preferred that they keep their roles fixed. Her house, her kitchen. He was a guest.

"We're working a pretty good bounty," Taite said.

"But something's wrong?"

"It has a lot of interested parties after it. Nyx thinks it's safer if we move our families away from the city for a while."

Inaya said nothing. She pulled a plate of something out of the icebox. Half a dozen ice flies fluttered out on gauzy wings, hit the warm air, and fell, dead, to the floor. They died more quickly in the summer.

"I was thinking it might be good for you to leave," he said.

"Where am I supposed to go?"

"I'm asking a friend if you can rent out a room at a place he knows."

Inaya made fists with her hands and turned to him. Her expression was grim. "Don't you dare. I'm not staying anywhere you and Khos, that filthy—"

"It's not like you're working there," Taite said hastily. "Where else was I supposed to find a cheap room? I—"

"I'm not staying in a brothel. Especially not one of *his* brothels."

"It's temporary." He dared not tell her that it wasn't Khos who recommended the room. Mahdesh had told him about the cheap rooms some months before when the rent on Inaya's flat had gone up and Taite was looking for places to move her to. Mahdesh, with the warm eyes and rough hands and passion for astronomy...

He had never told Inaya about Mahdesh.

Inaya hated queer men nearly as much as she hated shifters. Nearly as much as she hated herself.

"You know what they do to women in brothels?"

He shook his head. "This isn't Ras Tieg."

"It's the same everywhere."

She was deliberately wrong about that. How many men stood on the street here throwing rocks and broken bottles at her for being the daughter of shifter sympathizers? How many times had she been accused of being a murderer?

"I've put some money away so you don't have to work for a while. And your board is paid up for the next two months."

"The baby will come."

"What better place to be than a brothel? They'll get you to the best midwife, maybe even a magician. They won't care if you're a half-breed... or anything else."

She delivered a half-eaten tray of fried bread and grasshoppers to him and went back to the kitchen.

"No, of course not," Inaya said, frowning. "I am worth very little."

"You sound like Mother when you say that."

She brought over the tea and hesitated. He half expected her to throw it at him and winced. Some days he felt he should have turned out more like his father, but his father's arrogance and loud voice hadn't saved their mother, or Inaya, or Taite. It hadn't protected any of them.

Inaya firmed up her mouth and set the tray down neatly. She spent a good deal of time trying to sit comfortably. He had the urge to help her, but every time he had tried, she told him, "I'm not a whining Nasheenian woman." The longer they lived in Nasheen, the more Ras Tiegan she had tried to become. The sister he had known back in Ras Tieg would have asked for his help when she was tired, helped him fix the com, and told dirty jokes after dark. The woman who had crossed into Nasheen a decade after they parted felt like a different person entirely.

He had been in Nasheen far longer than Inaya had, and, unlike her, he had made his way alone and never regretted it. He held no love for Ras Tieg. Nasheen did not care much for half-breeds either, but Nasheen didn't call its women murderers and hold up bloody pictures of dead babies in the street. Nasheenians would not have killed his mother for being a shifter. They would not have called his family perpetrators of genocide.

When she was settled, Taite said, "I'd like you to leave tonight, if possible."

Inaya looked into her tea. "We have no help. I cannot move all of my things."

"You can leave them—"

"When I return, I will have nothing. My neighbors will steal it."

"I can replace it. All of it. I can—"

"Unless you're drafted." She looked at him. Her eyes were nearly gray.

"I have enough saved. And when this bounty comes in—"

"This isn't the first time you've said our circumstances would change when you received a bounty of Nyx's. We both know how that has turned out."

"You don't understand the business."

"I understand it very well." She still drank her tea cupped in both hands, like they did in Ras Tieg. "I would rather stay here."

"You have to go, Inaya. Please."

"Just as I had to come here?"

"Why do you say things like that? You could have crossed that border without any trouble. You chose to do it the hard way."

Her face reddened. Taite flinched but pushed on. "When was the last time you saw a midwife?" he said.

"With what money?"

Taite pulled out the notes Nyx had given him before she left and another buck besides, which he'd meant to deliver sometime earlier. "That's for the midwife. I can move you tonight and get the rest of the money to you tomorrow before we leave."

"Leave?"

"We have a safe house in Aludra with Nyx's friend Husayn. It's an old boxing gym on Shalome, a couple blocks down from Portage," he said.

"Aludra? Are you mad? That city is even closer to the border than Punjai. You'll be overrun or killed by some burst."

"And in Ras Tieg we could have been killed on the street for being shifter sympathizers."

"I sympathized with no one," she said.

The self-hate was so strong, so deliberate, that Taite felt as if she had slapped them both. He said nothing, only stared back.

She let her gaze drop suddenly, and he saw her face redden again. Humility this time. She looked at a tapestry on the far wall—a bright, detailed portrayal of a courtyard garden in Ras Tieg. There was more water in Ras Tieg. More green things, deadlier things. Nasheen and Chenja had only prospered once they'd blighted the world and rebuilt it. Ras Tieg was still wild, water-rich, and dangerous. But she would never forgive him for bringing her to the desert.

"We need to go," he said. "Khos has the bakkie parked a couple blocks away. He's waiting. Just bring what you need."

"I'm not going anywhere with that… man," Inaya said, "and I will not share rooms with whores."

"I'm sure you won't." Taite stood and held out his hand to help her up. What would his father have said? "We need to go."

She struggled up without taking his hand, using the makeshift table for leverage.

Taite waited at the window while she packed her things. The light inside was dim, and there was some light on the street, so he had a view. He saw no one outside.

He heard Inaya bumbling around in the kitchen. "Can you hurry? Do you need help?"

"I don't need your help," she said.

She had never needed his help. When his parents smuggled him into Nasheen, she was in the middle of getting married, her own attempted escape into anonymity as attacks on shifters and sympathizers grew worse. But when her husband died, an old man already when they married, Inaya lost her protection. She was a widow, and in Ras Tieg it meant she belonged, once again, to her shifter-sympathizing father. It made her a fair target.

"I did everything correctly," she yelled at him from the kitchen. He stayed at the window, did not reply. "I don't need anyone's help! I was a patriot. I was safe there, Taitie. I was a good woman, a proper woman. I covered my hair. I did not talk to other men. I went to church four times a week. I prayed for him. I was a good wife."

He heard her continue to bang around, now in the bedroom. She gave a strangled sob, and the sound cut at his gut, but he did not dare go to her. Let her alone, he thought. She will push you away.

"You need to hurry," he said.

She stepped out of the bedroom wearing her housecoat over her skirt and blouse, and had put on a hijab. She had carpet bags in both hands. Her face was red, but she had wiped her tears away. She stopped at the little figure of Mhari, saint of women scorned, that sat in the niche outside the kitchen. After going through the prayer rote, she bagged the statue of the saint as well.

Taite took one of the bags from her before she could protest, and headed down the stairs. He listened to her plod behind him.

Outside, they walked quickly. Inaya was stubborn and kept pace with him. She was breathing hard, and he slowed down. A couple of women hung out under the awnings of their buildings. A solitary dog trotted across the street.

Khos was still waiting in the bakkie. He'd slid down into his seat and pulled his burnous over his head.

"Hello, Inaya," he said.

"I'd prefer a quiet drive," she said without looking at him. "Where's your regular bakkie?"

"I'm borrowing a friend's," Khos said. He opened up the door from the inside and then started the bakkie. "Get in. There's too many dogs out tonight."

Inaya got into the back. Taite put the second bag in next to her, and sat in the front.

"Let's go," Taite said.

Khos turned into the street. A swarm of red beetles pooled across their path. A dog barked.

Taite looked back at Inaya, but in the dim light of the street, her face was unreadable.

16

An hour out of Punjai, Nyx hit a hastily erected security check-point. She slowed the bakkie and rolled down the window. The bakkie hiccupped and belched, and she caught the rabid stink of coagulant. There was another leak somewhere.

A couple of women carrying acid rifles stood in front of the barricade across the road. There were half a dozen military vehicles on the other side of the barricade, and as Nyx got closer, she saw that they were directing traffic away from Punjai. Nyx was a little drunk and sen-numb, so the whole convoy had the fuzzy half reality of a dream. She'd bought whiskey and sen at the mechanic's in Jameela before she got on the road again, and she hadn't been sober since.

She stopped, and one of the women leaned toward the bakkie. Nyx looked out past her, to the stir of figures around the military vehicles. They were men. Nasheenian men. Not old men or boys, but men in their prime, dressed in organic field gear and carrying standard-issue rifles and flame throwers on their backs. She had a jarring flash of memory—men all coming apart, bubbling flesh, melted field gear.

"We're redirecting through Basra, matron," the woman soldier said.

"What's going on?" Nyx asked. She tore her look from the men.

"We have a breach in Punjai. Minor skirmish. Should be cleaned up in half a day."

"What's the threat level?" Nyx asked.

The woman narrowed her eyes.

"I spent time in Bahreha," Nyx said. "I laid the mines that took out Lower Azda."

The soldier shrugged and looked blank, and Nyx realized all that had been a decade ago. A lifetime, in terms of the war. Thousands had died since then. Bigger cities had been contaminated or overrun or blown up. You're an old woman, Nyx thought.

"A couple of bursts contaminated the southern half of the city, and a small terrorist unit got through. Nothing serious. We'll have it cleaned up, matron. Go on toward Basra. We've cleared the road through to there."

The southern half of the city. Nowhere near the Chenjan quarter, which meant her storefront might be safe. Had her team gotten out before the quarantine? Fucking hell.

"Thanks," Nyx said. She looked again toward the men on the other side of the barricade. "You take care of the boys for me."

"Yes, matron," the soldier said. "We always do."

Nyx turned the bakkie down the temporary sticky-graveled road that the military had put down to bypass Punjai. Punjai under quarantine would buy her time. Anybody—even a bel dame—would have a tough time getting into Punjai, and once in, would have a tougher time wading through the chaos of contaminated quarantined quarters. If her team had gotten out, they might have bought enough time to regroup in Aludra and bolt the fuck off to Chenja without any bel dame knowing the wiser.

Maybe.

A whole heap of maybe.

Nyx ducked and rolled under Husayn's right jab and threw a right uppercut to her body. Husayn blocked with her left elbow and pushed forward again, throwing a left hook followed by another right jab.

Husayn had gotten a good deal more skilled with age. Not quicker—just smarter. Still, Husayn moved forward when other boxers moved back. Nyx should have remembered that before agreeing to a "friendly" spar with Husayn.

Nyx stopped trying to drive her back and stepped sideways instead. She threw a punch at Husayn's kidneys, but her heart wasn't in it. Husayn swung and caught her with a left hook to the jaw, another left hook to the face. Nyx saw darkness move across her vision. Something flashed at her from the back of her brain, some other fucked-up memory. She deflected a double right jab, but she didn't see the uppercut coming until it knocked her backward onto the dusty mat. Her head felt like it was floating.

Husayn laughed. "You're getting slow, old woman."

Nyx used the ropes to help herself up. She waited for her head to clear.

Husayn's gym had two rings, and a couple of kids were sparring in the other one, far more effectively than Nyx had been.

"I've been out of the ring for a while," Nyx said. She worked her jaw. She was going to hurt tomorrow. Hell, she hurt now.

Husayn grinned crookedly. She had gained a little weight and broken her nose a couple more times, but otherwise, she was the same Husayn. She'd stopped fighting for the magicians not long after Nyx went to prison, and she got leave from the magicians to start her own gym. Lots of young kids came her way hoping to gain some experience before testing their mettle in a magicians' ring.

"How's business been?" Nyx asked. She found one of the discarded corner stools and started unknotting her gloves with her teeth. Nyx's team was around, Husayn had assured her when she drove up just after mid-morning prayer; they'd shown up a day before the quarantine, then scattered their own ways. Probably to mosques and brothels, Nyx thought.

Husayn shrugged and pulled off her own gloves. She never laced them very tightly.

"Been good, as things go."

Nyx nodded at the sparring kids in the other ring. She let her gloves drop to the ring. "I thought you kept a busier gym."

"Huh," Husayn said. "Used to. Most of them headed out to Chenja. There's a fighting ring out there taking away my best fighters."

"You know where in Chenja?"

"I heard they're out of Dadfar."

"That so?" Nyx said. If they were going after Nikodem in Chenja, the fighting rings were a good place to start. And Husayn had spoken to the aliens before.

"Yeah, heard that from a couple girls now," Husayn said.

"You remember a fight in Faleen, about seven or eight years ago? You fought an outrider named…" Nyx realized she'd let the name slip again, and had to fish for it. "Jix. Jaks something, Jaksdij, maybe?" Fuck, Nyx thought, I cut up the kid's brother, and I don't even remember her name.

Husayn crinkled her mouth. "I fought a lot of girls, been knocked around a time or two." She rapped her knuckles against her head. "Don't remember all the girls I fought."

"How about aliens? You ever seen any of those?"

Husayn's face opened up. "Aw, hell, the aliens, yeah, I remember them. Aw, yeah, *that* fight."

"I might be looking for one of them. She met up with you at that fight in Faleen. Name's Nikodem Jordan."

"Blood and hell, Nyxnissa, what're you getting yourself into?"

"Nothing I can't handle."

"I heard that before."

"What did she talk to you about?"

Husayn sighed. She spared a look at the sparring kids and then went and picked up another of the corner stools and plopped it down next to Nyx. She sat, leaning in close, so her sweat dripped on the mat at Nyx's feet.

"She was a real strange talker, that one. Was pretty nice, hearing she was so interested, but those magicians, they said not to talk about boxing or bugs too much, you understand?"

"Magicians like Yah Tayyib?"

"Huh," Husayn said, and spit. She wiped at her face, grimaced. "He wasn't the one cutting black work. Can't fault somebody for doing their job."

"Let's say this isn't personal. What if I told you Nikodem was back—and missing—and the queen had me looking for her?"

Husayn guffawed, but when Nyx's expression didn't change, she sobered. "No shit?"

"No shit. It's cloak-and-dagger work though, all right?"

"Right, all right. This real spindly girl comes in and talks to me before the fight. I was pretty riled up, you know. I get all anxious before a fight, and answering questions—from dogs or aliens or whatever—is not something I got any interest in."

"What did she want?"

"Wanted to know how we trained, what it felt like to be a boxer, whether or not the bugs or inoculations got in the way. Best I could figure, she thought the bugs made us feisty or some shit, 'cause she couldn't imagine us going around bashing each other up for fun. She must live on a real dull world."

"She say anything about why she was here? What she was working on?"

Husayn shook her head. "Naw, and I didn't think to ask. Magicians all around, you know? I figured she was under their protection. Whatever project magicians got going, you leave it be. You remember."

"Yeah," Nyx said. "I remember."

"Something else she said, though—wanted to know if I'd ever fought a shifter. I told her we don't allow shifters in a ring, and she said why not? I told her it was 'cause they had an unfair advantage. She thought that was stupid, you know, since we'd fight magicians and all. I had to tell her being a magician just means you're using bugs. Magicians can stop using bugs. They can even drug up the bad ones to *keep* them from using bugs. But shifters, it's in their blood. They're half us, half something else. Told her the First Families used to call them angels. She was real interested in that."

"Huh," Nyx said. "She didn't know the composition of shifters?"

"Naw, she thought they were just like magicians. Called on certain bugs or something to change them up. I told her no, they were something else, something that got fucked up at the beginning of the world. Told her shifters live half in this world, half in the afterlife. Angels."

Nyx nodded. It was a popular idea—shifters being angels or demons—but she had known too many shifters to buy into that one. So Nikodem was interested in knowing about shifters. Bugs and shifters. *We're all trying to cure the war,* Kine had said. If shifting was genetic, in your blood, could you parse it out? Do something dangerous with it? Use it to make other things? Gene pirates muttered about that kind of shit all the time, but Nyx had stupidly believed it wasn't something Nasheen or Chenja would consider. Too fucked up.

"Thanks," she said. "I better clean up and talk to my crew."

"Yeah, I saw some of them come back in when you hit the mat. Isn't much of a safe house if they keep wandering around in broad daylight," Husayn said.

"Thanks. I'll talk to them," Nyx said.

"Nothing of it," Husayn said. "You spend six weeks here, I could get you back into shape, you know."

"We won't be here that long," Nyx said. The bel dames would burn them out.

Husayn shrugged. "Too bad. I keep wanting to whip that dancer of yours."

"In more ways than one, I'm sure," Nyx said.

Husayn winked. "That Chenjan accent turns me frigid. But you know, your little black man's not a half-bad boxer."

"Rhys doesn't box. He's a dancer."

"He *does* box. He's a magician, ain't he? And he's in good shape. A little small, maybe, but there are a lot of women at that weight. I've been working with him since he got in. I thought he was training with you."

Nyx knit her brows. "Not with me."

"Well, he's not bad."

"I'll keep that in mind."

So Rhys was boxing now, despite his long-suffering abhorrence for blood and violence. When had he started that up? It explained how he stayed in shape. He was probably taking lessons from Husayn just to spite Nyx. If she had fewer things to worry about, she might have let it get to her. As it was, she'd spent the last two nights mostly drunk and driving, trying to ward off nightmares of Kine lurching out of the tub, seeking her out with cold hands and bloodied eye sockets. It was not enough that she still dreamed of her dead brothers and her dead squad. Now her sister clawed at her as well. Too many dead.

Nyx hopped out of the ring. She landed badly and winced. She was hungover, and everything was starting to hurt again.

Nyx headed into the steam room. She cleaned herself up and slipped into the closet where Husayn had built a stairwell that went up into the attic.

Nyx found Anneke with her forehead pressed to the floor. Anneke prayed facing north in the center of a vast array of weaponry. Taite had set up a makeshift com center in a far corner, and he and Khos were playing cards on the console. It looked like they'd all slipped in while she fought. What, had they been at lunch?

Rhys had hung up a sheet to screen his sleeping area from the others. She heard him praying, too low to make out the words, as usual, and figured it must be about noon.

She was hungry. They must have eaten.

"What have you all got for me?" Nyx asked.

Khos leaned back in his chair. "What happened to the bakkie?"

"What happened to your face?" Taite said. They were playing for locusts, and one of the bugs was creeping off the table. They must have seen the bakkie in the garage.

"You still need me to fix that window?" Anneke said, coming up from her prone position.

Nyx found a seat on a threadbare divan at the center of the room. There were some deflated speed bags in one corner, and a lone punching bag hung from the long main beam of the ceiling.

"I missed you all too," she said.

"Anneke and I checked out some of the mercenaries on the note," Khos said, shoving his cards back at Taite. Taite poked at one of the locusts. If they were just a little harder up, he'd likely eat them. "Two more dropped their notes. If I didn't know better, I'd say somebody was convincing them it was a good idea. We're down to one bounty hunter and two mercenaries."

"The ones who dropped had pretty good money in their accounts after they did," Taite said. "I hacked into Raine's com for about a day before he patched the leak. As of three days ago, he's still after the note." Nyx saw the statue of Taite's little Ras Tiegan saint stuck up on the top of the com console. It was good to know that some things were constant.

"Where's Raine at?" Nyx asked. She wondered how much of her own gear they'd managed to get out.

"He has someone doing recon in Chenja. But he was just in Faleen talking with Yah Tayyib."

Yah Tayyib. Yeah, it was where she would have gone first too, if the old man would have seen her.

Rhys's praying died off, and he walked in, buttoned down as ever, though the attic was stifling. He'd cut his hair again, shaved himself nearly bald. She hated that.

"She isn't in any Chenjan districts I have contacts in," Rhys said. "All they know is that a lot of bel dames are looking for an off-worlder."

"Bel dames? Not bounty hunters or mercenaries?"

"Definitely bel dames."

So bel dames *were* looking for Nikodem. And if they were looking for Nikodem, it meant they didn't know where she was either. Were they trying to make sure Nyx didn't get to her first? Why? To keep Nikodem away from the queen?

"How about that transmission on our dead bounty hunter? Did you decode that?" Nyx asked.

"It's a transmission from someone who says they're on the bel dame council," Rhys said. He sat on the far side of the divan from Nyx. "They were asking him to drop the note on Nikodem in exchange for immunity. They knew he was smuggling out boys to Heidia and were threatening to cut off his head and turn him in unless he dropped out."

Khos grunted.

"Any idea which bel dame?" Nyx asked.

"No," Rhys said. "Taite ran it through our voice recognition reel and didn't come up with any matches."

Nyx raised her brows. "We should have every working bel dame's signature on that reel."

"Well, it was somebody from the actual council, not just a girl. Maybe she's too old to be on the reel?"

"She'd have to be real fucking old not to be on that reel—or pretty new. It took some skill to pinch that."

"Hopefully you didn't pay too much for it, then," Rhys said.

"I talked to Husayn," Nyx said, before he got cheeky. "No off-worlder has been asking about boxers or about the magicians in Faleen." She paused a minute and looked them all over. "She did say she's losing some boxers to a big ring in Chenja."

"You think Nikodem might be around boxers?" Taite asked.

"Either the Chenjans took her, with help from our magicians, or she went on her own to go sell something," Nyx said. "In any case, the boxing is a good place to start. It's something she was interested in last time, and if she's got as much of a thing for violence as her sisters say she does, yeah, I'd start with Chenjan boxing."

"If Raine's doing recon in Chenja, he might have the same idea," Taite said.

"We need to do better than Raine," Nyx said. And Nasheen wasn't exactly a friendly place to be right now. Not that Chenja would be an improvement, but she liked staying on the move, staying one step ahead of everyone. "I want to move operations to Chenja. Anneke, the bakkie is for shit, and you and I need to work on it tonight."

"I don't want to go into Chenja," Khos said.

"Then don't. I'll get another shifter."

"Nyx—"

A low, steady whine started outside. Fucking burst sirens.

Nyx raised her voice and shifted on the divan, turning back to Khos. "We already talked about this. You go or you don't. We're moving the day after tomorrow. Dawn prayer." She was done with all the sniveling. They were out of time for that.

Khos snorted and hunched in his chair.

The *whump-whump* of the anti-burst guns shook the building. A pause. Another thump.

Nyx tried to measure Rhys's reaction, but he was staring off into the air.

"Taite, I'll need you to stay here and work the com, keep an ear on what's going on in Nasheen. All right?"

"Sure thing," he said. "Does Husayn play cards?"

The siren started to mute out, then died.

Clear.

"No, but she can teach you to box," Nyx said, looking pointedly at Rhys. He didn't react, but Taite made a face at her. The idea of Taite doing anything involving vigorous physical movement was a running joke.

"Anneke," Nyx said, "let's go get that bakkie running properly. We'll need to give it new paint and put on the new tags. Rhys?"

He looked over at her. "Yes?"

"You here?"

"I'm here," he said.

"Good," she said. "We'll need you. I want to talk to you about some things."

Nyx pushed Khos and Taite away from the com and laid out the papers she'd taken from Kine's office. She motioned Rhys over. He walked up next to her. She opened her mouth to say something stupid about him, about gravy or prayer wheels or picnicking on the graves of the dead, but she realized she was too tired, and all she really wanted to say was that she'd missed him and his buttoned-up coat.

"When I went over to Kine's, I saw that they'd gone through her papers looking for something," Nyx said. "What they didn't know is that she doesn't keep her private papers in plain view, not when it has to do with her work in the compounds."

"So what is this?" Rhys asked, paging through the ciphered sheets.

"Her private papers. I figured you and Taite could decipher them and see what my bel dame sisters wanted from her. It could have been a hit on Kine just to get to me, but… well, they knew Kine and I weren't close."

"They aren't all ciphered," he said, pulling out a bound record book. "Looks like compound records. I'd have to know more about the technology they're using."

"Taite can look that up. You'll try?"

"I'll try."

"Good." Nyx made to move away from the com. They had a tight deadline, and she already had the litany in her head: papers, bakkie, call the contagion center, go to the bank, pick up gear and supplies.

"Nyx?"

"Yeah?"

"I'm sorry about Kine."

"Me too," she said. She saw the body again when she blinked: the sightless eyes, the rusty water, the white feather. "I'm going to go help Anneke with the bakkie."

"Nyx?"

"Yeah?"

"I'm a dead man in Chenja."

Something inside of her hurt, something she kept trying to dull with sen and whiskey. She pressed her fist to her gut.

"We'll be all right. Nobody out there knows you anymore. I can get you over the border and back." When she said it out loud, she almost believed it.

The way you got Tej over the border?

Rhys pursed his mouth and went back to the papers.

Nyx took Anneke by the collar, and the two of them went down into the garage and looked over the bakkie.

"Who the hell did you have go over this?" Anneke asked. She unshuttered the overhead light. The worms in the glass were dying, and the light was bad.

"Local mechanic in Jameela."

"I can heal up the front end, maybe replace the bumper if you want to spend the cash."

Anneke wrenched at the hood. It hissed open. She rolled up

the long sleeves of her tunic, showing off the jagged black lines of her prison tattoos, the most prominent of which was a shrieking parrot clutching a bloody heart. She leaned in. She swore. "Shit, how'd you get this back here? You need a new cistern. And your brake line is leaking. Fuck, that coagulant stinks. Who cut this line? You sewed it up twice."

"Rasheeda. The tissue mechanic patched it the second time. I didn't have the cash to replace it."

Anneke sighed and straightened. "You should just get a new bakkie, boss. A proper one with a real flatbed instead of a trunk, one of those ones with the reinforced cistern."

"Can't afford it."

"Can't afford the repairs neither."

Nyx handed her a portable light. "Lucky for me, my labor's cheap."

Anneke grinned. "Yeah, I know. I get the receipts."

"At least we know you're a good shot."

"Naw, if I was a good shot you'd have died in Faleen, proper."

"I hired you anyway."

"Bad judge of character."

"I know."

"Huh." Anneke moved to the back of the garage and pulled out a giant needle, some hoses, and a pair of clippers from the supply cabinet. She had to stand on a box to reach it. "You think you can get the boys back over the border?"

"Raine did."

"Raine had a lot of contacts."

"Yeah, I remember."

"Hand me some clips and some lube," Anneke said.

Nyx handed them over, and Anneke disappeared under the hood. Nyx heard the wet slurping of organic tissue as Anneke slid her hands among the guts.

"Why'd you keep running with Raine, after?"

"After what? The thing with you?"

"Yeah."

"Eh," Anneke said. "I've seen him do worse."

Anneke reappeared, poked her head around the hood to look at Nyx. She was covered in lube and bakkie bile up to her elbows. "We won't be able to get Rhys back over the border."

"Don't be so dry."

"I know your count. You never got a guy back over the border."

"I'll get Rhys back over."

"Yeah. Huh." Anneke leaned back into the guts of the bakkie.

"I'll get him over."

"Doesn't sound like it's me you're trying to convince. Hey, I get some cigars for doing this, or what?"

"Just remember to fix the window," Nyx said. She set the new tags for the bakkie on the front seat. "And put the tags on. I'm going to go look into getting a cistern."

"Hey, Nyx?"

"Yeah."

She straightened. "I've seen Raine do a *lot* worse."

"Me too," Nyx said.

"So how *are* you getting us across the border this time?"

"It's a surprise," Nyx said.

Anneke grunted. "I hate surprises, boss. The last surprise I got, somebody died."

"Yeah, well, the last surprise I got, I went to prison," Nyx said. "I sympathize."

17.

Rhys woke in a bad mood, and morning prayer didn't make him feel much better. He needed a clear head, but even after going through the salaat, his mind was still stuffed with list after list of chemical compounds and vat numbers and bug secretions. Kine had been a copious note-taker, but none of the names and numbering in her records made much sense to him—it likely wouldn't make any sense to anybody outside the breeding compounds. And he was out of time to decode it. He left most of it with Taite so he could work on it in their absence.

At least his immersion in Nasheenian organic tech had kept him from dwelling on the border crossing. Nyx kept telling him that she had a way to get over the border that wouldn't involve any of them inhaling chemical vapor and burning out their lungs.

But somehow, he doubted it.

Anneke—who was dark to begin with—rubbed herself down in bug secretions to stain herself even darker. Anneke was skinny in the hips and flat-chested and could pass for a boy. She had done the same a half-dozen times with Raine's crew, she said. She and Khos could drive right over the border—a particularly low-tech, low-security part of it, in any case. She had a couple of her relatives on the other side scout out a good stretch and assured everybody twenty times over that she could handle herself.

They were packed at dawn.

Rhys stood with the others around the loaded bakkie. He had his Kitab in one hand. He watched Nyx standing next to him, her face a cool blank.

"You keep your head down and report any deviations to Taite, got it?" Nyx told Anneke. Anneke rubbed down her gun while they all waited for Khos to shift.

"Yeah, boss. Me and Khos'll meet you in Azam, bright and shiny. You gotta take care of that wheel spinner, though." She winked at Rhys.

Rhys watched Khos stow his clothes behind the front seat and start his shift. Rhys had to look away when he did it. The contortion and contraction looked obscene. *Wrong.* As a magician, Rhys could feel the wrongness in the air, the bending of matter in ways it should not bend.

Anneke opened the passenger door, and Khos-the-dog jumped inside and settled onto the seat, tongue lolling. He was a yellow, blue-eyed dog now, cleaner than the wild mutts that scrounged for garbage in the streets but otherwise no different in appearance.

Nyx sidled up closer to Rhys and crossed her arms, and the two of them watched Anneke and Khos drive out of Husayn's garage and into the violet double dawn.

Rhys took a step away from her, to give himself some room. He was angry at her again, angry about this, about all of it. He wanted to find some way to tell her why he was angry, to explain it, but she tended to believe that every conversation involving strong emotion was full of words and resolutions that were not meant, as if he were a raving drunk. She saw every stated emotion as an admission of weakness.

"So where are we going, Nyxnissa?" he asked.

She spit sen on the garage floor. "The morgue," she said.

Rhys closed his eyes and prepared himself for horror. The last eight years had been an unending nightmare, starting with his flight across the desert. And it will end with my flight back into the desert, he thought. The globe the queen had given them had included a detailed summary of what she was willing to pay them in return for Nikodem—alive or dead. Nikodem, the alien with the big laugh. He had known her immediately upon seeing her stills but was uncertain about how he felt about hunting her. She was just an alien, and the sum to bring her in—even split five ways—was indeed enough for all of them to retire on. If they completed this note, he could leave Nyx, and this bloody business, forever.

He had no idea what he would do, after.

When he opened his eyes, Nyx had gone.

The dead that came back from the front were processed in filtered containment facilities expressly designed for the purpose. Chenja and Nasheen had signed and broken—and signed and broken and signed again—treaties requiring the return of the dead to the processing centers—the morgues—within thirty days of a soldier's death. The morgues were run by magicians who identified, cataloged, decontaminated, and burned the dead. The sterile remains were placed in ceramic jars and shipped home to mothers or sisters or merely sent to the war memorials on the coast—vast, shining walls of smooth metal that faced the sea. The largest of them was the Orrizo in Mushtallah, a monument dedicated to unidentified soldiers—dead boys and patriotic women.

After being reconstituted, Nyx had worked at the containment center just west of Punjai. She had to pay back the magicians for putting her back together, and the dirty, dangerous work in the containment center was the only work they had for her at the time. She had spent her mornings loading bagged corpses onto carts and her afternoons sorting piles of body parts that the magicians insisted all went to the same body. More often than not, the magicians were wrong, and she'd have to take out an extra arm or leg or the remains of a foot and throw it into another pile made up entirely of "unidentified" parts that were later burned up and dumped in the Orrizo.

It had been shit work, and she'd been hosed down and swept for organics three times after magicians suspected her of being exposed to contaminated bodies. Chenjans and Nasheenians alike had been known to plant bug-borne viruses in the flesh of the dead before sending them back over the border.

Even the dead were participants in the war.

Nyx still had some contacts at the morgue, so she and Rhys hitched a ride with a caravan going to Punjai, waiting out the hottest part of the day at a little cantina before walking the rest of the way to the center. An old woman named Ashana met them at the gates at dusk, after Rhys had finished his prayers and Nyx had finished her sen. Ashana brought them in through the filter at the rear of the compound, where the bodies selected for contamination—as opposed to decontamination—resided.

She led them to the containment room.

"You can't be serious," Rhys said as he stared out at the neatly numbered bags of the Chenjan dead, the ones the Nasheenians had taken from the field and planted with viruses to be trucked back into Chenja. These bodies would be stacked up and mixed in with the rest of the Chenjan bodies pulled out of the field that day and then delivered back to Chenja, carrying tailored viruses and nests of bugs primed to burst after they reached a populated area.

Rhys, as a magician, would be immune to just about everything. It was why only he and she could get across this way.

Even so, Ashana held out a beetle whose clear shell was filled with an orange fluid.

"Eat it," Ashana said to him, in Chenjan.

Rhys replied in Nasheenian, "Nyx first."

"I was inoculated against everything they have to offer when I worked here," Nyx said.

"And you're assuming they haven't come up with new viruses?" Rhys said.

"I'm sure they have, but there's a base contagion Nasheenian magicians use in all of their concoctions, and, yes, I checked to make sure that's still their base. It's the base that they inoculate all of their workers against. My body recognizes the base and destroys anything attached to it." She winked at him. "You aren't supposed to know that."

She supposed he could take a risk and try to save a few Chenjans by passing someone his now inoculated blood sample, but then he'd have to let them know why he'd been in Nasheen and who he was, and one call to the local security forces would turn up his name on their wanted list. Even if he avoided the security forces, the Chenjan magicians he gave the sample to would lock him up for conspiring with the enemy and then put him in quarantine for fourteen months. He knew that as well as she did.

If all went well, one of Anneke's kindred—six of her sisters had converted and married Chenjan half-breeds over the years—would haul them out of the mass of others based on the numbered tags that Ashana put on the bags. The driver would then give Rhys and Nyx false security badges so they could ride up front with her as far as the Chenjan border city of Azam. Nyx could pass for a eunuch when she needed to; castrated Nasheenian captives were sometimes used as a form of slave labor in Chenja. Once they were off the truck, she could pass for Rhys's servant if the two of them had to wait around the pick up point for a while if Anneke was delayed.

The containment room smelled only faintly of death. The tiny bugs that had been released into the chamber ate up all the bacteria that broke down the bodies, at least until they left the holding room. The ride out across the desert among the bags would not be pleasant.

Nyx looked over at Rhys. In the cold light of the holding room, he looked slim and fragile and more than a little sick. He had followed her for a long time, through some shitty situations, but she knew this was a lot to ask. She was not yet so much of a monster that she did not realize that.

"You don't have to do it," Nyx said. "I can run this without a magician."

He turned to her. Ashana began unzipping their bags.

"Is this how you're getting me back out?" he asked.

"Sure," she lied. She hadn't sorted that part out yet. Getting a Chenjan body into a holding center for Nasheenian dead would be tougher than getting a Chenjan body into a holding center for Chenjan dead. She needed another way to get him back into Nasheen. Her conscience had picked a hell of a time to nag at her.

"I hate it when you lie to me," he said.

"Sometimes I can get away with it."

"You won't be able to hold off bel dames without a magician, even a poor one," he said.

"No, probably not." That part wasn't a lie. He wasn't the most talented of magicians, no—but no standard could get her the communications and security he could. If somebody got poisoned or had a limb chopped off, well… he was less useful. That's what real magicians were for.

He waited. She waited. Ashana stood over the open body bags and waited.

"I need you to come with me," Nyx said, finally.

"Then I'll go," Rhys said.

"Good on you all, then," Ashana drawled. "Now get in the damn bags."

*

From a small hole in the body bag, Rhys could see the double dawn turn the sky gray-blue, then violet, then bloody. Punjai was still quarantined, and the body bakkies circumvented the city. A couple of miles west of Punjai, the veldt turned to flat blinding-white desert. Rhys was pressed up against the slatted side of the bakkie flatbed, half a dozen bodies below him, a couple on top of him, and Nyx next to him, at her insistence.

"Best we keep close," she had told him.

They passed signs warning travelers that they were on an unpatrolled road. The air started to turn sour. He could smell the yeasty stink of spent bursts, and he caught a faint whiff of geranium and lemon. There were no other vehicles on the road.

Rhys widened the slit that Ashana had cut for him to breathe through during the long ride. The bags were good at keeping their contents cool; they were all organic and fed off the body's secretions and the heat of the sun. Under the sun, the black bags turned green.

He saw a long column of smoke off to their left, too far away for him to see what was burning. Sometime later he saw the first burst, a green spray of light against the violet sky. He could feel the low thump of the bursts in his chest as the ground rumbled with the blast.

At the border station, the truck stopped for the drop-off, and Rhys held himself still and waited. He heard a couple of people speaking fluent Chenjan, and felt a swarm of wasps buzz by. Ashana helped with the transfer, and he felt the weight of the bodies above him ease as they were offloaded.

Someone grabbed hold of him by the hips and dragged him across the flatbed.

"Praise be to God," a male voice said from outside the flatbed, in Chenjan. Hearing the language spoken out loud so freely left Rhys with a feeling of half dread, half relief. "Where are you all headed?"

"Praise be to God," Ashana said. "I'm dropping this batch with your girl. Came straight from the front."

"Careful how you lift them, woman! Pay them some respect," the male voice said. The person holding Rhys let him go, and two big hands grabbed at him and pulled.

Rhys froze. He was lifted up and slipped carefully onto another flatbed. Another body was pushed on top of him.

He wondered what they would do to him if they found him out. Kill him quickly, he hoped. He closed his eyes. It must have been time for prayer. There was no call to prayer out here, no call that he could hear. Submit to God, he thought, and God will attend to the rest.

Ashana and the man began to bicker. He heard something thump on the ground.

"You tell me to show respect? I'm not the one dropping bodies, you fool," Ashana said.

"What are you packing these bodies with, woman?"

"Nothing you don't pack yours with. Cut it open if you want to find out. Half your bodies are contaminated with your own bursts."

Rhys felt something bump his feet again. He kept his eyes shut. Would they take him out and cut him open? He held his breath and sent out a call for bugs, but the tailored colonies inside the bodies were too complex for him. He could feel them but couldn't alter or direct them. Poor magician, indeed. He swore softly.

Ashana and the Chenjan spoke a few more heated words. Rhys heard the sound of a bag opening. More bickering. Then the sound of the body being dragged across the packed sand.

Then the bakkie started to move.

Rhys let out his breath.

They drove for what seemed like hours. They passed a couple of burned-out farmsteads. Every few decades some hard-up family, a man and his ten or twenty wives, would move out close to the front and try to make something grow, but most of Chenja's agricultural land was still along the coast, like Nasheen's. It was safer there, and less toxic than the wasteland in the north or the spotty, poisonous swampland in the south inhabited by Heidians and Drucians and Ras Tiegans.

When the bakkie stopped again, someone grabbed him by the feet and pulled.

The bag came open, and Nyx's sweaty face blotted out the hot white sun. She was grinning. He had never been so relieved to see her.

"You still in one piece?" she asked.

Rhys sat up and eased out of the bakkie and onto the hot sand. A tall, skinny Chenjan woman stood next to him, wearing work trousers, sandals, and long sleeves. Her face was half-veiled, and her eyes were black. She wore a pistol on one hip and a machete on the other. Rhys felt suddenly vulnerable. He and Nyx had left their gear behind. Anneke was smuggling it over.

"This is Damira," Nyx said.

"Your clothes are in the back," Damira said in Chenjan, "and your badge. You'll need to wear it in case we're stopped along the road." She didn't meet his eyes. It was the drop of her gaze, more than the language, that convinced him he was back in Chenja. No Nasheenian woman would lower her eyes in his presence.

He and Nyx changed into long trousers and dark vests with red bands around their arms signifying their role as ferriers of the dead. Damira was a quiet woman, and she left the radio silent. The inside of the cab was strung with gold-painted beads, and a prayer wheel hung from the rearview mirror. Rhys had the sudden urge to open up the prayer wheel and see what prayer she kept there. One was not supposed to ask God for anything, only submit to His will, but there were sects in Chenja who believed that God enjoyed granting favors. Chenjans had divided themselves into roughly two sets of believers and perhaps a handful of minority sects. This woman with her prayer wheel was a purist, not an orthodox. She would have been cut and sewn at puberty, bearing the marks of her faith and submission on her body while courting God for private favors during prayer. Rhys found the idea of female mutilation and begging favors from God distasteful, if not repulsive, but as an orthodox, he also believed in allowing others to worship as they willed, so long as their people respected God and the Prophet, performed the salaat, and respected God's laws about marriage—seclusion, respect, and moral purity.

And so long as they weren't Nasheenian.

The desert was still flat and white, and they passed burst craters and abandoned vehicles along the road. He expected the air to be different somehow, now that they'd crossed the border, but the air contained the same yeasty stink. Nyx sat near the window, a scarf pulled up over her face to keep away the dust and to obscure her appearance. She had cut her hair with Damira's machete when they changed clothes. It was a bit of a botched job, a ragged mop of thick, dark hair that did nothing to soften her face. She looked like a wild desert orphan, someone who'd grown up on an abandoned farm near the front after her family was slaughtered.

He sat in the middle, trying to give Damira some space. It meant sitting closer to Nyx, but after spending the morning inside a body bag, the idea of pressing himself against someone alive didn't seem so indecent.

Too long in Nasheen, he thought, and watched the flat desert rolling out before him. How long until it looked different? Until it wasn't just some long stretch of Nasheenian desert but the land of his birth? His father's land, the land they bled and died and prayed for?

Rhys glanced over at Damira again, then at the prayer

wheel. He had opened his mouth to form the question in Nasheenian when he realized he could speak Chenjan freely. The words came out a little stilted. "Can I ask what you pray for?" he asked.

She kept her eyes on the road. "I pray for an end to the war."

He could barely hear her over the sound of the tires on the gritty road and the chitter of the bugs.

They passed a hastily erected road sign along the edge of the scarred highway, its base covered over in lizards. The original sign was a rusted-out hulk, mangled and broken and half-buried in the sand behind it. The new sign announced distances to the nearest Chenjan cities:

Azam, 40 km
Bahreha, 86 km
Dadfar, 120 km

"Where did you live?" Damira asked him.

"Here in Chenja?"

"Yes."

"A little town west of Bahreha called Chitra," he lied.

"My mother heard that Chitra was once a beautiful city."

"I don't remember it that way," he said. He had never been to Chitra.

"No one alive does," she said.

The desert stayed flat and white all day. Rhys saw more evidence of recent fighting as they drove—spent bursts and abandoned artillery, black-scarred rents in the desert, pools of dead bugs. He saw a heap of burning corpses in the distance. He knew there were corpses because the giant scavengers were circling, despite the smoke: couple of sand cats, black swarms that must have been palm-size carrion beetles, and some of the rarer flying scavenger beetles with hooked jaws, the kind that grew to over a meter long and had been known to devour children in their beds.

There were human scavengers as well, walking along the road as they passed, asking for rides. One of them looked like a Chenjan deserter, his jacket torn from his body, long tears in his dark skin that looked like they'd been made by a sand cat. When the man turned, Rhys saw that half his skull was missing. He could see the gray-red wetness of his brains beneath the sand and dirt and cloud of flies. He wouldn't last long unless he found a magician. He must have dragged himself out from under the heap of corpses and was probably trying to walk home. They would patch him up and send him back.

Rhys looked away.

He had fled across the desert to escape this fate. Some part of him wondered if it had all caught up with him at last.

18

Damira dropped them off outside Azam, a bleeding border city. A half-dozen anti-burst gun towers ringed the swollen black sprawl of the city, half again as tall as its two minarets. Most of the gun towers were charred husks. Heaps of debris littered the roadway.

Rhys and Nyx walked with their hoods pulled up. Geckos skittered across their path. They passed a contagion sensor along the road, tilted at a hard left angle. The light at the top flashed yellow; the whole thing was covered in locusts.

The sun was low in the sky by the time they made it past the burst guns and into the city. It was dead quiet, like the streets around a magicians' gym before a fight. Rhys saw some moths under the eaves of the tenement buildings, blasted-out archways riddled with bullet holes. The city was teeming with wild and tailored bugs; they made Rhys's blood sing. Swarms of flesh beetles darkened the sky. A few ragged people stared out at them from the ruined buildings. Rhys saw a couple of scabby kids digging in the sandy basin of what had once been the city's central fountain and asked them where everybody was.

The boy sneered at Nyx, but as he turned to Rhys, his expression sobered and he pointed east, toward Nasheen.

"That fighting we passed was close," Rhys said.

He saw Nyx gaze down the deserted street. A swarm of wasps hummed over the rooftops. In the west, the primary sun was headed down, and the sky was starting to go the brilliant violet of dusk.

"We don't have time to get to Dadfar tonight," Nyx said, in halting Chenjan, probably for the child's benefit. Speaking Nasheenian would draw even more attention than the color of her face. "If Anneke's in, we have to hole up."

They walked past prayer wheels hanging in broken lattice windows, cracked water troughs, and abandoned bug cages. Rhys caught the distinctive smell of gravy over protein cakes, spinach and garlic.

Nyx led him down a narrow, refuse-strewn alleyway that smelled heavily of urine and dog shit. He had to pick his way around heaping piles of garbage and feces and rubble. They stirred up fist-size dung beetles and enormous biting flies. At the end of the alley, in a cracked parking lot, Rhys saw Nyx's familiar bakkie—new paint, new tags, but her bakkie nonetheless—squatting underneath a spread of spindly palm trees. One of the trees was splintered in half. The other bakkies he could see were all sun-sick, rusted-out wrecks—Tirhani made, just like the ones in Nasheen. A woman in a soiled burqua called to them from the scant shade of the palms. She had something in her hands—tattered lengths of cloth for turbans.

"Here it is," Nyx said, pointing to the green awning at their left. The way house was a leaning, three-storied façade of mud-brick and bug-eaten secretions. The tiled roof was coated in flaking green paint. A battered poster under one of the reinforced windows bled black organic ink all over the bricks, announcing the arrival of a carnival now four years past.

"Nyx," Rhys said, "we shouldn't stay in Azam." He had his own reasons for that. He had family in Azam.

"We'll be fine," Nyx said, and rapped on the heavy, bullet-pocked door of the way house.

A small peeping portal opened. Rhys saw one misty eye look back out at them.

Nyx glanced at Rhys.

"We have reservations," Rhys told the misty eye. He had to stop again, work backward from the Nasheenian. It had been too long since he spoke Chenjan at length. "My brother has preceded us."

The door opened.

A haggard old man stood on the other side, a long rifle in one of his bent, arthritic hands. "Anneke," the old man said.

Rhys looked at Nyx.

"Yeah," Nyx said.

A slim figure stepped toward the door from the dim of the reception area. Rhys recognized Anneke under the black turban that wound about her head and covered her face. Khos-the-dog trotted behind her, pausing in the light from the doorway to yawn and stretch.

"Any trouble?" Anneke asked in Chenjan. Rhys was startled at how smoothly she spoke, with no hint of an accent. Not for the first time, he wondered what she'd gone to prison for.

"I don't think so," Rhys said, also in Chenjan.

"Huh," Anneke said, and she pulled down the cover over her face so she could spit sen. A couple of male voices sounded from deeper inside the house, Chenjan voices. Rhys caught the smell of marijuana and a whiff of curry.

Anneke grinned at him. "Good to be home?"

"Under these circumstances? No. I think we should stay on the road."

The old man gestured with his rifle. "Get in, get in!" he said.

The call of the muezzin sounded, low but close, and Rhys looked out behind them. They were within a block of one of the city's two remaining minarets. The few speakers along the city street belched a green haze, the exhaust generated by the door beetles translating the call.

"That's handy," Anneke said, and pulled her prayer rug from across her back. "I put yours behind the cab in the bakkie," she said, and rolled out the rug to pray. "Sorry, didn't unpack all the gear."

"Do you have a fountain?" Rhys asked the old man.

"The hell you bother washing? Use sand. Don't go out there!" the old man barked.

But Rhys turned away from them and picked his way to the parking lot at the end of the alley. He passed near the woman in the burqua. She thrust the dirty turban cloth toward him, babbling at him so quickly, so desperately, that he could not understand her.

"Where is your husband?" he asked.

"Dead, all dead!" she said, and thrust the cloth at him. "Please, I need bread. Bread and venom. Please. Anything you like, anything." She stepped toward him as she said it, and began to clutch at her burqua.

"Stop," Rhys said. "Stop. You are not mine to look after."

He retrieved his rug and called for a wasp guard on the bakkie. It took a good minute to find a swarm. The contagions in the air confused them and made his already tenuous communication with them all the more difficult. He hoped they didn't turn around and attack him when he came back.

"Please, anything," she said, but Rhys pushed past her and walked quickly toward the way house as the amethyst sky became the true blue dusk of early evening.

He pounded at the door until the man with the rifle let him back in. Inside, he saw the cracked, patterned marble of the floor, what had once been a beautiful black and white mosaic of intricate script from the Kitab. The fountain at the center of the reception area was dry and silent.

Anneke already had her prayer rug out, facing north. It wasn't until he looked down at Anneke's bowed back that he remembered it was a sin to pray among women. He hesitated, looked behind him, but the old man was making his way up a worn set of steps, rifle in one hand, the railing in the other. Nyx stood at the end of the stairway, watched Khos shift. No one would see anything objectionable about kneeling next to any of these people during prayer. Anneke didn't look like a woman; here, she was just another small Chenjan man, underfed. Rhys let out his breath and rolled out his rug.

None would see but God.

But God had seen him commit this sin every day for the last eight years. Prayer in Nasheen was mixed, even in a magicians' gym.

Rhys hesitated a moment longer, then he knelt on the rug, and he surrendered. He took comfort in prayer, in recitation, in submission. After so many years of working for a woman he found it impossible to trust entirely, submission to God was a much welcome release.

When the prayer ended, Rhys raised his head and gazed off past the dry fountain, where three dead cockroaches rested beneath the broken head of a stone locust. Rhys saw political posters up on the walls. The mullahs who ruled Azam were up for re-election, though Rhys doubted any of them were out here tonight. Most local mullahs were related to the holy men who sat up in the high courts at the capital. Like Nasheen's elections on domestic issues, elections in Chenja weren't really elections. In Nasheen, the queen did what she wanted. In Chenja, the mullahs in the capital appointed all of the local officials, and the Imam, an orthodox, selected the mullahs.

Rhys tugged his hood further down over his face, to hide his eyes. There were other voices in the house. As slight as the chance of being recognized was, he didn't want to take it. The penalty for his crimes was torture, evisceration, and quartering.

As he stood, Nyx said, "I need you to put out a call to Taite. Think you can do that this close to the border?"

"Risky, but possible," Rhys said. "Do we have a room?"

"Up here," Khos said. He wore a dhoti and burnous now, nothing else. Rhys always marveled at the shape shifter's disregard for nudity. He was as bad as Nyx.

They walked up the dim stairwell to the third floor. There were a couple of dying glow worms in glass, but most of the ones they passed were already dead. Khos pushed open a battered door made of knobs of metal and bug secretions.

Dirty pallets were lined up at the center of the room. A dark gauze hung from one window; the other bled unfiltered evening light across the center of the room. A swarm of mark flies circled the center of the room.

Rhys waited for Nyx to come in and shut the door, then he called up a little swarm of red beetles. It took him three tries and nearly twenty minutes to get a link to Taite.

"Everything all right out there?" Taite asked.

"About as expected," Rhys said.

"That bad?"

Nyx cut in. She had pulled off the hood of her burnous and found some sen. She spit at her feet, next to one of the pallets, and Rhys grimaced. "Have you found out anything more in Kine's papers? Rhys wasn't much help."

"I've deciphered most of the pages. I did some research work on the compounds too. I have some contacts who used to work there doing recon and cleanup work."

"Spies?" Nyx asked.

"We don't call them that. Anyway, it looks like she was selecting for traits and working with a lot of magicians. You'll never guess whose name came up in these records."

"Yah Tayyib," Nyx said.

"Great guess," Taite said. "There's some information about

attempts at breeding kids in vats—you know, artificial womb tech—but they're not getting far on that. That's nothing new. The interesting thing is some kind of project called Babylon, or a project being done out in Babylon where they're splicing human and bug genes... or doing some weird stuff with viral contagions and genetics or something. They've got everything in here: blood roaches, fire beetles, cicadas, locusts."

"That's fucked up," Nyx said. "They breeding some kind of bug army?"

"They've got a lot of notes in here about shifters. Maybe trying to replicate a shifter's blood code?"

"Breeding for magicians and shifters," Rhys muttered. "But have they gotten anywhere with it?"

"You think they'd be so stupid to fuck with the world again?" Nyx said.

"It wouldn't be the first time," Rhys said. "There were no shifters on the moons. Magicians, yes, but no shifters."

"Where did you hear that?"

"Read a book sometime."

Nyx hocked up a wad of sen and spit it at his feet. This one hit the pallet. Rhys decided that was where she was going to sleep.

"He's right," Taite said. "Nobody in Ras Tieg could shift before they came here. We were all standards. It's Umayma that does it. In Ras Tieg, they say God cursed us."

"You have a saint for it?" Nyx asked, and Rhys suspected she was only half joking.

"We do, actually," Taite said. "Mhari, saint of women scorned and women's wombs. A lot of our church leaders blame women for all the shifters."

"That's the dumbest thing I ever heard. Those men think babies come from women and dirt?"

"You don't know much about Ras Tieg," Taite said. "From what my contacts say, this information would go for a real high price in any market from Ras Tieg to Tirhan. Even a list of failures gives them an idea of where not to go when they push forward."

Rhys glanced over at Nyx. She sighed. "All right. Anything else you can get out of it?" she asked.

"Maybe," Taite said. "Later, though. I have a limited window. They spray for foreign transmissions in that sector in half an hour. You're still too close to the front."

"Taite," Nyx said.

"Yeah?"

"I want you to burn all those papers. I don't want anybody using that against Nasheen. Have locusts eat whatever won't burn."

"And the transcriptions?"

"Nyx—" Rhys said. He had taken some of those papers with him for study. He hadn't left them all with Taite, and he certainly wasn't going to burn what he had bundled up and had Anneke smuggle in.

"See what you can do with them. If it's just a record of failure, again, get rid of it. But if they found anything out, if she mentions any names—magicians, bel dames—you let me know before you toast it. I want to know if they actually accomplished anything over there."

"All right," Taite said.

"Let's end this transmission," Nyx said.

"Peace be to you, Taite," Rhys said.

"And to you. I've been picking up a lot of other transmissions coming out of there. Be careful. God bless."

Rhys released the bugs. "Your bel dames might have good reason to take Nikodem if she's trying to pull information about the compounds," he said.

"I'm leaning toward the idea that we'll all be better off bringing back Nikodem dead," Nyx said. "If they're breeding magicians, we could bury your country in viral bugs in twenty years that'll eat everything organic. Men, women, dogs, kids, shit, trees—the whole fucking deal. We could fuck up the world with shit like this. No wonder the bel dames are clawing at the queen for this tech. Whoever owns it owns the world."

"I don't like that idea."

"It would end the war."

"In your favor. And what then, when all your Nasheenian men come home to a blasted wasteland? I'm not convinced they'll share power with you that easily," Rhys said.

"You don't have much faith in Nasheenian men," she said. "Are you asking how long it'll be until Nasheenian women all become slaves like the Ras Tiegan women and your Chenjan mothers?"

"It isn't like that." He hated it when she made her sweeping generalizations about foreign men. This, from a woman who had never known a father. That was the problem with Nasheenian women. They had all been raised without men.

"Why did you leave, again?" she said.

"That's not fair." And not, of course, true. If you wanted amnesty in Nasheen, you told them you were blacklisted for protecting a woman. You didn't tell them the truth.

Anneke walked in from the hall. "Hungry?" she asked. "I got real tired of sitting around here watching Khos lick his ass all day."

"Food sounds fine," Nyx said. "The old man got anything?"

Rhys heard a low whine start up from outside, too high for the muezzin. He cocked his head. He knew the sound but couldn't place it.

Anneke turned to look out the window, and Khos pushed himself away from the wall.

"Fucking incoming!" Nyx yelled, and before Rhys had time to realize what she was yelling about, he was on a pallet on the floor with Nyx on top of him.

A heavy thud and whump shook the whole house, and something rained against the unfiltered glass.

Anneke scrambled across the floor in front of him toward a gear bag stowed against the far wall. Nyx pulled herself off Rhys. His face was damp with her sweat. His whole body tingled. There was some bug in the air, something... He looked toward the window and saw centipedes crawling along the outside.

"Anneke!" Nyx said. She pulled off her burnous and grabbed a dual-barreled acid rifle from one of the gear bags.

Anneke threw Rhys his pistols.

Rhys shook his head. "I don't—"

"They're coming overland!" Nyx said, her shoulder pressed against the gauzy window frame, one eye on the world outside.

"Overland?" Rhys said.

"Means Nasheenians are in the city," Anneke said, scrambling past him, shotgun slung over her shoulder, sniper rifle in hand.

Khos said, "You see them?"

"I've got a scout in the alley," Nyx said. "Cancel that. He's waving his fucking squad through. Fuck."

Khos pulled both pistols.

Rhys's hands were shaking. He raised one arm, closed his eyes, and looked for a swarm. There were several, but his nerves made it hard to pinpoint them. Four wild, two locked and specialized. Whatever squad was coming down the alley, they had at least one magician with them carrying specialized swarms.

"Don't fire unless I call it," Nyx said.

"Boss?" Anneke said.

"They're Nasheenians. Don't fire without my call."

"Nyx—" Khos said.

"Nyxnissa," Rhys said, opening his eyes. He saw the sweat beading her forehead, her glistening bare arms. The gun was heavy, and as she stood against the window frame in her breast binding and knee-high trousers, baldric too tight, he saw the power in her arms, the muscle under her flesh. He had felt it when she pushed him to the floor, the weight of her.

She turned to them, outlined in the blue haze of the coming night, and in her face—the hard jaw and suddenly flat, fathomless eyes—he saw the woman who had burned at the front. He was breathless.

"I said you don't fire without my call. Those are my boys," Nyx said.

Anneke set up her sniper rifle at the window. She would have a clear view of the alley.

Rhys stayed on the floor. He could track the progress of the squad by the position of their wasp swarms. The swarms were sniffing out bursts and traps in the alley.

"Nyx?" Rhys said.

All her attention was at the window.

"Nyx?" he repeated.

He heard a banging on the door below them. Heard raised voices in the house.

Nyx turned to him. "I know," she said.

The other magician had sniffed him out.

Another high whine sounded, close. "Down!" Nyx yelled, and pushed herself away from the window.

Khos dove flat next to Rhys. Rhys covered his head with his hands.

The world trembled; the windows shuddered, and cracks appeared. When Rhys raised his head, he saw that full night had spread over the city. The room was dark.

"Got another squad," Anneke said.

"Khos, check the other window," Nyx said.

Khos got up and went to the gauzy window, looked out. "There's another patrol over here too," he said.

The voices downstairs rose in pitch. Rhys heard the sound of a rifle shot. Screaming. A woman's scream.

He tried to see Nyx, but in the darkness she was only a dim outline. Outside, he saw the pale green and red streamers of bursts trailing out over the city. God help me, he thought, and began to recite the ninety-nine names of God. He drew his pistols.

"Khos, check the stairs," Nyx said.

Khos picked his way toward the door and opened it. He crept into the hall.

"They're coming up," Khos said.

Nyx moved across the room, walked right past Rhys. "Get back in," she said.

Rhys heard a pounding on the stairs.

"Get back in!" she hissed.

Khos stepped back inside. He stood a breath away from her in the dark and said, low, "Goddammit, Nyx, they're fucking coming up. I'm not going to sit here like some martyr."

"You fucking hold," she said. "Move the fuck away from the door and listen the fuck up."

"I'm not going to—"

She shoved her gun against his chest.

Rhys opened his mouth to protest, then clamped it shut. Anneke said, "They've got backup in the alley!"

Rhys watched Nyx and Khos.

They were both shadows. He was taller, broader, outweighed her, and the outline of him—his wild mass of dreads, beefy legs, the breadth of his shoulders, the pistols in both his hands—was terrifying in the dark.

"I said hold," Nyx said, softly.

More shouts came from downstairs. Rhys heard another shot, then the familiar *bat-bat* of a pistol.

Khos turned his big body away from Nyx and moved to the window. "You're going to kill us all," he said.

"Not today," she said.

Rhys stood. He raised a hand, found a local swarm but couldn't call it. He could hear them singing in his mind, heard them acknowledge his call, but they did not change course. Useless magician, he thought. My God, why give me any talent at all if I can't use it now?

Something downstairs exploded. The house trembled again. Footsteps on the stairs. The smell of smoke, yeast, and the faint whiff of geranium.

Men in the hall, shouting. The squad was on the floor. Doors banged open. More screams.

Rhys kept hold of his pistols. He would not kill for her. He would never kill for her. But wounding… Sweat rolled down his back, between his shoulder blades.

Nyx had her gun pointed at the floor.

The ninety-nine names of God….

Lights. Movement. Shadows appeared in the doorway, green lights.

Nyx crouched low, raised her gun, yelled at them in Nasheenian. "Bel dame! Hold! I'm a bel dame on the queen's business!"

Wild cries, from the boys. They had green lights on the ends of their guns, and the flares swept the room. For a moment, Rhys was blinded. He turned his head away.

"Drop the guns!" the man at the head of the group yelled, in Nasheenian, then Chenjan. "Drop the guns!"

"We're yours! We're Nasheens!"

"Drop your fucking guns!"

"Drop the guns!" more yelling from the hall.

"I'm a bel dame, you drop your fucking gear or I'll cut off your fucking head!"

Rhys started to shake. A green light tracked along his breast. Why didn't she shoot them? She'd killed Chenjans and Nasheenians in droves. What were three or ten more?

And the boy said, "Who do you serve, woman?"

Nyx straightened and pointed her gun at the floor. She stepped in front of the squad, blocked Rhys and Anneke. "My life for a thousand," she said.

Outside, a huge purple burst lit up the sky, and for one long moment Rhys saw the whole room in violet light: Nyx and the squad, Anneke with her shotgun at her shoulder, Khos crouched at the window with his pistols, burnous discarded, as if he was getting ready to shift. The whole dilapidated room—the peeling paint, the dirty pallets, the bug-smeared windows—all thrown into sharp relief.

The man at the head of the squad raised a fist. The men behind him pointed their guns at the floor. He wore organic field gear gone black for night fighting, and there were black thumbprints beneath his eyes.

Then the room went dim again, lit only by the residual glow from the windows and the green lights of the guns.

More screaming sounded below. More pounding feet.

"This room is clear!" the squad leader shouted.

The men behind him fell back.

For a long moment more, Nyx and the squad leader stood eye to eye, the way she had with Khos.

"You're on the wrong side of the border, bel dame," the man said softly.

"We all are," Nyx said.

And then the man turned back into the hall. He kicked the door closed.

Rhys let out his breath.

"Fuck," Khos muttered.

The sounds of the men and the shouting receded, headed further downstairs.

"The second squad's holding," Anneke said, from the window.

Nyx turned back into the room. Rhys watched her. She looked at him. Khos walked across the room to keep watch at the window with Anneke.

"They're clearing out," Khos said.

"Yes," Nyx said.

Rhys sat back down on the pallet on the floor, suddenly sick. "What were you going to do if they didn't stand down?" he asked.

"Kill them," Nyx said.

Rhys shook his head.

Nyx crouched next to him and leaned in so their faces were a hand's breadth apart. "What were *you* going to do?" she said. "Where was my wasp swarm, magician? Where were the bugs I pay you for?"

Rhys didn't answer.

"That's what I thought," she said, and joined the others at the window.

19.

Nyx stumbled into a call booth after the others were asleep in the garret room she'd secured at the low end of Dadfar. The streets of Dadfar were dark, too dark, and they stank like Chenja. She hated the way their cities smelled, and she hated the sounds of their stupid language. It was enough like Nasheenian that when they started talking she expected she could understand them. Then she really heard them, and realized they were speaking something entirely different. The streets were wet; they had gotten into town the day before at the end of some local celebration, probably a mass wedding or a mass funeral involving decadent displays of water wealth.

She made a call. She was very drunk. The liquor wasn't local. Chenja was dry, as a rule, and she'd had Anneke smuggle in several bottles of whiskey. She was going to need all of them to get through this job.

She heard the faint whir of a burst siren, somewhere to the east. Burst sirens sounded the same everywhere. They were all manufactured in Tirhan.

The line opened up, crackled, spit, then:

"Yes?"

"I'm looking to speak to Yah Tayyib," Nyx slurred.

"May I say who's calling?"

"Nyxnissa so Dasheem." She nearly added, "Tell that fucker I'm coming for him, and I've got the queen's leave to do it if he's bloodied his hands with this." But she bit her tongue. A teenage boy ran down the street. Someone shouted from the rooftop. Fuck it all if it wasn't nearly midnight prayer. The street was going to be singing a dead language in about five minutes.

A long pause.

"One moment."

Nyx waited. There was some noise coming from the other end of the line—the low hum of bugs, the sound of somebody practicing on a speed bag.

"I'm sorry, Yah Tayyib is indisposed."

"You told him who this is?"

"Yes."

"Tell him again. Tell him I have a question for him."

"I'm sorry, Yah Tayyib isn't taking calls."

"Tell him I know what he's doing with Nikodem."

The muezzin cried. The speakers along the street took up the call. The world was full of prayer, social submission to God.

Nyx hung up.

Nyx woke just before dawn, as the call of the muezzin to dawn prayer sounded across Dadfar. The city pooled at the edge of the desert sea just northwest of the mining town of Zikiri in the Chenjan interior. When the wind blew the wrong way, Dadfar got misted over in a fine haze of toxic grit. The city used to sit along a broad river, maybe a thousand years before, but the river was gone now, and the sand had swallowed any record of it.

Nyx pushed off her sweat-soaked sheet and swung her legs to the floor, rubbing at her eyes. From her garret room, with the shutters open, she saw a sliver of bloody red light spread across the city's skyline and swallow the blue haze of the first sun. She felt stiff and sore. She stretched out as dawn broke.

In the main room, she heard Anneke and Khos stir. Rhys was already praying. She was tired.

She poured herself a shot from the bottle by the bed and sank it.

Something was pulling at her, something she was unhappy with. She couldn't name it. She had taken a risk with the call to Yah Tayyib, but if he thought she knew more than she did, he might try playing all his cards too soon—if he was the magician who ran off with Nikodem. Nyx would have bet her left kidney he was. Yah Tayyib was in the breeding compound records, and he'd been with Nikodem the night she disappeared.

She took another shot of whiskey and got dressed.

Nyx pushed back the curtain into the common room.

"Anneke, I need you to bind me up."

Anneke trudged in, tossed her scattergun on the bed, and re-bound Nyx's breasts. She yanked at the fabric and grunted as she fastened it.

"I'd like to breathe," Nyx said. "Ease up."

"Your tits are too big."

"I haven't heard any complaints."

"I'm complaining."

"Huh," Nyx said. She pulled on a long tunic and burnous and tucked her botched hair up under a gutra and fastened it with an aghal. She needed to cut her hair again properly. She hated short hair.

"You ready, Anneke?"

Anneke slung her scattergun over her shoulder and went back out into the main room for her rifle. "Ready, boss."

"You don't think that's a little much?"

"Not where we're going," Anneke said.

"Khos, you're doing recon today," Nyx said.

"Yeah," he said.

She glanced at the curtain Rhys had hidden himself behind. Didn't bother. Sometimes he just exhausted her. He wasn't happy about Chenja. Or the liquor. He was never happy about anything.

"Let's go," she said.

She and Anneke walked out to the bakkie. Nyx did a quick check for explosives, then they both got in and drove to a local teahouse.

Chenjans dressed far more conservatively than Nasheenians, and it was probably the reason they suffered from fewer cancers. The people they drove past and shared the road with wore brightly colored vests and long coats and trousers and aghals and burnouses, and even some of the men veiled their faces. She expected to see more men in Chenja than she did in Nasheen, but unless there was a political rally or she stood outside a mosque around prayer time, the people on the street were still mostly women. All of the women wore veils and covered their hair, and most wore chadors. The few men she saw were swaggering old men or boys young enough to be the grandsons or great-grandsons of the old men. In Chenja, all of the street signs were in the prayer language, not local Chenjan, which was a similar script but not identical. Nyx's Chenjan wasn't the best, but she was better with the prayer script.

Luckily, Anneke knew the streets of Dadfar pretty well. She and Raine had worked in Chenja for a couple of years, and she had family in the city, so when Nyx said they needed to find out about a boxing gym—violent sports and gambling were outlawed in Chenja—Anneke knew the right teahouse.

The tea house sold tea and marijuana, and business looked slow. A couple of prayer wheels hung in the window. Most of the patrons were men either too young to be at the front or too old to get sent back. The old men played board games and smoked marijuana. The boys talked about weapons and girls. A gaggle of chador-clad women sat at the back, laughing in high, loud voices. Like all Chenjans, they wore clothing in gaudy, mismatched colors, as if making up for the fact that they had to live without liquor.

Nyx found a table close enough to the rear door to comfort her and sat with her back to the wall. Behind her there was a massive flaking gilt frame with a picture of some Chenjan martyr on it. Maybe the owner's son. Nyx wondered why it was that the prescription against images of living things didn't apply to martyrs, just the Prophet and everything else.

"You sure this is the right place?" she asked Anneke in her broken Chenjan.

Anneke waved over the older woman standing behind the counter and started chatting to her in Chenjan. The woman, unveiled and pushing fifty, brought them tea and sat down and drank it with them. Nyx could follow most of what she said. The bar matron knew one of Anneke's sisters. She'd been widowed. Owning the teahouse paid the bills. She and her daughters kept it running. The man on the wall was her husband. He had been one of the suicide soldiers who bombed the Nasheenian breeding compounds three decades before.

Nyx looked up at the image on the wall again, examined the eyes. She wondered if she'd ever looked like that: the absolute faith, the grim purpose.

They exchanged a few more words about abandoned buildings and boxing, and then the bar matron lowered her voice and nodded.

Anneke said to Nyx, in Nasheenian, low, "Yeah, she's heard rumors of fights. Doesn't much like the idea of fighting in this town, but her husband used to do some of it."

They finished their tea, and the matron left to tend to the others. Anneke stood.

"We're good?" Nyx said.

"Yeah. There's supposed to be a fight in a few days about three or four kilometers from here at an abandoned waterworks. They hold a lot of illegal fights there."

"Good," Nyx said.

Anneke shrugged as they stepped back out into the heat of the day. "Well, that was easy. Let's get lunch. She owns the bakery next door."

"I'm not in the mood for sweets," Nyx said.

They picked up a couple of stuffed rotis at a food cart in the town square. It was market day, and the square was choked with merchants selling prayer rugs, scarves, hijabs, burnouses, baskets, dried meat, protein cakes, rotis, braided bread... just about anything Nyx could think of, and more besides. There were butchers and pseudo-magicians and what Nyx figured were probably gene pirates selling their services—real magicians didn't advertise in markets—and one of the fakes was hawking what he said were human organs in jars laced with ice flies.

She saw a long line of people—men and women—dressed from head to toe in white, making their way across the square. The white marked them as Tirhani pilgrims, and they bore their temporary visas around their necks. Dadfar was the death place of the Tirhani martyr, Manijeh Nassu, one of the daughters of the Chenjan caliph, back when they had one. She had led southern Chenja in revolt against the north and died trying to get water for her group of fighters after they were cut off from the only well for miles. Nyx remembered the water on the streets the night before, and wondered now if it had been some kind of Tirhani pilgrim thing.

"Bloody fucking dung beetles," Anneke muttered, following her look. "You watch them. Someday they're going to show up here, guns hot, telling us they're our bloody liberators come to save us from ourselves."

"After selling guns to both sides," Nyx said. "It's real easy to sit out there on the coast playing holier than thou and getting fat off someone else's war." It was Chenja's reliance on Tirhani weapons that kept Tirhani pilgrims getting visas, and Nasheenian reliance on the same that kept them ferrying bug tech and magicians by the boatload to Tirhan. Fucking dung beetles.

Across the square was a mosque, and the muezzin called out mid-morning prayer, bringing most of the activity in the market to a halt. Anneke dusted off the sidewalk in front of her and pulled the prayer rug from her back. Going into the mosque would have been risky. Always better to pray outside official spaces when you were cross-dressing in Chenja.

Nyx wandered through the market as it cleared out. She bought a couple of mangoes—Rhys liked mangoes—and another roti. Most Chenjan food was shit, but there was nothing better than a good roti.

She looked over the stalls nearest her and saw Anneke still prone on the sidewalk. She walked a little more until she came to the other side of the square, where a veiled woman sold prayer rugs. On the street behind the woman, a bakkie sat idling, its windows opaqued. Nyx started eating a mango as she watched the bakkie. Strange to leave your bakkie idling while you hopped into the mosque for mid-morning prayer. Chenjans weren't any more honest than Nasheenians, no matter what Rhys said. Somebody was liable to steal their transport. If not Nyx, then somebody like her.

The veiled woman who owned the stall was praying. The day was going to be hot. Nyx smelled curry over protein cakes and grimaced. Chenja.

She turned again to look for Anneke. As she did, she saw a flurry of movement out of the corner of her eye. She ducked and thrust her elbow behind her. She caught somebody in the gut.

A bag went over her head, and the light bled away.

Nyx kicked out, but she was already off her feet. Something hard hit her in the head. She let out a long scream, hoping somebody around her would note that she wasn't being kidnapped willingly.

Somebody shouted something. Nyx got hit in the head again.

A bakkie door opened, and she was shoved inside. Her captor took the bag off her head. Nyx had one dizzying moment to look into Rasheeda's grinning face before her sister thrust a toxic scarab beetle into her mouth and gagged her with a rag.

Nyx choked on the beetle as its poison trickled down her throat, turning the world gray and hazy, making her too drugged to move.

20

Nyx forced herself to focus. The poison was wearing off. She'd eaten most of the beetle while trying to breathe. Her head felt too heavy to hold up. She was strapped to a chair bolted to the floor. She was naked. She hadn't recognized the other women who stripped her and searched her, but she knew Rasheeda was working this with another sister. If Rasheeda had been working alone, she would have just killed Nyx.

Nyx tried raising her head again and looked around. The room was dim. The floor was gritty and oddly damp. The whole room felt too damp. It was probably a basement room dug just above the old riverbed.

She tugged at her bonds—organic rope that fed off her sweat and blood. The more she moved, the tougher it got. Over that, barbed wire twisted into some bizarre shapes on the arm rests. Rasheeda liked to twist restraining wire into grim parodies of faces. They'd trussed her feet as well and pinned her at her elbows and wrists so she had to sit a certain way or risk losing circulation in her arms. She wished they'd tied something around her head to keep it up. She let it sink again.

Time stretched. Her head cleared. She was cold and thirsty. There was something wrong with her legs. She held her urine as long as she could before finally pissing herself. That was part of the game, of course, leaving her in a pool of her own urine, so thirsty she'd drink it if she could reach it. The light globe above her was never shuttered. How long they waited until they came to her depended on how desperate they were for information.

But what information? About Nikodem and the boxing? They'd know about that. Rasheeda didn't want Nikodem anyway. Their goal was to keep her away from Nikodem, wasn't it? Or were they using her to find Nikodem? What was this, another intimidation game?

She waited. Her body stiffened. She tried flexing her arms, her back, her shoulders, her legs. She was going to start losing feeling in her limbs if she didn't find a way to move.

Nyx finally managed to get a look at her legs. Bloody wounds crisscrossed her flesh. The lines moved and wriggled. Alive.

They'd stuffed her wounds with bloodworms.

Her gut roiled. She looked up again. Something moved in the far dark corner of the room in the broken masonry. She briefly saw the shiny head of a giant centipede peek through. The pain would kick in soon—maybe another couple hours—when the bloodworms had excreted enough poison into her skin to start the slow burn. Her lower limbs already tingled.

She avoided thinking about her team. She didn't think about the interrogation, about what she'd seen Rasheeda do to people. Instead, she thought about the black sand of Tirhan, the kind she'd spun stories about back in Mushirah. She thought about sitting on a deck under a couple of broad-leafed palm trees surrounded in dark green foliage, sipping cool coconut drinks spiked with vodka.

She thought about counting stars with Tej, and she remembered the good nights with that girl, what was her name? Radeyah, yes. Radeyah, with the kind eyes and quick tongue who'd told her they'd spend a lifetime growing old together in the same bed in a little beach house in Tirhan, though all that water in one place scared the shit out of Nyx. But Radeyah's boy lover had come back from the front—most of him—and dreams of Tirhan and vodka and a lifetime of Radeyah's sweet tongue and soft hands had ended.

She had told that story again, though, wrapped in bed with another sort of woman, a desperate outrider. Told her all about Tirhani beaches she had never been to and never wanted to see—*"Don't tell anyone what I'm about to tell you…"*—but Nyx had lied and whispered to her Radeyah's dream, not her own, because Jaks loved the sea, dreamed of the sea. Nyx had learned that from one of Jaks's house sisters, the one who told her about Arran.

Arran. The note that killed Tej.

Nyx used them all to get to somebody else, to pick up some other note. It was her job. It's what she did.

The door opened.

Nyx raised her head.

Rasheeda walked in, wearing loose trousers and a short coat. Her black hair was pulled back from her cool, flawless face, and she was grinning. Her eyes were flat and black and, paired with the grin, she looked like some kind of demon, something come up straight from hell to inhabit a soulless body. She carried a bag and a stool.

Behind her was Fatima.

Nyx wasn't surprised. This was the sort of job Fatima would pull. Fatima was skinny—skinnier than Nyx had ever seen her—and her dark hair was shot through with white; very becoming on a Nasheenian woman. Fatima fixed a hard look on Nyx, then shut the door. Nyx hadn't seen Fatima since she sent Nyx to prison.

Rasheeda snickered and set the stool in front of Nyx, just far enough away so Nyx couldn't bite her nose off.

Fatima sat as Rasheeda unpacked her instruments from her bag.

"You look terrible," Fatima said.

Nyx only looked at her.

Fatima's mouth quirked up at the corners, not a smile. "You were much more difficult to track when you worked alone."

Fatima waited a bare moment, glancing over at Rasheeda as the other bel dame laid out a series of scalpels and straight pins and blinking syringes on a scarlet-colored length of silk.

"You were told to stay off this note," Fatima said. "Rasheeda and Luce were clear, as I understand it. Yet here you are, far from Nasheen, looking up an off-worlder. Where are Kine's papers? I searched your safe house. Are they in the country? Who else knows about them?"

Nyx clenched her teeth.

"Your team's dead," Fatima said.

"You're a bad liar," Nyx said. "If you toasted my team you'd have told me all about the street they were on and the way you killed them. You wouldn't stop with half-assed declarations. You're a bel dame."

Fatima's mouth quirked again. "You think so? If you leave this place alive, perhaps we'll see."

Nyx grunted.

"We know you were at Kine's," Fatima said. "Did you speak to her before her death? What do you know about her work?"

Kine and her goddamn papers.

Nyx shifted a little in her chair. If she started talking, she'd be in trouble. She could make up stories, sure, but she didn't trust that after several days of torture, she'd be able to keep the stories straight. But silence implied submission, and she wasn't keen on submitting to anyone—not Fatima, not the magicians, not the queen, not God.

"I have no wish to send you home in pieces," Fatima said.

Rasheeda squatted next to the instruments, giggling.

"Tell me," Nyx said, "what do bel dames want with information from the compounds? Thought you would be on good terms with their security."

"I want to know what *you* know about Kine."

"What do you know about Kine?"

"Oh, stop it," Fatima said, and her expression got ugly. "You want us to chop you up and leave you here?"

"You should have asked my team before you killed them," Nyx said. "They'd have known just as much about Kine as I do." Burning the pages had been a good idea. If the bel dames wanted the papers and wanted to keep Nyx off the note, it meant they were probably working with Nikodem. They wanted her to stay hidden. In Chenja.

Sweet fuck, Nyx thought, *are the bel dames working with the Chenjans?* Were they working some kind of deal together to topple the monarchy?

"I don't have any patience this afternoon, Nyxnissa."

Nyx tacked that down. Afternoon. Not of the same day she was brought in, though, right? So she'd lost a day?

"You never did have much patience, sister-mine," Nyx said, "and I don't have much patience for traitors. When did you all decide to sell out Nasheen?"

"Rasheeda?"

Rasheeda grabbed the back of Nyx's chair and tilted it. She turned Nyx around so she could see the tub of water behind her. A thin layer of ice coated the surface. The tub was padded around the base by a band of insulation that hummed.

"Those are expensive bugs," Nyx said.

Rasheeda pushed Nyx over.

Nyx went into the water face first. The lip of the tub caught her in the gut. Her head banged the bottom of the tub.

Cold hit her like a fist to the face.

The first time under, she didn't thrash, just shut her eyes and felt the cold eat into her bones.

Rasheeda pulled her back up. Nyx gasped and went back under, banging her head on the bottom again.

The third time under, she started to struggle, but Rasheeda had the advantage, and the cold was starting to muddle Nyx's head. Black ate away at her thoughts. It felt like descending into the bowels of Umayma. She opened her mouth to breathe, and sucked in cold water instead.

It went on for a long time. They hauled her out fully once or twice, left her gasping in the chair like a spent swimmer, asked her some questions that didn't make sense anymore, and then forced her back under.

Finally, Rasheeda got tired, or Fatima got tired. Probably Fatima.

Rasheeda hauled Nyx out of the water and let her chair fall sideways onto the floor, so Nyx had a watery view of Fatima's sandaled feet.

"Kine's papers," Fatima said. "I want them. Where are they? They belong in Nasheen, not here. You've run black work before. You think I'm a fool? Who did you sell them to?"

Rasheeda bent over and gazed into Nyx's face, blotting out the light. Nyx coughed up cold water. She shivered uncontrollably.

Fatima wrinkled her nose, said to Rasheeda. "Give me a couple of her fingers."

Rasheeda licked her lips. "I want her eyes."

Nyx's thoughts were dark and sticky. Fatima thinks I killed my sister. But Rasheeda killed my sister. Why doesn't Fatima know that Rasheeda killed my sister? Why was Rasheeda only slowing me down, but Dahab wanted to stop me?

Sticky thoughts. Black thoughts.

Something congealed. Rasheeda had slowed her down so she could kill Kine before Nyx got there. Rasheeda didn't have leave from the council to kill Nyx. Rasheeda was running something on her own. Fatima was doing clean bel dame work, retrieving stolen Nasheenian information she thought Nyx had. Fatima had no idea Rasheeda was running black.

"Let's save the eyes for later," Fatima said. She pointed. "Give me those two fingers."

Rasheeda set Nyx's chair upright. The wire had dug into Nyx's flesh now, drawn blood. She couldn't feel it, though, just pressure. What she did feel were the bloodworms boring into her flesh. Her legs were on fire, and the rest of her was numb.

Rasheeda picked up a cleaver. She pressed the heel of her palm onto the back of Nyx's right hand, made her splay her fingers across the armrest.

They're just fingers, Nyx thought. She brought her head up so she could look Fatima in the face.

"I didn't kill my sister," Nyx slurred.

Rasheeda brought the knife down on her ring and little fingers. Nyx felt pressure, heard the crunch. Pain. Just pain. Pain is a message. That's all.

Fatima flinched.

Nyx didn't.

Rasheeda hacked at Nyx's hand again. She hadn't made a clean cut.

Nyx kept her breathing steady, not looking at her hand. Her fingers—or where she was supposed to have fingers—ached. She coughed up more water. She wanted to claw at her burning legs. She wished it was her legs they cut off.

Rasheeda wiped something onto the floor with the knife. Nyx heard a dull thumping sound. Her fingers hitting the gritty floor.

Rasheeda licked the knife.

"Kine's papers. Or should I take the whole hand?" Fatima asked. "Another day or two and the worms will have your legs…"

The first time Nyx was tortured, Raine had done it.

She had been doing her own side work, her first contract with a gene pirate. She hadn't known what the woman was, at first, just knew she was paying well for an easy job—plug some organic material into Nyx's body and have Nyx drive it over to some shady dealer in a border town. The dealer had cut it out, no problem, and suddenly she had more money in her account than she'd ever seen in her life.

Raine had figured it out. How, Nyx never knew. Maybe he kept tabs on her account. He had beat her bloody, called her a traitor to her own country. He'd bound her and left her.

When he came back for her a day later, she lay in the dark, in a pool of her own piss, hungry and dehydrated. He had loomed over her and cut off her ear with one quick slice of a sharp knife.

"A souvenir," he'd said, holding her bloody flesh in his hand.

He kept a collection of ears in his freezer from every bounty he took. She had thought the collection was funny, until he'd added a piece of her to it, like she was just another thing to be used and discarded. Another body. Like a boy at the front.

He had expected her to stay on with his crew. It was just a little discipline, he'd said, nothing worse than what had happened to her at the front, right?

She had bided her time for three days, then went into his room in the middle of the night after a long, heavy day of footwork and drinking; a coward's fight. She'd trussed him up and cut off his cock. She considered the act her formal resignation.

"Just a little souvenir," she'd told him while he screamed and strained against his bonds.

The first notes she'd taken as a bel dame were for his sons. They had deserted from the front, following their father's radical politics. She had sent their ears to Raine.

Nyx was not a nice woman. She knew she didn't deal with nice women. But she also knew the worst sorts of things these women could do to her, and there was comfort in that.

There would be no surprises.

"You can take what you want," Nyx said, "but remember what I took from Raine. I'll take everything from you, Fatima. Your face, your license, your lover, your daughters."

Rasheeda snickered. "Such a funny woman! And what will you take from me, eh? Sitting there bleeding in your little chair!"

"Oh," Nyx said. "I'm going to *kill* you."

Rasheeda snorted.

"Bind her fingers," Fatima said, and stood. "Tomorrow we want Kine's papers. Or we take your hands. Then your eyes. Think about that. And the loss of your legs in thirty-six hours."

Fatima walked out. Rasheeda bound up Nyx's hand, then beat her until her face swelled and her ribs ached and she hacked up blood. Rasheeda left her, bruised and bleeding.

When the door closed, Nyx murmured, "Kine, you bitch."

She drooled blood and saliva into her lap and let her head hang. Telling them about Kine's papers meant telling them where Taite was. If they'd killed her team—and she had an image of the whole garret burning, of Khos cut into pieces, Anneke's face blown away, Rhys... she could at least keep them from Taite for a while. Just a little while.

21

Taite listened to the results of the vote come in over the com. He ate from a carton of take-out food, spicy even for his taste, a Nasheenian imitation of Ras Tiegan food.

All the news was bad.

As the provinces reported in, his hopes sank. Eighty-seven percent of Abyyad district in favor of drafting half-breeds. Sixty-eight percent in favor. Ninety-eight percent in favor. Ninety-eight percent? That was from a district out on the coast, where they'd never even seen a male over the age of six, let alone a half-breed. What did they care if he got blown up at the front?

Taite was getting sick. He turned off the com.

Taite had gone through Kine's collection and gotten rid of everything but three recordings, which turned out to be her dictation sessions. It took a couple of days to break her personal security code, but once he mastered that, it was easy to loop them into the com and read them back. He was only fifteen minutes in, but the voting numbers had gotten to him, and he had opened up his bankbook instead of listening to transcriptions.

The only way to make it work was to move Inaya to one of the factory compounds in Basmah and have her keep her job there. It meant no recovery time after the baby came. It also meant living dormitory-style with no security. She wasn't going to be happy, but unless they collected this bounty soon, he was out of extravagant options. Mahdesh had already loaned him more money than Taite knew how to pay back, and though Mahdesh asked for nothing in return, Taite worried over it—spending his lover's money to help the sister who would burn them both if she knew.

He heard someone coming up the stairs and stopped his work. He grabbed his pistol.

Whoever it was knocked three times.

"It's Husayn."

He stood, and opened the door. Husayn had a haggard, wide-eyed look, as if death itself had clawed at her from the desert.

"What's wrong?" he asked.

"Someone's here, says she's your sister."

"What's she look like?"

"Half-breed, like you. Pale. Pregnant. Real, real upset."

"Send her up."

Husayn walked back down.

Taite put the gun in his belt. He'd told her not to come unless it was urgent. Had something happened, or was she still angry at being roomed with whores? She couldn't stay here. There was no way to get her to work from Aludra.

He went to the covered window and peeked out. It was dark outside. At least she'd waited for dark.

He heard her huffing up the stairs and ran back to the doorway.

Sweat pouring down her face, she stumbled on the last step, and he caught her.

She was crying.

"What is it?" he asked. "What's going on?"

They both sagged to the floor. He held her as she sobbed and clutched at him.

"What happened? Did somebody do something to you? Inaya?" If they'd touched her, if anyone had touched her—

"Raine is looking for you," she said.

"What?"

"He came to the brothel. I don't know how he found me. The

mistress screamed at him, and he shot her. He shot her in the head!"

"What happened?"

"He said he'd take you in pieces, Taitie. He said… he said terrible things. I thought he'd cut me. I thought—"

"What did you say to him?" Taite started looking around the room for what he could grab and run.

"I said I didn't know where you were. I swear, I said it."

"Inaya," Taite said gently. He took her by her wrists and pulled her off him, looked into her red-rimmed eyes. "Inaya, thank you for that. But, Inaya, you've led him here." The sister he'd known in Ras Tieg would never have been so careless. What had become of her? Who had she become back in Ras Tieg, casting votes the way her husband told her to, turning away from her own kind, damning her own parents? He could understand her desire for protection. He could understand turning away from the movement that had cost them everything, but where was the woman he remembered, the one who could hack a com and retrofit a gun, the woman who had helped wash and soothe their mother after the worst of the attacks?

Her eyes widened. She looked over her shoulder at the door.

"We have to move," he said.

"He said he wanted you to tell him where Nyx was. He said… he said…."

Taite grabbed his pack, threw in some bursts, his wallet, and his bank book. He grabbed a couple of transceivers from the com and threw in Kine's dictation sessions.

He took Inaya's hand. "There's a back stair. Please, please hurry."

Inaya was still sobbing. "I can't. I can't get up. I'm so tired."

"You can. Come here. Get up."

Taite lifted her. He didn't know how he did it, picking up his older sister, this towering figure he had so admired before his exile. The strong one. The shifter. He dragged Inaya toward the hidden door at the back, opened it. He heard someone else on the stairs behind them. A lot of someones.

He was fucked.

He looked into Inaya's tear-stained face and took it into his hands. "Go to Nyx," he said. "She's in a garret in Dadfar, in the Rihaada district on Lower Maida and Seventh. Are you listening to me? You need to cross the border. Do you understand? You need to cross the border."

"I can't go to Chenja! They'll kill me on sight, the bursts—"

"You *can*," Taite said. He kissed her forehead, her lips, her eyelids. He had a memory of his mother doing the same to him, the last he ever saw of her. He could not remember her face. "You can… A bird can fly across a border."

"Don't ask me to do that. Never ask me to do that!"

He shook her. "Then you'll die here with me, do you understand?" He shouted at her, and his gut churned as he shouted. He sounded like their father. He threw his pack at her. "Take that. There's water in Husayn's bakkie, and a couple bucks in change in my pack. Get the fuck out of here! Right now. Right now!"

"Taite!"

He prodded her into the dark stairwell and shut the door behind her.

He pulled out his pistol and crept behind the com. In the sudden silence, the quiet dim, he looked up at his little saint, at Baldomerus, and he prayed.

When they walked in, Taite started shooting.

22

Nyx faded in and out of awareness. For a time, she thought she heard voices outside the door. The sound of moist clicking, the shuffle of insectile legs, roused her.

When she looked down, she saw a giant centipede gnawing at her left leg with its finger-long pincers. She yelled and jerked in the chair, scaring it back into its hole in the masonry. Her body was instantly covered in a sheen of cold sweat. She fought to stay conscious.

When she next came to, Luce was standing over her.

"Doesn't look like so much now, does she?" Luce said. She took Nyx by the hair and searched her face.

Nyx faded again.

She dreamed of water. Cool, suffocating water. She swam in a great lake so clear and blue she could see the ruins of old cities below. And then she was drowning in it, drowning in cold, pulled down toward the dead cities, cities full of sand. So cold.

Someone dumped a bucket of water over her. She came to with a start.

"You stink," Luce said, and set the bucket next to her.

Fatima was closing the door.

They had left the chair from their last visit, and Fatima sat in it again.

"Good morning, Nyxnissa," Fatima said.

Nyx licked at the moisture on her lips. Her hands had gone

numb. She tried to flex them—the fingers she had and the fingers she thought she had. Her whole body was stiff and growing increasingly unresponsive. One of her eyes was swollen shut. She peered at the bel dames and wondered where Rasheeda was.

"I believe I was asking you yesterday where Kine's papers were," Fatima said. "I think it's an easy question. One answer and we give you some water. What do you think of that?"

What Nyx thought was that her throat was so dry she couldn't speak. But she was no good to them dead.

She moved her mouth but didn't let any sound out.

"What's that?" Fatima said, leaning toward her. She gestured irritably at Luce.

Luce walked out and came back with a water bulb. She held it to Nyx's lips and let her drink.

Nyx gulped it all down, licked her lips again. She tried to grin, but it hurt to move her face.

"Kine's papers," Fatima said.

"I didn't kill her," Nyx rasped.

A sound came from outside the door, muffled.

"What was that?" Fatima said.

"Sounds like a dog," Luce said. "I'll check it out, but the filters are up. No shifter is getting through that filter."

Luce opened the door. She didn't close it, and Nyx heard her heading upstairs. From the open door came the unmistakable sound of a barking dog.

"Why bother holding out now, sister-mine?" Fatima said, and her voice softened. "There's no one in this world who will know or care if you live or die. I am your sister. This time next year, I'll be on the bel dame council. You understand that? Why not tell me what I need and we'll welcome you back, sister. Isn't that what you wanted? Kine's papers, and all's forgiven. Do you hear me, Nyxnissa? I have the power to make you a bel dame again. No one else would give you that."

Nyx was drooling on herself again. She blinked a few times and raised her head. "You think I'm fucking stupid?"

"The thought had crossed my mind," Fatima said, and her tone flattened again.

"Teams are replaceable," Nyx said. "I'll get another team. You want your seat on the council, you'll have to torture something useful out of some other woman."

"Your sisters were all you had, Nyxnissa, and in your greed you lost us. I've never met a woman so despised."

"Yes, you have."

"Is that so? I have three daughters and a son at the front," Fatima said. "My lover is descended from the First Families. You? You have nothing. No one."

Nyx heard a soft clicking from outside the door. She raised her head an inch, just an inch, and saw a fist-size black roach skitter into the room.

Nyx shut her eyes.

There was a pop and a flash that Nyx could see even from behind her eyelids. Flash bug.

Fatima cried out.

A gun went off. Fatima screeched again. Noise and movement.

Nyx opened her eyes.

Khos stood next to her, naked, and covered in mucus, still shaking off the last of his dog hair. Anneke was in the doorway. She threw him a pair of cutters.

He bent and worked at Nyx's bonds.

Fatima was crawling toward one corner of the room, clutching at her bleeding face.

Nyx looked down dumbly at her own ruined, swollen hand as Khos worked.

"Go, go! Hurry up!" Anneke said.

A swarm of locusts burst through the door, throwing it wide, and circled the room.

Nyx heard Rhys's voice then, from outside. "The other rooms are clear, but Rasheeda's heading back this way."

"Do we have another exit?" Anneke asked.

Khos cut the last of the wire from Nyx's elbows and started on her legs. Nyx tried flexing her fingers. Everything was numb. Even her legs now. She leaned over and coughed up blood.

Khos finished with her legs.

She tried to push herself up, tried to stand. Her whole body shook. Pain blazed up her legs as circulation returned. She looked down and saw blood leaking from the wide, wriggling wounds. If she let go of the armrest, her legs would buckle.

Khos scooped her into his arms. She had forgotten how big he was. She looped her bad arm around his neck and tangled the fingers of her other hand into his dreads.

He carried her outside the little room and up the stairs. They were in some kind of busted-out tenement building. It stank of piss and dogs and human shit. Anneke yelled something at Khos. Rhys was at the top of the stairs. A halo of dragonflies circled his head. He was very beautiful.

"Out," Rhys said. "Right now. She's coming in the back."

They barreled out the front of the building. Khos set Nyx in the back of the bakkie as if she were made of glass. Blood smeared the seat. Khos started the bakkie, and Anneke slung into the front. Rhys climbed in next to Nyx and held her.

It was strange, being held.

Anneke had her rifle pointed out the window. "Go! Go!" she yelled. She fired.

Nyx heard something scream.

Anneke fired again.

"What the fuck was that?" Khos said.

Anneke spit out the window. "It ain't illegal to kill bel dames in Chenja."

"Is anything broken?" Rhys asked Nyx as he ran his hands over her. "You know what day it is?"

She named a date, two days after her market trip with Anneke.

"That's about right," he said. He pushed her cropped hair out of her bruised face. "Did they break anything?"

"Been coughing up blood," she murmured.

"All right," he said. He touched her bandaged hand. "They put anything on this?"

"No."

"All right. I can put something on it. You'll lose the whole hand if it goes gangrenous." He passed his hand over her legs, and she felt a nasty prickling. The worms writhed.

Rhys knit his brows, splayed his fingers, and as the minutes slid by, the worms began to drop off, one by one.

My magician, she thought.

"Where are we going?" Nyx asked.

"I have a place," Khos said. "Don't worry about it. They'll give us harbor as long as we need it. We cleared out after you went missing. Before they searched the safehouse."

"Yes," Nyx said.

"They told you about that?" Rhys asked.

"They said you were all dead."

"We don't go down that easy," Anneke said.

"No," Nyx said as the lights outside blurred past, as Rhys sat with one arm holding her to him as Anneke kept watch at the windows, her rifle out, and as Khos drove to someplace she'd never been, in a foreign country that hated her and her people almost as much as she hated them. Her head felt like someone else's. Someone else's broken body. She had been here before.

"That's all right," she said.

"You need anything?" Khos asked. "You need some water? I've got some up front."

"No, no," Nyx said, "but I could use a whiskey."

She rolled her head against Rhys's shoulder and passed out.

23

Khos had spent his teenage years on the streets of Mhoria. He had spent one too many nights on the other side of the great divide that separated men's and women's worlds, and the priests—the rhabbams—had cast him out of polite society for it. So Khos had made his way as a petty thief and errand runner for a while, and had gotten into his fair share of fistfights. He had seen a lot of maggoty wounds, of bodies devoured by bugs and dogs. On Nyx's crew, he had seen and done worse. But he had never seen it or done it to anyone on his team.

Nyx looked horrible. He sat at her bedside and tried to tell himself it was her own fucking fault. She was the most Nasheenian woman he knew, and that made her headstrong and arrogant and skilled enough to cut his head off if it caught her fancy.

"How did you find me?" Nyx asked. He and Rhys had gotten her to take in some water, a little food. Rhys had done some bug work on her face and cleaned up her legs, but they had to hire a local hedge witch to do the rest, which Rhys seemed to find embarrassing. Useless fucking magician, Khos thought. He never understood why Nyx kept him on the team. He wished she'd fuck the little prick and get it over with.

She lay behind a gauzy curtain in a discrete room. He'd shown her the lock on the door, and told her she was at the top of the house. There was a narrow grill far up on the wall. He could hear the splash of the fountain in the courtyard.

"I tracked your scent," Khos said. There were no chairs in

the room. The mattress sagged under his weight. "From where Anneke said she lost you. I could only keep up until the edge of the city. After that, Rhys sent out some bugs."

"So what's this place? You just on good terms with every brothel mistress in three countries?"

"No," he said, and hesitated. Then, "All right, it's a brothel, yes, but it's also a safe house we use for the underground."

"We?"

It was stupid to keep her in the dark about it now, but it had become habit over the years. Nyx was a dangerous woman. The people on her team knew that better than anyone, and everyone else she met had a pretty good idea. If she took issue with who he helped, who he betrayed, and the laws he broke, she would murder him for it. He had seen her kill people. It was never pretty.

"I've been helping the local whores in Nasheen smuggle their boys out for the last three years," he said, all in a rush, as if he'd opened a vein.

"Oh, you fuckers," Nyx said. She put a hand over her eyes. "I used to cut off the heads of men like you."

"Yeah, I know."

"Who else is here?"

"We're all here. They agreed to take all of us."

"And of course it's a brothel." Nyx crinkled her mouth. It looked like it hurt. "You must have gotten a lot of grateful women into bed."

"Only the ones who were interested." But none of them was you, Khos thought. He'd had his one night with her in Punjai, early on, before either of them knew who or what the other really was.

She grunted. "Can the underground do anything to help us?"

"You mean besides giving us a safe house where we can help you recover your ass?"

"You know what I mean. I have a great ass."

"You do have a great ass," Khos said. He'd spent a lot of time looking at it over the years, and one night with his hands on it. "Yeah, they'll put us up, and, yeah, they can point us to the waterworks where we can check out fighters. The whores go with patrons to the matches."

"Are any of these whores Nasheenian?"

"Don't take this the wrong way, Nyx, but you couldn't pass for a Chenjan whore. Trust me."

"Not me. You should take Anneke."

"Anneke couldn't play a whore to save her life. In Chenja, she couldn't even pass for a woman if she tried. Rhys and I will go." He hesitated, added, "As *men*."

"All right. Where's Rhys?"

"He's all right."

"Good." She was fading. They'd pumped her with some local drug Rhys had, but she didn't talk or act like a woman who wasn't in pain. She'd rebound, though, he knew. She'd rebound and forget the whole mess, go back to swaggering around. For one sharp moment, he realized he liked her this way, mostly helpless and incredibly vulnerable. But knowing that he was that type of man, that he liked her this way, frightened him. He looked away from her.

"You call a magician?" she asked, moving her maimed hand a bit. "I mean, a real one."

"They're hard to come by, and expensive." Khos paused again. Repairing Nyx's hand was delicate work, and they needed someone far more skilled than a hedge witch. "We don't have the cash."

"Who said that?"

"Rhys."

"Can't I sell something? A kidney? My liver?"

"I think you'll need your liver."

"Maybe a lung. I don't have to run fast."

"I'm not bringing a butcher in here, and a butcher is all we could afford."

"You could just find my fingers and stick them back on."

"You need some sleep, I think."

Nyx tossed her head. "That little dancer will kill me yet."

"I'll have one of the women bring you something to help you sleep," Khos said, and stood.

"At least it was my right hand," Nyx said. Her eyelids began to close. "Rasheeda never could remember I'm a southpaw."

Khos stood over her, and watched her mouth go slack, watched her drift. Half dead and mutilated, and she was already thinking about her next fight.

24

Rhys waited for Khos outside Nyx's room, pacing the hallway. Rhys had done everything he could, called up every bug he had the capacity to control, and it hadn't been enough. Every time he ran his hands over her, the severity of her injuries made him tremble. For all his talk of her godlessness, of God abandoning her, he had never expected this.

I never wanted this.

"How is she?" Rhys asked as Khos came out into the hall. Khos shut the door behind him and gestured for Rhys to follow him back into their shared room.

Inside, Khos said, "She's ready and willing to sell off her body parts for bread, so about as expected." He sat on the bed and stretched out his long legs. "She's the most stubborn bitch I know. She'll be all right. Not for a while, but she'll be all right."

"Did you tell her we haven't been able to get a hold of Taite?"

"No, and she didn't ask about him, praise be. Still nothing?"

"Nothing." Rhys pulled on his burnous. It was almost dawn. None of them had slept, but he wanted to stop at the local mosque and pray before going to clean out the rest of their things from the garret. Khos had warned him that the bel dames had likely blown the place wide open by now, but Rhys needed to check. He had left the stash of Kine's papers back at the garret, and he didn't want the bel dames to find them. If they hadn't already.

Khos stood as well. "I'll drive you," he said.

They'd spent a couple of hours repainting the bakkie with some borrowed paint from the brothel mistress and replacing the tags. Rhys had balked at Khos's choice of safe house. Nasheenian brothels might have been places of political protest and intrigue, but in Chenja they were just brothels. They sold sex and liquor and little else. The whole house smelled of cheap jasmine perfume, liberally applied; it muted but did not cover up the smells of sex and bile and sticky opium.

But they were out of places to go on such short notice. Rhys had no contacts here, and Anneke said her friend's teahouse was too conspicuous.

So it was sex and jasmine.

"Are we going to scout out other rooms?" Rhys asked.

"Once Nyx is up for it," Khos said. "She'll want a say. She gets jumpy when she's not in a place she chooses."

They walked down and got into the bakkie. Khos dropped Rhys at the mosque and pulled out a cigar.

It was the best part of being in Chenja, perhaps the only part that made any of it worth it: There was a mosque at every corner, a call to prayer in every city.

Rhys joined the crowd of others moving into the mosque for prayer. The wave of women was far greater than that of men, a billowing tide of veils and burquas. He joined the trickle of old men, young boys, and the handful of household heads, and performed the ablution with them in the courtyard. He knelt with the other men in a neat row and praised God with them in one voice.

Rhys found a moment of peace in the madness, and he clung to it.

After, Rhys joined Khos in the bakkie. They circled the garret twice to look for movement or some kind of disturbance or for bel dames posting watch along the street. Rhys sent out a swarm of locusts to scout the area. They found nothing in the garret. No bel dames, no mercenaries. Nothing. He tried calling up some wasps to sniff out traps, but there were no local hives except for the one Rhys had set to watch Kine's papers. He'd have to risk it.

"You want to come up and help me detect explosives?" he asked as Khos parked the bakkie four blocks from the building.

Khos grunted. "How'd I be good at that?"

"All right." It was worth asking.

Rhys kept his hood up and walked to the door. The building manager had already replaced the lock that Rhys and Khos had broken while trying to get back in for their gear after Nyx was taken.

Rhys pulled out one of his bug boxes and used a squirt beetle to spray the lock. The metal began to dissolve. Rhys pounded the lock free with his burnous-wrapped hand.

He stepped inside.

There was a dirty, pregnant white woman huddled on the stairs. Either she belonged to one of the other tenements or she had snuck in before the lock on the door was replaced. She wore a dirty hijab. He wondered what she was doing out of the foreigners' ghetto.

Rhys headed up the stairs and made to squeeze past her.

She lifted her head. "Rhys?" she said, and tugged at his trousers.

Rhys's heart leapt. He reached for his pistols.

"I'm Taite's sister," she said frantically. "You remember me? Rhys?"

Her hair was a mess, partially hidden under the dirty hijab. The last time he'd seen Taite's sister, she wasn't yet showing her pregnancy. She had been beautiful and haunted. He didn't remember her being so pale.

"Inaya?" he said. "How did you get over the border?" A half-breed woman passing from Nasheen to Chenja? Across the border?

"I can't… I'm not…" She let out her breath.

"What's happened to Taite?"

"Raine came for him," Inaya said. "Taite told me you were here. I worked the way out."

"Worked out? How did you run the border?"

"I just… did."

"Did anyone follow you?"

"Not this time."

"Not *this* time?"

"They couldn't this time. But Raine followed me to Taite, back in Nasheen." Her eyes began to fill with water. She looked like she'd been crying a good long while.

"Has anyone else gone up past you? How long have you been here?"

"Before dawn. I haven't seen anyone but the man who came to fix the door."

"Good." A Chenjan man with a woman—who was to all eyes foreign—would get him noticed. "Stay here," he said.

"Don't leave me, please!" She grabbed his burnous.

He took her hands, leaned toward her. As he touched her, he felt a curious lack, something he could not name. She had the feeling of a woman free from disease or contagion or petty hurt. Completely free. It was a slick, oily feeling.

He released her hands. "It's all right. I'm getting Khos. We're just around the corner. Stay here. I'll come back. I promise."

She choked back more tears.

Rhys hurried outside. He found Khos and leaned into the bakkie window. "Taite's sister is here."

Khos choked on cigar smoke. He put the cigar out on the dash. "Inaya is here?"

"Yes."

"Oh, fuck." He started to get out of the bakkie.

"Don't," Rhys said. "The three of us walking around together—"

"Her and I together is all right," Khos said. He'd already gotten out. "I can take her. Is she veiled?"

"She has a hijab."

"Good enough."

"Khos, she *hates* shape shifters."

"Yeah," Khos said, and started tying back his dreads. "Did you ever wonder why?"

"I don't—"

"How do you think a pregnant half-breed crossed the border?"

"Oh," Rhys said, and then, "*Oh*. But that's impossible." He remembered taking her hands. He remembered when he first saw her. "I can sense a shifter at three paces. I would have known when I met her."

Khos shrugged. "You've always been a shitty magician."

"Not when it comes to perception."

"What happened to her? She's probably being tailed."

"Raine got Taite."

"Shit."

"Yes."

"All right. I'll take her to a diner in the Mhorian district. You finish up what you need to do here and go tell Nyx what's happening."

"Where will you be?"

"Don't worry about it. I'll make my own way back to the brothel once she's secure."

Rhys left a locust guard on the bakkie, and they both went to the building.

Inaya stood when they entered. When she saw Khos, Rhys saw something in her face harden.

"Khos will take you to a safe place, then we'll get you back to Nyx. We need to clear things with her," Rhys said.

Inaya continued to stare at Khos, her expression grim.

Khos held out his hand.

She turned her head away.

"Taite's probably dead," Khos said. "You come with me and maybe you live. You stay here and you get cut up by bel dames. You choose."

Khos walked back to the door and opened it for her.

Rhys waited a tense moment. He saw a complicated play of emotions on Inaya's face. Then she was moving to the door, awkward with her large belly.

Khos followed her out.

Rhys went upstairs and began the painstaking circle of their garret. It took him another half-hour, looking for traps, to convince himself that they hadn't been here. He pulled Kine's papers out of a hole in the floor that he'd covered over with a board and some more debris. He waved away the wasp guard. At least *that* had worked this time.

Rhys bundled everything into his pack and headed out. He drove the bakkie to the brothel and then went up to talk to Nyx.

Anneke said she was still sleeping.

"I need to get her up," Rhys said. He made to move to the door, but Anneke stepped in front of him. She barely came to his shoulder, but she had firmed up her jaw. Anneke's stubborn look.

"Let her be," Anneke said. "Unless the fucking world is burning."

"Taite's sister is here in Chenja. Raine has Taite."

"Raine?" Anneke said.

He heard Nyx's voice from inside, yelling for water and a pot to piss in.

Anneke opened the door, and Rhys managed to push past her.

Nyx didn't look much better. One eye was still swollen shut, and her head looked too big. She had herself propped up on one elbow.

"What the hell is this? You all want to watch me piss?"

"Raine has Taite," Rhys said, "and Taite's sister is here. She needs sanctuary."

"Can I take a piss first?"

Anneke brought in the pot, and helped Nyx squat over it. Rhys politely turned away.

"Khos is having her wait in a diner," Rhys said, "but we should bring her here."

Rhys waited until Nyx was done, then turned back. Anneke handed him the pot.

"Go dump this," she said.

Rhys wrinkled his nose and took it out, dumping it in the street. Half a dozen blue beetles lit out from the gutters and began to feed. When he returned, Nyx had been moved to the couch in the main room.

"Don't bring Inaya here," Nyx said.

"We can't—"

"Scout out another safe house. If you're still certain she's not being tagged, bring her there. We'll follow. We can't stay in a brothel forever. Underground or not, there are too many people who know we're here. I don't trust wagging Chenjan tongues."

"And what are we going to do about Taite?" Rhys asked.

"You let me deal with that," Nyx said.

Rhys didn't like her tone. "How are you going to deal with that?" he persisted.

"You let me worry about it."

"We could find a safe house closer to the waterworks," Anneke said. She had picked up one of her guns and begun taking it apart. "That's where the fights are."

"Have you been down there yet?" Nyx asked.

"Not yet," Rhys said.

"When we're packed, I want you and Khos to head down there and report back tomorrow. All right?"

Rhys nodded.

Someone knocked at the door. Anneke picked up a rifle from under the divan and answered.

The brothel mistress held a small package in her hands. "This came for you."

"You checked it for organics?" Rhys asked as he passed his hand over it.

"Of course," she said. "It came back organic, just not the sort you mean."

Anneke took the package and opened it up. She unwrapped a layer of stained gauze. Her expression was dark. She handed the package to Nyx.

Rhys leaned in to get a better look.

Nyx unfolded the gauze to reveal a perfectly formed ear, too pale to be Nasheenian or Chenjan. Underneath the ear was a note. Organic paper. It had eaten most of the blood. She held it up in her good hand.

"What does it say?" Rhys asked.

Nyx grunted. "Raine wants to swap Taite for Kine's papers. But if he has Taite, he knows we burned all of those."

"The dictation sessions," Rhys said. "Taite told me he was keeping them to see if he could get any names you wanted." Taite wouldn't have known what Rhys had kept.

Nyx grimaced. "And I bet I have a real good idea where they ended up."

Rhys pressed his hands to his face. There was only one person Taite would have given the dictation sessions to. Why else would he have sent her here?

"God be merciful," Rhys muttered.

"Inaya better hope so," Nyx said, "cause if He's not, Raine is headed right for us."

25

Nyx had Khos carry her into the bombed-out building he and Rhys had found on the south side of the city. She didn't like being carried, but she didn't like the idea of walking any better. She had him put her down on a tattered divan, and when Anneke was done bringing up the gear, they started playing cards while Rhys and Khos went to go pick up Inaya.

Nyx didn't want to make any decisions until she could recognize her own face in a mirror. She needed to run a swap for Taite, she just didn't know what kind. Raine wouldn't have asked about transmissions unless Taite had told him they existed, and there was only one person Taite would give those to without ratting her out by name.

She heard them on the stairs before she saw them but didn't look up when Inaya arrived.

Inaya came in yelling, quite a thing considering she had just come up four flights of stairs.

"You bring my brother back, you black bitch," Inaya said. She was still pretty. Fat and dirty, yes, but pretty.

"Black?" Nyx said. "I'm not black."

"—or I swear to every saint—"

"Cockroach brown," Anneke said. She crowned her king, and swapped Nyx for an ace.

"—I'll tear out your heart—"

"Cheap whiskey brown," Anneke said. "We always end up with three extra aces. Who does that, huh?"

"—and strip out your bones—"

"I like being cheap," Nyx said. "Anneke's the black one. What's this? Did you just steal my king?"

"—from your skin and grind them—"

"That's an illegal move. What are you talking about?" Anneke said.

"I'm just saying you're pretty dark."

"—and grind them. You hear me? Grind them—"

"What's this? I told you, look at it, that's another ace. That's five aces in this deck."

"—into flour and pound you into bread!"

"Are you done making dinner?" Nyx asked Inaya. Bread sounded real good about now. Food of any kind sounded good. What sounded less good was getting yelled at by some dumb pregnant Ras Tiegan. She took back her king and swapped out another ace. "I win," she said.

Anneke pounded the table.

Inaya's face was flushed. It wasn't often Nyx saw anybody that color. Inaya kept her fists clenched. "I swear—"

"I heard that already. Sit down before you bust something."

"Nyx," Rhys said. He moved protectively toward Inaya, which just pissed off Nyx more. He called Nyx godless, but Taite's sister with her Ras Tiegan bastard of a kid was virtuous? *Bastard* was a bad word in Ras Tieg. She wondered if Rhys knew that. "I think that maybe—"

"It's fine," Nyx said.

Inaya didn't sit, but started clutching at her belly. She clenched her teeth and started huffing through her nose.

"Yeah, hey, sit, would you?" Nyx said. A sudden sense of alarm sped through her. Pregnancy. Babies. Oh, fuck.

Rhys went over to Inaya and helped her sit. Her whole body went taut, and she cried out.

"Oh, shit," Nyx said.

Rhys put a palm to Inaya's belly. "How long?" he asked.

She thrashed on the couch, then went still, came back. "I don't know."

"That's all right." He looked at Nyx. "We'll need a midwife."

"With what money?" Nyx held up her right hand. "I'm still missing fingers and you think we can afford a midwife?"

"We won't find a respectable Chenjan woman who would do it," Khos said. "I could take her back to the brothel. It'll be tricky, but they know about babies."

"Don't worry about it," Anneke said, rolling up her sleeves. "I'll do it."

"What do you know about babies?" Nyx asked.

"My mom was a breeder, remember? Multiples are hard. Singles are easy." She eyed Inaya over. "I gotta have help, and Nyx ain't doing it."

Inaya's eyes widened, and Nyx remembered she was Ras Tiegan. Modesty and all that. Worse than Chenjans.

But the white girl grabbed Rhys's hand, looked him in the face. "Taite trusts you," she said. "Help me."

"Sure then," Anneke said, and started waving around her hands. "You and Khos wait outside, Nyx. Rhys?"

"I'll heat some water," Rhys said.

Oh, hell, Nyx thought.

Nyx and Khos sat in the main room and played cards and smoked a cheap cigar. They listened to Inaya shrieking. The room was stifling. The two of them swapped a sweat rag to wipe the damp from their faces. A swarm of flies circled at the center of the room.

At dusk, Khos went out and brought back food for everyone. Inaya was still shrieking when he got back.

Khos leaned toward Nyx over the remains of dinner, and whispered, "You think she'll die?"

"No more likely than with any other woman who gives

birth." She traded one of her cards. "Kid might die, though. No inoculations." She had promised Taite inoculations, she realized, back when she believed they'd all live to bring in this note. She looked at her mangled right hand. She already knew they wouldn't make it out whole.

"But women still die doing it, right, even in Nasheen and Chenja?"

"Of course, yeah. What, you thought this was going to be a party?"

"What about Taite?"

"I don't think he's coming."

Khos grimaced. "I mean, what will you do about him?"

"We don't have anything to trade for him." There was a lot going on with this note, and she was far enough behind to know that she was the player working with the least amount of information. It was a dangerous place to be. It got you mutilated. And dead.

"We know where to find Nikodem, or at least where to start," Khos said.

"Yeah, but we don't have her yet. I want you and Rhys to go to the waterworks tomorrow and ask around."

"You want to get her first?"

"I think trading Nikodem for Taite is a safer deal." And it would give her time to decipher the dictations and interrogate Nikodem when they found her. Trading Nikodem away without getting any information left her with exactly nothing…

Inaya let out a long, low sound of distress. It was worse than the shrieking.

"She sounds like she's going to die," Khos said.

"Well, it happens."

"How can that be natural?"

"What, death?"

"Birth."

"No more natural than death." She won the hand.

Khos threw in his cards. "You're making fun of me."

"You make it so easy."

Inaya's noises were muffled now. She'd worn herself out. Then there was a long silence.

Khos looked over at Nyx with his big, blue Mhorian eyes. "She's dead," he said. They were pretty eyes, if only because she didn't see the color that often, but right now, with a woman bleeding and shrieking in the next room, he wasn't terribly appealing.

"Would you get off the death thing?"

Nyx heard a baby cry.

It was a strange sound, like a cat crying.

And then there was another sound of crying—Inaya's crying. Not shrieking, just crying.

Nyx shuffled to her feet and opened the door into the little room with her good hand.

Anneke was rubbing down the purple-red mewling kid with a clean towel. Was it supposed to be that color? Rhys was trying to soothe Inaya, but she was still sobbing, great heaving sobs.

"What's wrong?" Nyx asked.

Anneke said, "It's a boy."

26

The waterworks was on the south side of Dadfar, which used to be an industrial quarter before Nasheen blew the hell out of it sixty years before. It had never been rebuilt. The south side was a morass of hulking, burned-out shells where squatters and draft dodgers made do. There were rude opium dens tucked into corners. The pervasive smell of marijuana filled the rubble-strewn streets. It wasn't the sort of place Khos would have picked for a proper fight, but then, fighting wasn't legal in Chenja.

And, in that case, Khos supposed the south side was perfect.

Rhys, as usual, was wearing too many clothes for the occasion. He had picked up a green turban sometime after they arrived in Dadfar, and that—paired with his long trousers, long tunic, and green burnous—made him look like some local man of importance. He kept everything too clean. And he was too pretty. If Khos drew attention for being a pale giant, Rhys drew it by being too well presented. If Khos had still been a thief, he'd have pegged Rhys as a perfect target, magician or not. Holier-than-thou men were smooth marks.

The night was dark; the moons were in far recession. Khos kept his high beams on and parked about four blocks away from the waterworks.

As Khos stepped out, he asked Rhys, "You ever fought a real fight, boxing?" Khos had learned all of his fighting from street brawls in Mhoria. The desert obsession with boxing interested him; he liked going to fights. "No. Boxing leads to gambling, and I don't gamble."

"It's not gambling if you don't bet on anyone."

"Yes it is. Others gamble."

"If you bet on yourself, you could call it being self-employed."

Rhys sighed. He spent a few minutes calling up his bugs to guard the bakkie. When the wasps were settled, Khos made his way toward the waterworks and Rhys followed. Dark shapes skittered along the edges of his vision. He heard the hiss and chitter of giant scavenging bugs.

There were two men sitting around outside a set of double doors leading into the waterworks. Khos smelled bug-repelling unguent around the doors. Fuck, he hated contaminated cities. Behind the men, a globe full of glow worms gave off a faint light.

Khos still found it strange to see so many men around, even though they were old. He had lived in Nasheen for most of his adult life, and he had gotten used to the presence of women and the sound of Nasheenian. Mhoria was still a strictly sex-segregated society, which he'd hated enough to compel him to cross the border into Nasheen. He did miss some things, though. The food was better in Mhoria, and nobody was as suspiciously frightened… of everything. Countries at war lived in a state of perpetual fear. It got to you. He wasn't sure why Taite had brought his sister out to the desert. She wasn't built for it, and she hated it. Taite had invited him over to her place a couple of times, and he and Inaya had gotten along all right until she realized he was a shifter.

"Take care of her," Taite had said that night in the Mhorian café.

And now Raine had Taite, and Inaya was Khos's responsibility.

Damn this note, Khos thought.

The old men at the doors of the waterworks asked for nearly a buck to admit Rhys and Khos.

Rhys made to argue, but Khos paid it. The less fuss they made, the less likely they'd be remembered. A giant white Mhorian and a draft-age Chenjan would get plenty of attention without making a scene over money.

They entered a narrow corridor that stank of piss. Khos followed some glow worms to his left. He heard men talking in loud voices, old men, men who'd been to the front. You could tell. They talked differently from the ones who stayed home—rasping, bitter.

Khos turned in to the room. There was a raised ring at the center with plain organic ropes and unpainted corner posts. Lights hung over the ring, but the rest of the place was dark, except for a few globes at the end of the room where the bar was.

"You want a drink?" Khos asked Rhys.

Rhys just looked at him.

Khos shrugged. He had never much cared for Rhys and his buttoned-down coats and upturned nose. It was like he thought he had some kind of special relationship with God, like he was one of the First Families. Why didn't Raine take *you*? he thought, but that just led to thinking about Taite again, cut up and tortured in some Chenjan offal house.

Khos remembered the first time he figured out Taite was looking a little too long at him, that his eyes spent a lot longer on the few young men they passed than the fleshy, friendly women. It had amused Khos to find somebody who thought bedding a man was some kind of sin, something you'd get beaten up or killed for. It was illegal in Ras Tieg, Chenja, and Nasheen, for no good reason except that it scared the shit out of people, and Khos had laughed and laughed about it, until he saw a young boy stoned in the street for kissing another boy in Ras Tieg.

Bloody fucking barbarians, he thought. In Mhoria, men were brothers and lovers and friends. Denying that was like cutting out a piece of yourself. What Mhoria didn't get was that cutting women out was like cutting out a piece of yourself too. A society needed balance, Khos thought, but a society at balance was harder to control, and Umayma had been founded and built on the principles of control. You controlled the breeding, the sex, the death, the fucking blood that ran in your veins. The government thought they could control the world through will alone.

Like Ras Tieg and its war against the shifters.

You'll never bother to understand how any of it works, he thought, pushing his way after Rhys through the crowd. You'll never control a world you don't understand. They'd been bleeding and dying for three thousand years on this planet, and nobody'd taken the time to understand it. They just wanted to control it.

Rhys found them a pair of rickety seats. An old man came around asking if they wanted to bet on any of the fighters.

Khos could follow most Chenjan and asked who was fighting.

"Good fight tonight," the old man said, and grinned. He was missing most of his teeth. "We've got an outrider named Afshin Ahben fighting our own Khavar Puniz. Good fighters, both. You seen them? After, we have the really good stuff. We have Barsine Shifteh and Tarsa Zoya."

Khos wondered if he'd heard right. "These are men boxing?"

The old man laughed. "Men? No, no. Barsine, you think that's a boy's name? Your Chenjan needs work, boy."

"How did you find women to box in Chenja?" Rhys asked.

"You haven't seen much boxing," the old man said. "We've been getting in some Nasheenian girls this last year. Why do you think our entrance fee's so high? We don't risk our boys in the ring anymore. Too dangerous. Makes them unfit for the front. Gets people suspicious."

"Husayn said she was losing fighters to this ring," Rhys said, in Mhorian. Khos had only heard him speak Mhorian a handful of times. There were days when he wondered just how important Rhys's family was. Chenjans and Nasheenians didn't bother learning Heidian, Drucian, Ras Tiegan, or Mhorian, as a rule.

Those were the lesser people, the latecomers who they fed the planet's scraps. "But I didn't realize they made up the entire card."

"So you want to bet on anybody?" the old man asked. His eyes were eager. Khos wondered what his cut was.

"Yeah, sure," Khos said. "I'll put a buck on that second one, Tarsa."

Rhys said, "A buck? Are you—"

"It's my personal take," Khos said. He counted out a buck in change and handed it over to the man. The man punched out a receipt with a dumb stylo on organic paper. If you wanted to make some contacts, you had to start by passing out money.

When he'd gone, Khos said, "You see any magicians in here yet?"

"No. We're early, I think."

"I'm going to the bar. Want anything?"

"Only if they have clean water."

"Doubtful."

Khos moved through the crowd to the bar. The advantage of being big and foreign was that most people got out of your way.

Khos ordered a bloody rum. The bartender was a stooped old man with half a face and a crusted black hole where one of his eyes should have been.

"You Mhorian?" the man asked.

"Yeah," Khos said.

The man contorted his face in what Khos took to be an attempt at a smirk. Maybe a grimace.

"What's it like, never seeing women?" the man asked.

"It's why I left," Khos said, and found himself thinking of Inaya. Why had she left Ras Tieg in the first place? Taite always said she was happily married back home.

The man coughed out a laugh and handed over Khos's drink. "I like my women in private spaces. Can't get away with it much anymore. Not like old times."

"But foreign women are different?" Khos asked, nodding at the ring.

"Foreign women are dogs," the man said.

"I'm a shifter," Khos said. "I take some offense at that." He didn't, really, but it was worth the fearful look on the man's face. Khos was a head taller and thirty kilos heavier than he was.

"They're just bad women," the barman sputtered.

Khos turned away from the bar and bumped into a tall man wearing a long blue burnous cut like Rhys's. He was old and too pale to be Chenjan. Khos saw a locust clinging to his cuff. When the man opened a hand and ordered a drink, roaches scuttled back up his sleeve.

Khos stepped away and looked over the press of people around the magician. He saw no one familiar, so he widened the sweep of his gaze around the tables to see if anyone was looking at the man. A veiled woman and a tall unveiled woman glanced at the bar from their places near the ring.

"Khos Khadija?"

Khos started. He reached for the short pistol at his hip with his free hand.

A lean, ropy-looking Nasheenian woman with a long, mean face stepped in front of him. She had a boxer's face, one whose nose had been mashed in one too many times. She squinted at him.

"I thought that was you," she said.

"I know you?" he asked. In his line of work, he knew a lot of women.

"No, but some of my women do. You helped some of my whores in Nasheen get their boys out."

"You run a brothel?"

"It's among the many things I do," she said. "Have a drink with me."

"I'm with someone."

"He can wait. I have a private room."

Khos hesitated. She wasn't an attractive woman, certainly not the type he'd want to have a drink with under any other circumstances, but he was here to scout out news and make contacts, and she was offering. He'd also be interested to know how she was going around unveiled without an escort in Chenja.

And how she knew his name.

"All right, then. One drink," he said. "You have a name?"

"In Chenja, I go by Haj."

"Seriously?"

She grinned. He saw dark circles under her eyes. Nyx would say she was a bleeder. "Seriously."

Haj led him up a winding set of stairs to the balcony over-looking the ring. She opened a battered metal door and revealed a lushly appointed viewing box with windows overlooking the ring.

Two young women slumped on the raised benches set against the windows. The benches were covered in an assortment of pillows that matched the gauzy veils the women wore. Both were Chenjan dark. They looked up at Haj and Khos with heavy-lidded eyes.

"Get this man a drink," Haj told one of the women.

The woman got to her feet with the practiced ease of a dancer. She went to the private bar at the other side of the room and poured out two glasses of dark liquor.

"Sit," Haj told Khos.

He pushed some cushions out of the way and sat next to the other woman on the bench. She smelled good, some kind of heady, flowery scent peppered with cinnamon. Haj was well off, but not well off enough to have boys.

Haj sat in an armchair across from him and took the liquor the woman offered her.

"I'd heard you were in town," Haj said.

Khos felt the hair on the back of his neck rise. Who else was tagging them? "Is that so?"

"I run the brothel on East Babuk," she said. "Oversee it, actually, for my employer. I found out they're giving you sanctuary."

"Is that so?" Khos repeated, still too startled to come up with anything else. He couldn't imagine Mahrokh selling him out, but he'd been wrong before. Who the hell *was* this woman? "Who's your employer?" he asked.

"Local magistrate," Haj said, waving a hand. "No one important. I hoped to thank you for services rendered. You helped some good men dodge the Nasheenian draft. I'm grateful for that."

"Kin of yours?"

A knock came at the door.

"Enter," Haj said.

A bulky Nasheenian woman pushed into the room. She wore a set of dueling pistols, and one arm was paler than the other.

Khos tensed. He knew that woman.

A stocky kid came in behind her.

"You entertaining again?" Dahab said to Haj. She spared only a glance at Khos. Something else was on her mind, praise be. "I need to talk to you about Nikodem."

Khos forced himself to drink more.

"Over here," Haj said.

"You're such a voyeur," Dahab said. "I don't have time for this shit."

"So long as I pay you, you'll make time. Come on."

Haj moved to the far end of the room with Dahab. The girl who'd come in with Dahab hung around pretending not to look at Khos and the women.

"You're a good man," one of the women next to Khos murmured, in Chenjan. She put a soft hand on his shoulder. He didn't feel so great at the moment.

He took another drink and kept his head tilted toward Dahab

and Haj. He'd seen Dahab two or three times around the Cage, but it looked like she hadn't recognized him.

"I can't protect a woman who goes out to fights," Dahab said.

"You could have protected her just fine if you brought me that bitch you said you had in Jameela."

"I ain't God."

"Neither is she."

Dahab and Haj said something else, and then Dahab was marching past him and out the door. Her squirt followed after her, sparing one last look back.

Haj sat across from him as the Chenjan woman next to him kissed his neck. Memories of his night with Nyx, years before—the smell of her skin, the strength in her legs, her perfect naked ass—showed up in the strangest places.

When the woman pulled away from him, he saw a smile touch Haj's plain face.

"Now," she said, "let's talk about what I can offer you for Nyxnissa's head—and the safety of your little white bitch."

Khos took another drink.

27

"You sure about that?" Nyx asked from her seat on the tattered divan. Her fingers throbbed—the ones that weren't there. She had lost an arm in a tangle with a sand cat once, but she was under the magicians' protection then, and after passing out from blood loss, she'd gone only half a day without an arm before getting fitted with a new one. Ghost pains were new to her.

Rhys shifted his weight from one foot to the other. Khos leaned against the card table in front of her, chewing on his thumb. Anneke was wandering around the room, holding the brat in her ropy arms and muttering in low tones. She was probably telling the kid prison stories.

"We tailed Nikodem and the magicians after the fight," Khos said. "They're living in an upscale hotel on the east side. Rhys got a list of the tenants, and there's a party of three under Yah Tayyib's name."

Once again—Yah Tayyib. Nyx supposed she should have been gleeful. Instead, she was exhausted. Being right didn't make it any easier.

"But you didn't see Yah Tayyib at the fight?"

"No," Rhys said. "I called Yah Reza, and she has Yah Tayyib written in as being under residence at the gym in Faleen."

"That just means his name's on a docket. Doesn't mean he's there," Nyx said. "When's the next fight?"

"A week from now. You don't want to nab her at the house?" Khos asked. He started fussing with his dreads. Always a bad sign. Something had gotten him worked up at the fight.

"It'll be easier to take her at the next fight. I'll be in better shape then. If we move now, we're one person short."

"Two," Khos said. "There's Taite."

"I haven't forgotten about Taite." Nyx nodded at Anneke, who had settled the kid on the floor in a spill of blankets. Anneke pulled out her shotgun and started polishing it, still nattering. She was telling the kid how to take apart an X1080 assault rifle. "Kinda hard to forget, isn't he?"

"Sure," Khos said, and grimaced at the floor.

"Anneke, I want you scouting out this building of hers. Get me as much information as possible," Nyx said. "How about *that* woman? She ready for visitors?" She nodded toward Inaya's room.

"Not really," Anneke said.

"Too bad," Nyx said. She hobbled to her feet and waved away Rhys's help. It was time to move. In every sense.

She knocked on the door with her good hand and entered before Inaya said anything. The room was too hot, airless, and dark. She needed to open some of the lattices.

Inaya raised her head, then turned toward the wall.

"I know you don't want to speak to me, but I need answers that might get Taite back."

Inaya looked at her.

"Did he give you anything before you left? Supplies, papers, stuff like that?"

"He gave me some things from his desk. And food. There was food and water in the bakkie."

"Where's the stuff from the desk?"

"In the bakkie. I put the transmission canisters under the rug beneath the gas pedals, if that's what you're after."

"The bakkie? Who's bakkie?"

"Husayn's. I left it parked by that place. Your other garret."

Nyx tried to get her head around that. "You got yourself *and* a bakkie over the border?" Khos had said something about Inaya being a shifter, but shifters couldn't shift bakkies, for fuck's sake.

"That's my business," Inaya said.

Well, shit, Nyx thought. "Thanks," she said.

She dragged herself back into the main room.

"Rhys?"

"Yes?"

"I need you to go and find Husayn's bakkie. Inaya parked it outside that garret. I have no fucking idea how she got it over, but I need whatever you can find inside it. Look under the gas pedals. If we're lucky, nobody else looked there."

Khos sat next to the kid and Anneke. He counted out violet bursts from his gunnysack. "That thing's been gutted by now. Or stolen altogether," he said.

"I need to risk it," Nyx said.

Rhys pulled on his burnous. "Do we need anything else?"

"Pick up some rotis," Anneke said. "And milk."

Rhys dug some money from their coffers and headed out.

Nyx lay on the divan and waited. There was nothing worse than giving orders from a divan. She pulled up her trousers and looked at the ruined flesh of her legs. They were healing up. Not prettily, but healing up.

Inaya stayed hunkered in the dark bedroom. Anneke brought the kid in to Inaya when he started to fuss. The kid ate a lot. Nyx played cards and thought about Yah Tayyib. She dozed and dreamed of the war.

Rhys was back a couple of hours later. He carried a paper bag. He dumped four rotis on the table and pulled a bulb of condensed milk from the paper bag.

"Anything?" Nyx asked.

"They gutted most everything," he said. "Except these." He pulled two transmission rectangles from the paper bag.

"Can you read them?" Nyx asked.

"We don't have the equipment for it."

"Who does?"

"I know a man in Bahreha who might do me the favor. He's a very old… friend."

"You going?"

"If these can bring Taite back, I'll go." He did not look pleased. Nyx knew what Chenjans did to criminals. If Rhys's man wasn't as friendly as he hoped, Rhys would sit out his last days in a hole in the floor before getting both his heads chopped off.

"Don't be idle. A day there, a day back. You need to take transit. We can't spare the bakkie."

"I know."

"Then go. Do it."

Rhys packed up. "I'm taking some coin with me. We're running low, but I'll need to buy water."

"Yeah," Nyx said.

Khos watched Rhys walk out. "What's next?" Khos asked.

"Rhys gets us some information. I recover. Then we go get Nikodem."

"And Taite," Khos said.

"And Taite," Nyx said. Or whatever was left of him.

28

Rhys wiped the dust from the window inside the bus with the already dusty end of his burnous. The clasp mechanism at the top of his window was broken, so hot air and red dust blew in from the road and covered him in a fine mist. He pulled his burnous over his nose and mouth. Red ants crawled along the floor. A man in a blue turban sat next to him, clinging with arthritis-knotted hands to a carpetbag. Rhys wanted to take the man's hands in his and soothe them, but healing without provocation might get a Chenjan magician killed, even if his poor skill had done any good. Chador-clad women sat three to a seat in the back of the bus, juggling luggage and children in their laps. The front was nearly empty. A few old men with wisps of gray hair and a young man just old enough to enter combat training took up a few seats.

He didn't know why the man with the turban sat next to him when there were so many empty seats, not until the man started speaking.

"I don't see many men on the roads," the old man said. "Not whole men, anyway. I sit alone in the teahouses. Most are run by widows, did you know? Have you come from the fighting?"

"No," Rhys said. "I keep a family in Dadfar."

It sounded like the truth.

"Is that so? How many sons do you have?"

"Just the one," Rhys said, and thought of his father.

"Just one? Just one? A great misfortune, many men would say.

You must punish your wives or take another."

"It is not their fault alone," Rhys said. Most rural men still believed that women had some control over the sex of their children and bore girls for spite. It gave them someone to blame for their misfortune. Someone besides God.

The turbaned man tapped his head and pushed up the blue turban to reveal a bald head. One-half of the visible bald skull was a pale green. His head must have been blown apart at the front. Organic fixes often replaced missing or shattered skulls.

"You see this? Too many boys in my family. I was first to the front," the man said.

"And the rest of your brothers?"

The man dropped the turban, crinkled his face. "Twenty brothers in all. Gone now. All gone. Gone to God."

"Yes," Rhys said. He thought of all the men at the front. Thought of the genocide of a gender.

Bahreha lay in a wide river valley about thirty-five kilometers west of Dadfar. The bus wound down a low rise of mountains that looked out over the wasted river plain. Rhys's father had shown him pictures of Bahreha before the first wave of bombings. Bahreha had been a desert oasis, one of the major trading centers along the border. What little trade that came down the river from Nasheen now consisted of shipments of black goods. They came in under the cover of darkness and departed in the same manner. Bahreha sold more slaves and illegal organics than it did bread, or silk, or lapis. The great palms that once shaded the river had been cut or burned, and the tremendous tiled fountains of the market and government districts were broken and dry. The green parks where children once played were now sandy brown lots infested with small dogs, feral cats, and refugees.

The bus pulled into a busy transit station packed with informal taxis, bakkies, and rickshaws. Vendors dressed in colorful but tattered clothing swarmed the bus when it arrived and pushed fried dog, hunks of bread, hard candies, and more useless items at the passengers as they disembarked—shampoos, bath caps, costume jewelry, fake leather belts, and cheap cloth for turbans. A couple of creepers lurked at the edges of the crowds, carrying their drooping nets and collections of bugs in little wooden cages.

Rhys pushed through the heaving tide and started walking through the center of the ruined city toward the riverfront. Ten years before, he would not have dreamed of walking through these streets. His mother would have wailed at the thought. The city was full of Chenjeens—Nasheenian and Chenjan half-breeds—but also Nasheenian refugees and Chenjan draft dodgers. They were a seething mass of the unemployed and the unemployable. The few businesses still open had security guards with muzzled cats on leashes posted out front. Those businesses that had retired from service entirely had heavy grates over the windows and wasp swarms humming just behind the barred doors. Rhys could feel them.

He walked the kilometer to the riverfront high-rises. Two decades before, the buildings had been the most sought-after property in Bahreha. Inside their now-barred courtyards, overgrown thorn bushes hid the blasted patterns of old succulent gardens.

Rhys buzzed at the gate of a wind-scoured building that needed a new coat of paint and a long visit from an exterminator. Geckos skittered in and out of crevices along the outside of the building, shielded by thorn bushes, and colonies of red ants pooled out all along the foundation.

He buzzed twice more before a tinny voice answered, "Who's there?"

Rhys hesitated. "Am I speaking to Abdul-Nasser?"

There was a long pause.

"You an order keeper?"

"No. Kin."

Another pause. Then, "Come in quickly."

The gate swung open.

Rhys crossed the dead courtyard, and went up a set of wooden steps. Someone had applied new paint to the center of the steps, but neglected the edges. Under the awning at the corner of the building, down a short open corridor, was door number 316. Rhys raised his hand to the buzzer, but the door cracked open before he pressed it.

Rhys saw half a face; one dark weeping eye peering out at him. The cloying, too-sweet stink of opium wafted into the corridor, mixed with the old, heavy smell of tobacco.

"Rakhshan?" the old man said.

Rhys felt something stir at the name. No one had called him that in a long time.

"Abdul-Nasser Arjoomand?"

"Hush. Peace be with you."

"And with you," Rhys said, his response automatic, like breathing.

Abdul-Nasser opened the door just enough for Rhys to squeeze past him. The room was dim, and Rhys paused a moment in the door to wait for his pupils to dilate. Yellow gauze covered the windows.

He heard the door close behind him and turned to see Abdul-Nasser bolting it with three heavy bars. After, Abdul-Nasser swept his hands over the bars, and a stir of red beetles swarmed the edges of the doorway.

"Now we can speak privately," Abdul-Nasser said, and offered his hands to Rhys. Rhys took them.

The sockets of Abdul-Nasser's black eyes seemed to sag in his lined face, like an old dog's. The sleeves of his threadbare tunic were pushed up, so when Rhys took his hands he saw old and new bruises on the man's wrists and forearms.

"You're still taking venom," Rhys said.

Abdul-Nasser shrugged, but he pulled away his hands and pushed down the sleeves of his tunic. "You know what I need for my work," Abdul-Nasser said.

"I do," Rhys said.

The little one-room flat was a ruckus of equipment: bits of old consoles and bug pans, piles of disintegrating boxes and papers, worm-eaten books, tangles of leaking wires, and cracked bottles of organic feed and roach fluid. Bug cages and aquariums took up one wall. Dead locusts littered the floor. The dim lighting was in part due to the strain on the room's internal grid—most of the power was being rerouted to the water pumps that fed the frogs, cicadas, mark flies, turtles, tadpoles, water skimmers, and multitudes of fish in various states of living and dying that clogged the aquariums.

"How have you faired? Let me get you something," Abdul-Nasser said. "Tea, something."

"Thank you," Rhys said.

Abdul-Nasser wended his way around the cluttered room to the wall of the kitchen. Dishes overflowed the tiny sink. Flies circled the dirty plates. When Rhys followed after him to help with the tea, he saw something crawling in the sink—the damp, filthy plates bred maggots.

"Maybe we can just sit and talk," Rhys said.

Abdul-Nasser shook his head. His hair was tucked under a turban, so Rhys did not have to look at the state of it, but Abdul-Nasser did stink, as if he did not wash even for the ablution.

"No," Abdul-Nasser said. "I am still civilized. We must have tea."

He clattered around, rinsed out a dirty teapot, and tried to get the fire bugs in his hot plate to stir.

In the end, the tea was lukewarm, in dirty cups, set on a tea table that had once been a com counter. There were no chairs. They sat on old cushions that stank of dogs.

"So you are a magician now," Abdul-Nasser said. "Those old women took you in?"

"They did."

"No doubt they agreed with what you did."

Rhys sighed. "It was some time ago."

"Yes. I have not seen your father since."

"Have you been home?"

"A time or two."

"You've seen my sisters?"

"Yes, all married now."

"To whom?"

"Best I can recall, a local magistrate. The one who mooned over them."

"Nikou Bahman. The one my father hated."

"Yes, that man."

Rhys stared at the tea. He could not bring himself to drink it. He kept thinking of the maggots in the sink.

"He already had eight wives," Rhys said.

"Did you expect it would go differently? Your sisters, the household, were disgraced when you did not follow your father's will. God's will. Your father thought no one would take them, not even as a ninth or twelfth wife."

Rhys took a deep breath. "But they married."

"Yes."

"Good. Children?"

"All boys. You have four nephews." Abdul-Nasser picked up his tea but did not drink it. He peered at Rhys. "But you did not come to me for news of your house. Not after eight years."

"No," Rhys said. He pulled the transmission canisters from his tunic pocket and set them on the table. "I need to read these. Our com man may have died for them."

Abdul-Nasser set down his tea and took one of the rectangles into his hand. He rubbed it between thumb and forefinger, pressed it to his ear and shook it.

"Ah," he said. "This is expensive." He bit it. "This is government. Nasheenian."

"Can you read it?"

"Yes." Abdul-Nasser stood, and went to a tangle of equipment piled at the far end of the aquarium wall. He unpacked some material, uncovered a com console, and inserted the rectangle into the panel. He tapped out a signal to the chittering bugs in the console.

Rhys got up and stood next to him.

A strong female voice bled out from the speakers; the cadence and inflection were like Nyx's, only more stilted, more educated.

"Don't tell anyone," she said, *"what I'm about to tell you…"*

They only listened to half of the first canister.

It was enough.

"Can you get me a transcription of this?" Rhys asked with a growing sense of dread, as Nyx's dead sister talked about the end of the war, the end of Chenja. He thought of Khos and Inaya, and the alien with the big laugh.

Abdul-Nasser pressed a button on the console. "Put your hand here," he told Rhys, and Rhys put his hand on the faceplate next to the printer plate. He felt a soft prickling on his hand.

Blank organic paper began to roll out of the console.

"It will respond only to your touch," Abdul-Nasser said. "I've locked it as well, for forty-eight hours from now. It won't open until then. Keep it close until you need it. I hope you have a trustworthy employer."

Rhys stared at the paper as it came out of the machine, even as Kine's voice continued to assault him from the speakers.

"What sort of trouble have you gotten yourself into?" Abdul-Nasser asked, staring at the speakers as if the voice would take on human form and step from the machine with a flaming sword.

"More than I know," Rhys said. "You'll destroy these?"

"Oh, yes. The moment it's done transcribing. You best not stay long."

"I'm sorry, Uncle," Rhys said.

"You were bound for trouble. Born under an inauspicious star, your mother said."

The printer stopped. Abdul-Nasser tucked the papers into an organic case and handed them to Rhys.

"This is important," Rhys said. "I need to get this back to my employer and decide what we're going to do with it."

"Your employer is Nasheenian," Abdul-Nasser said.

"Think what you will," Rhys said. He tucked the organic case into his satchel. "I should go. I said I wouldn't be long."

"Said that to a woman? How old are you, Rakhshan?"

"You sound like my father."

Abdul-Nasser grunted. He rubbed at his arms. "Eh," he said.

Rhys moved to the door. He waved the red roaches away and unbolted the doors. They moved easily. He wished all bugs were as well-trained as his uncle's.

Abdul-Nasser stayed close behind. Rhys could smell him. Rhys turned, looked into his uncle's weeping eyes.

"I did the right thing," Rhys said.

Abdul-Nasser said, "That is between you and God."

Rhys gripped the old man's arms. "Stay away from the venom," he said.

"Be careful among the women," Abdul-Nasser said.

Rhys made to pull away, but Abdul-Nasser held him.

"And know this," Abdul-Nasser said. "You are our last boy, the only one with our name. Whatever you do, whatever you need, you come to me. Ten hours or ten years from now."

"I know, Uncle," Rhys said.

"Good." Abdul-Nasser released him, and quickly shut the door.

Rhys pressed his hand to his satchel and the transcription, reassuring himself it was still there. He started back through the corridor and down the open stair. He could still hear Kine's voice talking with antiseptic clarity about the things Ras Tiegans had done to shifters, the things Nasheen would do to shifters. The eradication of a people. The end of Chenja.

He walked back to the taxi ranks. The call sounded for afternoon prayer, and he found the mosque nearest the ranks and knelt. He unrolled the prayer rug from his back. He submitted to the will of God and hoped he was not praying for the end of Chenja, and Nasheen, and the shifters; hoped he was not praying for the end of the world. After, he went for lunch at a Mhorian restaurant that served halal food; the bus was not due for hours. The afternoon heat kept the crowds away from the taxi ranks, and after lunch he sat out under the shade of the weather stalls at the ranks and waited.

He read from the Kitab and pushed away thoughts of Kine and bloody shifters. A bus pulled up ahead of him. When he looked at the sign in the window, he saw that it was headed for the city of his birth.

Rhys stared at the bus. He thought of what his mother would say if she saw him. Would she ignore him? Shriek? Turn away? He wanted to think that she would open her arms to him and invite him to her table. She and his aunts would cook a heavy meal—eight dishes—and his father would come home and laugh and smoke and tell him how proud he was to have a magician for a son.

"Rhys Dashasa?"

He stirred from his dream, then jerked himself awake. How had he done that? It was dangerous to fall asleep in public, even while sitting on your purse.

Rhys squinted up at the bulky figure in front of him. He did not recognize him. Two more dark figures stood off to the man's right. Rhys saw very little. The sun was directly behind them.

"What do you want?" Rhys asked, raising his hand to his brow. "I think you have me mixed up with someone else."

"No, I don't think so," the man said.

Rhys's fingers twitched. He searched for a local swarm of wasps.

"Let's not be hasty," one of the other figures said, and something rolled toward him, blowing smoke.

Rhys coughed and raised his hands.

The large man grabbed Rhys by the burnous and dragged him to his feet. Rhys reached for his pistols, but the man twisted both of Rhys's arms neatly behind him.

A magician stood just to the left of him, one hand raised, a swarm of wasps already circling her head.

"So you're her beautiful boy," the man said. "I didn't see you much at the Cage. Thought you were just a rumor."

"You're mistaken—" Rhys began.

"No, I think not," Raine said. "Let us see if she cares any more for you than she does her little half-breed."

29

Khos sat outside the diner in a too-small wicker chair, a pistol at his hip and the taste of excrement still in his mouth. Children played in the dusty street beyond the cool shade of the billowing red awning that cloaked the sidewalk. Little Mhorian girls, too skinny and already veiled, scurried among the poles that propped up the awning, shooing hungry bugs from the twine grounding the poles. The girls slathered a thick bug-repelling unguent on both pole and twine. The acrid stink of the repellent made Khos's eyes water.

It wasn't much past dawn, but the day was already hot. Khos sweated beneath his burnous. A girl came by with a tray and served him a tiny cup of tea, black as pitch. She lowered her eyes as she served him. He was careful not to touch her. She tucked the tray under her arm, pressed her palms together, bowed, and backed away from him.

Khos wished the chair was larger. He stared out at the children and the passersby. This early, the only people on the street besides the dirty children were the creepers. They slunk along the sidewalk with giant nets over their shoulders, their faces hidden by their floppy hats.

He saw Mahrokh crossing the street. She stood out easily among the dregs of the blue dawn. She went veiled when she wasn't working, and that was just as well. Chenjans—male and female alike—had been known to stone whores in the streets when they appeared during the day without an escort. But he marked Mahrokh by her significant height—nearly as tall as he was—broad shoulders, and confident walk which reminded him of Nyx. She carried a rectangular package under one arm, and the sight of it made his heart skip. He looked back up the street she had appeared from and into the long morning shadows between buildings, but saw no one following her.

She stepped around the refuse in the streets and up onto the sidewalk, and then he saw her eyes: blue-black and already squinting to make out his countenance, though he couldn't imagine she would mistake him for anyone else, even with her fuzzy sight.

He stood and pressed his palms together, bowing.

Mahrokh set the package on the table, and did the same.

They sat, and Khos called over one of the Mhorian girls. "Another tea," he said.

"No honey," Mahrokh added.

When the girl had gone, Mahrokh turned to study him. "You look better. Still terrible, but better."

"I hope that improves," he said. He sipped at his tea to clear the taste from his mouth. Shifting into a dog to bathe had its advantages, but a clean tasting mouth wasn't one of them.

Mahrokh reached beneath her burnous and pulled out several glossy papers. She pushed them across the table to Khos.

Khos stared at them. The edges were already beginning to disintegrate.

"They're tailored to destruct in several hours," Mahrokh said.

Khos fanned the images out on the table. A few pieces from the ends of each flaked away as he did. A beaming young boy, seven or eight years old, peered out from the pages. He was the color of the desert—far too pale and flat-nosed to pass as anything but what he was. And though his hair was dark, his eyes were unmistakably blue.

"We've had to transfer him," Mahrokh said. "To avoid the Chenjan draft."

"They're drafting half-breeds here as well?"

"Yes. It started last year."

"Where is he going?"

"Tirhan. They've been a neutral country since they broke away from Chenja. We send our highest risk boys there."

Khos tentatively touched the face in the picture. He imagined what it would be like to grow up in fear. His heart ached. He pushed the pictures back at Mahrokh.

"Keep them," she said. "They'll be gone soon enough."

"Is there danger in the crossing?" Khos asked. "I've never tried to get into Tirhan."

"Our network extends deep into Tirhan. I already have an interested family. His look is a little off for Chenja and Nasheen, and no doubt he'll be a little odd in Tirhan, but he will not stand out as much. I think he'll be happier there. And certainly safer."

Khos nodded. He did not trust himself to speak. He slipped the pictures into his vest pocket.

"And do you have news for me?" she asked.

"Three boys are coming in from Nasheen in three days," Khos said. "One of my contacts will be escorting them from Azam to Dadfar. You'll need to take them from there."

"I will tell my women," Mahrokh said.

Khos nodded at the package. "Should I ask about that?"

Mahrokh's body seemed to shrink. She gazed long at the package. "That was sitting on our porch this morning. Addressed to your woman."

The Mhorian girl arrived with Mahrokh's tea, then pressed her palms together and bowed her head. Mahrokh returned the gesture and drank.

Khos continued to stare at the package. "You and your women need to be careful," he said.

Mahrokh did not look at him. "We are careful. Those who trouble your woman would not trouble us. We have protection."

"Protection? You mean Haj?"

Mahrokh looked up at him. "You know of Haj?"

Khos felt his cheeks flush. He tugged at the hood of his burnous in an attempt to hide his face. Why did he still react like that, after all this time among women? Haj, who knew something about Nyx and just enough about Inaya—and too much about him.

"I've met her," Khos said. "How much do you know about her?"

"She's quiet. Since she's sympathetic to the cause, I assume she lost a man at the front. All of us have."

"What do you know about who she runs with?"

"Those she uses to protect us?"

"Yes."

Mahrokh shrugged. "Very little. Mostly Nasheenian women, as she is. They're reliable, efficient, effective."

"Could you ask around? Tell me what you can find out about her?"

"Certainly. Does she concern you?"

"I'm just interested. Thank you, Mahrokh." Khos finished his tea and stood. "Would you like me to walk you to your street?"

"No, no. I know my streets far better than you do. I'll finish my tea."

He reached for the rectangular package, and tucked it under his arm. He bowed his head to Mahrokh. "Take care. And remember what I said about being cautious."

"I am always cautious, my Mhorian."

Khos walked back onto the street, through the cluster of children. They held out their hands to him as he passed and called to him in Chenjan. He had no money to spare, or he would have spilled it into their hands. Looked into every beaming face, and thought of his boy.

Tirhan. On the other side of the continent. The end of the desert.

The way to the safe house was long, and by the time he arrived, the package was starting to stink. His stomach knotted.

Khos went up the narrow stairs. As he climbed, the air got hotter and closer until he longed for a window, a breeze, a view of the ocean. When was the last time he'd seen the ocean? He pushed into the room.

Nyx sat on the divan with her feet curled up under her. Her cropped hair was loose. She had just washed it. She and Anneke sat over a set of what looked like blueprints for a residence. Anneke was scribbling things onto the margins.

Khos set the box down in front of Nyx, on top of the map.

Nyx stared at the box.

"What the fuck is this?" she asked.

"From the brothel mistress. Addressed to you."

Anneke grimaced.

Nyx reached for the box and pulled off the brown paper. The stink coming from the box got stronger.

"Shit," Nyx said, and yanked the lid free.

Inside was a severed hand lying in a pool of blackish congealed blood.

No note, this time.

Khos looked away. "What are you going to trade for him?"

"Throw that out," Nyx told Anneke. She thrust the box at her.

Anneke frowned at it. "Better not tell Inaya."

"She's sleeping?" Khos asked.

Anneke nodded.

Khos looked toward Inaya's door, and the worry crept up on him again. A stupid promise he'd made, to protect a woman who did not want his protection, but a woman who had nothing in the world now. He could buy her freedom, and his, but he feared that would cut her heart far worse than losing her boy to the front when he came of age. Khos wasn't so sure he liked his solution either.

"I don't give a shit about Inaya right now," Nyx said. Anneke took the box outside. "We need Nikodem to trade for Taite. If we're going to get her, we need to go now. I can walk well enough. I've waited too long."

"You're just going to let Taite die?" Khos asked.

"Nobody's dead yet. Did you hear what I said?"

"He *will* be dead. How are you going to get Nikodem after all this waiting?"

Nyx regarded him as if he were an annoying insect, something she'd found plastered to the bottom of her sandal. "Have some faith."

Khos clenched his fists. "In what? You? You don't even have faith in yourself."

"Remind me again, did I renew your contract?"

Khos walked away from her, and sat in a ratty chair. Too small for him. Nothing fit him in any country.

Anneke returned and squatted next to Nyx. "If he ain't already dead, boss, we should bring him in like we brought you in. Fair's fair."

"Life isn't fair," Nyx said.

As he looked at Nyx, at her mutilated hand and scarred legs, Khos realized that Rhys, her shadow, wasn't in the room. Unless Rhys had gone out for food, that made him late from his trip to Bahreha. Khos looked again at Nyx and tried to read her. Was she worried about her tardy magician? Or did she care as little for him as she did for the rest of them? They had risked their lives to go after her, pitted themselves against bel dames. But she sat here on the divan and refused to bring back Taite? It'll be me who has to tell Mahdesh, he thought. Me who has to tell him his lover is dead.

And Khos would be the one left with Inaya.

"So lay this out for me again," Nyx said to Anneke.

"Low security up front," Anneke said, pointing to the hand-drawn blueprints on the table. She'd been running recon since Khos and Rhys came back from the waterworks. "The back has an emergency exit. The alarm's working, so we can get out, but our getaway needs to be right outside the door, 'cause if security don't know we're there by then, they'll know once that alarm goes. Nikodem has magicians with her. All the time. Mid week, all but one of her magicians goes out to socialize at the local boxing gym. That's the best time to move."

"When does she go out with the magicians?" Khos asked. "Just during fights, like when we saw her?" Nikodem would get them Taite. He needed to keep his mind on the fucking note.

"So far as I can tell," Anneke said. "It's not like I've had a lot of time for recon, and you've been… occupied."

"So once we get past the security at the desk, we need to separate Nikodem from her magician," Nyx said.

Khos ignored Anneke. "That's a tall order," he said. "We don't have a magician."

"No, but Anneke and I have firepower and some bug repellent. It could give us the time we need."

"How do you want to get in the back?" Anneke asked.

"We'll go in the front."

Khos shook his head. "How we going to get past security?"

"Trust me," Nyx said.

Khos sighed. Trusting Nyx never turned out well.

From the other side of the door, Inaya's son began to cry.

Evening prayer came and went, and Nyx found herself standing at the window of the main room, looking out over Dadfar through the lattice. Looking for Rhys.

Inaya crawled out of her room for the first time all day and sat with Anneke and the kid. She looked skinnier—and paler, if that was possible. Anneke fixed her some condensed milk and force-fed her a roti.

Khos walked up next to Nyx. "See him?"

"He's tougher to see in the dark," Nyx said, and smirked, but something clawed at her belly. Rhys was late. Very late. How long until Raine started to send him back in pieces too? She'd been a fool to send that stupid magician out on his own. A bloody fucking fool.

"He'll be all right," Khos said. "He's a magician."

Khos towered over her. Even in the warm room, she could feel the heat of him next to her.

"We both know what kind of magician he is," Nyx said. They stood a long moment in silence. Then, "You know I intend to bring Taite back."

"Sometimes I don't know you, Nyx," he said softly.

She looked up at him. The light in the room was low. Anneke kept a couple of glow worms in a glass. Lanterns used fuel, and gas was expensive. In the dim light, Khos's expression was difficult to read, but Nyx always thought he looked sad. She had signed this big sad man because she had sensed something in him that she'd never had—a protective loyalty toward her and the team that transcended petty disagreements about sex, blood, and religion. When she looked at him now, she wondered what would happen when those loyalties conflicted. Would he choose to side with her or with Taite? Taite or the whores? And where did Inaya fit into this? She had seen him stare long at her door and go rigid when her baby cried.

"Nobody knows anybody," she said. "We're all working on blind faith."

She watched a hooded figure come down the street and strained to see, but the figure passed by their building.

"You're saying your secret to getting up and going forward is blind faith?" he said, and she heard the amusement in his voice.

"No," Nyx said. "Lately, it's been whiskey." She peered down at the street again.

"I've been thinking about how to get past the desk," Khos said. "I think I know some people who will help us."

"Khos, the only people you know in Chenja are whores."

"Exactly," he said.

"We'll have a problem with com, not having Rhys and Taite."

"So we'll put together something else."

"Is there something wrong with your communications?" Inaya said from behind them.

Nyx and Khos both turned. Anneke was lying in a pile of blankets on the floor, working with her guns. Inaya stood at the end of the divan, her son in her arms.

"We usually use Rhys. Taite receives his transmission through the com," Nyx said.

Inaya hadn't washed her face in a while, and her hair was greasy. She looked like some street beggar. "You don't have regular transceivers?"

Nyx shrugged. "Anneke, Taite give you any manual transceivers?"

"I have a box of com gear," Anneke said, "but transceivers take a long time to synch up. Don't have the time or the money to take them in and have somebody do it."

"I can do it," Inaya said.

Nyx smirked. "*You* can do it?" She looked her up and down, pointedly.

Inaya narrowed her eyes. "Where do you think Taitie learned to repair a console? Did you think that fat man employed him for his looks?"

"You're kidding me," Nyx said.

Inaya said to Anneke, "Show me the box." She glanced back at Nyx. "I assume Taitie didn't tell you why we had to leave Ras Tieg."

"I don't pry into the affairs of my team," Nyx said.

Anneke walked over to their pile of gear and started moving boxes and duffel bags around.

"Our parents handled communications for the Ras Tiegan underground, rebels against Ras Tieg's tyrant, the uncle to your foolish Queen," Inaya said. "They were also shifter-sympathizers. My mother was a shifter, and my parents' politics were… frowned upon. When they killed my mother, my father took her place and trained Taitie and I. When things got bad politically, when the streets…" She choked up, and Nyx thought she was going to cry again, but, remarkably, she swallowed it. "I could marry. Taitie was too young."

"So when things got hot, you smuggled him out of the country."

"He did the same for me, later."

"You don't act like a rebel."

"We rebel in our own ways."

"Here," Anneke said. She dragged a box toward Inaya. "Should be a couple transceivers in here. Some might be broken."

"All right, then," Nyx said. "If you can give us com, then maybe we're ready to run. Anneke, I want you to get me a couple of empty cake boxes from that friend of yours who owns the teahouse."

"Cake boxes?"

"Khos," Nyx continued, "I want to talk to some of your whores tomorrow, early. I'll need a half hour of their time and yours."

"I'll go down and tell them," Khos said. "Where do we want to meet them?"

"That diner in the Mhorian district, just before dawn prayer."

Khos put on his burnous and headed out. "It's about fucking time," he muttered.

"Anneke?" Nyx said.

Anneke straightened. "Eh, I'll go get her up. The teahouse is still open." She concealed her shotgun beneath her burnous and followed Khos.

"Hey, you fucker!" Anneke called after him. "Give me a ride!"

Nyx turned and watched Inaya open the box and pick through its contents. She kept the kid in a sling so he had easy access to her breast. Unlike a Nasheenian woman, she didn't keep the breast bared. Instead, she kept an old tunic slung over one shoulder so it covered the kid's head and her breast. An odd affectation, as it wasn't as if Anneke, Nyx, and Khos hadn't seen breasts before.

Nyx sat on the divan and watched as Inaya set out the transceivers. She opened the little tool kit with her small deft fingers. She shook a couple of the transceivers and frowned.

"This equipment is in terrible shape," she said.

"So Taite always told me," Nyx said.

Inaya did not look at her but pulled out one of the com picks and began prying open one of the transceiver cases. "You're doing this to bring him back?"

"That's the idea," Nyx said.

Inaya worked in silence for a time. Nyx pulled out the diagram of the residence.

"So why wouldn't Taite tell me you were rebels in Ras Tieg?" Nyx asked.

"You used to cut off the heads off Nasheenian rebels. Why would it be different with us?" A low buzzing sound came from the transceivers. Inaya poked at its innards.

"Seems like you hate me a lot for somebody who doesn't know me."

"I know all about you. You're an ungodly, sex-crazed woman."

"I'm a… what?"

"I've read all about women like you, the sort who use everyone around them for pleasure. You're worse than the sort who cavorts only with women. At least they're honest. Ungodly, but honest."

"I'd say I was doing a great job submitting to God by submitting to my desires. Who do you think gave me desire in the first place?"

"God does not want us to kill, yet we are able to kill. If you were truly following God's desire, you would repress your own desires and marry. Marry a man."

Nyx settled back on the divan. "Tell me your marriage was happy."

Inaya's cheeks flushed faintly. Ah, yes, that color. Nyx covered her mouth. She's fixing your transceivers, Nyx thought, be nice.

"Is that why it takes a near-death experience to get you to shift?" Nyx said. "You like it too much?"

Now Inaya's face went bright red. "Do not judge me. You know nothing about me."

"If God wanted you or me different, He'd have made us that way. I'd think you'd be more unhappy with all the killing I do than with all the men and women I fuck."

"Sometimes killing is necessary."

"Sure, of course. Bloody God and all. You and Taite must get into some pretty good arguments."

"Taite doesn't kill people."

Nyx said, "I mean about the sex."

"Men have certain needs, needs that are unnatural in women. Brothels are a sin, but I can understand his needs for female companionship."

Now Nyx laughed. It was a full-belly laugh, and she laughed so hard it hurt. "*Female* companionship?" she gasped. "Oh, hell, you want a drink?"

"I don't drink liquor."

Nyx got up and poured herself the last of the whiskey in the bottle. "Inaya, when we get Taite back, you and your brother need to have a talk."

When, she had said. Not if.

The lie tasted all right.

30

The next day, just before mid-morning prayer, Nyx drove the bakkie to the east side on her own. Nikodem's residence was in a decent part of town, not one where a bakkie like hers prowled the streets. A few blocks north, the blue and green tiles of the business buildings at the city center reflected the new dawn as it bled to violet.

Nyx parked a block from Nikodem's residence, partially hidden by a gaudy fountain splashing at the center of the square. She had a clear view of the entrance and the sidewalk just north of it. Nyx pulled out her transceiver and rubbed it absently.

No sign of Rhys.

She hadn't touched any sen all morning, so she was a little shaky, but having red teeth and numb fingers for this job would be about as stupid as being drunk. She glanced at the cake boxes on the seat next to her and rubbed the transceiver again.

The transceiver buzzed.

She shook it, put it to her ear.

"Yeah," she said.

"I'm moving in, boss," Anneke said.

"Good. You see Khos?"

"Not yet."

"Khos?"

"We're on our way," he said over the line.

"All right. Go in."

Anneke severed the connection.

Nyx hated manual transceivers. They were easier to eavesdrop on, easier to trace. If Raine or Rasheeda or Fatima ran a transmission sweep, they were fucked.

She watched Anneke move in and gave her ten minutes by the fountain clock. Then Nyx locked the bakkie and walked up the street to the residence. She nodded at the armed, veiled woman playing door guard as if she'd known her all her life and stepped through the sliding doors.

Anneke's voice hit her as the doors opened.

"I asked for a head-of-household room three months ago. Is this how you treat your heads of household in this residence? How do you lose a reservation—"

The bewildered desk clerk kept opening her mouth and closing it again. She was little, young, veiled, and neatly dressed. The murals on the wall were glass mosaics of dense jungle and jeweled bugs. A chittering mass of soarer beetles sprayed a fine mist of water from their cages along the edges of the room. The whole residence felt humid, dense.

Nyx hurried up to the counter and mustered up her best Chenjan. "Excuse me," she said, nudging Anneke aside. "Has a delivery arrived? My employer is having a party on the third floor. There should be two pastry deliveries—"

"I'm sorry sir," the clerk said. "There have been no deliveries—"

"Your reservation policy clearly states—" Anneke continued.

"I'm sorry, but without a state-approved confirmation—"

"Pastries. The bakery on this street. Are you sure?"

"There have been no deliveries, sir, I—"

Nyx went back out into the street. She sat in the bakkie and waited.

Five minutes, tops. Anneke was a good catshitter, but not that good.

Nyx saw Khos and four women dressed in the gaudy colors of

whores, their hair uncovered, approaching the residence. Khos stared down the door guard, and they walked inside.

Nyx pulled the two cake boxes out of the back. They were filled with bags of sand. Sand was cheaper than cakes.

She walked back to the residence, carrying the boxes. When she went through the sliding doors this time, she heard a wave of angry voices.

The front desk clerk looked like a cornered animal.

The whores yelled at Anneke. Khos yelled at the clerk. Anneke's color had deepened, and the veins in her neck stood out. She was having far too much fun.

"This is a disgrace! A disgrace! Whores! You offend my—" Anneke yelled.

"I'm sorry. There's some misunderstanding—" the clerk said.

"No misunderstanding," Khos said. "My women were asked up to a gathering on the fourth floor. This is a highly important client—"

"If you could just tell me the client's name—"

"That's confidential. He has a state stamp. I cannot—"

Nyx angled toward the faceplate door and called to the clerk, "I have the pastries. I can't reach the plate. Could you—"

"If you simply buzz our client—" Khos said.

"I need a name before—"

"Can you just open this door?" Nyx said.

"First you lose my reservation, and then you intend to put me on the same floor with these dirty—"

"I can't reach the plate," Nyx said. "If you could just buzz me in—"

Sweat beaded the clerk's face. She reached under the counter.

The door slid open.

Nyx stepped in.

The door closed and cut off the sound.

Nyx did not allow herself a grin. The clerk would call for help soon, and Anneke needed to get in before that happened.

The stairs were adjacent to the main door. Most residences kept bugs in the lifts. Nyx ditched the cake boxes in the stairwell and headed up.

She pushed into the short hall. The floor of the corridor was hard wood, and moaned under her sandaled feet. Nyx pulled her burnous up and followed the dimly lit signs to room tres-bleu-chose. The whole place had a Ras Tiegan theme. She passed the door and walked to the window at the end of the hall to wait for Anneke. She dared not go in on her own to face a magician.

Nyx waited a couple of minutes, then heard a door open behind her. She turned and saw a woman walking out of the room. The woman spoke Nasheenian to someone still inside, asked if they wanted something from a vendor.

The woman spared an incurious glance at Nyx, then started off toward the lift. The door shut behind her.

Nyx looked back out the window.

If the magician was gone, that should leave Nikodem alone in the room.

Nyx clasped her hands behind her back. The window gave her an inspiring view of the cracked parking lot and rusted roofs of a sprawling shantytown, broken only by the occasional serrated palm. Beyond that, low desert hills shimmered in the rising heat.

The call sounded for mid-morning prayer.

Nyx looked behind her again. No sign of Anneke. A soda run wouldn't take the magician long. Without Rhys next to her, Nyx would be shit in a fight with a magician.

She pulled the crowbar from the loop at her belt and wedged it into the doorjamb of room tres-bleu-chose.

Tej once told her that sometimes the old tricks were the best ones.

Nyx popped the door lock, and front-kicked the door.

The door swung open.

Nyx dropped the crowbar and released her whip. She needed Nikodem undamaged, for now.

A small dark woman stood at the center of the room, wearing calf-length trousers and a thigh-length green tunic. She turned her face to the door, and Nyx knew her in an instant. Gray eyes met hers—too big-eyed for beauty.

Nyx strode right toward her without clearing the room. A mistake. She knew better.

"Nikodem? I'm here to get you out," Nyx said. "Your sisters have a bounty on you. We need to move."

Nikodem smiled, and, watching that smile split the broad-cheeked face, Nyx knew that everything she'd worried about was true.

"Oh, I know," Nikodem said, "and you're terribly hard to get rid of."

Nyx heard the unmistakable whir of an organics gun being powered up.

She looked toward the bathroom.

Dahab pointed a double-barreled organics gun at Nyx with her good arm.

"Good morning," Dahab said.

Nyx stepped left, crouched low, and snapped out her whip at the gun. The whip caught. Nyx pulled. The gun went off and sprayed the chair behind Nyx. Smoke rose from the upholstery.

Nikodem sprinted for the door.

Nyx jerked the gun from Dahab's grasp, freed the whip. The gun clattered across the floor. Nyx lashed her whip out at Nikodem's ankle.

The whip caught again. Nyx pulled again. She took Nikodem off her feet and yanked her forward.

Nikodem reached beneath her tunic and came out with a throwing dart.

Dahab ran for the gun on the floor.

Nyx heard the floorboards in the hall groan. If the magician was back with the soda, she was fucked.

Nyx yanked out her pistol, and fired off a few rounds at Dahab with her bad hand, but—as was typical—didn't hit anything. She felt a sharp pain in her shoulder and saw Nikodem's dart jutting out of her flesh. She yanked it out and threw it back at her. She hit Nikodem in the face, with the flat ass-end of the dart.

Nikodem yelled at her in some alien language, and then Dahab was on her feet and pumping the organics gun to reload it. The gun whirred.

Nyx shot at her again.

Dahab ducked.

Nikodem started pulling at the whip around her ankle.

Somebody stepped into the doorway.

Nyx prepared to be assaulted by a swarm of wasps.

Instead, Anneke shot Dahab in the head with her shotgun. Dahab's brains splattered the wall behind her.

The woman crumpled.

Anneke pointed the gun at Nikodem. "We get paid even if you ain't breathing," Anneke said.

"And how will you get a dead body out of this hotel?" Nikodem said coolly.

"Want to find out?" Nyx said.

Anneke slung her gun over her shoulder and put her knee into Nikodem's back. She bound her with sticky bands and then gagged her.

"Move, move," Nyx said. "Everybody heard that goddamn shotgun."

They fled into the hall. A few doors stood half-open, and when the residents saw them, all the doors swung shut. Nyx supposed that if she had seen herself running down the hall dragging a gagged woman ahead of somebody carrying a shotgun, she would have shut her door too.

Nyx pushed Nikodem down the stairs. If they wanted her dead or alive, they wouldn't mind getting her with bruises.

On the second floor, Nikodem stopped walking and sagged. Nyx threw the woman over her shoulder, and her whole body screamed at her. She stumbled. Nikodem tried to bite her ear.

Anneke punched Nikodem.

They ran down the stairs, and pushed out onto the first floor. Order keepers generally took anywhere from eight to forty-five minutes to show up after a call was placed, depending on the neighborhood. The on-premises security would be heading up.

Anneke sprinted down the corridor and pushed open the back door. The alarm went off.

Nyx stumbled into the hot, dusty parking lot.

Khos waited in the buzzing bakkie. "Inaya says the keepers are two minutes away."

Nyx wrapped Nikodem in a cooling tarp, and stuffed her into the trunk. Nyx squeezed in up front next to Anneke.

Khos hit the speed but slowed once they cleared the parking lot, to avoid suspicion on the street.

"She alive?" Khos asked.

"Does it matter?" Nyx said.

Anneke clenched her jaw and squinted at Nyx.

"You should be happy," Nyx said.

"You about bit it that time, boss."

"Not for the first time."

"No," Anneke said, "but it was the first time you almost bit it for doing something real stupid."

"You all want Taite back? This is how we do it." Her leg throbbed. She had fucked up her ankle on the stairs, and Nikodem was a lot tougher to carry with only three fingers on her right hand.

"Khos, you have your whores tell Raine's messenger we're ready to make a deal for Taite."

"I'll drop you off and drive over there. You both all right?"

"Swimming," Nyx said.

She had her bounty. She should be full of grim optimism, but Taite was in pieces and Rhys was missing—and she had no fucking idea how she was going to pull a slick switch for Taite and get Nikodem back across the border alive.

Good thing she didn't intend on delivering her that way.

31.

Khos unloaded Nikodem from the back. Her legs were bruised from trying to kick out the trunk. Once she had a clear view of him, she kicked out at him too.

Her nose was already bloodied from a hit she had taken from Nyx or Anneke. Khos hit her again, hard this time. She went limp.

Khos put her over his shoulder, shut the trunk, and walked up the long flight of stairs to their room. Nyx was just pushing in the door. Khos heard a shriek.

Nyx swore, and Anneke darted inside.

Khos pounded up the stairs.

Inside, Nyx was on the floor with Inaya on top of her. Inaya screamed and pulled at Nyx's butchered hair. Nyx caught both of Inaya's wrists and told her to calm down.

"You godless whore!" Inaya cried. "You dirty godless whore!"

Anneke walked over to a soggy box sitting on the tea table. The unmistakable reek of death clung to it. Anneke used the end of her shotgun to open the lid of the box. She grimaced, and slid the lid back on.

Khos deposited Nikodem on the divan and pushed Anneke aside. She grunted.

"You bloody bitch! You bloody bitch!"

As Khos reached for the lid, Inaya's voice began to fade. The baby was crying. Crying and crying.

He pushed the lid back and let it fall to the table.

Khos half-hoped, right up to that moment, that it would be Rhys's head.

But, no, the head inside the box had been severed from its body recently enough that it was still recognizable as Taite's. Bloody, covered in sand, discolored, yes... but still the head of his friend.

Khos felt unsteady. He pushed Nikodem's bruised legs out of the way and sat down on the divan.

Sound started to come back—the screaming baby, Inaya's sobbing. Nyx was speaking in low tones, and when he swung his head to look at her, he saw her kneeling next to Inaya.

"I'm not perfect," Nyx said.

"You bloody bitch," Inaya murmured.

Khos wanted to take Inaya into his arms and say something profound and comforting, but a part of him still wanted this all to be some kind of mistake. Some part of him still wanted Nyx to be right. He wanted them to win.

But Nyx was just a woman—no more, no less. He turned to Inaya, to hold her, but her body language warned him off. He feared that if he touched her, she would claw him.

"Who brought it here?" Khos asked.

"Some magician," Inaya said.

Khos felt the hair on the back of his neck rise. "A what?"

Nyx stood. "A magician? You're sure?"

"Yes, they all look alike," Inaya said, wiping at her wet face. "What does it matter who brought it?"

"What did she say?" Nyx said.

Inaya's expression got dark, mean. "She said that if you want your own magician back, you're to meet him in Bahreha. She left a map."

Anneke pushed the box aside and found a bloodied newsroll beside it. "Got it, boss."

Nyx took it from her, and unrolled it.

A misty image took shape in front of her. Raine's familiar face formed and spoke.

"You've taken up a better note," he said, and Khos felt his skin crawl at the sound of Raine's voice. It brought back memories of a service he liked even less than his current one.

"But you're still only a bloodletter," Raine continued. "If Taite didn't get your attention, maybe your dancer will. You don't know what you're doing with this woman, just as you never knew what you were doing as a bel dame. You were more of a terrorist than the boys you brought home. I'm waiting for you in Bahreha. Meet us here—" Raine's face dissipated, and a map of the terrain surrounding Bahreha materialized. The image eclipsed, and Khos saw a familiar landform: a low valley set between two rocky hills just west of them, in Bahreha. "Trade her for him, and what's left of your team goes home alive. If you aren't there by dusk tonight, I kill your black dancer. And then I kill the rest of you. I offer you this because of our former partnership.

"Your sins don't make you cleaner than I, Nyxnissa. I kill for the good of Nasheen, but you kill indiscriminately, with malice. That is the difference between us. Now I ask you to think of our country, our boys. Think of ending the war."

The particles making up the image began to come apart and diffused through the room until nothing was left of Raine's message but the smell of burned lemon.

"How the fuck did he know we had her?" Khos said.

Nyx threw the empty newsroll across the room. "Because our fucking transceivers are hackable," she spat. "Anneke, pack up. Now."

"But, boss—"

"Now."

"Boss, we ain't going to trade, are we? Taite's dead. Rhys's dead too, wager. I worked for Raine. That old man—"

"You think he hurt—" Khos began.

"Don't think about Rhys," Nyx said, and something came into her voice, something that twisted Khos's gut, because it sounded like fear. "Pack. Both of you. We're going to Bahreha. Anneke, did you pack my sword?"

"I *wasn't* thinking about Rhys," Khos said. "I was thinking about Mahrokh and her house."

"Don't worry about the whores."

"I got it wrapped up in the back, boss. You want it?"

"Yeah. You got the baldric too?"

Khos gritted his teeth. He walked past Taite's rotting head to get his rifle. Anneke shot past him, stuffing extra transceivers into a gunnysack.

"If he knows where we are, he'll have the place staked out," Khos said. "Why didn't he take Inaya?"

Nyx didn't look at Inaya. She took the bundle Anneke handed her and unwrapped her sword and baldric. "Because she isn't worth anything. Anneke, pack the bakkie. Go. Now. We don't need those."

"Boss, this is the biggest gun we've—"

"Leave it. Downstairs. Now." Nyx tightened her baldric and turned to Inaya. "Are you coming or not?"

Inaya looked back at the box containing her brother's head. From the other room, her son still cried.

"I'm better off here," Inaya said.

"You're not," Khos said. He strode up to her, despite Nyx's look, and pressed his hand to her shoulder. He didn't care, in that moment, if she hit him. "Come with us, or he'll kill you. If he doesn't, Nyx's sisters will. You're tied to her now, and if you're tied to Nyx, you're dead without her. We all learned that a long time ago."

"I don't belong to her," Inaya spit.

"I don't either," Khos said, "but if you have to choose sides, choosing Nyx might keep you alive awhile longer."

"Like it kept Taite alive?"

"He wouldn't have made it this far without her. I'll tell you about it sometime. Come on, get up."

"Leave her," Nyx said. She was pulling loops of bullet rounds over her head. She had a scattergun in one hand.

Khos ignored her, kept his attention on Inaya. She was far too pale, her eyes hollowed. It was as if someone had pulled something from her, drained her dry of blood and passion. He remembered Taite telling him stories of his brash, arrogant sister, the one who had once driven in from town with a stolen bakkie she had cut up and rewired, her hair butchered because women weren't allowed to drive. In her haste, it was the only way she could think of to pass for a boy. In the back seat of the stolen bakkie was a dying shifter who'd been stoned in the street.

"*She cried,*" Taite had said. "*She cried and cried, but she saved that woman's life.*"

But this Inaya would not look at him. This Inaya said, "Take my son. Your women will get him a place."

Khos took her by the arm, a surprisingly small arm, and pulled her—not ungently—to her feet. "Stand," he said softly. "Your son is yours, no one else's. Don't deprive him of a mother because you're too scared to stand."

"We're going!" Nyx shouted from the door. "Grab Nikodem!"

"We ain't all gonna fit in the bakkie, boss."

"You ride up top," Nyx said. Anneke was already pounding down the steps. Nyx hesitated in the doorway, turning back to look at Khos and Inaya.

Khos met Nyx's gaze, and for a long moment they stared at each other. Her burnous was tied only at the neck and hung behind her like a cape, so he saw her without any pretense, any added bulk, no deception. Her eyes were hard and black, and she looked at him the way she looked at everything else in her life—with cold determination, a willingness to part with whatever she knew, she saw, she had, to accomplish whatever she set herself to. She would leave him. She would leave Inaya. The wounds snaking up her legs were almost healed. He noted the missing fingers on the hand that clutched the scattergun, and the worn hilt of the sword sticking through the slit in her burnous. The world could burn around her, the cities turn to dust, the cries of a hundred thousand fill the air, and she would get up after the fire died and walk barefoot and burned over the charred soil in search of clean water, a weapon, a purpose. She would rebuild.

"Yes or no?" Nyx said. "It's a long drive."

Inaya gazed up at Khos, her face a mask of mourning. Her son cried.

"Yes," Khos said.

Nyx started down the stairs.

"Get your son," Khos said.

Inaya went back to her room, and Khos helped her pack her carpetbag. She put her son into a sling and held him to her.

Khos herded her and her son down the stairs. "I'll be right behind you," he said.

Inaya stumbled downstairs.

Khos walked over to the box containing Taite's head. Nyx couldn't protect them. She had lost Taite, and she would lose Rhys.

Khos had promised to look after Inaya.

Damn him and his bloody fucking promises.

He pulled the transceiver out of his burnous pocket and called Haj.

"What do you have for me?" she said.

"Everything," Khos said, and put the lid back on the box.

Something inside of him hurt, and he thought about why he'd come to Nasheen four years before. He thought about the

32

Nyx drove them out of Dadfar and into the desert. A fine dust coated the interior of the bakkie and the seams of their skin. She wore a pair of goggles and a scarf tied over her butchered hair. Nyx left a long trail of dead and dying beetles in her wake and tried not to think too much about a dancer on the other side of Bahreha.

Inaya sat next to her, her little body tense, clutching her baby to her breast. She stared out across the flat plain of the desert, the monotonous line of the road, and said nothing.

Sitting next to the door, Khos kept his rifle in his lap and his elbow jutting out the open window.

Anneke tapped on the windshield when the heat got too bad, and they stopped to wait out the worst of the day at a little roadside oasis.

The place was empty except for a couple of stray cats and some black tumbleweeds rolling through the empty courtyard of a long-abandoned market. Nyx knew Bahreha. In the spring, this whole blasted desert heath turned green. She had laid mines just north of the city and dug trenches out here, somewhere real close. The whole place looked different in the summer. It was like she was traveling on some long road, headed full circle.

Nyx popped the trunk and pulled off the cooling tarp she'd thrown over Nikodem. Despite the tarp, Nikodem was sweating a lot, too much. Her face was swollen, and when the tarp came up, she didn't do much more than loll her head back and squint. Her eyes looked funny.

Nyx pulled her out and hauled her over to the relative shade of the massive stone arches bordering the courtyard. A couple of mangy palm trees jutted up from the sandy ground near the fountain. She saw some termite mounds in the far distance, but no trace of acid sprayers or centipedes. Inaya moved after them to stand in the shade. Khos shadowed her.

Anneke trudged up to the fountain and returned with a half-filled bucket of brackish water. Nyx doused Nikodem in it. Anneke went back for more, and the two of them wet Nikodem through until the off-worlder shivered and her eyes started to focus again.

"What did you give her?" Anneke asked.

"Nothing. She's overheated," Nyx said.

"Fool," Nikodem murmured, and her speech was slurred. "You don't know what you're doing."

"Why don't you tell me?" Nyx said.

Nikodem firmed up her mouth.

Nyx slapped her.

Nikodem slobbered all over herself and started shaking. "Oh, it's much better than you could imagine," Nikodem said, and grinned a stupid grin, then winced. Her lip was split and bloody. She was brutally heat sick.

"You wanted to play Nasheen and Chenja for fools, and now you'll die for it," Nyx said. "I'm not the one looking the fool here."

"I've created whole armies on our world, the real world," Nikodem said. "Dumb beasts. I could create armies here. Different sorts of beasts, beasts you could never imagine. Your magicians and shifters…. You have no idea of their potential. We just need to understand… The Chenjans are more advanced than you are, did you know it? All that holds them back is their religion. They fear God's wrath. But I could breed you the sorts of creatures you couldn't even imagine. Armies. I can breed them full-formed, like baby foals."

Nyx had no idea what a foal was, but it didn't sound good. "Anneke," Nyx said, "more water." The water would keep her talking.

Anneke walked back to the fountain. Khos stood by, watching Inaya more than the road. Nyx didn't like the way they looked at each other. She didn't like a whole lot of things right now.

Nyx crouched next to Nikodem but kept one eye on the road.

"Listen, woman, listen," Nikodem said. "No longer will you have to see your sons and daughters, brothers and sisters, dying at the front. You can manufacture these beasts and send them out in your stead. Let God decide."

"Beasts?" Nyx grimaced. "Shifters aren't beasts. What do you and the Kinaanites get out of this?"

Nikodem turned her head away again. Nyx punched her this time. Closed fist.

Nikodem hiccuped and shook. She bared her bloody teeth and spat. "You'll find that ours is the only way to understand God. There was only one prophet, one Son of God, and He bled and died for *us*! Yours was a warmonger, just as you are, and you will fight your war unto death. You say you are people of the Book, but your religion is black, corrupted."

"Yeah, your Prophet's such a pacifist he sends you to other worlds for weapons and tells you to keep us fighting each other? Fuck that, you hypocrite alien."

Nikodem coughed and hacked. "We have a war to fight. You don't understand. We fight in God's name."

"I understand just fine," Nyx said.

Nikodem rattled off something that sounded like a curse. "With shifters and magicians, we could pound our enemies into submission. We can do much, blending your genes with ours."

So Nikodem was just another gene pirate, a fucking *interstellar gene pirate*, manufacturing weapons for her own God's war, calling Nasheenians and Chenjans dung beetles, like some holier-than-thou Tirhani.

"I should cut your head off right now," Nyx said.

Anneke returned with more water. Nyx dumped it over Nikodem's head.

The woman shivered, then spat, "Oh, what do you know? You're just an uneducated bloodletter. What do you know about God's plan, about the salvation of your soul?"

"No more than a butcher," Nyx said. "But a butcher knows how to serve it halal." She stood. "Anneke, put her back in the trunk."

Two-faced, two sides, like Rasheeda.

It all made her head hurt. She had one good solution to this problem, the same old solution, but Raine wanted Nikodem alive. Nyx could kill her later.

After Anneke dragged Nikodem back into the trunk, Nyx turned to her and Khos. "Khos, I'm going to need your shot. It's not as good as Rhys's, but it'll do. Can you work your way around from the other side of the hills? I want you to fire on Raine if he pulls first."

"And if he doesn't pull?"

"We walk away."

"And leave Nikodem?" Khos said, and she heard the surprise in his voice.

"When we walk away, I want you to shoot her."

"I won't do that."

"I'm a bad shot, Khos. I can't do point."

"I'll do it, boss," Anneke said. "I'm a better shot than the old dog anyway."

"Fine." Nyx pulled a ball of sen out of her pocket, rolled it between her fingers. "He'll have his own shooter up there. You take that one out. When me and Khos are clear, I need you to shoot Nikodem."

"And Raine?"

"You leave Raine to me."

"You know he travels with a magician," Khos said.

"We'll have ours there."

"He'll be drugged," Khos said. "And he's hardly a magician even when he's sober."

Nyx pocketed the sen. "I've got some unguent in the back. We'll slather ourselves with it before we go in. It'll slow the bugs down, at least. Confuse their sense of smell.

"Keep your transceiver on you. If the plan changes, I'll let you know," Nyx said. "When we have Rhys—after we get some distance—you take Nikodem out. Or, if Raine tries to pull when we back up, you shoot whoever pulls the weapon. You can try shooting at the magician, but she'll likely have some defenses up. Lay down some cover fire, and I'll deal with Raine. Me and Khos can take Nikodem's head and wrap it in the organic burnous. Then we get the fuck out of here and go home and collect our money."

"Sounds thin," Anneke said.

"Sounds like all we've got," Khos said, and pulled up the hood of his burnous. "Can we go now?"

They drove out past the shrine marking the sandy road that headed up toward the hills. Nyx dropped Anneke off with a good burnous and a bag of water, and Anneke loped off toward the hills with her rifle slung over her shoulder.

Nyx looked over at Inaya and her kid, at Khos. He was staring out the window. "You ready?" she asked.

"Let's get it over with," he said. Inaya's kid started crying again.

"Give Anneke a minute to set up," Nyx said. She got out of the bakkie and walked around the shrine. She needed some space.

Nyx sat down on the other side of the shrine, in the shadow of the great curved slab, and watched a couple lizards scuttle away from her. She took a deep breath and clenched and unclenched her hands, taking a good look at them. She thought about Raine. Tried not to think about Rhys, about what Raine had done to him.

Raine knew her, knew how she worked. He'd taught her how to work that way. He knew all about Bahreha. It was why he asked her out here.

She rubbed at her eyes with her palms.

"Nyx," Khos said.

She looked up. He stood over her, too tall and too broad, a foreign man in a foreign country. But, then, here in the Chenjan desert, she was a foreigner too. And an infidel. An enemy.

"Anneke's reached the top," he said.

"Yeah. All right."

She pulled out the unguent from one of the gear bags. They wiped themselves down with it and then got into the bakkie and drove out to the base of the hills, until the road got too rocky to drive on.

Nyx parked, and Khos helped her move some stones behind the back tires.

"I want you to stay here, Inaya," Nyx said. "When you see us heading back, I want you to take the stones out from behind the tires and start the bakkie. Understand?"

"Yes," Inaya said.

Nyx checked all of her gear and cleaned her pistols. Khos cleaned his own. They did not speak. She nodded at him when he was done, and Khos popped the trunk and pulled Nikodem out. Nyx gave her some water, but the alien could barely keep her feet.

Nyx and Khos got Nikodem to walk by holding her up between them.

They stumbled through some low-lying scrub and into a rocky gully. The hills reared up on either side of them, a pair of heavy breasts that Nyx might have found comforting under different circumstances.

"Let's keep out of the gully," she said. The sky was clear above them, but there were dark clouds just north, and that meant it was raining up in the mountains. Gullies filled up hard and fast in the desert. The water might be coming their way already. She didn't trust the weather. She didn't trust much of anything.

They killed a couple of acid-spraying chiggers along the way and surprised a centipede eating what looked like a sand cat kitten, but they were all wild bugs—nothing Raine had thrown at them.

Nyx and Khos—with Nikodem still between them—skirted the edge of the gully, which meant treading through waist-high brush. Long scratches lined Nyx's already scarred legs, and a flurry of biting bugs rose in soft clouds around them.

They cleared the scrub and rounded a bend in the path along the gully, giving Nyx a clear view past the base of the hill. She saw a tall, solitary figure wearing yellow robes. Bugs crawled along the hem of the robe. Magician.

Nyx told Khos to hold up.

Nikodem sagged between them. Nyx left her in Khos's grasp and stepped forward to the lip of the gully. Sand and stones tumbled down the soft slope and into the ditch below.

Nyx surveyed the surrounding hilltops—there were plenty of rocky, scrub-filled places to hide. Why show his magician up front? To keep her from doing something stupid? Raine knew it was already too late for that.

Something moved just across the gully. Nyx reached for her pistol with her bad hand. What had appeared to be another swath of uninteresting brush blurred and morphed into a dark, bare-headed man in a tattered robe lying in the rocky sand. Behind him stood the hefty, barrel-chested Raine.

Nyx saw another man step out far to the left of them. She

recognized him as Dakar, a mercenary from the Cage. He was broad in the shoulders and narrow in the hips, with a crop of black hair and legs that looked too big and beefy to carry him very far. Nyx remembered that he was also a shape shifter, and a good shot.

Nyx held her pistol in her bad hand. "You tell him to stand down!"

"Why?" Raine said.

Nyx grabbed Nikodem by the arm and jerked her close. She put the gun to Nikodem's head. "Because I'm a better shot from here."

Khos's hands moved toward his pistol.

Nyx dropped her gaze to Rhys. Rhys's face was turned away from her, and one arm rested limp on his chest. He had not moved.

"He alive?" she barked.

Raine nudged Rhys with his sandaled foot. Rhys put up a hand as if to ward off a blow.

"Alive enough," Raine said.

"You get him up and push him across the gully," Nyx said. "I do the same with mine, and we walk off. You keen?"

"I'm disappointed, Nyx. No threats? No lectures?"

"You've always been the blowhard. You played this dirty from the start. I want this over."

"You pass me the mark, and we'll see about your magician."

"Don't push, Raine. I've got nothing to lose." She tightened her grip on Nikodem.

Raine pulled a small curved blade from his belt. Even from across the gully, she recognized it. It was the knife she'd taken from him the night he took her ear. She'd cut off his cock with it.

"There are plenty more pieces of him I can cut off," Raine said.

Nyx took Nikodem by the collar and pushed her toward the lip of the gully. The alien stumbled and muttered something in her language. She was going to need more water. Her skin was loose and dry.

Raine made no move toward Rhys.

Nyx tensed. She kept her hold on Nikodem's collar. She wanted to throw her into the gully and be done with her.

Nyx licked the sweat from her upper lip. The sun was low in the sky. She saw something glinting up there on the hill, maybe ten yards up.

She heard a shot.

Nikodem jerked and crumpled. Nyx let her fall. Another shot rang out. Khos yelled at her. His gun went off.

Nyx leapt into the gully, and as she jumped she pulled one of the poisoned needles from her hair and flung it at Raine.

The needle bounced right off him, but he clawed at his left breast and stepped back. By the time he recovered, Nyx was up over the lip of the other side of the gully. She grabbed Rhys by one arm and one leg and yanked him down with her. They tumbled back into the ditch in a hail of sand and gravel.

Shots sounded behind her, close. She heard a dog bark. She regained her feet and turned just in time to see a brown dog leap at her.

Nyx dropped low and reached behind her. She pulled her sword from its sheath in one clean stroke with her good hand and brought it down in front of her. The dog met the blade, and another shot from the other side of the gully felled the dog. It collapsed at her feet and choked on its own blood while shedding hair and slowly half-morphing back into the form of Dakar.

Nyx heard a soft cascade of sand and stone behind her and turned with her blade to see Raine bearing down on her, sword drawn.

She put herself and her blade between Raine and Rhys. She heard more shots. Somebody was going to run out of bullets.

Raine hacked at her. She stepped left, caught the blow. She had to use both hands on the hilt to push him back. He outweighed her and he had the higher ground, but if she tried to reverse their positions she would leave Rhys unguarded.

She saw a blur of tawny blond lope up at her right. Khos had shifted. The dog grabbed Rhys by the ankle and started dragging him.

Nyx stepped back and tried to find solid footing on the gully floor. Raine swung again. She parried and moved her feet. Boxing and sword fighting were their own sorts of dances, but you learned the footwork for one and you knew how important footwork was for the other.

She thrust forward and ducked and moved again. The problem with Raine being bigger was that she couldn't take many heavy blows. And she was missing two fucking fingers on one hand. She needed to avoid those blows at all costs.

For Raine the problem with being bigger was that he couldn't move as fast as she could.

She danced back toward the other side of the gully. Raine pulled his knife again and came at her with both blades.

Nyx stumbled on a twisted bit of wood. She crouched and blocked a blow from above. Raine cut toward her with the knife in his other hand.

Nyx was already too close to the ground. She rolled and caught him around the legs. He toppled, and she used her grip on him for leverage. As he fell, she shot back up and thrust her blade down.

He twisted and rolled, and then she lost her feet.

Raine dropped his sword and used his free hand to take her sword hand by the wrist. He struggled on top of her, trying to pin her so he could use the knife.

Nyx caught his wrist in her bad hand and wrapped her legs around his torso. Stones bit into her back. Dust clogged her mouth. Raine's sweat dripped into her face.

She pushed herself up on her right shoulder and rolled him over.

She let go of the sword—it was too long, this close.

Beneath her, Raine was a barrel of heat, fat, padding-thick muscle. He stank of old leather and fermented wine and the distasteful funk that was Raine—a scent altogether too spicy, too strong, like a musk that had gone sour.

He had her by one wrist, but with her other hand she had his left wrist, the one with the dagger. He gritted his teeth. She kept him locked between her legs.

While they grappled, she heard a distant sound. Somebody calling her name. A wasp landed on her arm. Another buzzed past Raine's head.

And she realized there was only one reason Khos would have shifted in the middle of a firefight.

Bullets could kill dogs as well as people.

But bugs were tailored to go after humans.

Fucking *magician*.

Raine's expression was grim, and sweat poured down his darkening face.

Bugs. Well. Let him send bugs.

I have lived through worse, she thought, and she said it aloud, bit through the words: "I've survived worse than you."

"You have," Raine gasped, and he made to roll her again. "But in the end I realized I made you, and because of that, it's my duty to end you."

She twisted her other hand free and grappled for the dagger, two-handed now.

They rolled again along the gully floor. The blade cut the inside of her left arm. She pushed back.

He was on top of her again. Her arms shook as she held him away. His free hand came down on her throat. She pressed her chin down and pushed her body back a half inch, enough to get a breath.

"Look at what you've become," he said, and he was sweating into her face again, big salty drops that fell onto her cheeks, her lips. The veins in his neck stood out. "Do you realize what you've become? You have no honor, no purpose. You bleed others for money with no idea of the consequences. What a fool you are to think that killing this woman solves anything at all."

His grip tightened on her throat. She stabbed her foot into the sand again and pushed back, caught her breath.

"And you're a fool for thinking that killing me is some kind of epic duty," Nyx said.

How many men had made her? Her brothers, by dying? Yah Tayyib, by rebuilding her? All those dead boys whose heads she brought back to the clerks? Raine, by teaching her how to drive and how to die? Tej and Rhys and Khos and all Raine's half-breed muscle? They were just men. They were just people. They had made her as surely as Queen Ayyad and Queen Zaynab, Bashir, Jaks, Radeyah, and her sisters had. Her hordes of sisters, Kine and the bel dames and the women who kicked her out of school for getting her letters fucked. No, she could have gone either way; followed all or none of them. It wasn't what was done to you. Life was what you did with what was done to you.

"You didn't make me," Nyx gasped. "I made *myself*."

She released her bad hand from the dagger and wrapped her fingers around Raine's face. She shoved her thumb into his eye. Press and pop. She dislodged the eye from the socket and punctured the orb. Blood and fluid leaked into her face. He jerked away from her before she could sever the optic nerve. The eye bobbed against his face.

Raine swore. He grabbed at his smashed eye.

Nyx heard a buzzing sound above her, and something dark moved across the sun.

Nyx jabbed her knee into Raine's side and pushed him over again. He started to bellow at her, just nonsense. She couldn't make anything of it over the buzzing of the bugs and pounding of her heart. She wrapped both hands around Raine's knife and plunged the dagger down at him. He pushed back at her. She leapt off him suddenly, rolled left, and grabbed his forgotten sword. It was better than hers.

He'd lost his vision on that side, and while he tried to scramble to his feet and turn his head to catch sight of her, Nyx took up the blade and brought it down where he still floundered in the sand. The blade slid right through him, through fat and muscle alike. She pressed into him until the hilt lodged against his chest and the length of it buried itself in the sand.

Raine grunted.

Above her, a cloud of wasps circled.

Nyx was breathing hard. Blood trickled from the cut in her forearm. Her knees and elbows were bruised and bloodied. She took up the dagger.

Raine gasped. He had both hands on the hilt of the sword. She pressed her knee into his chest and leaned into him. His eye dangled from its socket. Blood leaked from the corner.

Nyx grabbed his ear. A dozen wasps buzzed around the hood of her burnous. Three of them crawled along her arm. She felt more of them alighting in her hair.

The knife was sharp. Raine kept his gear in good shape.

She sawed off his ear, and he writhed and bellowed at her. She leaned over him so he could see her tuck it into her dhoti.

"Deliver her to the Queen," he said, spitting blood. "Don't kill her."

"I'll be as merciful to her as you've been to me," Nyx said.

She put her other hand on the hilt of the sword, pressed on it as she moved her face within inches of his. She whispered, "I intend to collect you in pieces."

"Nyx!"

Her name, on the wind, above the buzz of the bugs. A cloud of wasps circling her. One of them stung her arm.

Nyx pushed herself back up. She stood amid a swarm of wasps. She could not see either side of the gully. The world was a buzzing, hissing swarm. She put a hand over her mouth, tried to breathe without inhaling wasps.

But what did it matter? What did it matter?

Raine's ear cooled against her skin. She felt the blood leaking down her belly.

"Nyx!"

Why did they call her? Why bother? They were all dead anyway. They should have died the night Fatima and Rasheeda took her. Then she would be dead too, and all this would be over.

"Nyx!"

She stumbled toward the voice without knowing why. She felt the wasps sting her face, her arms, her legs. She had sweated away most of the unguent. She kept her hand over her face.

She fell, and banged her knee on a stone. She dropped the dagger and put both hands down to catch herself. Her hands came away wet.

Water. Why was there water in the gully? Unless…

Nyx ran blindly toward what she hoped was the other side of the gully.

Water rushed past her ankles. As she ran, the water rose, and then she was slogging through it. The wasps stung.

She hated it when she was right about the fucking weather.

She lost her fight with the water.

Nyx let herself drop under. The buzz of the bugs abruptly stopped. Her burning skin was suddenly cool. The current was strong. Bits of stone and wood and some dead thing smashed into her. She broke the surface, tried to stand. The water was chest-deep now.

She could not swim, of course.

When she looked up, the cloud of wasps was somewhere behind her. She tried to find her footing, but the current was too strong.

Nyx collided with the side of the gully. She groped for a hand-hold and found a loose root. She held on and hauled herself out of the water. She rolled onto the other bank like a beached log and gasped. Anneke was running over to her from just upriver, her gun slung behind her, bumping against her ass.

"Where's Rhys?" Nyx asked.

"You breathing, boss?"

Anneke crouched next to her, cloaked in a sheen of sweat.

"Where's Rhys?" she repeated.

"Still upstream, boss." She looked over her shoulder at the raging water in the gully.

Nyx pulled herself into a sitting position and gazed out at the gully as well. Raine had been in there. Pinned to the ground with a sword. She reached for the ear she'd tucked into her dhoti, but it was gone, torn away by the water.

She looked for the cloud of wasps but saw nothing upstream.

"Where's Khos?" Nyx asked.

"Last I saw, the fucker was running back toward the bakkie."

Nyx knitted her brows. Her arms and face stung. "Go see if the bakkie's still there," she said.

Fucker, she thought. Cowardly fucker. And perhaps something worse. If Khos had headed out before the end of the fight, it was more than possible that he had either set himself up with a back exit or, worse... Please, fuck, she thought, let that not be it. That's not it. He wouldn't do that. Nobody on my team would do that.

She got to her feet. Anneke ran off toward the bakkie.

Nyx stumbled along the bank toward the scrub, searching for Rhys. She saw one dark arm flung out from a line of scrub, palm open toward the sky. She had a sudden memory of her sister, Kine, in the tub, bloodied, eyeless.

She fell to her knees and scrambled toward him. He opened his eyes, squinted at her. Closed his eyes.

"You," he said.

"Me," she said.

"I saw you fall."

"Thought you could get rid of me so easy?"

"Hoped," he said, and opened his eyes again.

"I think I killed Raine."

"Never liked him anyway," Rhys said.

"You still drugged?"

"Yes. But it should wear off. I was due for another dose."

"They fuck you up?" Nyx asked.

Rhys closed his eyes again, grimaced.

"We need to go," she said.

"Their magician was shot, but she'll be coming around."

"It's not the magician I'm worried about," Nyx said. She looked behind her at the raging water in the gully. Where was Nikodem? Had she fallen and washed down the gully too? Or had she scrambled back up the way Nyx had, heading for the road?

She glanced back down at Rhys, at the shallow rise and fall of his chest. She saw now that there was something wrong with his hands. The fingers looked twisted. Broken.

She wanted to kill Raine again. Even dirtier this time.

Nyx closed her mouth, leaned back away from Rhys. Her heart ached. This wasn't the time for petty sentiment. She had spent so long trying not to feel anything.

"We need to go. I'll carry you," she said.

She squatted and pushed her arms underneath him. She was nearly the same size as Rhys, but as she lifted him, she had to go easy, find her balance. She was exhausted.

The stings hurt, and her vision was going blurry. Her knees nearly buckled. The heat was rapidly sucking the moisture from her hair and clothes.

She followed the gully back down through the hills. The water was already lowering, bleeding off. She looked behind her and no longer saw any storm clouds. At least when it rained up there it didn't last long.

Sand stuck to her skin. She'd lost a sandal somewhere in the gully. She walked with a limp. As she walked, she became increasingly certain that Khos had taken Inaya and the bakkie and fucked off. And Rhys was getting heavier. Her breath came hard. She stumbled.

She looked at Rhys, in her arms. A couple of hours. Could he walk in a couple of hours, after the drugs wore off?

A shot sounded ahead of them. The sound of a rifle.

Nyx stopped, and was going to drop Rhys and reach for her pistol when she realized she didn't have it. She was down to two poisoned needles in her hair and a razor blade in her one remaining sandal.

She had to make a decision. The shot had come from the direction of the bakkie, which likely wasn't there anyway. Behind her was more Chenjan desert, a desert she had last seen a decade before, in the spring. A desert she had blown apart. Something flew over her head, circled them, flew back toward the bakkie.

A white raven.

Nyx looked behind her. They could skirt the other side of the hill, hole up in a cave until dark, and wait for Rhys to get his strength back. They could walk out.

Someone snickered.

Nyx turned.

Rasheeda strode toward them, naked and still shivering. A hail of white feathers blew out behind her.

Nyx tensed.

She needed to run. Taite was dead. Anneke probably was, too. They'd kill Rhys and her, eventually. If they caught her.

Run.

Drop the fucking Chenjan and run, she thought. Fucking run. Oh, God.

Everything was burning. She was burning in the desert.

Someone moved on the other side of the gully.

Dahab carried a rifle. Half her face was a mass of scar tissue and badly healed bone. One black eye, not her own, peered out from the wrecked half of her face.

Bel dames were hard to kill… especially when there was a magician just down the hall when they were shot.

Run, Nyx thought. Bloody fucking hell, why can't I fucking run? She started to shake.

Rhys opened his eyes. They didn't focus right. She wondered if he even saw her.

She wanted to say something stupid and profound.

But all she managed to say was "Don't die."

She choked on the rest.

They wouldn't kill her, not yet.

Whoever wanted her wanted her alive.

Rasheeda flexed her fingers and licked her lips. She stopped three paces from them, one arm akimbo. "I missed you, sister," she said.

Nyx heard another shot. Something hot and heavy slammed into her back. She lost her balance and tumbled, Rhys in her arms. She tasted dust. She writhed in the sand and reached toward Rhys. He tried to get up. The bel dames were laughing. Another gun went off.

She wanted to hold his hand.

33

Rhys lay on his side on a hard, gritty floor. The air was hot and oddly humid. His shattered hands were bound behind him, and they throbbed. Someone lay across from him. Shiny darkness pooled on the stones under her.

"Nyx?" he said. "Nyx?"

They were in some kind of cell. He saw pale orange light between him and Nyx, seeping from beneath the door. He thought it was Nyx. Was she dead? Had they killed her?

"Nyx," he said.

The figure moved and moaned.

Nyx.

His hands bled pain, but he tried to move them anyhow. The knots were tight. His head still hurt. He closed his eyes and tried to find the bugs, tried to call out for something, anything. Some wasps or some pinchers, preferably roaches to gnaw through the sticky bands. But he met only a wall of blackness, emptiness. His whole world had gone silent.

"Nyx," he said again.

She turned toward him. His eyes were adjusting to the low light coming in from under the door.

Her hands were bound too, but in front of her. She reached toward him.

"They shot me," she said.

"You make a good target," he said.

She made a strange hiccuping sound. It took him a moment to realize she was laughing.

"God, that hurts," she said, and gasped.

"Where did they hit you?"

"You can't feel it?"

"I'm blind like this." How long ago had Raine drugged him? His head swam. Memory bit him, memories of blood and needles and the sound of bone crunching under boots. His hands twitched.

"It's bad," she said.

Fear choked him. Suddenly and completely. Nyx never said it was bad, even when it was. "How bad? Where is it?" he said.

"Where's Anneke? Is she in here?"

"Where are you shot, Nyx?"

She reached out and grabbed him by the collar, pulled him close. They lay a breath apart on the dirty floor. There was something wet underneath him now. Her blood.

"You're bleeding," he said, stupidly. She was shivering.

He needed his hands. He twisted his wrists, tried to loosen the bands again. His hands throbbed. Pain blinded him.

"I can stop the bleeding," he said. "I just need my hands. If I can—"

"My sandal," she said.

"Did they—"

"It's here." She brought up her leg and kicked something from the sole of it. The razor blade. He heard it clink across the floor. "Lie on your belly. I can cut you out."

He turned onto his stomach, and she cut his hands free from behind him.

Rhys tried to flex his ruined fingers. White pain shuddered through him. Something tapped at the corner of his mind. He heard a chittering sound—the delicate flutter of a moth's wings. He closed his eyes and concentrated.

Where were they? It was like reaching through a dark gauze.

"I'm dying," Nyx said.

"No," he said. He put his hands on her. She rolled over onto her back. More blood escaped from beneath her. Too much blood.

"I fucked it up," she said.

He couldn't disagree with that. "Yes," he said.

"I wanted to be brave," Nyx said.

"Brave? I heard about the front. Did you forget I knew that? How much more brave—"

"That's a lie," she muttered.

"What?" He could almost feel the hurt in her. He closed his eyes again. If he just concentrated, just willed the drug out of him...

"I'm not a hero," Nyx said. "I shouldn't have been reconstituted. They should have buried me in the Orrizo. Fuck, I was stupid."

Rhys opened his eyes. "What?"

She was still shivering.

"I was a sapper," she said. "We went in and exploded bursts, cleared minefields. I told you I was too good to kill. I could cut out a mine and make four better ones from the guts. You give me a magician and some bug juice and I could take out half a city. And I did, you know, I did... I watched a lot of boys die. A lot of good boys. I killed a lot of good boys. Women, kids. Everyone."

"It's a war, Nyx. None of us did things we're proud of." Rhys caught himself.

"I was good at it. It made me somebody else, though. I didn't like what it made me."

He heard them, then. The bugs. Close. He needed more time. How much time did she have?

"Nyx, you can't—"

"I was doing a sweep at the edge of some agricultural compound out here. Bahreha, back before I blew all these compounds. It didn't used to be desert. Oh, I was so good. I took out whole cities, Rhys, whole cities full of your people, women and girls too. I was just doing some stupid job with my squad, clearing these flesh mines, and I fucked up.

"I set off a burst. Just one burst, clumsy, and when I did it I fucking froze, and then I just clawed past those boys in my squad, those boys I fought and bled with, and I didn't even warn them. Didn't even call out. Just ran.

"There was acid everywhere. My boys blew apart and melted. I crawled out with their bloody steaming guts all over me. When I got out, they had to spray me off with a neutralizer.

"What kind of a woman does that, Rhys? Lets boys die? We're supposed to protect them. I let them die. I killed my own boys."

She fell silent for a long time.

In the silence, Rhys heard the hiss of a nest of cockroaches. Then nothing. Only the labored sound of Nyx's breathing. How badly was she hurt? He needed to *know*.

"I burned myself," she said in the darkness. "I got drunk and went out into the fields. The moons were in progression back then, and, oh, they were so big and bloody and there was plenty of light. I dragged out a keg of fuel oil, the kind we used for fire bursts, and I set myself on fire. I just set myself on fire, Rhys—"

"Nyx—"

"I judged myself."

"Judgment is God's task, not yours."

"I left God in Bahreha."

Rhys heard footsteps outside the door. The light changed. Rhys fell back onto his side and tucked his hands behind him.

The door started to open.

Nyx used her thumb to push the razor blade under him.

A woman stood in the doorway, a black shadow.

"Get her up," the woman said, and Rasheeda padded in behind her and took Nyx under the arms and hauled her out.

"What are you doing with her?" Rhys asked.

"That's not your problem, kid," the woman said. He knew her

voice. Was she one of the bel dames? He squinted. There was something about her, something about her hands…

Rasheeda dragged Nyx out of the cell.

"Where are you taking her?" he persisted.

"Don't you worry," the woman said, and when she turned into the light, he knew her. "We'll come back for you soon enough."

34

Khos's father had been afraid of three things: dancing, women, and wine. He had told Khos that what made men from boys was a man's ability to drive well, shoot straight, and tell the truth.

For thirty-four years, Khos had heeded that advice with a fervor he would call religious. He followed that creed long after he had violated every law in his country and some others besides and found himself pining after women with the sort of blind affection Mhorians were supposed to reserve for those of their own sex. Women were not the same people, his father and uncles said. They did not feel the same, did not love the same. They bled and gave birth and died according to their own rules. Their hearts were great deserts of secrets, and those deserts were not a place a man could ever hope to cross, let alone conquer.

When he shifted to human form in front of the bakkie, he paused only to kick out the rocks from behind the tires and pull on an extra burnous from the back.

Inaya was nursing her son, and she said nothing to him until the bakkie was belching and grinding down the barely passable road, toward the shrine.

"What happened?" she asked.

"They're dead," he lied, and the lie tasted bad, like blood.

"Where are we going?"

"Tirhan."

"Tirhan? Are you mad? How will you get there?"

"I know some women who can get us there." She would kill him if he asked her to shift. In any case, her son wouldn't be able to shift at all, even if he'd been born with the talent. Most shifters didn't get the knack of shifting until puberty, though there were exceptions.

"Where's Nyx?"

"I told you." He did not look at her. In her face, he saw too much of Taite. How would he tell Mahdesh? "We go on until dark. I have some money stowed in the back, some side work I've been doing. We'll be safe in Tirhan. Your son will be safe in Tirhan."

And mine, he thought. My son is safe in Tirhan.

The dust blew in from the road. He once heard that when the men at the front marched in formation, those at the center got dust in their nostrils, and their lungs started to seize. They started getting nosebleeds. It got so bad sometimes that the men just dropped out of formation and died there along the road, casualties not of the war but of the desert.

"Khos," Inaya said.

"We'll be all right if we can get in and out of Dadfar fast. We'll need to pick up a few things, some supplies—"

"Khos?"

He hooked a right past the shrine and back onto the main road. Another bakkie screamed past him, spewing red beetles from its back end. There were armed women inside. He was glad they drove too fast for him to make out their faces. He kept his gaze on the road. The long, too-bright road.

"Once we're packed, we can—"

"Khos, where's Nyx?"

He chanced a look at her.

Inaya had pulled the baby from her breast. The boy whined in her lap. Her pale breast hung out the front of her robe. He had a sudden impulse to take the nipple into his own mouth, to close his eyes and ask for comfort.

He gazed back out at the road, shifted pedals.

"We were ambushed. She died."

"You're a terrible liar, Khos."

"This was the only way," he said. "They're letting us go. They only wanted Nyx. I can get us out." He spared a look at her again. Her face... there was something hard in her face, something unexpected. "Inaya, I can save you and your son. He can grow up in Tirhan. There's no war in Tirhan. No mercenaries. No bel dames. No bounty hunters. You can wear a veil and live properly. You can live safe. You can—"

"Do you know where they're taking her?"

"Who?"

"Nyx."

"What?" This wasn't the way it was supposed to go.

"Where are they taking Nyx? Are they killing her or capturing her?"

"I—"

"You can't just leave her back there."

"What are you talking about? She let Taite die. She'd sacrifice me, you, your son, all of us. So long as we're with Nyx, we're dead. It took me a long time to figure that out."

"I heard what that alien said. Nyx isn't doing this for herself."

"What?"

Inaya sighed heavily. She shifted her son in her arms, covered her breast. "You want to run away? Nyx believes that killing this Nikodem woman will stop something much worse. The sort of tech Nikodem has could exploit people like..." And Khos realized she was about to say "us." Instead, Inaya pushed on. "What she's doing won't end with Chenja and Nasheen. Umayma is scarcely habitable. To stir up more bugs, more bursts, more hybrids, more... monsters, will upset everything. How long until it burns through Chenja and Nasheen and moves on? How long before Ras Tieg enslaves shifters and sends them to fight in Nasheen's war? And Tirhan? Mhoria? How long do you intend to shield me? And how long do you think I'll go on, after you're dead?"

"Inaya, Taite—"

"Taite is dead," she said, and he heard a finality in her voice. "I do not love Nyx, but Nikodem and her people are gene pirates, going planet to planet collecting pieces of what they want and need while dropping off reckless alien technology. Things that will destroy us."

The words of his father and uncles came back to him. Unknowable. Irrational. And he remembered Taite's story again, about Inaya driving a stolen bakkie from town, pulling a dying shifter from the backseat.

This Inaya.

"Inaya, Nyx isn't going to save the world—"

"No, perhaps not, but neither are we, by running away from her and the rest. If she cannot succeed in killing the bearer of this knowledge, then one of us needs to. As far as I'm concerned, Nikodem is a gene pirate, and if that's so, someone should stop her."

"Inaya—"

"Do you know where they're taking her?"

Khos tightened his grip on the wheel. "Yes," he said.

"Take me there."

"Inaya—"

"Take me there. Or is this a kidnapping? Don't confuse rescue and kidnapping. I have not asked to be rescued."

He felt suddenly ridiculous, angry. "I'm doing this for Taite! And *you*!"

"Taite is dead. And I don't want it. So who's being served?"

"Fuck!" Khos yelled.

35

Nyx had wanted to be the hero of her own life. Things hadn't turned out that way. Sometimes she thought maybe she could just be the hero of someone else's life, but there was no one who cared enough about her to keep her that close. Hell, there was nobody she'd let that close. No one wanted a hero who couldn't even save herself.

Nyx opened her eyes, but everything was still dark. She heard people talking really close.

"With the information we've gotten from Nasheen and what you can get me from Chenja, all I need is to meld my work with what they're doing in Tirhan, and we'll have hacked this planet like a blood bank."

"Don't know why you had to do it all on the sly."

"It wouldn't be sporting to offer two sides of a holy war the same technology. I had to disappear. You and the magicians gave us that. How were we supposed to deal with Chenja when the only docking bays on the planet are in Nasheen? You know how long this has taken us? Decades."

"Well, you take whatever you want. I give you your pieces of Chenja, and you give me Nyx. I've done work with pirates before. Just take your shit off the planet."

"Our worlds have no shifters, no magicians. The sort of codes you offer us will transform our world. I've been fascinated by some of the mutations I've seen in Mhoria and Ras Tieg. I can't imagine the wonders they're keeping from us in Tirhan."

"Well, you're on your own with Tirhan and the red desert. Tomorrow you'll get your access to the Chenjan compounds. The magicians will arrange it the same way they arranged your disappearance."

Nyx knew one of the voices, the strange accent. She tried to squint. She wished for sight. A gray wash bled across her senses. She squeezed her eyes shut.

"I am endlessly fascinated with Nasheenian magicians."

"Yeah, I got that."

Nikodem laughed. It was a big laugh, far bigger than should have come from the body of such a little woman. "We are even, you and I."

Nyx opened her eyes.

Light flooded her vision. She squinted again. For a moment, everything was blurry light, too intense. Then she started to make out shapes and figures. The world smelled of damp concrete and ammonia.

Nyx struggled to sit up, but someone had bound her to a cold slab at the wrists and ankles.

"Here she is," Nikodem said. She wore a black scarf over her hair, but instead of a robe, she wore loose trousers and a long tunic. She had two pistols belted at her hips.

Nikodem placed a hand on Nyx's arm. Behind the alien, Nyx saw someone else, a tall, brown Nasheenian. White hair, lined face, and his hands... his magician's hands.

Yah Tayyib.

So this was where everything met up. Yah Tayyib turned back into the shadows and left them before she could speak.

There were big lights overhead. Flies circled them.

Nyx was in some kind of converted storage room. Jars of organs lined the walls—jars covered in cooling bugs—and there were two giant, silvery vats against one wall whose sleek sides pulsed. A long table next to Nyx was covered in instruments.

Some tendon worms writhed in a white bowl, trying to escape. She saw a com unit next to the shelving and a dozen bugs chattered in a cold glass case just above it.

Nikodem would keep a laboratory someplace safe. Somewhere magicians and bel dames wouldn't look. Nyx amended that: where *some* magicians and *some* bel dames wouldn't look.

Another woman walked into view from the shadows along the edges of the room. She wore loose trousers and a thigh-length tie-up tunic that she had failed to knot up top. Her small breasts were bound in purple silk. She was a lean, long-faced woman, with the dark circles under her eyes of a bleeder and the confident bouncing walk of a boxer.

Nyx thought the woman reminded her of someone but couldn't place her.

The woman cocked her head at Nyx and grinned. "I can see you trying to figure it out," the woman said.

The grin. Nyx knew that grin, the way it didn't improve the face. There was less joy in it now.

"I know you," Nyx said.

"You do," the woman said.

But the first name Nyx said aloud was "Arran."

The boy Tej had died for.

"You're Jaks," Nyx said. And some old wound throbbed. The old bullet wound in her hip. "Jaksdijah. The boxer. I killed your brother."

"You remember." She placed a rough hand on Nyx's forehead, tenderly, though her eyes and teeth were predatory. She smoothed back Nyx's hair.

"Nikodem had Yah Tayyib patch you all up, one last time," Jaks said.

"For what?" Nyx said.

"For me," Jaks said. "Then for your sisters. I'm told they'll do far worse, but I wanted you first. It turns out someone on the bel dame council has wanted you for some time."

Nyx grunted. "Who?"

"I'm just a businesswoman. Your sisters say someone on your council wants you. They said they'll take you dead if they have to. I needed you alive, but I don't need to deliver you that way."

"You can't do worse to me." Nyx tried to think, tried to get her muddled brain to push back the gauze of sleep and drugs. She had the queen's protection. Somebody on the council was going over the queen.

The council was split.

Jaks pulled her hand away, kept grinning. "I have your team," Jaks said.

"Why should I care?" Nyx tried moving again. Flexed her remaining fingers. She ran through the inventory of her team. Rhys had been in the cell. She figured Khos took off with Inaya, Anneke had been in some firefight with the bel dames. Taite was dead. The only one she was certain they had was Rhys.

"Because I'm going to let you fight me for them."

"What?"

Nikodem broke in. "You and that other hunter were the last I had to concern myself with. Your little magician had some transmission transcripts on him, I heard, and I needed those in order for my work to continue. Your queen is not as forthright with her information as she should be. I'd have preferred to get them myself. Rasheeda was assisting me."

"Kine's records," Nyx said.

"On my world, you two would never have been called sisters. Impossible, with your differences in class. She wanted to make life. You want to destroy it."

"You don't know shit about either of us," Nyx said.

"I know enough. You have an interesting past, Nyxnissa. It was fortunate that your past served me so well."

"I'm half dead. You expect me to fight?" Nyx said.

"No," Jaks said. "I want you dead. At my hand."

"I have a good team," Nyx said.

"For a woman who prides herself on her independence, you sure do rely a lot on a bunch of gutter trash," Jaks said. "Let's see how well you do without anyone to hide behind."

"I did well enough with your brother."

Jaks didn't punch her; she smacked her, hard, across the face. Blood tickled Nyx's nose. She sniffed.

Jaks leaned over her. "And what a noble, powerful woman you must be, with the strength and courage to murder a boy in his bed."

"He was contaminated and he ran."

"And you didn't?" Jaks said. "Rasheeda, get her up and taped. I want my fight." Jaks took Nyx by the chin. "Let's see how well you do in a fair fight."

Nyx put those names away in her head. Dahab and Rasheeda. Rasheeda and Luce had been the ones to warn her off the note back in Mushtallah. If they were telling the truth, it meant they'd come from the bel dame council. Fatima, Luce, and Rasheeda had tracked her down and tortured her, looking for Kine's papers, but *not to give them to Nikodem*. They had said nothing about Nikodem. They'd said they needed to get the papers out of Chenja. So Luce and Fatima were working for the council members that wanted Nikodem back and Nasheen's secrets safe, and Dahab was working for Nikodem and Chenja or whatever part of the council believed in whatever Nikodem was doing, and… Rasheeda was playing both sides.

Which was why Rasheeda played dumb when Fatima accused Nyx of killing her sister. Rasheeda had killed Kine for Nikodem, then turned around and played Fatima.

Well, fuck.

"Fair?" Nyx said. "I'm half a corpse."

"Then all I need to do is kill the other half," Jaks said.

Rasheeda and Dahab unstrapped Nyx from the table. Dahab

glared at her with her new, foreign eye, a bland point of darkness.

Rasheeda was making strange chirping noises.

"I don't want your squirts taping me up," Nyx said. "Where's Rhys?"

"You'll see your magician soon enough," Jaks said. She was already at the door.

"You want to fight me?" Nyx said. "Rhys knows how to tape hands. Your bel dames aren't boxers. They're bloodletters." And Nikodem loved magicians.

Jaks paused.

Nyx waited.

Nikodem stood next to the slab, collecting what was left of the bands that had bound Nyx to the table. "Let her have him," Nikodem said, turning to Jaks. "He's been drugged."

Jaks looked them both over with her black eyes, hesitated for a long moment. Cool air blew in from the doorway, oddly humid. The hall was dim.

"Sure," Jaks said. "Dahab, you get him. And stay here with them. When you're done, you and Rasheeda bring them both out to the ring. Got it?"

Dahab and Jaks walked off into the hall, leaving Nyx with Nikodem and Rasheeda.

Rasheeda found a chair, turned it backward, and straddled it, facing Nyx. "Long time, sister," she said.

"Not really."

"When we cut off your head, I'm going to eat your eyes," Rasheeda said. "Like I ate your sister's."

"Must have been tasty, my sister."

"Mmmmmm…." Rasheeda licked her lips.

"Not much you could get from her, though."

"Protein."

"Uh-huh." Nyx kept her face slack. Rasheeda could smell discomfort. Worse, she fed on fear. "Don't know what the fuck a bunch of bel dames were doing casing the house of a government worker."

"Mother's orders," Rasheeda said, and chirped. What was with the chirping? When did that start? "The papers were for Nikodem, but the blood was for you."

"How thoughtful. How long have you been working both sides?"

Rasheeda snapped her teeth. "It keeps me honest," she said.

Dahab walked back in, but the only thing she had a hold of was her gun. "Nikodem, his hands are broken. He can't wrap shit."

"Then get Tayyib to fix him," Nikodem said.

"I don't like magicians."

"If he troubles you, sever his head," Nikodem said. She gathered up some instruments lying next to the sink and put them into a black organic bag. "Come, I want this over with. I have things to do tonight."

Dahab and Nikodem walked out.

Rasheeda continued to peer at Nyx.

"Your sister told us all about you," Rasheeda said, leaning over the back of the chair. Her eyes were empty. "Died screaming in the end. She was a bloody fucking screamer. The worst kind."

Nyx wanted to watch Rasheeda's eyes bulge and pop out of her head, wanted to watch her face darken and her tongue hang out like a dog's.

Instead, they waited for a long time, in silence.

Then Dahab's voice from the hall: "Here's the wraps and tape. Come on, let's go, black man."

Rhys appeared in the doorway. Rasheeda snapped her teeth at him and uncurled from her seat. She sauntered back into the hall. They had stripped him of his tunic and burnous, and dark blood was still smeared across his bare chest. Nyx had never seen so much of him outside of an organics search before.

She looked at his hands. The fingers were straight, and he

held two long lengths of cloth and a roll of tape. Fine red ants crawled along his knuckles, his wrists. As she watched, they began to drop to the floor.

His face was impossible to read—his jaw was set, and the dark gaze that met hers was fathomless.

But he was not broken. No, that look was not the look of a broken man.

He nodded at the operating slab.

Nyx sat up on the lip of it. Her body protested. She winced.

Rhys put the tape and wraps next to her. He did not look at her but started wrapping her right hand. He was slow, methodical, professional. How many hands had he wrapped when he worked with the magicians? How many fights had he prepared fighters for? Fights he never watched?

"You all right?" she said softly, and felt stupid for saying it. *All right?* What did that mean, here?

"When you fight her," Rhys said low, not looking at her, "goad her into using her left. Let her hit that hard head of yours."

And something clicked.

Yes, how many hands had he wrapped? Had he wrapped Jaks's hands, that night in Faleen? Rhys knew hands.

"You trying to make me fall?" she said.

He raised his head and looked at her. "Do you trust me, Nyx?"

"I don't trust anyone."

"You didn't answer the question."

Nyx met his look. His was a face she could gaze into forever. She knew it the night she watched him dance, the night her sisters pursued her and her womb bled—the night she reached the end of everything. She supposed she thought that if she could keep him close, she would be able to look at him forever and forget everything else. Sex with him, she could take or leave. But she wanted him. Wanted him in a way she couldn't explain, and tried hard not to think about.

She had no magical ability, so the face he gazed into carried no illusions. She'd never tried to be anything but what she was, for him or anyone else. She was thirty-two years old, and looked ten years older. Born on the coast, raised in the interior, burned at the front, a woman who was alive only because behind her was a long line of dead men. And women.

"You're too thin," he said. "You look hollow."

He took her right fist in his palm and squeezed it. He leaned in to her.

"I have no love for you," he said.

"I never asked you to."

He took up her left hand and started wrapping. There was a noise in the doorway. Just behind him, Dahab turned. Roaches scuttled along the floor.

Dahab swore and stomped at them.

Rhys flicked his wrist toward the band of his trousers, and the razor blade Nyx had given him appeared in his hand. He tucked it between the middle and index fingers of her left hand. He looked only at her hands.

They said nothing more. He finished wrapping.

She made a fist to keep the blade in place, all but the barest hint of the edge hidden in her palm.

"You done, boy?" Dahab said.

Rhys squeezed Nyx's left fist. "Done," he said.

The bel dames escorted them out into the hall, up the stairs, and into the ring.

36

Sometime after Khos came on board with her team, Nyx had gotten drunk and fucked him. She hadn't been to bed with a man in years, and though he was too big and coarse for her taste, when she was drunk, she didn't care. He was warm and tasted good and kissed her like a man who breathed women, dreamed of women, found bliss in the arms of women. And for Nyx, who had never known bliss or surrender with or toward anyone or anything, seeing him submit to sensation—to lust, desire—was one of the most intensely erotic things she had ever witnessed.

After, while she pulled on her dhoti and braided back her mussed hair, he had asked her about Rhys.

"You should see the way the two of you look at each other," he said.

"We don't look at each other. He's just a kid."

"A pretty kid, by anybody's standard. And if even I can see that, I imagine you sure can."

"Well, no amount of looking is going to make any difference. He's still godfull, and I'm still godless."

"Maybe you should find God again."

"Maybe he should become godless."

"You compromise for no one."

"No."

"That's a lonely place to be."

"You trying to open me up? You're nobody special."

"Haven't I already opened you?"

"The cunt is not the heart," she said, standing, "though a lot of people get the two confused."

He sat along the edge of the bed, behind her, and she could feel the heat of him, though his skin did not touch hers. He was a big man. Why did big men make her nervous?

She left him naked and alone and slightly bewildered on the thin mattress of his raised bed. She always left them bewildered, wondering if they had said something differently, or had said nothing at all, if she would still be in their arms, if she would have surrendered.

The next time she got drunk, she went to a brothel, and resolved to stop sleeping with people on her team.

Now Nyx stood inside a boxing ring, for real, for the first time since she'd left the magicians, since she ran off with Raine and his crew. She had taken this woman to bed too, and she hadn't surrendered then. She wouldn't now.

I use you all, she thought bitterly. I use you and then I cut you out like a cancer, like my womb… but they were still there, sticky and hot in her dreams, like the detritus of a butcher's shop, memories of blood and sand. And she remembered Rhys drawing the shape of a perfect heart in the air.

The air was wet and tasted like copper. Two overhead lights were on, lights that weren't made to be ring lights but had been rigged for it. She suspected she was in the abandoned waterworks that Rhys and Khos had told her about. This was where Jaks and all the Nasheenian boxers she smuggled in fought. They broke rules and risked their lives to bloody each other in front of an audience that loathed them as women and foreigners. They got bloodied up and took Chenjan money and fucked off to gamble or drink it away and come back the next week, a little hungover, a little stung, and ready to do it all over again.

Dahab and Rasheeda herded Nyx and Rhys into the converted

room. Nikodem was already sitting at a table ringside, and Dahab bound Rhys's hands again and shoved him down next to the alien. Anneke was balled up on the floor next to him, hands tied behind her, a short line connecting the bonds on her hands and feet, so she was bent backward. Her face was swollen. So, they'd gotten Anneke after all. Gotten her alive, even.

Jaks was already waiting in the ring. Behind her, working as her cut man, was the magician Nyx had been waiting for.

"Yah Tayyib," Nyx said. "Missed me so much you wanted to help put me back together again?"

Dahab prodded her into the ring.

Nyx ducked under the ropes and stood under the hot lights.

Yah Tayyib stood in Jaks's corner. He was hard-faced, and neatly dressed.

"This whole thing your idea?" Nyx asked. She looked at her own empty corner. "I get a cut magician? Or we still going to play this pretending I'm in boxing shape and have a whole right hand?"

"That's not the point," Jaks said.

"Give her the boy," Nikodem said. "It will remind her of what she's fighting for."

Nyx eyed Yah Tayyib. "This clean work?" she asked him, and couldn't keep the bite from her voice. "You pinch on me for running a womb for a couple of gene pirates and now you're selling us all out to some space pirate? Who do you think you're saving, old man?"

"I'm ending your war," Yah Tayyib said.

"I spent time at the front too, old man. Don't pretend only you boys are martyrs."

"I have never pretended," he said.

"You smuggled Nikodem into Chenja. Why?"

"I owe you no explanations."

"You fucking patched me back together, old man. You gave

me back a life. You *do* owe me answers. What did you bring me back for? So you could see me fucked up now?"

"Quiet, please," Nikodem called from her table.

Nyx swung around and peered out at the darkness. She could barely make out Nikodem's form. "Then give me some idea! Give me some reason why I'm dying. Why you're willing to slaughter my team! Why you're staging this bullshit for some jilted kid's benefit."

"Shut up and fight," Jaks said.

"I don't even have any fucking gloves," Nyx said. She was buying time for Rhys to recover from the drugs now, but she didn't think they knew that yet. "Why not slit my throat and be done with it?"

"Because tomorrow Yah Tayyib gets me into the Chenjan breeding compounds," Nikodem said. "Because after that day my people will have all we need from your shitty little world. When we're gone, you can stay here and destroy one another far more efficiently. Then I go and win the war for my people."

"Your sisters know about that?" Nyx said.

"Sisters? They're just here for show. When I go home, it won't be with those pawns."

"You want a good show?" Nyx said. "You want a real go-ing-away? You give me a proper magician."

"He'll work old-fashioned," Jaks said. "No magic, but he can keep you from bleeding in your face. Maybe get me a little longer with you."

"You never could accept your death," Yah Tayyib said.

Nyx turned on him. "You're right. That's why I came to you. I *trusted* you."

"A bel dame can trust no one."

"I'm not a bel dame anymore."

It was the first time she'd ever said it out loud.

Dahab pushed Rhys up into the ring. Under the lights, he

looked bigger, his shoulders broader. In the ring, for a brief moment, Nyx could have mistaken him for a fighter.

Nyx stepped toward him, grabbed his wrist with her bad hand. "You can do this?" she said softly.

"I've spent much of my life in one ring or another," he said. He looked her in the eye. She held the look for a long time.

God, why didn't I find you sooner? she thought.

Jaks tossed a pair of gloves across the ring. "Come now, bel dame," she said.

Nyx handed the gloves to Rhys. "You lace them on," she said, and bent forward so their foreheads touched. He did not draw away. So close, he smelled of blood and sweat and something even more intimate. Perhaps it was fear she smelled, or the biting chemical odor of a magician. But it was something uniquely Rhys. I'll miss you, she thought.

"Keep the laces on the left loose," she said. "I want to be able to get them off with my teeth. You know."

"I know," he said.

Rhys slipped on her gloves and took his time lacing them up. He was good with the knots on the right, but he tied a simple bow on the left and tucked the ends into the seam of her left glove.

"Good?" he said.

"Good."

Nyx was in no shape for a fight. She was worse off now than she had been back at Husayn's gym. She wanted to believe that Jaks hadn't had much time to box either, but as she looked across the ring and saw Yah Tayyib take off Jaks's coat, that hope went right out of her head.

Jaks was lean and muscled, and under the lights the contours of her body were that much more dramatic. She was also young, six or seven years younger than Nyx, and though she had lived a hard life, there was no way she'd been rebuilt as many times, in as many ways, as Nyx had.

Nyx didn't look out at Rhys or Anneke. And she would deal with Yah Tayyib later.

She looked at Jaks.

Yah Tayyib was rubbing Jaks's arms and shoulders. Nyx had no illusions that this would be a proper fight with proper rules. She saw no one at the buzzer. It was going to be one long round, with a moment or two for Rhys to patch her back up if she got too bloody. Maybe.

Nyx stood with her hands down and her left toe forward. She waited.

Jaks didn't put in a mouthpiece, and she didn't offer one to Nyx.

"Don't get hit," Rhys said.

"I'll try to keep that in mind," Nyx said.

Yah Tayyib took his hands off Jaks and waved at the buzzer. A thousand hard-backed beetles exploded into movement, sounding the bell.

Jaks leapt forward.

Nyx left her hands down until Jaks was within hitting distance. Then she ducked and blocked Jaks's wide, wild left hook. As Nyx ducked, she pivoted behind Jaks and caught her with a left jab to the back of the head.

The dull edge of the blade she held in her fist jarred her palm. She sucked in a breath, stepped back into a fighting stance.

Jaks stumbled and turned and moved away, reassessed.

They circled, hands up.

Nyx watched Jaks gnaw on strategy. She had opened too eager, just like she did eight years ago, hungry for a quick fight, for first blood.

Most people who watch a fight think it's all about the muscle: hitting harder, moving faster. And, yeah, sometimes it looked that way. But telling somebody that you won a fight by hitting the other person harder and more often was like telling somebody that the way you kept from drowning was by moving your arms and legs.

Once two fighters knew how to fight, they stood pretty even. What made one win and the other fall wasn't about blood or sinew or sweat. It was about will.

Jaks was old enough to know that.

So was Nyx.

Nyx dropped her hands again.

Jaks made as if to hesitate, then stepped in and fired.

Nyx ducked and blocked. The blow glanced off her forearm. She had only enough strength to take a couple of good hits. She needed most of these to bounce off, but she needed them to bounce off in a way that made Jaks think she was winning. Nyx was tired. Not all of the hunched posture was feigned. Her body ached. It didn't feel like her body anymore. Hadn't for a long time. She sometimes wondered who she belonged to: the queen, the magicians, the front; Raine had thought she belonged to him, thought he had some responsibility.

But in the end it was just Nyx in a ring.

Jaks sent out a double right jab, a left cross. Nyx kept her hands up. Nothing got through, but she let Jaks keep at it, keep pounding at her forearms and shoulders. Jaks tucked in an uppercut to Nyx's midsection.

Nyx huffed air and stepped left, tried to get herself out of the corner Jaks was trying to push her into.

"Hit me!" Jaks yelled at her. She batted at Nyx's raised hands, and Nyx peered between her gloves at Jaks's pinched face. "Hit me, you fucking coward!"

"Your brother was the one who wouldn't fight," Nyx said, pushing back at her with her gloves. "Your brother was the coward."

Jaks swung, a wide right hook, double left jab, right uppercut. The combination was too fast for Nyx. The uppercut caught

Nyx hard under the chin. She fell back and caught herself on one knee.

Jaks brought a gloved fist down. Nyx rolled out of the way and staggered back up, brought up her hands. Sweat poured into her eyes. The bell didn't sound. It had been longer than two or three minutes. Too long.

That was all right. Nyx didn't intend to fight fair either.

"Look at you, broken up over a dead boy," Nyx gasped. She sucked more air, tried to concentrate on her breathing. Remember to breathe, remember to breathe….

You kept yourself from drowning by breathing air.

Jaks swung again, a wild swing. Nyx caught her in the belly with a hard right uppercut, pummeled the side of her face with a left hook.

Jaks reeled and swung. She caught Nyx across the ear.

Nyx grabbed her in an embrace, locked their bodies together.

"You rigged this whole thing for a dead kid, a coward," Nyx murmured in Jaks's ear, "and you're no better."

Jaks pushed her away and tried forcing her backward. Nyx pushed back.

The lights were starting to flicker. Nyx thought maybe her sight was going. She tried to blink the sweat from her eyes. Her face was starting to swell up. She needed both eyes. She tried to protect the bad side, the one with the swelling eye, but Jaks saw what she was trying to do and swung away at that side with her right.

Nyx stumbled again. She saw darkness at the edges of her eyes. Jaks pounded at her. Still with the right.

Nyx staggered back, put her hands up again. Blood leaked from a wound just above her eye. She blinked, rubbed the side of her face against her shoulder, smeared blood.

"Let me clean her up!" Rhys yelled. "Let me clean her up!"

The lights *were* flickering. What *was* that? Nyx tried to look up, but Jaks was on her again.

Nyx hung back on the ropes and let Jaks pummel her shoulders and forearms. She let the force of the blows bleed into the ropes.

"You want to know how he died?" Nyx said. "He was a bleeder, just like you."

But of all the things she remembered, vividly, from her last night as a bel dame, the death of Jaks's brother was not one of them.

Just another boy, another body, to Nyx.

But to Jaks: the world.

What had Nyx done, what had she given up, for her brothers? Her mother?

Jaks pounded at her again. Sweat poured down her face. Her body shone.

Nyx's arms were tired. She waited out the shaking and the pain, kept taking the hits. She didn't look directly at Jaks's face but kept her eye on the left side of Jaks's body, just below the collarbone. She watched the muscles move there from between her gloves. She didn't need her peripheral vision so long as she had a good look at the way Jaks's muscles and tendons moved under the skin.

She remembered to breathe.

"You can hit me harder than that," Nyx said.

Jaks's assault slowed down. She was losing momentum.

Nyx used the ropes to push herself up against Jaks. She forced the younger woman back and yelled at her, "He bled out like a dog."

The swing came from the right. Nyx blocked and saw her move left.

Bel dames didn't trust anyone.

Lucky she wasn't a bel dame.

Nyx dropped her guard on her right and ducked and turned her head. Instead of smashing her in the temple, Jaks's left caught

Nyx full force on the upper right side of her head. The hardest part of her head.

Light exploded behind Nyx's eyes. She dropped to her knees.

Jaks cried out and fell back, clutching her bad hand to her chest.

Nyx curled over her hands and pulled at the knot on her left glove with her teeth. Her head spun. Black juddered across her vision.

Jaks dropped next to Nyx and grabbed her by her butchered hair, jerked at her throbbing head.

Nyx wedged her left glove between her knees.

Jaks forced Nyx to face their audience. "You could have cut and run from your team. You could be in Tirhan now, living on that beach you told me about in that shitty cantina outside Punjai. But you didn't run, and this is where it left you."

Jaks's left hand was limp at her side. She spoke through her teeth, whispered into Nyx's ear, "You think dying for your team makes you a hero? No, Nyx, heroes *live* for what they love. It's what separates the heroes from the cowards. Arran and I weren't the cowards. You're the coward."

She let go of Nyx.

"What do you think I've been doing my whole life?" Nyx said. "Giving up?"

Nyx jerked her left hand free of her glove and caught Jaks in the throat with her left elbow.

Jaks choked and clutched at her throat. She made a clumsy swing with her bad hand, but the knock on Nyx's head had broken something deep, and when her bad hand hit Nyx's head, it felt like a halfhearted swipe, a slap.

Somebody yelled something. A dog barked.

Nyx pinned Jaks. She brought the razor blade across Jaks's throat. It was a ragged cut, rough and desperate. She pressed hard, sliced. Blood ran, Jaks thrashed, and Nyx sprang for the edge of the ring.

Rhys leapt across the ring and punched Yah Tayyib full in the face. It was a beautiful, unexpected hit, and the old man toppled off the edge of the ring. Rhys jumped after him. Nyx rolled under the ropes and came up in a crouch among the startled spectators, drooling spit and blood.

People were moving, just shadows in the dark. Nyx was momentarily blind after stepping from the glare of the ring and into the dim. Nyx moved before her eyes adjusted. She heard Rasheeda snicker. Nikodem was already standing. Yah Tayyib yelled.

Dahab's gun went off.

Nikodem drew one of her pistols. Nyx slammed the palm of her hand into Nikodem's face. Nikodem fell back onto the table.

Nyx pulled a poisoned needle from her hair and jabbed it hard into Nikodem's arm.

Anneke still lay under the table. Nyx used the razor blade to saw Anneke's bonds. She gave Anneke the razor blade. Anneke crawled to her feet.

A tawny dog darted past them. Khos? Where had he come from?

Nyx yelled at the dog. "The gun on the floor! Give Rhys the gun!" She didn't see Rhys. Where was Rhys? She squinted and wiped the blood and sweat from her eyes.

The dog retrieved the gun with its mouth and took off across the dim room.

Nikodem was holding a hand to her gushing nose while stumbling toward the door.

Nyx heard Rasheeda snickering and looked up.

Rasheeda carried no weapons. She merely reached out and clawed at Nyx's face. Nyx stumbled back and fell.

Anneke scrambled past Rasheeda toward Nikodem and the other pistol.

"I'm hungry, sister," Rasheeda said. She stalked forward like a cat.

Nyx tried to get up, but the floor was bloody and slick. She grabbed one of the chairs.

Rasheeda leapt at her.

Nyx got to her feet and pulled the chair between them.

Rasheeda grabbed the chair and held it up.

Nyx ran.

Dahab stood at the corner of the ring as Nyx ran past. She shot at her. A chair kicked back and splintered an arm's length away.

Nyx covered her head and ran toward the other side of the boxing ring, where the magicians had gone.

Rasheeda strode after her.

As she ran, Nyx saw Rhys and Yah Tayyib; a cloud of beetles, flying ants, and wasps circled them. The floor was covered in roaches. She crunched across them on bare feet. She saw someone run past the struggling magicians. Beside the figure ran a tawny dog.

Somebody hit her on the back of the head.

Nyx sprawled on the floor, scattering roaches. The dog barked. Somebody yelled at her. Why was everyone yelling?

Rasheeda stood over her, grasping the broken leg of a chair. She swung it again.

A gun went off.

Nyx looked out into the darkness.

Rasheeda dropped the chair leg, and clutched at her throat. She started to shiver and morph.

Dahab appeared from the other side of the ring, trained her gun on Nyx. "You fucking—"

The pistol went off again. Dahab jerked back. The rifle fell from her hands. A line of blood appeared from a hole at the center of her head.

Rasheeda was squawking and bleeding feathers.

Nyx watched Rhys step out from the darkness, pistol trained

on Rasheeda. Rasheeda screamed and finished morphing into a raven. She flapped twice.

Rhys shot her again.

Rasheeda-the-raven dropped like a stone to the floor. The body shivered and changed back into the form of a woman, naked and bleeding, covered in feathers and mucus.

Roaches swarmed over Nyx's legs. She looked up at Rhys. He'd always been a good shot.

He turned away from her, gun still in hand, still ready, and pointed his pistol toward Yah Tayyib, who was struggling to his feet. Yah Tayyib had sent up a cloud of wasps to obscure him. Rhys bolted into the cloud. He held up his hands to call back the swarm.

Nyx crawled toward Dahab's crumpled body and found a dagger. She ran after Rhys, into the cloud.

As the cloud began to collapse, Yah Tayyib pulled himself toward the door among the remnants of the swarm.

"No you don't, old man," Nyx said.

But he was covered in wasps as he reached the door, and all Nyx had left was a dagger and a powerful desire to fall down and press herself against the cool floor. She tried one last sprint, but her legs buckled. She caught herself with her bad hand.

Oh, fuck it, she thought.

She threw the dagger at Yah Tayyib just as he turned to look back.

The curtain of wasps shuddered. Nyx didn't hear the dagger hit the floor.

The curtain swayed.

Yah Tayyib collapsed, and the wasps buzzed angrily above his head and began to dissipate. The magician clutched at the dagger in his chest.

For a moment, Nyx was so startled that the dagger had hit him that she stared at him stupidly, awestruck at her own throw. She crawled toward him. He had one hand on the hilt of the dagger, and with the other he dug into his robe, probably looking for a boxed flesh beetle or killer roach.

Nyx grabbed his wrist and pinned him beneath her. She was breathing hard. Blood had congealed on her face. She still outweighed him.

"Who are the bel dames who want Nikodem alive? Why?" she demanded.

"I don't know."

"Tell me, old man, or I'll tear your head off with my bare hands."

"Nyxnissa, I do not know."

"Who told you to bring Nikodem here?"

"She came to me with an offer. Rasheeda and Dahab said they spoke for the council," he said. His mashed nose was bloody from the hit he'd taken from Rhys, and moisture collected at the edges of his dark eyes. An old man. A war hero. One of the few who came back, making backyard deals with bel dames. "They told me the queen was selling out Nasheenian samples in exchange for help from the aliens with the extermination of the bel dame council. With the council out of the way, the queen will have no one to argue against her weapons programs."

"What?"

"This is what they told me."

"The queen told me that Nikodem can end the war."

"With whatever technology Nikodem's people give us in exchange for our genetic material, no doubt that is true. The queen will also gain absolute power over Nasheen, and then Chenja. Then the world."

"You expect me to believe that a magician who's spent time at the front moved without knowing what everybody's cards were? You think I'm stupid?"

"I've always thought you foolish."

She gripped his throat with her good hand.

He gasped and squirmed beneath her. "You have the potential to be more than you are," he whispered. "You always have. And you chose *this*. How did I fail you?"

"Fail me?" she said, disbelieving. "Fail me? You fucking *betrayed* me. You acted like some kind of fucking father from a historical drama and then sent me to prison. How did you *fail* me? You fucking *killed* me! You took away everything I had, you fucking fuck!"

"Nyx?"

Rhys's voice.

"Nyx, let him up," Rhys said. He had walked up beside her. She saw his bare feet.

"I intend to eat him," Nyx said.

"Clever," Rhys said. "Then you can be just like Rasheeda."

Nyx looked up at him. He had pulled Jaks's neglected tunic over himself. It was a little short, but otherwise a good fit. It was like Rhys, to think of modesty in the middle of a firefight. He still had a gun in his right hand.

"I'm not letting anyone walk out of here," Nyx said.

Rhys grimaced. "Have I murdered monsters only to save something worse?"

Khos padded in from the doorway in front of her, human again and naked. "Unless you want the others coming after you, you better cut off their heads," Khos said, "just to be sure."

Nyx eyed Rhys. There was something in his face that had not been there before. He looked at her differently. His look made her feel cold.

"You and I need to talk," she said.

"We do," Rhys said. He pressed a hand to her shoulder. "Let Yah Tayyib up. It'll take him time to recover. He won't attack us alone. By the time he's fit, we'll be away from here."

Nyx kept her hand on the magician's throat. She gritted her teeth. "Rhys—"

"Let go," Rhys said. He squeezed her shoulder. "It's all right. We're all right. Let go."

She slowly released her hold on Yah Tayyib.

Rhys helped her stand.

Khos got out of the doorway and let the magician stumble into the corridor. The dagger still jutted from his chest. Where would he go now? To his Chenjan friends? The ones who were going to help him get Nikodem into their compounds? Would they give him some kind of a life here? As a Nasheenian man? A Nasheenian war veteran?

"Where's Anneke?" Nyx asked.

"Here, boss."

Anneke strode over. She had a pistol in her hand. "I got the alien," she said.

"Dead or alive?" Nyx asked.

"Don't know for sure. Pretty dead, likely. But you know how it is."

Nyx limped back toward the boxing ring. The others trailed her. She stood over Nikodem and gently nudged her body over with one foot. Anneke had shot her at least three times in the chest. Hard to tell with all the blood. A few paces away, Rasheeda's twisted body still lay on the floor, and at the far corner of the ring, Dahab lay in a pool of blood.

"We need to clean up these bodies," Nyx said, turning toward the others. As she did, she saw their faces change. They were all at least three paces from her: Rhys next to Anneke, who had the chamber of her gun open as she cleaned it, Khos close enough to spit at, his grim face on the ring.

"Nyx—"

She didn't know which of them said her name first, but the

startled looks on their faces made her swing back and stare into the ring.

Jaks stood with Dahab's rifle in one hand, her other hand clutching at her bloody throat.

No, Nyx remembered, it hadn't been the best cut.

Jaks had her point-blank. The rifle would blast a hole in Nyx's torso big enough for Anneke to put her head through.

Nyx opened her mouth. At least she could try to give off some last witty thing. Something grimly optimistic.

Somebody else shot first.

Nyx jumped at the sound and grabbed at her chest, but it was Jaks who collapsed into the ring.

From the darkness on the other side of the ring, a woman stepped toward them, rifle in hand, a kid slung over her back. She was a pale ghost in the dim light.

"In Ras Tieg," Inaya said, "we bury our bodies. We know when ours are dead."

37.

They had one last thing to do.

Nyx sat with Jaks's body, in the ring. Rhys stood next to her, still holding his gun, as if he'd forgotten it wasn't a part of him. Khos and Inaya stood along the ropes, and Anneke was looting the dead below.

"I want to burn the lab," Nyx said.

"What lab?" Anneke said, looking up from Dahab's splattered body, bullet necklaces in hand.

Rhys sighed. "Nyx, what's—"

"Nikodem never did get into the Chenjan stuff, but she'll have some Nasheenian information here that no Chenjan needs to find. Fatima and Luce were working with the council to make sure none of Nasheen's secrets got out of the country. That's why they were tracking us. I don't think they know about Rasheeda and Dahab or even the black part of the council they were working with. I don't want any of our stuff here either, so burn it."

Rhys stared at her.

Anneke loaded her gun.

Inaya's kid cried.

Khos shrugged. "This is the last thing I do for you, Nyxnissa," he said.

"I won't ask anything else," she said. "You still have those transmission transcripts she talked about, Rhys?"

"Raine had them."

"Then hopefully the desert has them," Nyx said.

Nyx couldn't make the walk back to Nikodem's lab. Instead, she stayed in the waterworks and cut the heads off Jaks and Dahab. By the time she started sawing at Rasheeda's, her fingers were trembling and sweat blurred her vision. She stopped hacking and crawled back into the ring next to Jaks's headless body. She pressed her forehead to the cool organic matting.

It was a bit like praying, she supposed. She felt as if she were sinking into the ring, surrendering to it. Maybe that's what it was to surrender to God: to just let everything go, to give it all up. Submission to God meant a submission of one's desires, of one's will, to God's will. Maybe that's why surrender, submission, scared her so much now—it felt too much like dying, and she'd had enough of dying. She wanted to live.

God, she wanted to live.

She heard someone approach and looked up.

Anneke walked toward the ring, wearing a pale tunic and tattered burnous, both too big for her, but she'd found a belt somewhere and tucked a couple of pistols into it and slung Dahab's bullet necklaces over her head. Her feet were still bare. In one hand, she carried a burnous stuffed with Nikodem's head.

"You ready, boss?"

Nyx could smell the smoke.

"Yes."

Anneke helped her down, and they walked to the door. Khos and Inaya and Rhys came after them a few moments later and the five of them—and Inaya's kid—stepped through the halls of the waterworks and out onto the street.

Outside, the world was stuck in the hazy blue half place between darkness and dawn. Though there were no streetlights, Nyx saw the outline of everyone's faces in the dim.

"You have the bakkie, Khos?" she asked.

He handed over the keys.

"I can't drive," she said, looking at his outstretched hand. "Why don't you drive?"

"We're not going with you," Khos said. "I have some friends picking us up."

"You and Inaya heading out?" Nyx said. "I wouldn't have renewed your contract anyway."

"I'm going with them," Rhys said.

Nyx started. "What?"

Dawn crept up on them, bled across the eastern sky, the first rays of the blue sun.

Rhys reached out and almost touched her face. The gesture was so strange and unexpected that she jerked away from him.

He smiled thinly, dropped his hand. "You won't be able to get me back over the border, Nyx."

"You're wrong, I—"

"Nyx, don't," Rhys said.

"I know some people who are very good at getting people over the border," Khos said. "I've been helping them out a long time."

"The whores," Nyx said.

"The underground, yes," Khos said.

"So you'll meet me at the keg?" Nyx said, and her voice broke. She wasn't even sure why. She just choked on the end of her sentence, like it hurt.

"We're going to Tirhan," Rhys said.

"I have a son in Tirhan," Khos said. "And some contacts."

"I can get you all amnesty," Nyx said. "From the queen. That's what this is all about. Money and amnesty."

"No, it's not," Rhys said.

"You signed a contract with me—"

"And it wasn't a writ of sale!" Rhys said, biting. She saw his jaw work. He looked away from her, then back, and relaxed his posture. "Good luck to you," he said, and she remembered how he had looked at her as she pinned Yah Tayyib, as if she was some kind of monster.

Maybe she was.

A bakkie turned onto the street, illuminated by the blue wash of first dawn.

The group instinctively took a step back into the doorway.

"That's Mahrokh," Khos said. "I know her bakkie." He touched Inaya's shoulder tentatively. She looked up at him. There was something in her face too, but Nyx didn't understand it.

Khos hailed the bakkie, and it stopped. A veiled woman leaned out. Khos opened the back door.

Inaya turned to Nyx. "You're a filthy, godless woman," Inaya said lightly.

"I've been called worse," Nyx said, "but not from anybody who killed for me."

"I didn't kill for you," Inaya said. "I killed for Taite. For people like… all of us. I would do it again."

Her son cried, and she moved his sling under her arm and carried him in front of her. She stepped into the bakkie.

Rhys looked at her. Last time.

Don't go, she thought. He wouldn't go.

He turned away from her. He got into the back seat.

Khos shut the door for Rhys and then opened up the front. He gave Nyx a little wave. "The bakkie's parked two blocks down, on West Maheed."

He got in. The woman at the wheel pulled back onto the street.

And just like that, it was done.

Nyx watched them drive off into the pale dawn. The second sun was coming up, and a brilliant band of crimson and purple ignited the sky.

Anneke snorted.

"You too?" Nyx said.

"Fuck no," Anneke said. "Who do you expect to drive you out of this shit hole?"

Anneke looped an arm around her waist, and they limped down the street as the double-dawn broke.

"Is the radio busted?" Nyx asked.

"Yeah. Been a little busy, thanks to you."

"It's a long drive," Nyx said.

"No problem, boss. Unlike you, I get my buddies back over the border."

"Right," Nyx said. "Not like me."

She looked back up the empty street.

She felt as if something had been cut out of her, an organ she would miss.

"Boss?"

"I'm fine," Nyx said, and got into the bakkie.

38

Rhys watched the second sun rise while Mahrokh drove them out of Dadfar. Next to him, Inaya sat quietly, and her son slept in her arms. Khos had the window down. Rhys heard the sounds of the waking city: mothers calling their children from sleep, old men hacking out the night's dust, the faint buzzing of wasps and beetles and the chittering of roaches as the sun warmed their lethargic bodies. He smelled curry and fried protein cakes and the peculiar spicy jasmine scent of red dye, the sort used for turbans. Rhys saw a woman step out onto her balcony and hang a prayer wheel. Three young girls robed in yellow and red ran out ahead of the bakkie and crossed the street to a bakery whose matron was just pushing open the door for the day.

But inside the bakkie, the only noise was the chitter of the bugs in the cistern. Rhys wanted to look back toward the waterworks, but they had turned away from that district three streets ago, and there was no one and nothing behind him.

Let me go back, he thought, and squeezed his eyes shut. No. This was for the best. He had fled into Nasheen because he didn't want to fight Nasheen. Some part of him had believed that if he ran to them unarmed, they would not harm him. He had been wrong.

As his father's only son, Rhys had grown up knowing he was immune from the draft. He would marry twenty or thirty women and inherit his father's estate, his father's title.

But his father had been a mullah. A powerful one. And unlike some of the more powerful, he had wanted his son to perform the ultimate submission to God, the submission that he himself had never had the courage to perform. He had wanted Rhys to atone for his own sins.

Rhys remembered the way the air tasted that day: oranges and lavender. He remembered the sound of the cicadas. The water bubbling in the fountain in the courtyard just inside the gate. He remembered the sound of the servants and slaves outside, the intermittent cries of the overseers in the fields.

"It's time to speak of your future, boy," his father had said, and put his smooth hand on Rhys's head. He had smiled, his teeth so white, and sat across from him. His father was a tall man with a short beard and broad, generous face. You could stand near him, listen to him speak, and feel as if you were in the presence of some wiser man, a true mullah. His uncles were the same. Rich, powerful men whose influence allowed them to profit from the war, not fight in it.

"I have consulted with your uncles and spoken with your mother," his father had said. His birth mother, he meant. The others, Rhys called "Aunt." "We have prayed often to God so that we may find the best path for you, the most humble. A boy of our house has not served God at the front for three generations, and yet we sit on our hill and call ourselves pious men. How can we be pious without sacrifice?"

Even now, huddled in the back of a bakkie—a Chenjan deserter, dead if they found him—Rhys didn't understand the feeling that had overcome him at his father's words. The mounting terror. The knowing. War happened to other people. Other people died in God's war. Poor men. Nasheenian men. Godless women. Like Nyx.

Not Rakhshan Arjoomand.

He would no longer kneel and pray with his father, no longer climb the crooked tree at the far end of his father's land and stare out over the city. In his mind, his whole life, he had built up and planned out his path, worked out ways to manage a household, playfully picked out wives from among the girls in the village below, and, above all, he had studied the teachings of the Prophet and spent long days trying to learn to submit his will to God's.

He believed, until that day, that he'd succeeded. If this was the life God wanted for him, submitting to that will was not such a terrible thing. His will and God's will were one.

The shock of this other life, this other path—blood and death in a foreign country—was so horrifying, so unexpected, that he did not have time to wonder at his own lack of humility. He had explained the impossibility of that other life. He had cursed his father. He threatened suicide. He sobbed. Seventeen years old, and he had sobbed in front of his father like a child. He had watched his father's generous face harden like a cut gem.

"I am worth more than this!" Rhys had cried.

"More?" his father had said, as if Rhys had told him he needed water in order to breathe. "More than a sacrifice to God? We must submit our desires to God's will. We are fighting a holy war. God's war. Every one of us. We fight. We die. This is who we are."

"It's not who I am," Rhys had said.

"Then you do not belong to God. You do not belong to me."

Rhys had summoned the bugs that night. He showed more skill in that one night than he had during his entire career as a middling magician in Nasheen. He confused and reprogrammed his father's security system and sent wasps ahead to sniff out his way. But his father had sent the blood bugs after him. The chittering creatures, large as dogs, caught him in their jaws and dragged him back, and it was as if the talent bled out of him in the face of these impossible monsters. When Rhys returned, his father had smashed Rhys's hands with a metal pipe. Smashed them bloody. Broken.

It was one of his sisters, Alys, who helped Rhys escape the

second time. She called her friends, members of Chenja's own underground, and they had gotten him as far as the border. At the border, their vehicle hit a mine.

Bloodied faces. Body parts. He remembered the smell of burning flesh. Not his own.

After that, he ran.

Ran and ran and ran, until his skin peeled off and his lungs burned.

He had not gone to the front to sacrifice himself to God. He had not gone there to save anyone. In the end, he did not even believe he would save himself. He was just running, fueled by terror, a man running from God, from His will.

But Nyx had not been afraid.

She had volunteered for the front to protect her brothers. She'd protected the boys and women in her squad, until the end, and when she'd failed at that, she burned herself. Carried out the punishment she believed God would have meted out for her sin.

She drank too much, shot up and swallowed drugs, had sex indiscriminately with both genders, did not bend her knee to God, but which of them had been more pious? Which had been stronger before God? The woman who had given her brothers and body to God and then rejected Him, or the man who pretended godliness but could not perform the ultimate act of submission?

Khos put his meaty arm up on the seat and looked back at Rhys. "You sure you don't want us to drop you off with somebody in Chenja? Must be somebody doesn't want you dead."

"No," Rhys said.

Khos nodded and turned again to the road.

Rhys felt a knot of fear in his stomach and reached instinctively for his copy of the Kitab, but it was not there, of course. Raine had taken everything from him during the interrogation.

Rhys closed his eyes. He did not think of Nyx's offensive

remarks, the heat of her next to him, the way she looked at him when he read to her, her filthy fingernails and stained teeth and the terrible way she mangled her Chenjan. Instead, he thought of her hair. Long and braided, botched and unbound. Black glossy hair like the deepest part of the sky where there were no stars, just darkness. Umayma, at the edge of everything.

And he thought of Kine's words then—the voice that spoke with the same inflection as Nyx's, the voice that told him she had been making black market deals with Khairian nomads and interstellar gene pirates who sold her the base ingredients for winning the war.

"*These are old-world powers that must be controlled,*" Kine had said, her voice even, a little distant. "*To take the red sand out of its natural environment, to transport it out of the wastelands, could mean a disaster beyond our imagining. But handled the right way, correctly understood, it could win us the war without the need to alter our shifters. We could, effectively, cure the war by wiping out its cause.*"

But if she could not wipe out his people, she would find a way to enslave and modify the shifters.

Rhys opened his eyes and looked over at Inaya, her pale, dirt-smeared face, and tried, again, to see something of the shifter in her. But there was nothing. The air did not bend or crackle around her the way it did around Khos, as if he existed outside the world.

"I have wondered," Rhys said, "how you got Husayn's bakkie over the border."

Khos turned to look at them.

Inaya shifted her son in her arms. "How do you compel bugs to send your messages? How do you use them to mend flesh?"

"I could say it's a matter of examining the air, tasting it, and telling it what to do," Rhys said. "You would have to be a magician to understand."

"It is like that, then," Inaya said. "There is some knowledge one just has. That just is. There are things the people of this world can do that no one should know. Your bel dames know something of that. Nasheen's bel dames have existed in one form or another since the birth of the world. Before they cut up boys, they were responsible for killing rogue magicians and mutant shifters. Did you know that?"

"Yes," Rhys said, "I'd heard of it."

"It's no secret."

"How is it you know?" Rhys asked.

Inaya finally looked at him; her eyes were gray. "When you're born with a number of talents you do not understand, you spend your life looking for others like you, to understand why it is you've been cursed by God. You do this so you can receive forgiveness for whatever it is you've done. You will go to great lengths to find the knowledge you seek and will cross many borders."

"So what are you?" Rhys asked.

"A mistake," she said.

Khos said, "We're all mistakes. God's or man's."

Rhys resisted the urge to say something grimly optimistic in turn. The silence stretched, and he realized that Nyx was no longer there to fill it with some sarcastic remark about blood or sex or the inevitability of human failing.

"It's so quiet," Rhys said.

"Yeah," Khos said. "It's nice."

"Yes," Rhys said, but there was a hollow place in his chest, a strange absence, as if some part of him were missing, a piece he never knew he had, or needed, or even wanted. But he missed it nonetheless.

39.

The queen's palace in Mushtallah was about what Nyx remembered. Or, at least, she knew nothing had changed much, even though it *felt* different. Maybe it was just different because getting into it without a Chenjan man was a lot easier. Maybe it was because people looked at how she was dressed and treated her better—money and power and all that catshit.

She sat by a little fountain in yet another reception area, gazing out at a mural of the veiled Prophet receiving and reciting the words of God. The air was cool; the season had turned, though it never stayed cool in Mushtallah for long. Cicadas sang from the trees lining the interior of the courtyard, and three locusts rested on the lip of the fountain.

Nyx wore a green organic silk burnous over long black trousers, a white tunic stitched in silver, and a black vest. The hilt of a new blade stuck up from a slit in the back of her burnous. She wore Tej's baldric, Nikodem's pistols, and a new whip attached to her belt. Her sandals laced up to her knees. Some lovely kid back in Punjai had done her braids for a couple bits. Good thing, too, because her hair was longer now and far better for having the ends razored.

She reached out and flicked one of the locusts into the fountain with the ring finger of her right hand. The new fingers were a good match. Most people didn't even notice a difference. She still woke up sometimes and clutched at them, expecting to find an absence.

A woman in yellow appeared from one of the inner doors.

"She will see you now," Kasbah said.

Nyx stood. "You going to disarm me first?"

"I will take your things as you pass, but let us excuse the formalities of the organics search."

"Come, now, Kasbah, we're already on such intimate terms."

"Are we, now?" Kasbah smiled thinly. "We have a long path to tread to clean this house," she said. "Come."

Nyx left her pistols and her sword with Kasbah and walked down a short hall, through a low curtain, and into a big spherical room. Nyx stopped short as she entered. She looked up. The whole room was glass. Above her, she saw that she was enclosed by or beneath some kind of tank filled with water. Strange creatures, some kind of fish or animals or something, swam lazily above her, around her. Rocks and seaweeds and odd tentacled things covered the bottom of the pool. The water was so deep, the tank went so far back, that she could not see past the first ten feet or so. Nyx's palms were suddenly damp, and she had to push herself to walk farther into the room. All that water….

The queen sat on a bench at the center of the room. When Nyx entered, the little woman turned and smiled at her with her round, too-young face.

"Nyxnissa," she said, and raised her hand.

Nyx moved inside, and Kasbah entered behind her.

"Queen Zaynab," Nyx said, and came around the other side of the bench.

"Sit, please," the queen said.

Nyx sat on the other side of the bench. The weight of the water in the tank surrounding the room made the air feel heavy. It smelled faintly of peppermint and ammonia.

"I heard you returned my woman."

"What's left of her, yeah."

"You were unable to bring her to me alive?"

"She was a fighter." That part wasn't a lie, at least.

"I did prefer her death to the alternative, of course. It is best that the knowledge she possessed stays in Nasheen."

"The bel dames would probably agree." Some part of her wanted to know how much the queen knew. Yah Tayyib's words about the obliteration of the bel dames had shaken her. She didn't believe any queen could be so bold, not even this one.

"Indeed. Nikodem's sisters did not relish the idea of her spreading our secrets or theirs. Nikodem was a bit of a rogue."

"Was she, now?"

The queen smiled. "It is best that no one knows how my puzzle is put together, Nyxnissa. Nikodem was merely young and foolish and infatuated with a new world. Now she has been reined in. Now we can continue with our work."

"My sister—"

"Your sister's work was not for Nikodem's eyes, or Chenja's. I'm glad they've been destroyed, though I am sorry for the loss of your sister. I heard the bel dame council had several rogues working against you. How much did you learn of your sister's work?"

"Didn't even try to get past the security," Nyx said. "I had enough on my plate." This lie was outright, but she looked the queen in the face when she said it, and when the queen met her look, something hung there between them—the knowledge that they were both lying their asses off.

"That's best for all involved, I'm sure." The queen placed her hands on the edge of the bench and turned away to stare into the tank. "It is best you do not concern yourself with certain things, Nyxnissa. Do you wish to discuss money?"

"You've already been pretty generous."

"I'm unable to provide properly for you, but perhaps a yearly allowance is in order for a few years, at least, to keep your work honest."

Or to keep me in your pocket, Nyx thought. She watched a giant creature with a great tail fin and enormous teeth snake by. The room was too cold. She didn't like not being able to see the sky.

"That's pretty generous," Nyx said, "but I think I'll be all right."

"I heard you have a love of the ocean," the queen said, gesturing to the tank. "I heard a rumor that you'd like to retire to the coast."

Nyx started. A love of the *ocean*? Of *water*?

"Yeah? Who told you that?"

"There are many such things in your file."

Nyx frowned. She remembered a hot, dusty night, tangled in the arms of a young, losing boxer, leaning into her, saying, "Don't tell anyone what I'm about to tell you…" She had told Jaks all about the dream of fruity drinks on the beach in Tirhan that night when Jaks took a dive in the cantina outside Faleen. She had lied and told Jaks she loved the ocean and cool water, because Jaks loved the coast and Nyx needed to build up her trust, win her over. Hardened boxers didn't take just anyone home—especially not if their brothers were wanted by bel dames. Jaks was the only person she'd told that lie, besides Radeyah. Who had Jaks worked for before she started working for Chenja? Had she been one of the queen's little roaches, purged and exiled for working with the aliens? Working with rogue palace magicians like Yah Tayyib? Had the queen driven her to betray Nasheen? Or given her blessing?

"I suppose you have all sorts of roaches," Nyx said. "Must be useful to have people like that around when you need something done quietly."

"Don't pretend you know what I do and do not have my fingers in, Nyxnissa. Know that what I do, I do for the good of Nasheen."

"When I was a bel dame, I believed I was killing boys for the good of Nasheen too."

"And weren't you? You prevented the deaths of thousands by neutralizing contaminated boys."

"There are some days I think I would have done us all a bigger favor if I let them kill us."

"That's not very optimistic."

"Oh, I'm an optimist," Nyx said. "A grim optimist. In any case, it's your business."

"I see. So what is it you want? I was curious as to why you wished an audience. I assumed you came seeking more money. It's what I expect of a hunter."

"I want a favor."

"Certainly."

"I want you to pardon me. Give me back my bel dame license."

"Only the bel dame council can do that." Cool fact, no malice, no hint that she'd expected that kind of request.

"Then tell me about the split in the council and why half of it wanted me and Nikodem dead and the other half wanted me and Nikodem alive. Tell me who else is running rogue and who took my license."

"I'm afraid I don't know."

"The Queen of fucking Nasheen *doesn't know*?"

The queen smiled; a warm, matronly smile. Nyx saw Kasbah saunter closer to them, one hand twitching. Nyx wondered what kinds of bugs a magician would tailor for palace security. Highly specialized. Highly lethal.

"You should be very careful, Nyxnissa," the queen said, "that you, too, do not become an enemy of the crown."

"I want amnesty for my crew. Amnesty from the draft and from past offenses."

"You know I can't do that."

"I thought recompense was negotiable?"

"We're negotiating. How much did Nikodem tell you before the end?"

"Enough."

"I see."

"Do you? Do you know what we're fighting for anymore?"

"Ah," the queen said. "What we've always fought for. Power. Control. Immortality. The world. My mother forgot that. Sometime during the long war, we all forgot that, and the war became our lives. We can't imagine a time without it. That time needs to end."

"You think anybody really knows why the war started anymore?"

"Like most Nasheenians, most Chenjans, I don't care how the war started. I care how it ends."

"Maybe that's the problem." Nyx stood. "You'll let me know about the amnesty?"

The queen shook her head. "I heard you lost your team."

"I promised them they'd get amnesty. All of them." God help her, she thought of Rhys.

She turned to leave.

"There is an assumption," the queen said, and Nyx turned back to face her, "that saving as many people as possible is the right thing to do. Soldiers are taught that at the front. It's why one soldier will throw herself on a mine to save her boys. It's why a bel dame will track down and kill a frightened young boy whose only crime was fearing death. But sometimes it is necessary to sacrifice many to save a few. We send three hundred into the breach so a squad of elite may get past a city's defenses. We must decide, in the end, whose life matters most and how many can be sacrificed to preserve those few."

"Who decides who the best few are?"

"We do, Nyxnissa. We are not so different, you and I."

"From where I'm standing, you and me don't have much in common."

Nyx bowed her head. Kasbah moved to follow her out.

"Nyxnissa?"

She looked back at the queen. "There are no happy endings, Nyxnissa."

"I know," Nyx said. "Life keeps going."

Nyx met Anneke at a little café just around the corner from the palace. Nyx ordered a Green Beetle and thought of better times. Anneke ordered a whiskey and water.

"So, we rich or what?" Anneke asked. She pounded down the whiskey and asked for another.

"Probably so," Nyx said. "You want to cut and run, set something up for yourself? You've got enough to retire on."

"Might be. Might take me a recreation. Visit some of my sisters, get a place on the coast, do some homesteading. Still got some homesteading out there in the southeast. Would be funny, wouldn't it?"

"Maybe."

"You heard the bel dames are clearing out of Mushtallah?"

Nyx quirked an eyebrow at her. "Where you hear that?"

"Around. They sold the place on the fifth hill, you know, where you trained. They're relocating to Amtullah."

Removing themselves from the queen's city. Finding a safer staging area. Nyx took a long drink. It was going to be an interesting couple of years.

"What about you, boss? All this moving around. You got money now. Where you going?"

Nyx shrugged. "Don't know. Maybe it's time I retired too. Some other hill. Not sure what I'd retire to, though. Not much else I'm good at."

She sipped her green drink and grimaced. Too sweet. How the hell had Rasheeda swilled these things?

Anneke finished her second drink and called for another.

Nyx didn't bother reminding her it was a café, not a cantina.

"Maybe you should go to Tirhan," Anneke said. She didn't look at her, but became suddenly interested in the cooling bugs in her glass.

"Should I, now?"

"Dunno. Might be some work there, maybe running boys out of Chenja and Nasheen. Something a little different. Or same thing, different side."

Nyx leaned back in her chair. There was nothing for her in Tirhan. They wanted their own life out there. She would leave them to it.

"I'm not a good woman," Nyx said.

"I never wanted to be good," Anneke said.

They went back to their hotel, but Nyx couldn't sleep, so she spent the evening out walking in the cool night air, listening to the hum of the cicadas. Big women bustled past her, some veiled, most not. She heard the call for midnight prayer, and she stopped just outside a mosque and thought, inevitably, of Rhys.

She remembered him lying there on the rocky ground next to the gully in the Chenjan desert, his face bruised, his fingers broken, barely breathing. She remembered kneeling next to him, thinking, "Don't die. Don't die. Take me. Take my heart. Yah Tayyib says I don't need it. I don't use it. Take my heart."

She had opened her mouth to say it, had nearly broken down and grabbed at Rhys like some kind of crazy woman, a girl losing her lover to the front.

Take my heart.

"I am such a fool," she said aloud. The worshippers moved past her. A couple dogs barked in the street.

She pulled her burnous more firmly around her and turned away from the mosque and back into the street. She walked with all of the other godless women and young men, the ones who fueled themselves on the strength of their own will. Sometimes she wondered who she had turned away from first, her world or its God, abandoned somewhere in Bahreha, like an organ at the butcher's.

The haunting cry of the muezzin faded away. A burst trailed across the midnight sky. The faithful were at prayer.

Nyx went on.

ACKNOWLEDGMENTS

I wrote most of this book during the year I was dying.

I'm dying a lot less quickly these days, but neither I nor the book would be here without the support of a small army of folks who saw me through that year and beyond.

Big thanks to my first readers: Patrick Weekes, Julian Brown, Miriam Hurst, and David Moles. Finding good first readers can take a lifetime, and this bunch are among the best you'll ever dig up. I can always count on them to call me on my bullshit. I hope they'll continue to stick with me, even if sometimes I ignore them and leave in all my bullshit.

Special thanks to Jennifer Whitson. Though we're no longer friends, I wouldn't be writing this today without her love, enthusiasm, energetic support, and a particularly expedient 911 call.

This book also would not exist without the friendship, encouragement, financial advice, and ass-kicking of my adopted family, Stephanie and Ian Barney. They have saved me in every way a person can be saved.

But just creating a book and getting up after a knockout doesn't get the book to print. For that, I have my tireless agent, Jennifer Jackson, to thank. She dusted off the book after round one and passed it into round two with all the professional aplomb of the best boxing manager. Thanks also to my purchasing editor, Jeremy Lassen, and the posse at Night Shade Books. Both Jennifer and Jeremy took a big gamble on a bloody little book.

Hats off as well to all of the editors who had a hand in this book along the way, including Juliet Ulman, David Pomerico, and copyeditors K.M. Lord and Marty Halpern. Special thanks also to David Marusek, Colleen Lindsay, Greg Beatty, Jeremy Tolbert, Tim Pratt, Geoff Ryman, Shana Cohen, Kaitlin Heller, and the generous-and-always-inspiring Jeff VanderMeer for various and sundry professional advice, shout-outs, and writing opportunities that have sustained me over the last ten years.

Many thanks to my friends and family for their financial and emotional support. My Clarion experience and Master's work at the University of KwaZulu-Natal in Durban, South Africa was made possible in large part by the generous contributions of Roger Becker, Edward Becker, and Ernie Rogers. Additional contributions were also made by Steve and Kris Becker, Annie Hurley, Jeanne Mack, and Jacqueline Hurley (*Je t'aime grand-mère*). It takes a village.

To Jayson Utz, who stumbled into this whole process mid-fight, thank you for supporting me during many long nights of uninterrupted writing time when we'd both rather be doing something else. Thank you for the incredible patience, fortitude, strength, and love you have generously shared with me during our partnership.

Finally, many thanks to my long-suffering parents, Terri and Jack Hurley, who told me—back in the hazy 80's—that they would be happy to encourage their dorky kid's writing career, so long as I knew I'd always be poor.

Over the years, I found out that poverty wasn't such a catastrophe. The real tragedy would have been dying before I'd ever published a book.

There are some things worth coming back for.

St. Anne's Hill
Dayton, Ohio
Fall 2010

ABOUT THE AUTHOR

Kameron Hurley currently hacks out a living as a marketing and advertising writer in Ohio. She's lived in Fairbanks, Alaska; Durban, South Africa; and Chicago, but grew up in and around Washington State. Her personal and professional exploits have taken her all around the world. She spent much of her roaring 20's traveling, pretending to learn how to box, and trying not to die spectacularly. Along the way, she justified her nomadic lifestyle by picking up degrees in history from the University of Alaska and the University of KwaZulu-Natal. Today she lives a comparatively boring life sustained by Coke Zero, Chipotle, low-carb cooking, and lots of words. She continues to work hard at not dying. Follow the fun at www.kameronhurley.com

†.

The smog in Mushtallah tasted of tar and ashes; it tasted like the war. Mushtallah was nearly a thousand miles from the front, but the organic filter surrounding the city couldn't keep out the yeasty stink of spent bursts and burning flesh blowing in from the desert.

Nyx pulled on a pair of goggles and stepped over a dead raven. Dusty feathers, dog shit, and edible receipts clogged the gutters. Ahead of her, the pale, stupid-looking Ras Tiegan kid she was charged with keeping alive made her way down the crowded sidewalk, swinging her shopping bags ahead of her. Her name was Mercia, and she was daughter to the Ras Tiegan ambassador to Nasheen. The ambassador's kid covered her hair like most Ras Tiegans, though on choking days like this one, most everyone did. Mercia had big dark eyes and a flat nose like her mother's that gave her a distinctly foreign profile. The rest of her was awkward and gangly. Her hips were so bony she could have forced her way through the crowd without the bags. Rich Ras Tiegan girls were all too skinny.

Nyx moved around a tangle of women dancing outside a cantina blaring southern beat music. The tangy smell of oranges and saffron wafted out over the sidewalk. Nyx kept track of the time by counting the number of wasp, locust, and red beetle swarms buzzing by, delivering messages of a far higher caliber than she'd been entrusted with in years.

A bedraggled young vendor sat at the corner on a mat, holding up a "Paint your own prayer rug!" sign in one hand and a jar of zygotes covered in a sheen of ice flies in the other. Nyx's footsteps slowed as she passed. If she'd still been a bloodletting bel dame, she'd have chopped off the woman's head and collected the inevitable bounty on her. These days, women selling illegal genetic goods were policed solely by bel dames. There was a time when the vendor would have been spooked at Nyx's approach. Nyx had been better dressed, better armed, and better supported, once: running with her bel dame sisters instead of a cocky boy shifter and reformed venom addict. Now, instead of collecting blood debt, she was babysitting diplomats and cutting up petty debtors when the First Families paid her in hard currency. It felt more honest. But a lot less honorable.

The woman shoved the jar of zygotes at her.

"Ten hours of viability left," the woman babbled. "Good price in the pits for these!"

"Fuck off," Nyx said, "Or I'll call the bel dames."

Invoking their name produced the desired effect. The woman's eyes got wide. She jerked away from Nyx and collected up her illegal genetic material and her prayer rugs, then disappeared quickly and quietly down an alley.

Nyx looked up to see Mercia stepping into the doorway of a boutique selling conservative swimwear with tunics and hoods, oblivious of her spat with the vendor. Nyx slowed down. They were already in a better part of town than Nyx was used to— illegal merchants aside. With her whip at her hip and the hilt of a sword sticking up from a slit in the back of her burnous, she looked about like what she was: a bounty hunter, a mercenary, a body guard. Somebody hard up and dishonorable, like a woman just discharged from the front.

Nyx leaned against an unguarded bakkie—real risky, leaving them untended—to ease some of the pain in her back and knees. She wondered where she could get a hit of morphine this early in the day. She'd slept ten hours the night before, and thirteen the night before that. Too much sleep, even for a woman who bartered her organs for bread on occasion—one more reason she wasn't a bel dame anymore. Yet here she was, rubbing at her eyes before noon. She thought about going back and seeing her magician, Yahfia, and getting swept for cancers. Frequent trips to the magician kept her team relaxed. Eshe, her kid clerk, and Suha, her broken-nosed weapons tech, were a good crew, but they still had a lot of blind faith in magicians and bug tech. They thought that anybody who could afford to get patched up by a magician lived forever. Nyx knew better.

Nyx's charge walked out of the storefront. Mercia's pale face, flat features, and the cut of her clothes drew the stares of small children. A pack of adolescent girls in chain mail and boots snickered at her. The Queen was half Ras Tiegan, and since the brutal turn in Nasheen's war with Chenja five years before, the Queen and Ras Tieg weren't nearly as popular as they'd once been. The war hadn't been going well for Nasheen in almost a decade; there were boy shortages, rogue magicians, problems with the bel dame council, and one of Nasheen's primary munitions compounds had been bombed out the year before; a blister burst that would keep the area contaminated for half a century at least.

Bad for Nasheen—good for business.

Nyx watched the Ras Tiegan kid. She wondered what the hell the kid had found in there that required another three bags. Shit, probably. The foreign kids were all buying shit these days.

"Carry this, will you?" the kid said, holding out the bags.

Nyx crossed her arms and spit a bloody wad of sen on the sidewalk. She was trying to give up whiskey. Replacing it wholesale by upping her sen habit had seemed like a good idea. Better to dull pain than dull thought. The kid, though, said she was allergic to sen and didn't like the smell. Ras Tiegans were frail little roaches.

"I'm not a sherpa," Nyx said.

"A what?" the kid said. Daughters of diplomats took to languages like terrorists to water reservoirs, which meant the kid didn't have an accent. Nyx sometimes forgot that most Nasheenian slang was beyond her.

"I don't do shopping," Nyx said.

The kid looked put out. "My mother says you're to do what I say."

"Well, you and me can chat with your mother about that when we next see her," Nyx said. Nyx had acted babysitter to the daughters of diplomats enough times during the Queen's summits to know that the bugs would be silent for a good long while yet. Hopefully after the kid's mother deposited Nyx's fee.

"You need a sherpa, I'll hire a girl for you," Nyx said, and eyed the tail-end of the pack of girls in boots. Nyx wasn't so washed up yet that getting one of the girls into bed was all that ridiculous an idea. Young girls loved old bel dame stories.

"You're not very accommodating," the kid said. She sounded like some rich nose, one of the First Family women who lived up in the hills and sneered down at the sprawl of humanity they still called "the colonials," a thousand years after the last battered ship of planetless refugees was allowed onto the planet. Anybody who happened to bump into Umayma these days en route to somewhere else was either rerouted or left to orbit the planet and die a slow death by asphyxiation. Nyx had heard that when they still had the ability, the Families had the magicians blow up the ships. On those nights there was enough light in the sky to read by. That's what the old folks nattered about, anyway.

"My mother says you're the best in the business," Mercia said.

Nyx started moving down the street again, and the kid tagged after her. "No, just the cheapest," Nyx said. That was mostly true.

"But not easy to buy out?" the kid said slyly. Nyx had already considered pulling out the kid's sharp tongue. Probably be some monetary penalty for that, though.

"Sadly, no."

"My mother wouldn't have hired you if you were." The kid pulled out a berry-smelling sweet stick and started sucking at it like a coastal infant. How old was she? Ras Tiegan girls all looked younger than Nasheenians. She might have been eighteen or nineteen, but didn't look or act a day over fifteen.

"Takes some faith in your mother's smarts to trust that," Nyx said.

"She's a diplomat," the kid said, like that meant something.

"I've known some stupid diplomats." Hell, Nyx had *killed* some stupid diplomats. Countries like Heidia and Druce paid good money to diplomats who "lost" family members while on foreign assignments, especially in Nasheen and Chenja. The first illegal note she took during her short bel dame career was for a Heidian deputy ambassador's husband.

"My mother isn't one of the stupid ones."

Nyx watched a woman stepping out of a storefront ahead of them. The pitch to her walk as she came out told Nyx that she'd begun the movement from a standstill, loitering in the doorway, and the bag at her hip was holding something far heavier than the shoe brand it advertised.

Ahead of them, Nyx saw two more women standing alongside an otherwise unguarded bakkie. Never could say what made her watch some women closer than others. Maybe they tried too hard to look like they had nothing to do.

The bakkie was missing its tags. Missing tags meant the women were either bel dames or somebody doing black work. Generally, the sorts of people who illegally trafficked in bugs, people, and organs were gene pirates, mixing and matching blood codes and selling them illegally to the breeding programs in Nasheen and

Chenja. Nyx had run that kind of black work before. She knew enough about it to know she didn't want to have anything to do with the people running it.

As Nyx moved to get herself between the kid and the sidewalk, the women hanging around the bakkie too-casually turned their backs to her.

Nyx rolled her shoulders. The kid said something about a Ras Tiegan holiday where children wore funny hats.

Nyx saw a gap in the sidewalk traffic and grabbed the kid by the elbow. She steered her into the street.

Ravens' feathers stirred around their ankles. The kid tensed under her fingers and went real quiet. One of the benefits of working with kids used to kidnapping attempts was that they knew when to shut up.

With her other hand, Nyx reached behind her where she kept a scattergun strapped to her back. She was a bad shot, but a scattergun would hit just about anything in the general direction she aimed it.

As they walked into the street, Nyx felt a rush of dizziness, as if her head was floating somewhere over her right shoulder. A gray haze ate at the edges of her vision. She shook her head and blinked. Too old for this, she thought.

A cat-pulled cart rolled past. A rickshaw driver swore at her. Dust clotted the air. The cats stank. The kid started sneezing. Mercia's mother had said she was allergic to cats, too. And oranges. And cardamom. And a hundred other things. Nyx half-expected the kid to burst into hives at the sound of raised voices.

Nyx pushed the kid ahead of her and glanced at the cart window. She saw the reflection of the sidewalk behind her where the woman with the shoe bag was hastily stepping after them.

The kid dropped the slobbery sweet stick into the street.

"Suha," Nyx said. Saying Suha's name triggered the bug tucked into the whorl of cartilage at the entrance to her ear canal.

"Where are you?" Suha's voice had the tinny whine of the red beetle in the casing. "Eshe lost you back on south Mufuz."

Mufuz, near the cantina. Nyx remembered the stir of women hanging around outside, the smell of saffron and oranges. Saffron put shifter-dogs and foxes off the scent, and the smell of oranges confused the parrot and raven shifters—magicians, too. She should have noticed that. She was getting too tired and dizzy to think straight. Muddied heads in her business got chopped off.

Nyx chanced a look behind them, just over her right shoulder. Her head felt light again, as if attached to a string.

Hold it together, she thought. You don't make forty notes a day if your charge ends up dead. She tightened her grip on the kid.

"Nyxnissa—" the kid began, her voice low and cautious.

Nyx heard angry voices behind them, and moved.

She drew her scattergun as she turned. A hooded woman with a leashed cat in hand cried out and ducked. Several more women scurried out of the line of fire, leaving the woman with the shoe bag in the open. The woman crouched low and reached into the bag.

Nyx put herself between the woman and the kid and fired.

The woman on the ground pulled and rolled. Nyx ducked away and pushed the kid ahead of her, behind another rickshaw. She heard the shot. The back end of the rickshaw exploded.

"Move, move!" Nyx said, choking on yellow smoke. Pain blistered across her skin. She half-feared she was on fire, but the smoke in her nostrils didn't stink like scorched hair or flesh. She'd been set on fire enough times to know what it smelled like.

Nyx kept shoving the kid through the crowd. People were panicking now, screaming about terrorists and timed bursts as they flooded up the street. Nyx pushed the kid into the melee and tore off her burnous, leaving it to be trampled by the mob. The kid had dropped her bags.

Nyx needed to split from the kid, but Suha was holed up back at their storefront half a kilometer away, and there was no sign of Eshe. She didn't have anyone to pass the kid to.

Not for the first time, Nyx resented not having a bigger team.

Nyx put an arm around the kid's waist and hauled her back onto the sidewalk and into the doorway of a Heidian deli that stank of peppercorns and overcooked cabbage. Nyx went right on past the counter and through the kitchen, eliciting startled cries from squat, tawny Heidian immigrants. A big matron held up a bigger knife and swore at her in Heidian.

Nyx pressed right past her and kicked through the back door and into the reeking alley. She heard the breathy flapping of wings, and turned in time to see a black raven descend from the rooftop. Her vision swam. Her heart pounded in her chest as if she'd run five or ten kilometers. She gulped air. The kid wasn't even out of breath. Some vague part of her registered that something was wrong.

The raven alighted on a dumpster and shivered once, shook out a hail of feathers, and started to morph. Dusty feathers rolled down the alley.

Watching the tumbling feathers made Nyx's stomach roil.

She kept hold of the kid, who was saying something Nyx figured should make sense. Some other sound droned in Nyx's ears.

The raven shook off the rest of the feathers and flapped wings that were now mostly arms. It jumped off the dumpster lid and landed on two human feet while it took on the body of a teenage boy. The ends of his fingers still looked too long and bony. He was covered in a thin film of mucus.

Eshe was still getting used to morphing quickly, but he wouldn't be good at it for another couple years, about the time he got drafted for the front.

Whether or not the army made better use of raven scouts than Nyx did was debatable.

Nyx let go of Mercia's arm and pushed her toward Eshe. He wiped off the last of the mucus and feathers as his fingers finished taking on human proportions.

"Take her to the safe house," Nyx said. "Stay away from our regular front until I figure out who these women are."

"But you—" Eshe started, his eyes still black as a raven's, head cocked. Sometimes watching him shift put her off dinner.

"I'm going back and finding those—" Nyx was unsteady on her feet. She pressed a hand against the back wall of the deli to catch her balance. She closed her eyes, shook her head.

"Nyx, are you—" Eshe began again.

She opened her eyes and waved him away. "Get her out."

Eshe glanced at the girl. "You up for running?" he asked.

Mercia nodded.

Eshe started off down the alley, naked, and turned sharply left down another. Mercia took off after him—surprisingly fast for a soft diplomat's kid.

Nyx heard the door behind her bang open. She turned and fired her scattergun.

The woman at the door had pulled it half-closed, fast enough to catch most of the gun's spray on the door instead of her belly. She was young, slight, and fast. Her burnous was dusty, and she wore a dark tunic. Nyx wasn't sure how much damage the scattergun had done.

The woman launched herself at her. Nyx fired again and drew her sword. The woman fell into a roll and came up with a knife.

Screams sounded from inside the deli.

Nyx caught the first thrust of the knife with the gun, pushed it back. She thrust at the woman with her sword. The woman leapt back.

Bloody fucking fast for a mercenary, Nyx thought. Her head swam.

The knife lashed out at her again. Caught Nyx on the cheek. Nyx flinched, retreated. The woman grinned.

Cocky, Nyx thought.

Nyx let the woman push her back to the end of the alley. She parried most of the knife thrusts, but caught a couple on her forearms. There was nothing worse than a knife fight. Fuck around too long and you'd be in ribbons.

Nyx was within an arm's length of the wall. The knife flicked at her again. The woman's eyes were shiny—she must be new to the game—and sweat beaded her upper lip. Nyx caught the knife with her blade and pushed—hard. In the same motion, she threw her left hand out—the hand holding the gun—in a hard left hook.

The gun connected with the woman's temple. Her head lolled to one side. She stumbled. Her hands sagged. Then she crumpled like a drunken kitten.

Nyx raised her head and looked back toward the deli. There had been two of them. Where was the other one?

She slipped just into the next alley and kept her sword out. Sweat trickled into her eyes. She wiped it away, blinked furiously. She heard a noise in the alley, and chanced a look.

The second woman was up on the roof, taking in the full measure of the alley. She had a scattergun drawn. Nyx made herself flat against the wall, waited.

Nyx was a terrible shot from any range.

"Suha," she said softly. The name triggered the tailored red beetle in her ear. It opened the connection.

"What you got?"

"Two women. Possible assassins. Bagged one in the alley. I got another one on the roof of the deli behind me. You got my position?"

"Yeah."

"You still on point?"

"I'm moving to intercept. Eshe says you're in shit shape."

"I'm fine. But I've got a second shooter. I need you to intercept."

"On it. Got a description?"

Nyx gave her a description of the second shooter. When she looked back, the woman was no longer on the rooftop. "Lost visual on the roof of the deli," Nyx said. "Check the street outside."

"I'm six blocks away."

"Watch your ass. They're good. Young, but good."

"So am I," Suha said.

Nyx ducked back into the alley behind the deli and sheathed her sword. She crouched next to the woman and patted her down. The clothes were worn, dirty, but good quality. The burnous was organic, which wasn't cheap. She found two more knives and about five bucks in loose change—not an insubstantial amount of cash.

"Who the fuck are you?" Nyx muttered. A wave of dizziness passed over her again. She breathed deeply through her nose.

The woman began to stir. Nyx pulled out some sticky bands from the pack at her hip and bound the woman's hands behind her. As she pulled up the burnous, she saw a flash of red. She paused. Stared. A red letter was tucked into the back of the woman's trousers.

Nyx went very still for the space of a breath.

Then she pulled out the red letter and yanked it open. It was a bel dame's assassination note. The note wasn't written up for

Nyx or Mercia, but for some inland kid with a smoky face and big eyes. Only a bel dame would carry one of these notes. What the fuck was a bel dame doing hunting down the daughter to a diplomat without a red letter order to do it? Or was she running some kind of black work?

The woman was groaning now.

"Bel dame, huh?" Nyx said, and snorted. "Might be illegal to kill you . . . But a buck says you're running a black note."

Nyx shoved the note into her pocket. She stood and grabbed the bel dame by the hair.

"This'll hurt," Nyx said.

It took three whacks of Nyx's sword to take off the bel dame's head. Blood splattered her feet and swam in lazy rivulets down the alley. She tugged off the woman's organic burnous and wrapped the head with it. The body shuddered.

Bloody fucking bel dames, Nyx thought, and stumbled out the alley and across the next street.

Dust quickly covered the blood that coated her from hip to feet, but she still got cautious looks on the street. She turned down another alley and tried to catch her breath. She set down the head. Fuck, she needed a drink.

Nyx fell against the alley wall. She turned and pressed her forehead to it. Her stomach heaved. She vomited, tasted acid. Blue beetles lit out from beneath the wall, swarmed toward the steaming bile and blood splattered across her sandals.

She moved away from the wall and staggered. She needed to move before somebody else showed up. She needed to take this head to the bel dame office. Might be they'd pay her to bring in a bel dame running black work. She needed to check her account. She needed to bring home a nice girl. She needed a drink. She needed to call Rhys, she. . . .

Time stopped.

The world went dark.

"Nyx? Nyx?"

She was staring at the pale lavender sky from the floor of an alley. Eshe was staring down at her, a skinny little Ras Tiegan half-breed with a soft face and pouting mouth, too plain and unremarkable in looks for much of anything but disappearing into crowds.

He pressed a hand to her forehead, like he was trying to measure something.

"Whose head is that?" he asked.

Dark smears blotted out the boy's face. "I don't have time for this shit," Nyx slurred. She tried moving her arms. Everything felt heavy. Something stank like vomit.

"I think you need a magician," he said.

"What?" she said, but searching for the word took a long time, and even saying it seemed heavy, too difficult. "I think I'm a little tired," she said.

"I'll take you to Yahfia."

"The kid . . . ." Nyx said, and then stopped, unsure about what kid she meant. Some kid. Something important. Maybe it wasn't so important. "I need to call Rhys," she said.

"Who?" the kid said. "I'll get Yahfia."

"There was a little black dog," Nyx said.

"A what?"

Eshe started to look like someone she didn't know. What was a boy doing on the street unchaperoned? Shouldn't he be at the front?

"I just need to sleep, Fouad," Nyx murmured. "A little sleep, and maybe Kine can get me some whiskey . . ."

Something wasn't right. She saw a body in a tub, bloody, no eyes . . . Yes, that's right, Kine was dead. Her sister was dead. "Fouad," she told her brother, "Kine is dead. I think you're supposed to be at the front."

"I'm getting Yahfia," Fouad said. He stood, and that was fine, because she was tired of talking. She just wanted to lie there a little longer. Blackness clawed at her, but it felt good, like giving in to sleep after a long, hard day.

It didn't feel like dying at all.

Coming soon from Kameron Hurley:

INFIDEL

The only thing worse than war is revolution.
Especially when you're already losing the war...

Nyx used to be a bel dame, a government-funded assassin with a talent for cutting off heads for cash. Now she's babysitting diplomats to make ends meet and longing for the days when killing was a lot more honorable.

When Nyx's former bel dame "sisters" lead a coup against the government that threatens to plunge the country into civil war, Nyx is tasked with bringing them in. The hunt takes Nyx and her inglorious team of mercenaries to one of the richest, most peaceful, and most contaminated places on the planet – a country wholly unprepared to host a battle waged by the world's deadliest assassins.

In a rotten nation of sweet-tongued politicians, giant bugs, and renegade shape shifters, Nyx will forge unlikely allies and rekindle old acquaintances. And the bodies she leaves scattered across the continent this time ... may include her own.

Because no matter where you go or how far you run in this world, one thing is certain: the bloody bel dames will find you.

Book Two in the Bel Dame Apocrypha

Also available from Del Rey:

A RED SUN ALSO RISES

by Mark Hodder

A man without faith. A woman without hope.

My name is Aiden Fleischer, and today my assistant and I awoke on another planet. On Ptallaya, we are welcomed by the Yatsill. The creatures transform their society into a bizarre version of our own, and we find a new home beneath the world's twin suns.

But there is a darkness in my soul, and as the two yellow globes set … A RED SUN ALSO RISES … and with it comes an evil more horrifying than any on Earth.

'An exhilarating romp' Michael Moorcock

Also available from Del Rey:

THE SUICIDE EXHIBITION

by Justin Richards

WEWELSBURG CASTLE, 1940

The German war machine has woken an ancient threat – the alien Vril and their Ubermensch have returned. Ultimate Victory in the war for Europe is now within the Nazis' grasp.

ENGLAND, 1941

Foreign Office trouble shooter Guy Pentecross has stumbled into a conspiracy beyond his imagining – a secret war being waged in the shadows against a terrible enemy.

The battle for Europe has just become the war for humanity.

The Thirty-Nine Steps *crossed with* Indiana Jones *and* Quatermass. *Justin Richards has an extremely credible grasp of the period's history and has transformed it into a groundbreaking alternate reality thriller.*

Enjoyed *God's War*?

January 2013 saw the launch of Del Rey,
a brand new imprint dedicated to readers who love
SF and Fantasy.

To find out more, visit us at:

www.delreyuk.com

Or follow us on twitter:

 @DelReyUK

DEL REY

Del Rey: bringing you the best in Science Fiction,
Fantasy and Horror.